SHADOW OF CAIN

W. W. NORTON & COMPANY
NEW YORK   LONDON

A NOVEL
BY VINCENT BUGLIOSI
AND KEN HURWITZ

SHADOW
OF CAIN

Library of Congress Cataloging in Publication Data

Bugliosi, Vincent.
    Shadow of Cain.

    I. Hurwitz, Ken. II. Title
PS3552.U393S5 1981   813'.54   81–4863
ISBN 0–393–01466–5   AACR2

W.W. Norton & Company, Inc. 500 Fifth Avenue, New York, N.Y. 10110

W.W. Norton & Company Ltd. 25 New Street Square, London EC4A 3NT

ISBN 0 393 01466 5

1 2 3 4 5 6 7 8 9 0

ACKNOWLEDGMENTS

THE AUTHORS WOULD LIKE TO EXPRESS THEIR SIN-
cere gratitude to: Dr. Kenneth Richler, Director, UCLA Neurobe-
havioral Clinic; psychiatrist Peter B. Gruenberg; Benjamin Baer,
U.S. Parole Commission; Subu Iyer; Irv DePriest, parole agent,
State of California.

PART ONE

CHAPTER 1

All murderers walk the earth
Beneath the curse of Cain.
　　　—Thomas Hood

WITH WINTER'S EARLY DUSK SETTLING ON PASA-

dena, a glowing sense of anticipation began generating inside the
gated mansions. By five o'clock, lights were flicked on in the high
beamed living rooms of English Tudor homes and the courtyards
of Spanish villas overlooking the sycamores of the meadowy arroyo, the first Scotches were splashed over ice, logs in the fireplace
set ablaze, appropriate neckties laid out on the beds. Especially at
Christmas time, it was a more colorful attire that ushered one
downstairs into the evening's mood.

　　As with most people of fortunate circumstances, there was a
natural sense of physical security. An aperitif could be enjoyed
while walking the grounds. The people feared for their paintings

and silverware, but not their lives.

For the clique of 1959 Pasadena High graduates who had dubbed themselves the " '59 Fine," Christmas Eve offered a special allure—the first time since they had gone off to college in the fall that they would all be together again for a black-tie party at the Pasadena Hunt Club. Pamela Husting, Bill Lippencott, Teddy Delbert, Laura Kenendael—the list went on. During the course of their senior year, credentials had, as one of them once put it, perhaps loosened a bit much.

Paul Morrison stood talking on the phone in the foyer off the dining room as he swilled an Old Fashioned, the first drink he had not had to sneak at home. (What a grandly understated moment it had been when his parents had offered it to him.) With the phone cradled against his shoulder, Paul listened as his friend, Teddy Delbert, told him how self-absorbed and uncaring of the world they had all been, of the whole universe of real issues that had already opened up for him after just three months back east at Colgate.

"Then don't come tonight," Paul shot back, "if you think that'll save some kid in China from starving. And give your T-bird away, too, while you're at it. You know?"

"That's not the point," Teddy answered, exasperated.

That *was* the point, as far as Paul could see. He was not about to apologize for pledging a beau monde fraternity at USC, or for having campaigned for Ike three years earlier or, for that matter, still thinking his parents were pretty damn good people.

After they had hung up, Teddy Delbert felt he had not articulated the points quite right—at least not as well as his roommate from New York had.

In her bedroom at her parents' grey-stone, eighteen-room manor, Pamela Husting pondered the yellow chiffon gown she had bought for the evening. It was gay and airy, like her room itself —a pink carpeted haven with sashed diaphanous curtains, the only brightness in a home whose rooms were as cavernous and drafty as a medieval castle. More perseveringly than her mother, Pamela fought against the secure, but massive gloom of the home chosen by her father, a Cal Tech scientist who had, at least as far as Pamela could understand, single-handedly designed the computer system for the B-52 bomber. Pamela, who was all for the country's strong defense, but fidgety under the pall of concern her father brought home with him every evening, had been happy to be sent off to Mills College up north, where afternoon tea was served in cheerful Victorian parlor rooms. Mills was her mother's alma mater and the only place that had nodded understandingly at Pamela's high school grades.

To pass the time until the party, Pamela talked on the phone for an hour with Laura Kenendael, who had a private line in her parents' house. It was only one of the additional incentives that her folks offered her to live at home while going to USC. Not that any more were needed beyond the royal breakfasts and dinners prepared by their maid, having her room straightened up before she arrived home each day from school, and total reign of an old but elegant, Spanish-tile pool where she and her friends would not be disturbed. Laura was a fount of conversation with Pamela, all of it weightless as space. There was the tall sandy-haired graduate student who took her to homecoming but was half an hour late. And the Lanz jumper and blouse her mother had bought her but had to return because the light in the store was different from that outside, or at home, or . . .

Mary, their maid, was pregnant, almost ready to deliver, and Laura told Pamela of the increasing feeling of warmth she had for the woman. Maternal instincts were already simmering in Laura herself, even if she did not recognize them as she sat out on the pool terrace waiting to be swept up off her chaise lounge by a square-shouldered, handsome young executive who would place her down gently alongside a pool of his own—realistically, not quite as big as her father's.

★ ★ ★

In his rented, ramshackle cottage on the island of Catalina, twenty-six miles off the coast from Los Angeles, Raymond Lomak sat at a tilted wooden desk, reading his diary. At five-feet-eleven, his knees pressed up against the middle drawer. His broad forehead leaned over the hot, metal-cup reflector of an inexpensive lamp. Although there was a sturdiness to Ray Lomak's frame, his skin bore his father's Croatian paleness—not one suggestive of ill health, but of generations of hard, east European winters and visionless factory work. His pallid blue eyes and wheat-blond hair came from his grandmother, who was said to have been conceited about her own. Ray had little interest in his physical appearance; he wore his own flaxen hair in one heavy shock pushed to the side and lopped off, as if his barber had used the single stroke of a paper cutter.

It had been only one week earlier that Lomak had moved to the craggy, one-town (Avalon) island, which centuries before had been a refuge for sloppy-toothed sea pirates, and whose more recent decades of big-band dancing and weekend diversions had also faded. He had come in answer to an L.A. *Mirror* ad for a night orderly at the island's twelve-bed hospital. He was glad to get away from the mildewed wealth of Pasadena—and to have an out-of-the-way place to return to when this night was over.

From a passage he had written in his diary months earlier, he read: "There's nothing wrong with wealth and power as long as the people who have it did something to deserve it. A lot of them did. They were intelligent and worked hard. What's wrong is that too many of their children are worthless, arrogant do-nothings, but they still are on top because they started there. Even if they're lazy and barely know how to think, and don't care about anyone but themselves, they get into all the finest private schools, and take over businesses. They're inferior people, but unlike the inferior people among the poor, who don't stand in anyone's way, and live and die in their . . ." (here Lomak had consulted his newly bought thesaurus) . . . "debased condition, the inferiors of the rich are the downfall of society!"

He shoved the diary away.

On the scabbed wall just above his clarinet case was a small shelf of alphabetized books he had read parts of, disagreeing with their authors at every other turn. (Marx, the soft-hearted, would give it all away equally, and therefore indiscriminately, whereas Gobineau thought it could simply be decided by race.) While he had on his own read philosophers (at least synopses), the others at Pasadena High had handed in their mindless geography assignments in between building homecoming floats. " '59 Fine." It was a farce! Charging gas to credit cards their parents paid for, and going off to Lake Arrowhead every summer—did that make them better than he? They were the type of non-productive people who contentedly reminded themselves several times a week that their family name was the one on the new wing of the city's indoor botanical gardens.

The thought of all the parties he had never been invited to, the jokes he had overheard about his out-of-style saddle shoes, his January-sale khaki pants, his father's working at a Pasadena service station, now made Ray Lomak's blue eyes froth angrily and pumped up a vein on his forehead.

From a bottom drawer he took out the sheet of paper he had been working over and revising for months. On it were over a dozen names of his former classmates (the most vacant-headed ones), their parents' names, prestigious addresses, his estimates of their wealth. He folded the sheet, put it in his pocket, and looked at his watch.

He rose from the desk, unbuttoning his shirt. Having rehearsed this night a hundred times in his mind, he went about the preparations without a beat of hesitation. Taking off his clothes, he put on (almost ritualistically) a pair of black pants, black socks, and a hooded, pullover sweatshirt which he had dyed black. Lastly, he laced up a pair of canvas-top shoes he wore at the hospital. White and antiseptic looking just the day before, with an aura of healing and benevolence, they were now also as black as tar pitch.

The head-to-foot blackness would not only help him move through the night with less detection, but curiously, the mantle of darkness gave him a sense of slightly added power.

From the fogged-in harbor, just a five minute walk from his cottage, came the mooing horn of the S.S. *Catalina*'s second to last boarding call. The five o'clock trip would be the "great white steamer's" last passage over to Los Angeles that night.

Lomak got a .45 caliber automatic from the dresser. Tucking it into his waistband, he put the extra, already loaded magazine clips into the sweatshirt's pockets. He also dropped in the pair of dark brown surgical gloves he had purloined from the hospital's emergency room.

After turning off all the lights inside, he locked the front door behind him and stood for a moment on the sagging porch, the light from the bare yellow bulb next to the door dissipating into the mist. Putting his hands deep into the sweatshirt's pockets and holding the items he carried there, he walked through the chilly, particled air down the hill to the harbor.

Ray Lomak was one among hundreds on the large steamship that churned its hour and forty-five minute path toward Los Angeles' old San Pedro landing. While many walked the deck with cocktails in hand, Lomak sat by himself toward the front, his eyes fixed straight ahead on the thick fog that fell away from the ship's prow. The day's dusk went out quickly this dead-of-winter night, and in what seemed only a span of several minutes the ocean became black. The ship's engines moaned below. A few seagulls that did not return to shore with the others at nightfall were caught momentarily in the lights from the captain's bridge above as they swooped close to the railing, looking for tossed scraps of bread from the children on board. Lomak stared straight ahead.

The fog stopped several miles short of the mainland. When the sharp twinkling of the vast city that sprawled out before him came into view, Lomak stood up. For the last fifteen minutes of the trip, he shifted his weight slowly from one foot to the other. Like a strange black-garbed monk, head down and vowed to silence, he followed the feet of the others down the metal gangplank.

A quarter mile from the dock, he came to his used little VW. It, too, he had painted black. Once inside and behind the wheel, he lifted the hood of his sweatshirt over his head and tightened the strings until only his eyes and a small oval portion of his face showed. On the third try the car sputtered, and started.

Lomak steered his VW onto the Harbor Freeway heading north. Traffic flowed swiftly, up past the rows of spindly flagpole palm trees, and later past the lights of Los Angeles' brief downtown. At the Interchange, where five freeways swarmed into a maze of cloverleaves, he headed onto the Pasadena Freeway, the narrow, bending, oldest freeway in Los Angeles. As he emerged from the last of the hillside tunnels, arched cement street overpasses began to loom above. At the city limits of Pasadena, he glided onto a familiar off-ramp.

Pulling over and parking for a minute, he used the bottom of his sweatshirt to wipe off any fingerprints already on the gun, and then put on the stretchy surgical gloves. Without the talcum powder normally used by doctors, they squeaked with their tightness.

When he believed all was ready, he drove off. Pasadena was a heavily foliaged community. Many of the streets had no sidewalks and even more of them were without streetlights for some distance. It was the way the people there wanted it, private and discommodious to strangers. Several blocks from his first destination, he turned off the car's headlights.

An elderly resident, out walking his Great Dane, heard the sound of the car and looked up, but saw nothing. There was only the sound—of a small, puttering car moving on in the dark night.

★   ★   ★

Paul Morrison, on his way to pick up a corsage for his date, was walking through the well-barbered expanse of grass toward his Alfa Romeo parked on the far side of the circular driveway when his mother called to him from the front door.

"Paulie, don't forget to tell them I need my azalea centerpiece by Thursday."

Without stopping, Paul merely raised his hand to indicate that he had heard her.

It was the explosion of gunpowder and, in the darkness of the night, the flash of it from behind the driveway hedges that brought the first shriek from Mrs. Morrison. By the time she looked back toward her son, he was a shadowy heap on the ground. His hand grasping his neck, Paul had dropped to the grass exactly where he had stood. Immobilized at the doorway, Mrs. Morrison screamed hysterically, then rushed toward her dying son.

Fifteen minutes later Pamela Husting, who wore only a slip and stockings, put a dab of perfume on her wrist. She thought she heard a noise outside her gabled bedroom window, but paid it no attention. Squirrels often dropped acorns there. In another moment the glass of the window shattered, and as she turned she saw the black muzzle of a gun poking into her bedroom. It was only a split second that she stood petrified, unable to move, but in that split second a .45 caliber bullet with a velocity of five hundred, eighty miles an hour ripped through the center of her belly, through the first lumbar vertebra of her spine, and into the oakwood dresser behind her. With a raspy groan, Pamela doubled up and stumbled backward, but caught her balance before falling. The second shot missed and took a chunk out of the wall, part of the powdery plaster raining down into an aquarium of tetra.

By the time an ambulance arrived twenty minutes later, the gay pink carpet was dark red beneath Pamela's body. All the while the paramedics were there, four tetra poked at the surface of their resettled world, tasting and spitting out bits of plaster.

Some in Pasadena heard the ambulance siren rushing toward the Husting home, while others heard only the wailing squad cars of the Pasadena Police Department in the arroyo neighborhood where the Morrisons lived. A few heard all the sirens and assumed it was a multiple alarm fire.

By the grace of fate, Jay Horton and his parents were out dining at a restaurant when their darkened home was circled twice, peered into, and finally left.

Five blocks away, Laura Kenendael carried a large box of old baby clothing out to the maid's car in the driveway. Mary, the maid, was just a few steps in front. At the car, Laura started to rearrange the cluttered trunk to make room for the box of clothing.

"You go back inside and get ready for that big party of yours, Laura honey. I can do this," Mary said.

"Oh, you know how much I enjoy doing things for people," Laura offered.

Mary smiled to herself.

She and Laura shuffled the items around together. Bent over the trunk, neither of them felt the presence of the person who walked up right next to them.

Laura was felled by a single bullet in her right side. Mary was in the bullet's path as it raggedly exited Laura's body. The two of them became the night's third and fourth victims.

Seven year old Timothy Sandston was about to come down from his back yard tree house, where his parents never wanted him to go at night after dinner, when he saw a stranger dressed in black get out of a dented little car and walk soundlessly up the Helstroms' driveway next door. At the end of the driveway the man climbed over the padlocked wooden gate and into the neighboring Lippencotts' garden of fruit trees. When Timothy saw the stranger scuttle through the yard in a low crouch, he grinned slyly and called down, "I see you!"

The man looked up momentarily, then disappeared from view as he moved toward the Lippencotts' back porch. A minute later, Timothy heard two loud reports that echoed off the stone walls of the nearby homes.

Bill Lippencott was shot twice as he stood in front of the kitchen window, about to lift a mug of eggnog to his lips. Alone in the house (his parents and sister having gone to visit friends in San Marino), he lay on the kitchen floor coughing up a bullet that had lodged in his lung. Trying to crawl to the phone, he collapsed and died.

"Oh, my God, they're killing the kids!" Mrs. Saltor, a sixty year old neighbor of the Lippencotts, cried into the phone to her nephew. She had already seen a flash bulletin on television of the four other murders in Pasadena within the hour.

In a community of 116,000, it would be several hours before most became aware of what was happening, and took refuge inside their locked homes.

The phone circuits in Pasadena became jammed. Some families huddled in dens with the lights turned off and dialed frantically, trying to reach relatives. As if in a fictional horror movie, a monster of a human being was on the loose. Seldom had a single community experienced such a night of terror.

"She's not home, she should have been home by now!" a Martha Turner screamed at her husband, who was still at the office. Their daughter Janice was barely ten minutes late getting home from ballet class. "Oh God," Mrs. Turner sobbed, "there's some crazy person still out there."

At the corner of Gordon Terrace and Waverly, Pasadena police patrolmen Edward Koren and Mark Bailey saw a young dark-jacketed man trotting down the street. Bolting from their squad car with drawn guns, they ordered him to halt with his hands up. The man, who had been on a pleasant jaunt to his girlfriend's house, was stunned and terrified, but no more so than rookie officer Koren, who shouted, "Keep your hands up, goddamit!" He pulled the speechless fellow to the ground by his collar when the unidentified man, too shaken for much presence of mind, did not put his hands as high as the trembling cop wanted them.

Like an armored battalion chasing a small field gopher, the Pasadena police were in helpless confusion trying to catch up to a killer who was no more than a fleeting shadow cutting across pool verandas and back yard terraces. No sooner would they respond to one homicide report than they would receive an incredulous radio dispatch about another a half mile away.

Parmer Cale was the only one who had had any chance at all that evening of December 24, 1959. Having heard rustling sounds in the boxwood hedges that hemmed the rose beds, he came outside and stood beneath the front portico, looking about. The first shot only wounded him in the right hip.

"You," he moaned and fumbled for the front door. He tottered backward, though, and hearing the gun jam once, then twice, he turned on his assailant in a rage. With a desperate lunge he knocked him to the ground, where they struggled about. Parmer had his arms around his attacker's waist and one of his arms pinioned, but the fellow whom he had never even exchanged more than a few words with in school placed the gun's barrel against the top of Parmer Cale's head, and again pulled the trigger.

It was outside the home of this sixth and final victim, in the freshly watered rose beds, that a telltale shoe print, which would furnish the police with their first lead, would later be found—a unique print made by a shoe with a graphite strip down the center of the sole, the kind of shoe often worn for electrical grounding by hospital personnel.

CHAPTER 2

AS THE NIGHT OCEAN'S WAVES POWERED AGAINST
the rocks directly beneath his bedroom, Richard Pomerantz lay
sleeping, happily comatose to the world, hugging his pillow as
though it were his first love. Between waves, when the sandied
water slipped back, Richard heard the phone's second ring.

"H'lo."

"Hello, Dr. Pomerantz? It's Harold. I'm sorry, did I wake
you?"

"That's all right, Harold. What's wrong?"

As a psychiatrist, Richard snapped almost automatically from a dead sleep to a sense of urgency; nighttime was when fragile humans, his patients, crawled to the brink.

"I know you said only in case of an emergency, but—"

"It's all right, Harold. It's why I give out my home number. What's happened?"

"I . . . I fell out of bed."

Richard eyed the clock. Quarter of four.

"Are you hurt?" he managed to ask evenly.

"No . . . I think I'm okay."

Richard dropped his head to the pillow, and closed his eyes. For seven months he had been dealing with Harold's syndrome of diurnal reversal, his sleeping during the day and living by night to avoid contact with other human beings. Seven months to get him back in bed at night, and all for this.

"Are you unhappy about my calling you?" Harold asked.

Richard chuckled dispiritedly. "Harold, can you think of any way that I could be happy about your waking me up at four in the morning to tell me you fell out of bed? Now, Harold, you're an adult. You don't have to engage in this kind of silliness to test my concern about your well-being."

Richard told Harold he would see him at his next weekly appointment, and Harold went back to bed satisfied.

As he was falling back to sleep, Richard once again asked himself whether there was such a thing as making headway in psychiatry—whether, at age thirty-three, it was still not too late to go to law school.

The next morning he showered and shaved early, looking forward to his day of volunteer work with the ex-cons. There was something inside him that liked the action down there.

★ ★ ★

The small, metal fold-out chairs strained beneath the frames of men like Bernard Townsend, a six-foot-four-inch armed robber, and Hector Artez, a hyperkinetic junkie who bounced around in his seat like a small-bladdered child. Richard, only five-eight but of tough ply, sat in the circle of ex-cons who sniped at each other regularly, groaned about lost women, and pawed at their knees in frustration over parole regulations. Richard saw his Tuesday job as that of a lion tamer, though with his dark inquisitive eyes, black curly hair, and shadow of a beard by mid-afternoon, he looked more like a young Parisian artist who gently broke models' hearts.

This week's group therapy session was now in its third hour without a break.

"I don't give a damn," roared Bernard Townsend, his thick black finger planted in his thigh. "The man mess with my toolbox again, he gonna have a wrench for a necktie."

James Monroe, a slender stem of a man in his early twenties, the only other black in the group, inched forward. "Do you know for a bona fide, shadow of a doubt fact he took your tools, or is this a cognitive deduction you have made, based on the fact the man is white?"

"Shee-it."

"Hey, doc," Lonnie Brownsmueller piped up for the first time that day, "how 'bout scorin' us some stuff next week? A little weed, maybe. Huh?"

"I think James has got you dead to rights," Richard said to Bernard, ignoring Brownsmueller. Picking a thread from his suit pants, Richard gave Brownsmueller half a glance. "I'm nobody's bagman."

"You've got to relate to the dynamics of the situation," James Monroe continued with Bernard. "The man in your shop is your boss, and this is an intrinsic fact you must relate to."

"Why don't you talk straight, nigger?" Bernard growled. He cocked his thumb toward Richard. "All those words gonna impress whitey? Why don't you pull the brotha's coat, doc, and tell him it don't matter how he talks, you're still gonna be a racist honky."

Richard looked the big man smack in the eye and said casually, "Fuck you."

After a few seconds of silence in the room, an accepting grin touched Bernard's face, and the men, shuffling their feet nervously and laughing, returned to their grievances about matters outside the therapy room.

Richard's pluckiness was never foolhardy. In a cubicle of the building a week earlier, he had put his hand on Bernard's shoulder while the big hulking man cried his eyes out. "You got the right, Bernard," Richard told him. "A lot of people been screwing you over, and got you half-believing you deserve it. Come on now— it's a crummy world, but the ground rules for dealing with these people without winding up back in jail aren't that tough. It's time you learn them."

In lunch hour traffic it was a forty minute drive from the graffitied halfway house in East Los Angeles back to his office in Beverly Hills. Whenever Richard looked over to the dour, tense faces behind the wheels of the Mercedes and Porsches at the longer red lights on Wilshire Boulevard, he was always reminded of how universal anxiety and disappointment were, different only in the ways they were manifested. With his hamburger and Coke, Richard edged forward with the rest of the traffic, taking a certain pleasure in moving through the tony Beverly Hills shopping district of chic imports and high fashion in his 1969 Buick Skylark. The freshly painted vehicle spoke to his tenacious sense of Americanism and, though he had a private practice with an income approaching six figures, to his predilection for utility and maintaining a sense of proportion.

When Richard arrived at his office, his answering service (like most psychiatrists, Richard had no need for a secretary) had an "important" phone message waiting for him. It was from Howard Reiner, his father's shipmate during their hitch in the navy, and now senior member of the state's parole board in Sacramento. Richard called him immediately.

"Afternoon," Reiner muttered above the grainy sound of a cigarette being ground out. "How are all my westside liberals getting on?"

"About usual, Howard. Pulling for you guys to let as many dangerous people as possible back out on the streets."

The two laughed, and not without some affection for each other. The gravelly voice of the fifty-eight year old former Republican legislator turned serious.

"We have a situation up here that I'm afraid is no laughing matter. Raymond Lomak is up for parole again, and I think he's going to make it this time."

Richard did not speak right away. It sounded impossible.

"How does it work—two out of three votes or something to let him out?" he finally asked, fingering his necktie.

"That's precisely correct," said Reiner, as he lit another cigarette. "I don't have to go into my reasons for being the vote against, do I?"

"Hardly."

"Several of your colleagues up here testified before our board that he's fit as a fiddle. Or at least they . . . you know, I realize it's a little more complicated than that . . . they say . . . hold on, I've got it right here someplace . . . quote, he no longer constitutes a threat to society, et cetera, et cetera . . . also, he suffers from neither delusion nor paranoia, unquote, and then something here about something-something echopraxia, but that was fifteen years ago. He's been in twenty-one years, you know."

"Yeah, I remember I was a kid when it happened. Even back in Connecticut, it shook people up."

"It shook people up everywhere, for Christ's sake," Reiner rasped. "Dornan, the San Quentin chaplain, claims Lomak's a born-again Christian who's been a 'deeply religious man' the last five years. I think Dornan is smart enough to not loosely toss around a term like born-again. But who knows?

"I'll get to the point," Reiner said. "Lomak has stated that if he's released, he plans to resettle in Los Angeles. Because of who this guy is, we intend to tack on the additional condition to his parole that he see a designated psychiatrist. He's going to have to satisfy that psychiatrist, and if need be, a psychiatric board up here in Sacramento, that he's continuing to be a safe parole risk.

"So the thing is this. If I can arrange it, will you be Lomak's psychiatrist?"

"Well . . ." Richard hesitated.

"Pomerantz, I know there are hundreds of psychiatrists in this state with more experience than you, but you're one of the few goddamn shrinks I feel I can trust to play it straight with us. If something starts to smell bad, I think I can count on you to not pussyfoot till it's too late."

"I'm not a cop, Howard. I'm a psychiatrist."

"I'm not asking you to be a cop," Reiner asserted. "I'm asking you to be fair—to *all* people concerned. For as long as I've known you, you've been a fair and objective person. If I didn't sincerely believe that, I wouldn't be calling. Since Lomak is supposedly well-adjusted now, we're not asking you to be his psychiatrist in the typical sense. What we want you to do more than anything else is to act as a psychological monitor."

Reiner paused, then sighed heavily and spoke in an earnest voice. "I'm not a compassionless man, I think you know that. If this parole does take place—and I'm still hoping it doesn't—you can believe me when I say that the moment Ray Lomak walks through those gates I'll do anything to help make that parole decision the right decision. I pray to God for all of us it will have been the right thing to do."

"He was only nineteen when it happened," Richard observed, cautiously.

"So the other board members have stressed," Howard Reiner said. "I realize this. Will you do it?"

"Yes, of course I will."

"Thank you, Pomerantz," Reiner said. "I'll be in touch with you."

Richard sat a moment at his desk, unable to immediately collect himself for discussions with his next patients about compulsive eating, or writer's block, or the loneliness of a housewife whose voice was beginning to resemble her myna bird's. Looking out toward his waiting room, he thought of who would probably be sitting there within a matter of weeks—a man who had nightmarishly struck at five different locations in a single community in one night, creating in the people a panic and terror that would never be forgotten.

Richard could not help thinking of his first, odd response whenever he was in the presence of a killer. Always, he stared a moment at the hands. The mystery behind one's actions, of course, lay in the mind. But still, there was the common curiosity-seeker in him that made him look at the murderer's hands, and almost see the mystery in *them*—those two simple anatomical parts just like his own. He wondered how they could have ever done such a thing.

$$\star \quad \star \quad \star$$

The walls of the austere little room at San Quentin where parole hearings were held were a dismal yellow, stirring no prisoner to think he was almost out. On the front wall was a portrait of the governor; next to the side window hung a black and white picture of inmates playing volleyball in the main yard. The warden's nephew, before becoming a policeman, had wanted to be a photographer.

Howard Reiner and the other two parole board members sat behind a dark wooden table, three glasses of water and copies of Lomak's case history before them. Facing them, at a smaller table whose varnish was dulled from years of nervous hands rubbing at the surface, was Raymond Frederick Lomak.

Ray Lomak, forty years of age and having lived over half of his life in San Quentin, sat quietly but intently in his chair. He stared at the glass of water set before him. Though no specific provisions distinguished the parole hearing from any other, the very uneasiness of the men who now sat across from him would have told anyone that this day was different. Ray Lomak was one of the most famous mass murderers the country had ever known, a man whose aura had caused even the most hardened convicts to look curiously at him from a distance in the prison mess hall.

Seated to Lomak's left at the hearing were Reverend Charles Dornan, and Norris Woods, a public defender. Reverend Dornan, the popular prison chaplain with an oriental patience, was the first to be given the floor.

"There is scarcely a doctor who cannot tell of a patient of his where every known medicine and drug was used without results," he intoned, "but then for reasons unknown to us, began all on his own to get better. Call it a miracle, if you like, or call it just the intangible reservoir of strength in the human body, the will to surmount all odds and live. The soul, gentlemen, has a will too."

Reverend Dornan clasped his hands serenely, what he even considered beatifically, in front of him, and spoke, looking each of the board members in the eye. "The natural life process of regeneration. This is what I'm talking about. We all pay lip service to prison rehabilitation, but I think most of us are beginning to question its efficacy, and with good reason. It wasn't twenty-one years of working in a metal shop that changed Raymond Lomak, and it wasn't twenty-one years of living with other criminals, either. No, it was Ray Lomak who changed Ray Lomak.

"For sixteen years I attempted to do all *I* could, and gentlemen, it wasn't my words, either. Oh, perhaps a little. No, it was five years ago when Raymond Lomak came to *me*. Came to me and spoke of the emptiness in his heart. Asked if he could pray with me. Why it happened and why then, I can't answer. I can only say that the truest healing is that which comes from within. Cures from outside, whether they're medicines or words, are often only temporary. But when a man begins to heal from within his own body and heart . . . then . . . well, then I think we can rejoice."

Having made his point rather eloquently, the chaplain began to rephrase his message for another fifteen minutes, each rendition a little less on target and more annoying than the last, his voice seeking more sonorous levels as he went. The board members nodded politely.

Norris Woods reviewed the case from the legal standpoint,

pointing to other multiple murder cases throughout the country in which life sentences had not been fully served. Parole, he said, had to be maintained as a viable tool of the prison system, an incentive for all prisoners, lest they lose hope and thereby become unmanageable while incarcerated.

Woods, at age fifty-five, lent scant passion to his words. He was overworked, and had been ever since he joined the public defender's office in 1950. A heavy breather because of his portliness, he sat hunched over his papers and tugged at his shirt cuffs as he spoke.

"Four years this man was on death row," he said. Then glancing at his watch and pressing his coat pocket to make sure he had not left his plane ticket back to Los Angeles in the motel room, he skipped to a closing which he felt was effective with parole boards. "Consider this. As you gentlemen know, it costs around $11,000 a year for every person we keep in prison. Now in this case here, three psychiatrists have said in their reports that Mr. Lomak could be returned to society as a productive member. Taking that into consideration, I think it would be a great waste for us to not do so . . . that is, to not return him to society."

Gathering up his papers, he looked over at Raymond Lomak with a nod, but Ray, sitting straight in a starched white shirt and nicely pressed slacks, only looked down at his own pale hands as they rested on the table.

Howard Reiner asked the prisoner if he had anything to say, but Lomak shook his head.

"No . . . no, I don't think so."

As Reiner turned to the other board members, however, Ray worked his mouth as though to speak again, then looked back down.

"Something?" Reiner asked.

"I only wanted to say . . ." Ray touched a hand to the side of his hair, which once flaxen and youthful, was now less blond and almost brown from lack of sunlight. Webbing out from his expressionless blue eyes were the small creases of early middle age, but they were creases without history behind them. There was no wear of weather in them, as in a merchant marine's, nor were they the deepening lines from late nights of decisions and compromise, like a forty year old politician's. As a prison loner for the most part, left to his reading and solitude by even the most aggressive inmates, his aging had simply been a biological process in a twenty-one year void, and his face still had a virginal naiveté to it.

". . . I only wanted to say that if you decide to not grant me parole, I understand."

Before adjourning to deliberate and take a vote, two of the board members declined to make any public statement. Howard Reiner, after asking the newspaper reporters outside to come in, picked up his reading glasses and placed in front of him a single typewritten sheet of paper. Just as he had when he delivered trenchant speeches from the floor of the state legislature—sleeves rolled up, necktie loosened, balled handkerchief clutched in one hand—he had the look of a man who has been negotiating all night with hijackers. Only grave, preferably publicized situations interested Howard Reiner.

"Certain people," he said, flat and sober, at the conclusion of his speech, "because of their unusual history of violence, because of the particularly horrendous crime they committed, should never be set free. They may very well have within them a murderous germ that can never be eradicated. To release them on a vulnerable society is to take a risk that we, as representatives and guardians of the people, do not have the right to take."

✳ ✳ ✳

Sixty days later, on a fresh and salty San Francisco morning in early October, Ray Lomak walked across the San Quentin yard accompanied by a prison guard on each side, both carrying a large carton of books for him. Wearing the same trench coat he had worn going into prison over two decades earlier, and the black, round-brimmed hat his father had brought from Croatia, Ray carried a small suitcase in one hand, his clarinet case in the other. He moved at a deliberate, unhurried pace, thinking perhaps a few inmates might want to stop him and wish him well. None did. The only three fellow prisoners Ray had spent much time with these last few years—Stennit, the forger; Haas, the cat burglar; and Horace Conley, a lonely, obese plumber who had fornicated with his eleven year old stepdaughter—were all queuing up for the last breakfast line, asking each other idly whether Lomak had left yet.

The guards steered Ray toward the prison's sally port, the old stone, fortress-like tower that provided the access between the yard and the prison's outer grounds. Only after the tower's inner door had closed behind them did the port guards slide open the second, exterior door. Few rules at San Quentin were stricter than the one providing that both doors were never to be open at the same time.

The three continued down the outside walkway and through a second gate that was swung open for them from a chain link fence. Getting into the guards' car, they drove the rest of the way through the prison grounds, the fire and gas stations off to their left, the rocky shoreline of San Francisco Bay with its poetically ironic black ravens in tree perches, on their right. After passing the gift shop where prisoners sold items like boats in bottles and little wooden stagecoaches they had crafted, they rolled through a third and final gateway in the prison's outer wall.

Because no one was meeting Ray, the guards drove him the three miles to the San Rafael bus station. What greeted him as he stepped out of the car at the station stunned Ray. Outside the front entrance was a crush of reporters and photographers. All three networks had sent porto-pack video crews. Cameras clicked, shoulder-slung tape recorders were set running. A fusillade of questions came at once.

"Please," Ray importuned quietly, shaking his head.

"What are your plans, Ray?"

"Do you fear for your life at all, Ray?"

Ray quickly got back into the car and rolled up the window.

"Could I just stay in the car until my bus leaves?" he asked one of the guards.

The guard thought a moment, then nodded. The reporters continued their bleating questions through Ray's closed window, but Ray only looked down at his lap.

"Come on, come on," the guard behind the wheel raised his voice at them, "everyone's entitled to a little privacy, huh?"

After about fifteen minutes, realizing they were not going to wheedle a single statement from Ray, the reporters began dispersing. Some of them ran to their cars and vans, eager to get in what few morsels of information they had for the evening papers and newscasts. When they had all gone, and the guards had taken his belongings to the bus, Ray got out of the car and said to the deputies, "God be with you in your difficult work."

The parole board's two to one decision became a final reality as Ray Lomak turned and walked alone to the bus—to again move in society as a free man.

CHAPTER 3

ALL THREE TELEVISION NETWORKS CARRIED STO-
ries about Ray Lomak, and nearly every evening paper in the
country carried somewhere in its first five pages, if not on the front
page itself, an AP wire service photo of Ray standing outside the
guards' car.

Beneath the picture of the surprisingly harmless looking man,
the captions varied from a matter-of-fact, "Raymond Lomak
leaves prison after twenty-one years," to a more indignant, "Mass
murderer set free," to the most sensationalistic and widely used
one, written by a UPI correspondent who recalled the nickname

chewed over by the press back in 1959: " 'Socialite Killer' comes out a born-again."

Scorching letters addressed to the Governor's office of the State of California were dropped in mailboxes from Oregon to New Jersey; the switchboard at the state parole headquarters in Sacramento stayed lit up for five days; the staid *New York Times* vented an uncharacteristic pique in a Sunday editorial; in North Dakota, the mayor of Fargo received a phone call threatening his life for having "probably been involved" in paroling Lomak.

But passions were not all of the same heart. Over the next few weeks, officials at San Quentin would receive several dozen letters, many of them in childlike scrawls, inquiring how they could get in touch with Ray Lomak; "a far out guy," said one of them; "a love sign for the universe," gushed another. And though a barber in Pittsburgh shook some hair lotion into his hands and muttered, "Shoulda been shot, an animal like that," and a Baptist minister in Jackson, Mississippi, began composing a sermon for the next Sunday about the "moral lassitude" of the judicial system, a priest in Baltimore made plans to speak from the pulpit on the inspiring example of a redeemed sinner. And there were clergymen elsewhere who read the newspaper articles and nodded, feeling that if anyone should have a sense of forgiveness, it was they. Many of these men of the cloth lived a safe two or three thousand miles from where Ray Lomak intended to settle.

★   ★   ★

It was in a pink, flimsy-walled motel on Pico Boulevard that Ray Lomak woke up to his first full day in Los Angeles. From across the alley, the kids' high pitched shouts in Spanish had awakened him at 6:30. Out of habit, he made his own bed.

He sat fully dressed at a small writing table, the previous day's classifieds of available apartments, a map of Los Angeles, and the city's entire bus schedule spread out before him. It had always been crucial to Ray Lomak to know how, when, and where everything around him worked, to reduce intimidating systems to their more simple, predictable, controllable elements. The one time he had gone to Disneyland as a youngster, he had studied the amusement park's map and brochure for a half hour before proceeding to his first ride.

By eight o'clock he had finished planning out his day—at least until four in the afternoon, when he was to check in with his parole agent—but still it was too early, he guessed, to start knocking on apartment managers' doors. He stripped away a sheet of blue paper from the pad he was using for his origami, the art taught to him at San Quentin a dozen years earlier by Kushawa, the bright eyed, ever smiling wife beater who could only throw up his hands and laugh bitterly at American laws. With a methodical precision, Ray made the twenty-one folds of the *hakucho* (the swan), securing each crease with a firm stroke of the flat of his thumbnail. After the twenty-first fold, he pulled gently on the delicate beak and tail feathers, and the once rectangular piece of paper puffed out into a beautiful blue swan. Ray placed it atop the bed's headboard, and looked at it a moment.

He took from his suitcase the plain white envelope that contained all the money he possessed. One last time he counted it— seven hundred, forty-two dollars and eight cents plus the two hundred dollars he had been given upon his release. At one point, he had saved over two thousand dollars from the work he had done in prison. But five years earlier, with a miniature Bible sticking up out of the breast pocket of his prison work shirt, and a feeling of joyful cleanliness in his heart, he had sent off six cashier's checks for $350 apiece to the people in Pasadena, whom he referred to in his conversations with Reverend Dornan only as "the families." Accompanying each check was a letter acknowledging that no amount of money could atone for his crimes, but stating that he, like post-war Germany, had no other means for reparations. The analogy, he thought, and not without some conceit, had been an apt one.

The check intended for the pregnant maid's husband and for the son born to her as she lay dying on the surgery table, came back from the post office stamped, "Forwarding Address Unknown." When every one of the five other checks was returned— the one to Laura Kenendael's parents coming back with a scribbled note from her father with the single sentence, "All I want from you is your death"—Ray plummeted into a depression that so alarmed Reverend Dornan he asked that guards make a special check on Ray in his cell each night in case he attempted suicide. The fact of the matter, however, was that although Ray all but stopped eating and slept very little, discontinued reading his Bible, and for four months uttered few words to anyone, the thought of suicide had not once crossed his mind.

Jolted from his faith in God and the notion of expiation for all acts, Ray crept back to his religion sheepishly, like an adolescent who has run away for three hours in the middle of the night. He again began reading his pocket Bible late at night, solemnly swearing he would never again pity himself. The returned cashier's checks, he gave to Boys Town.

Feeling little sense of security from the motel room, Ray put the envelope of cash in his trench coat. When he opened the door of his motel room and was confronted by the sun-bright, chilly autumn day, he was forced to pause momentarily, struck by the queer sensation of seeing no additional doors or walls sealing him off from the world. Although the moment lifted him euphorically, there was an almost instantaneous puncture in the feeling—a shrinking fearfulness, a vanished security which the dreaded doors and walls had provided for twenty-one years.

The people on the bus which took him toward Santa Monica sat glumly oblivious to him—all except one older woman who stared at him, and then looked back down at her purse, nervously pressing her caked rouge lips each time he returned her glance. Ray was keenly aware of the hostility and fear in her eyes, a look he had not seen since the trial. He kept his eyes to the dirty floor of the bus, hoping she would get off soon. He caught himself beginning to feel some contempt for her, but chastised himself for it; she's old, he thought. She did not get off, and as his discomfort grew, convinced as he was that others were also beginning to look, he waited for the next stop, then sprang to his feet and exited quickly via the bus' rear doors.

Once out on the sidewalk, he breathed deeply. In all the months of pondering what his life would be like if he were released, never had it occurred to Ray that the media would once again make his face recognizable to many people. With his spirit floating ethereally these past few years in search of truth and meaning amidst the words of the prophets and disciples, and even with the more earthly anchored side of his mind planning the details of everyday life on the outside, he had, like a fly meticulously cleaning its wings in the shade of a descending swatter, simply never looked up to see the larger picture.

At times like these, when he had not seen the obvious, he touched on an angry memory or two of his father, a man who could please gas station customers with his work until they discovered the water pump he had neatly rebuilt for them had not been put back in the engine. Or who, when working for a security firm, would arrive swiftly at a house whose alarm had been accidentally triggered, only to realize his ring of ninety-one keys was still dangling from the door of the last home he had inspected.

Without the bus, Ray had ten blocks to walk to the first apartment house, a complex of boxy units facing each other across a walkway and crabgrass lawn.

Ray's knock on the manager's door was answered by a tall, ambitious-eyed young man in a T-shirt.

"I would very much like to see the available bachelor apartment, please," Ray said very formally, having convinced himself behind bars that proper and courteous speech would eventually be recognized and rewarded.

"Sure thing," the manager said, letting the screen door close in Ray's face as he went to fetch his keys.

The furnished bachelor apartment was small but clean, and the durable looking, if graceless convertible couch accommodated

Ray's spartan inclinations. But the two hundred dollar a month price for the tiny place jarred him. In prison, inflation was merely read about, like a foreign war.

"Take my word for it," the manager told Ray, "you're not going to find any cheaper."

"Well, okay," Ray said. "You look like a truthful person."

Back at the manager's quarters, Ray, steeling himself with the assurance that America was a country of protected rights, even for ex-cons, drew himself high in the chair at the kitchen table and boldly printed out on an application his name and former address of San Quentin.

"I just do this for free rent," the young man said, skating his fingernails on a counter top while Ray carefully worked over the application. "Actually, I'm an actor."

Ray looked up with an impressed smile. "Really? That's very interesting."

When he finished the application he handed it to the manager, who perused it under Ray's steady gaze. A change of expression flitted subtly across the manager's eyes. The lips twitched but once.

"I . . . uh, of course have to send this into the company for approval," he said, looking up from the paper to a random spot on the greasy stove top, catching Ray's eye only for a split moment on the way.

"May I leave a deposit?" Ray asked.

"Sure. Sure thing, why don't you do that? Only thing is, if like they already decided to rent it to somebody else, you'd just have to come back and pick it up."

"Has someone else put a deposit on the apartment?" Ray inquired, a knowing edge to the innocence.

"Well, I don't know. I have to call, see?"

Ray nodded. "Could I prevail upon you to call them now, before I look at other apartments?"

The manager wiped the palm of his hand across his T-shirt. "Sure. Sure thing." His eyes moved quickly along a row of kitchen drawers as he thought of the knives they contained, and then he walked briskly into another room, casually nudging the door part-way shut, as if it had not really been his intention.

"Mr. Strather? This is Jim Hogan," he said mutedly into the phone. "You won't believe this, but Raymond Lomak is here . . . yeah, right, and he wants to rent the bachelor."

"You tell him it's already rented," Strather said gruffly, sound-ing unfazed, though it would become a stock conversation piece of his just who had come by wanting to rent at one of his apart-ment buildings.

Jim Hogan decided on what he believed to be a more prudent course of action.

"You just leave the application here, and if it's accepted I'll leave word at your motel tonight," he said, but not until he had walked Ray back out onto the lawn, in view of neighbors and passers-by.

Ray looked down at his new, polished brown shoes sunk low in the crabgrass, then up at the sky, and finally into the face of this callow young man for whom he tried not to feel any anger. "It's not fair," he said quietly. "I have to live and eat and have a roof over my head like anyone else."

"Hey, look," said Jim Hogan sprightly, "they'll probably ap-prove the application, and I'll give you a buzz."

Ray did not smile. "I believe you know in your own heart that it's not fair. . . . Well, I sincerely wish you the best in your career."

He turned and walked back out to the street, where he bent down and pulled a stalk of dead weed from the toe of his shoe. He licked his finger and rubbed the shoe where the weed had scratched the shine. A sense of goodness and charity filled him for his having risen above the petty human impulse to lash back. With an expansive feeling of self-esteem, he continued on to the bus stop.

✷ ✷ ✷

Los Angeles was a locked and shuttered city to Ray Lomak as he rode the buses and walked the streets by himself that day. In his shapeless trench coat and black hat, he looked like a newly arrived foreigner. The apartment managers and landladies who recognized him talked to him through latched screen doors and peepholes. And even though it was only a few people who knew his face, most knew his name.

At a duplex across the street from the Santa Monica airport, in a neighborhood where factory storage tanks and power lines fenced the human spirit into a world of concrete and noise, a friendly man with a Missouri drawl and beltless trousers invited Ray to have a seat in his living room. When he heard Ray's full name, he went into his bedroom and brought out a rifle, snarling, "You get out of here before I blow you away. What right does a scumbag like you have coming into my home?"

Ray backed slowly out of the room and, once outside, ran down the street. "Make him burn in hell, God!" he cursed the man to himself.

Ray was turned away, in one fashion or another, from seven places on his first day of searching for an apartment. The world, Ray saw, was unforgiving of his sins, but oddly, he felt no lingering hostility. In every cold and implacable face, he began to see only frightened human beings who were all too aware of how delicate their connection to this planet of life really was. Neither courageous nor cowardly, but like soldiers in first combat who raise their rifles over their heads and shoot blindly without ever poking their noses up out of the foxholes, they were merely average people. The more he was rebuffed, the more Ray believed he understood them better than they understood themselves. Even the man who had driven him off with a rifle, Ray believed, was only chasing out his own demons, his fears of his own base instincts and murderous fantasies. How self-deluding human beings were, Ray told himself that afternoon. They were as weak and phobic as field mice, and in need of the Greater Hand to guide and reassure them.

Ray read his pocket Bible on the bus, a passage from Proverbs: "The fear of man bringeth a snare; but whoso putteth his trust in the Lord shall be set up on high."

Fifteen minutes early to his appointment with Calvin Neale,

his assigned parole officer, Ray sat outside the drab office in downtown Los Angeles folding another strip of paper, this one into the form of an ox. When he finished, he left it as a gift on the table with the half year old magazines.

"How are you today?" said Calvin Neale as he opened the door to his office. He was a trim, black man in his mid-forties whose navy blue blazer and striped, collegiate tie attempted to force an elegance between the water-stained walls. He offered Ray a chair and cigarette. At the latter, Ray shook his head disapprovingly.

"Ray, since you've never been on parole before, maybe I should point out to you," Neale began, once seated, "that this idea some people have about our liking to be police just isn't so. Now, okay, I'll grant you our main job is to make certain you're complying with your parole conditions—seeking gainful employment, not consorting with known criminal elements, no possession of firearms or carrying knives with blades longer than two inches—I'm sure you've read over all of them. But I hope, Ray, you'll come to trust me as a friend, as I know I'll be able to trust you."

"Would it be all right for me to change my name?" Ray asked, having been intently thinking of this question and, until he got it out, nothing of what Calvin Neale had to say.

"No, that wouldn't be possible."

"I'm having trouble, you see, renting an apartment. Everyone knows my name. . . . Are you sure?"

"Yes . . . uh-huh."

Ray nodded resignedly, and Neale, realizing he had spoken a bit hastily, tried to recall the rules about aliases. He made a mental note to look it up later.

The interview was concluded in a little less than twenty minutes. Ray was told to report back to the office every two weeks and to inform Neale immediately of any permanent residence or employment.

Two days later Calvin Neale received a phone call from a man asking where Ray lived.

"I'm sorry," Neale told him, "but we don't give out that information."

The man chuckled, coarsely. "Why the big secret? For all you know, maybe I just want to send him some flowers."

"May I tell him who is calling," Neale inquired.

"No. That's okay. Don't worry, I'll find him on my own."

The man hung up.

When Neale promptly phoned Ray at the motel to notify him of the caller, Ray said only, "I appreciate your telling me."

Ray sat down slowly in his chair, uneasy. He tried to imagine who the caller could have been, but he had no idea.

That night, trying to put the call out of his mind, Ray stood on the threadbare carpet of his motel room, playing his clarinet until midnight. Even at nineteen he had played respectably. Now, after twenty-one years of jamming with some fairly talented inmates in a small room off the prison's old gym, his technique approached a professional level. The notes slid out clean and resonant. His fingers raced nimbly over the keys and rings; maybe, he imagined, almost as fast as the legendary Barney Bigard's had.

Ray loved all forms of jazz—from the early New Orleans days of King Oliver, Louis Armstrong and Kid Ory, to the string accompaniments Artie Shaw put behind his own clarinet, to the cool jazz of Lennie Tristano, whom Ray had always admired for having suffered as an avant-garde musician.

When Ray played he stood nearly as straight as a Marine Corps band member, eyes open, foot tapping once every few measures, incongruously immobile considering the rolling, plaintive melodies that came out.

Though he believed he was good enough to earn a living with his clarinet, he also knew he would never be given a job as publicly visible as that. Often he told himself he did not want one, anyway. Jazz for a living meant the accoutrements of smoky clubs, boozy-eyed listeners, and in some places, Ray was sure, under-the-table transactions for drugs. No, he would never set foot in a place where souls were lost. He disliked those people for what they made of jazz.

Ray stood in his motel room by himself, playing for himself.

CHAPTER 4

RICHARD POMERANTZ SIDESTEPPED MOST CALIfornia Medical Association conventions, except when they were held in San Francisco. An original city to nearly all who have tasted its charm, it played to a mounting priority in Richard's life. San Francisco, they said, was where people fell in love. At thirty-three and still single, Richard was now as unabashedly direct about that subject as his great-great-grandfather, who packed up his suitcase and walked a hundred eleven miles to Kiev to take himself a wife.

As Richard sauntered from the cobblestone atrium into the

lobby of San Francisco's fashionable Stanford Court hotel, he was greeted near the registration desk with a hug and a kiss from Dr. Stephanie Gold, a plump, red-headed psychiatrist who had been giving Richard indicating hugs since their medical school days back at Yale. Richard gave her a squeeze and said he'd ring her up for breakfast, choosing the meal that was safely sexless, with its orange juice for dry throats and discussion of morning headlines.

Stephanie was the kind of woman Richard felt he should fall in love with, but chemistry was chemistry, and theirs was charcoal in a glass of water. It was not her slight overweight—there was even a certain lustiness in those few extra pounds—but rather the relentless, almost self-effacing goodness to her. The wholesomeness had no tang to it, like fresh broccoli without lemon or salt. Women like Stephanie, he had observed, were by age thirty-eight more comfortable with their children than with the threatening passions of their husbands. They put on their Brownie troop leader uniforms as if to camouflage their exits from the house with the pack of little ones.

Richard wanted a woman who could mother with the best, all right, but he looked for a few provocative corners in the nurturing heart as well. When reading about unspeakable atrocities abroad, she would do more than sigh at the tragedy of human life being lost, and then turn to the home and gardens section. She'd root for the dictator and his henchmen to get theirs, by God—then turn to the home and gardens section.

"Probably unfit to be a psychiatrist," had been one pacifist psychoanalyst's offhand observation of Richard. He thought there might be some benefit were Richard willing to undergo analysis with him, and being only a second year resident at the time, Richard acquiesced. After a dozen sessions of rambling on about everything from his Connecticut boyhood of traumaless summers playing golf and tennis to a rather regrettable year in college of heavy drinking, to a handful of typically unremarkable anxieties (all while the analyst remained virtually silent—that being the standard psychoanalyst's tool which irritated would-be psycho-therapists like Richard who preferred give and take), Richard stood up, straightened his tie and announced, "That's about it for me. My kind of problems, I think I'll be better off spending these afternoons practicing my backhand."

At the convention, speaking to an evening study group of the psychiatric section, Richard compared the relatively embryonic field of psychiatry, which in the final analysis he was proud to be a part of, to the primitive periods of surgery four hundred years ago.

"Let's just not boast more than we can deliver at this point in the game," he told them with no discernible air of chastisement, rocking back on his heels, hands in his pockets.

Richard, never one to subscribe to what he called the emerging national ethic, 'I came, I saw, I concurred,' saved his most incendiary observation for the end of his politely tolerated speech. "I've been giving a little more thought lately," he said, "to the proposition that just possibly, the only people who benefit from psychiatrists are the ones who don't have genuinely serious psychiatric problems in the first place. The ones who do, need neurologists."

When he finished, the study group carried on that night unperturbed, and for his part, Richard, the growing speculator in neurological, chemical explanations, went into the hotel's bar.

More than a lounge, it resembled a gentleman's club, with its clusters of high-backed easy chairs set discreetly out of earshot from each other. A few well-dressed couples were scattered about, and several unattached men and women sat at the bar. The tinted blonde with the tanned, beckoningly bare back caught Richard's needing eye.

So much for lasting love this trip up.

At a table by himself Richard ordered a bourbon on the rocks, then a second. It hadn't changed since he was eighteen—he still needed the liquid confidence.

Halfway through his third, he strolled up and asked with a pleasant smile, "Join me for a drink?"

Her bright teeth were later explained by the fact she was a dental hygienist. "Is that right?" Richard said back at the table. "I was reading not too long ago that . . ." Someday he would have to compile a list of all the interests he had feigned in his life in order to get laid.

Sun-lamp tanned Cindy Wilmeth had one of the smoothest bodies Richard had ever touched. She slithered over him that night like a playful otter beneath the tight covers which never came untucked.

When she showered and left his room early the next morning while Richard lay awake in bed, he thought they had achieved the perfect brief encounter. A few minutes later she returned with a baby rose in a slender little glass vase from the hotel's gift shop. The gesture ran Richard through the heart.

Tinted blond, artificially tanned Cindy Wilmeth was no one's breezy interlude. She invited Richard to have breakfast at her apartment, but from just his half moment of hesitation, she rose with a smile and said maybe some other time. After turning the towel-warmer on for him in the bathroom, she left Richard to his miserable self—to wonder how he could be a compassionate soul to dozens in his practice, but after a few drinks in a bar be anesthetized to the human feelings and hopes that pulsate outside his damn little office—beneath low cut suggestive dresses, and brusque lawyers' three-piece suits, and the hairy chests of macho construction workers. Why was it so difficult to remember that his lack of malice was no free pass? That most of the things people did to each other were not out of malice, but out of a simple lack of restraint, out of quieting their own insecurities and needs.

Richard had breakfast with Stephanie Gold that morning. Afterward, he called Cindy Wilmeth and asked whether she would like to spend part of the afternoon with him in Golden Gate Park. Cautiously, she accepted. On the way back from the park they dropped in on a friend of Richard's who lived nearby, and as Richard had hoped, Cindy and his friend, a gregarious, sandy-haired lawyer who owned a forty-two foot ketch, were getting along exquisitely when Richard excused himself to make his flight back to Los Angeles.

* * *

But for a few tasteful pieces of furniture, Richard's office was intentionally unelaborate. A mahogany desk with simple lines dominated one side of the room, while a brown leather couch and service cart with a hammered copper tray for coffee and ice water occupied the far corner. Two straight-back chairs, his and the patient's, faced each other across the desk, and except for some bookshelves and a couple of Hockney lithographs, the beige walls were bare. The atmosphere Richard sought to create for his patients was one in which to wrestle with problems, not luxuriate.

As Richard sat a little slouched in his corduroy jacket behind the desk, Ray Lomak held himself properly in his chair, his legs uncrossed. In his V-neck sweater and crimson, clip-on bow tie, he had a churchgoer's mien, though Richard soon learned that Ray considered the Bible his religion and was not of a mind to join any organized church.

In responding to a question from Richard about the people he most admired, Ray spoke ardently.

"And then he said, 'I consider myself the luckiest man on the face of the earth.'"

"Have you always been a baseball fan?" Richard asked.

Ray looked at him quizzically. "No, I've never been a baseball fan. But Lou Gehrig was one of the very best ever."

"Yeah, I know," Richard said with a smile.

"His speech when he said farewell was very . . ." Ray's eyes moved off Richard's for one of the first times as he seemed to hunt for a word, but one he could not find. ". . . interesting. He played in 2,130 consecutive games, you're aware. They say he didn't have as much natural ability as a lot of the other players, but he worked very hard."

The conversation continued for several minutes before Richard realized he was strangely uncomfortable in Ray's presence, a feeling unfamiliar to Richard around his patients, even the toughest ex-cons. After a moment, it came to him. Ray had the extraordinary habit of resting his eyes for minutes at a time on the person he was speaking to. It was not a stare, or even an unpleasant look. In fact, it was one that might even flatter someone for a short time because of the attention it connoted—but after the first minute or so, it became terribly unnerving. People simply did not do this.

Richard mostly listened during this maiden, learning session, already aware that Ray needed no prompting to talk freely.

"When I was on death row, before my sentence was commuted, I often had a dream. This is a very interesting dream, I think. I was in the chair they have in the gas chamber, and my hands and feet were bound, and a stethoscope was strapped to my chest. You know how they do, so the doctor can tell when you're dead? And everyone was looking in at me through the windows, and all I remember was trying to free my hand so I could rip the stethoscope from my chest. I tried with all my strength, but I couldn't get my hand more than part way. You see, I thought I could save myself if I could just get the stethoscope off my chest in time. I would never be dead as long as they couldn't pronounce me dead."

Ray looked at Richard with an air of satisfaction and asked, "Is my hour almost up, doctor? You'll tell me when my time is up."

"We have plenty of time left, don't worry about it," Richard said. He always allowed fifteen minutes between appointments so no patient would have to be cut off abruptly. "Your dream sounds like a case of how we fight letting other people define who and what we are—being declared dead or alive is an extreme example, of course. A philosopher by the name of Sartre would have approved."

"I know about him," Ray declared touchily. "I hope you're not being condescending with me."

"Whoa, Ray . . . lighten up. My apologies. You're probably one of only five people in the world who really understand the guy."

Ray attempted a brief smile.

"Aren't you going to ask me about my childhood? For the last twenty-one years in prison, psychiatrists have been wanting to know what ways my parents were responsible for what I did."

Richard couldn't suppress a grin.

"I tried to tell them they had nothing to do with it. My folks were very moral, even in little ways," Ray went on. "They never even smoked or drank or swore. Morally, they gave me a good foundation. They weren't responsible for my . . . illness. We respected each other in our family. We weren't always touching— they never embarrassed me in public like that, the way some kids' parents did. My mother was kind of pathetic with her oil paintings, but that's another matter.

"Until I was thirteen and we came to Pasadena, we moved around a lot. Our moving is the reason I never did that well in school. It wasn't . . . conducive to good grades. Am I using the word correctly, doctor? Always tell me if I'm not."

Near the end of the hour, Ray had relaxed considerably, and walked about the office, picking up and inspecting the few knick-knacks as he talked.

"I get along very well with people now," he said. "I had quite a few friends up at San Quentin, you know." He hesitated, and added, "I'm a very complex person. I'll probably have to go to psychiatrists all my life."

"Oh, I don't know about that," Richard answered him. "We're going to have to pump some optimism into you."

At the end of the session, Richard reached up to the top of his bookshelf to get an article on post-prison readjustment for Ray. Several books tumbled down, including a thousand-page volume on neurology which clipped his ear.

"*Damn* it," Richard winced from the sting. Looking over at Ray, he saw Lomak's face turning red trying to contain his laughter. Pausing, Richard could see the humor, but not as much as Ray obviously saw. Barely emitting a sound, Ray's face twisted with merriment until tears actually filled his eyes.

"S-sorry," Ray said.

After Ray stood up and put on his coat and black hat, a kind Richard had never seen before, Richard showed him to the office's back door, the one patients used for leaving so they would not come face to face with the next patient in the waiting room. Conditioned by years in prison, Ray stopped short of the door and waited for it to be opened. Richard swung it wide for him, saying, "Good session. See you next week."

Not long into his next appointment, Richard thought he heard something in the hallway outside the office's back door. When he went over and opened it, he got a chill finding Ray standing on the other side. Ray glanced down nervously.

"I . . . I apologize. I just didn't want you to talk about me to other patients."

"Ray," Richard said, covering a clinging uneasiness, "I can assure you I would never do something as flagrantly unethical as that."

Ray nodded, and as he hastily buttoned his coat, Richard caught himself staring a moment at his hands, at the seemingly ordinary hands of a mass murderer.

CHAPTER 5

BECAUSE RAY LOMAK ALWAYS TOOK IMMEDIATE
notice of people on the street who wore official looking uniforms,
his eye was drawn to the man standing aimlessly on the sidewalk
the afternoon Ray came out of his second meeting with his parole
agent. The man, short and squat, appeared to be in his midfifties,
though his black hair was kept in a crew cut. He wore a dark
zipper jacket with a green badge on the shoulder, the kind
granted to private guards more for effect than authority. Ray left
the man looking desultorily into store windows as he headed past
him toward the bus stop.

An after-work crowd of people pressed into the bus with Ray, and a nearly equal number streamed off with him at the main intersection several blocks from Ray's motel. Hungry after having completely forgotten to eat lunch during another long and focused day of apartment hunting before his parole meeting, Ray hurried toward his motel room where he would save some money by having a dinner of cereal and a couple of oranges. It was only as he turned up the motel's walkway that he caught sight of the man with the green badge walking a half block behind him. Ray's legs slowed and his muscles stiffened as he stared back at the stranger, believing he had been followed. The man, however, seemed to pay Ray no attention. He put his hands in his pockets and looked at a dog across the street, as if he were merely out for a stroll. At the corner he turned and ambled in another direction, away from Ray's motel.

At the little kitchenette table, Ray sat and stoked cereal into his mouth, thinking of the call someone had made to the parole office two weeks earlier. A pall of fear began to descend over him, and he repeatedly got up to peek out the window. The man was nowhere in sight. Ray slipped the door's chain lock into place, in addition to the already secured dead bolt, and sat back down. Again and again he turned over two thoughts in his mind: 'The man lives around here, it was just a coincidence'; and, 'I have to move.'

It was in West Hollywood that Ray finally found a place to live. Although it depressed him having to move that far inland from the ocean, to where the air became a yellowish brown, Ray soon discovered that people paid less in rents to live that way. And the landlords, used to dealing with pimps, sporadically employed actors and rock musicians, and the likes of miracle diet drug inventors who worked by mail order, were decidedly less discriminating.

The attractive two-story building with louvered windows (and even a pool, which Ray had no use for) that caught Ray's eye was on Harper, an older and still proud street with languorous palm trees. Incongruously, it was just below the lively, hip Sunset Strip. The sign staked into the foliaged garden out front listed a "very reasonable" single for rent and a number to call. The number belonged to Hal Lewin, owner of a busy liquor store on La Cienega, where Ray called and had to leave his name for an appointment.

The kid at the front counter rang the back office on the phone when Ray arrived, and after talking in a low voice for a minute with his back turned, told Ray that Lewin would see him. Ray walked down a long aisle of expensive looking wines with foreign words on the labels, but came to an abrupt halt several paces from the office, where two large German shepherds lay ominously in the doorway.

"Come on, come on," ordered a small, oriole-faced man with a shameless black wig. "They only hurt when I tell them to hurt. Just don't step on them."

Ray held onto the doorjamb as he looped one leg, then the other, over the furry mound they made. One of the dogs opened its eyes halfway, just enough for Ray to see that its left eye was cupped by bluish opaque cataracts and obviously sightless. Hal Lewin sat at a cluttered desk that faced a wall panel of six television monitors which showed every aisle and corner of the store out front.

"You know who I am, and figured I'd rent you an apartment. Is that the story?" Lewin asked.

"I saw the sign outside the building," Ray answered. "Could you tell me how much the rent is?"

Lewin's phone buzzed. He had a guarded, even intimidated way of answering it.

"Yeah . . . ?" Then almost immediately bolder, "Yeah? How much does she owe? Uh-huh . . . uh-huh. For thirty bucks I'm not gonna get tough. She's been coming in here for years. Send her another bill."

Lewin hung up and looked at Ray briefly. His eyes never lighted on anything for long.

"The place is ninety-five bucks a month."

Ray did not smile, lest he make Hal Lewin think the price was foolishly low. But inside he exulted at this first sign that his travail was ending.

"I'll take you over there in a sec," Lewin said, his little hands gesturing quickly. "I used to have a resident manager, but he tried to be cute. I had to get tough with him. I don't have to tell you, I know 'em all in this town. Did you ever know Mickey Cohen? Mickey was up to my place once. We had mutual friends. Everyone comes into my store here—the Duke when he was still around, all the big stars.

"I'm going to need first and last month, cleaning fee . . . *and* a security deposit. And don't go horsin' around, I also got a law degree."

Ray was duly impressed by this man who had not finished eighth grade, and stepped back when Lewin rose to get his jacket. A softening came into Lewin's eyes, and he put a hand on Ray's arm, saying, "We'll forget about the security deposit. It's gotta be tough first getting out, huh?"

Ray nodded, feeling uncomfortable at being touched.

The single turned out to be a penny-sized room in the basement, formerly used for the liquor store's extra storage. A few empty club soda cartons still littered the floor.

"You do a little sweeping up and save yourself the cleaning fee," Lewin said.

"Thank you," Ray nodded.

At one end of the narrow room was a waxy, blue-striped mattress on box springs, along with a knee-high icebox and a hot plate. Behind a simulated wood panel partition were the toilet and small sink. Ray saw the feet of a tenant go by outside the one slatted window which, being in a subterranean room, looked up only to the sidewalk level. When an engine started up a moment later in the carport area just outside the room, the smell of exhaust wafted up from under the door.

"Just when people are takin' their cars in or out," Lewin told Ray.

"Listen, I'm trying to be a good guy, but I gotta ask for a little cooperation. I don't want your name out there on the front mailbox. Other tenants . . . you know, they do their own thing, they got their own ideas. You tell the mailman to just drop your stuff outside the door here. Get yourself a toaster, maybe a little TV, you'll be all set. Fix the place up kinda homey, live like a real person. You understand what I'm saying to you?"

"Maybe I could put some carpeting in," Ray volunteered.

"Whatever."

Ray now began to look around the room appraisingly. In truth, the place was no bigger than two prison cells put back to back, and just as damp, but it would be his, a place to live, a place to start. He had always felt an almost mystical union between himself and the ground and walls that had ever surrounded him. As a kid, he had skipped school a few times and hitched rides back to some of the colorless houses he and his parents had lived in. He would sit across the street and gaze at the windows and porches and doors, the dry stunted shrubs and walkways, all of which he felt were inextricably part of his soul. After an hour he would amble away feeling lost and forsaken, melancholy and wondering where life was leading him.

Ray sat down on the mattress and, turning the back of his shoulder to Lewin, privately counted out the one hundred, ninety dollars. After Lewin had left, Ray paced the room, realizing he had forgotten to ask for a receipt.

That afternoon Hal Lewin dropped the receipt in the mail to him, just after he had walked cockily back into his store and gathered his young witless employees in his back office to tell them, "Okay, you all saw me with Ray Lomak. He comes in here, you be cool about it. He won't cause any trouble. He knows I don't want to have to get tough with him."

✳ ✳ ✳

In prison Ray had learned the life of asceticism. While other inmates were gambling, sexualizing, dealing and bribing for the pleasures Ray had no interest in—cigarettes, one hundred and ten proof pruno, extra conjugal visits with their wives, their share of the marijuana smuggled in by the dope mules—Ray got by on the food, work clothes and precious little more provided by the prison. But only in the last five years, when he came to religion, did Ray accept his lot, not with resignation, but with self-esteem. How many shirts could one man wear at a time, he had asked Stennit, the forger. The bright, silk-screened jerseys which the blacks, Hispanics and long-haired white hipsters hustled for and were allowed to wear in the yard, were not Ray's style, anyway.

On the unpainted walls of his basement single, Ray put up the strips of cardboard, with their admonitory messages, that he had brought with him from his prison cell: "He that had gathered much had nothing over; and he that had gathered little had no lack. (II Corinthians 8:15)" and "They that will be rich fall into temptation . . . for the love of money is the root of all evil. (I Timothy 6:9–10)." Above his bed, Ray put the words of Solomon that had been over his cell cot: "He that loveth pleasure shall be a poor man. (Proverbs 21:17)."

At times, when he walked in his new neighborhood down the several block posh section of the Sunset Strip, with its spanking new Rolls-Royces and sky blue Cadillacs parked in front of the boutiques, Ray wished from deep under that one of those cars were his—not for the material possession of it, but for the voice in the world that came with that life. There was nothing quite so vivid as the glimpse he had had of a man on the phone in the back seat of a limousine.

Taking seventy-five dollars from his envelope of cash, which he had hid by taping it beneath the bathroom sink, Ray rode the buses to the discount stores on La Brea. When he occasionally bumped into other shoppers in the crowded aisles, he excused himself with a lowering of his head, for fear of being recognized.

Cleanser and scrub brush, broom, dish towels, a boxed set of plastic dinnerware—all his purchases were tangible symbols to him that he really was a free man and the steward of his daily life.

For two uninterrupted days he scrubbed his room's floor and

walls and, to lend a warmth and coziness to his new refuge, took seven dollars and bought burnt-orange colored curtains for the window. Sitting out front in the sun one afternoon, he wiped every crevice of the hot plate with pungent ammonia until it shone. There, perched on the retaining wall to the front garden, he soaked up a feeling of community and belonging he wished he could have more of. As he cleaned his hot plate, two towheaded kids on skateboards said hi as they passed, and an older man walking his collie nodded a good morning. Ray's picture on television and in the papers was already three weeks past—the memory of it fading, he believed.

The evening Ray was at last satisfied with the presentability of his room, he went to bed early for a good night's sleep. The next morning he would go in search of work.

In prison Ray had chosen to learn welding. He welcomed the solitude it gave him from the other prisoners. It was usually the young ones who had just come in for murder-one who wanted to talk to him—the man in for the biggest murder-one rap of all. He shuddered to think he had even been placed in the same legal category as these wild-eyed killers—unbathed gang members to whom violence was only a sport, pockmarked delivery boys who had lusted after unsuspecting housewives, two-bit hoods who had made seventy year old liquor store proprietors kneel down so they could shoot them in the back of the head and empty the till of its thirty-four dollars.

Questioning whether he was not supposed to feel brotherhood for all, even these boisterous, sordid creatures, Ray had retreated to his Bible for the answer and was gratified to find passages that said he did not have to. "For whosoever shall do the will of my Father which is in heaven," read Matthew 12:50, "the same is my brother." There it was. Only he who did the Lord's will did Ray have to consider his brother and his equal.

Now, with a sack lunch in hand each morning, Ray rode the buses to almost all eleven welding companies within commuting distance from his apartment. Even at the places where they did not recognize his face or name, he quickly discovered another dilemma to his situation. At San Quentin he had learned on equipment that used either the acetylene torch or the electrode "stinger," but the equipment had been donated by industry for the tax deduction because it was already old and in many cases even obsolete. The companies Ray now visited were interested in welders who had been trained not only on acetylene and the electrodes, but were certified in heliarc as well.

Ray nevertheless went to more companies, but stopped the day a flannel-shirted foreman took him aside and confided, "Forget about your lack of training, pardner, it wouldn't make any difference. Very few companies around hire ex-cons."

For several days, Ray brooded about his room, wondering whether he'd ever be given employment—wondering whether he could even end up someday sleeping at night on park benches. After he had been turned down at three more companies, he wrote a longhand letter to the President of the United States.

Dear Mr. President,

I think you probably know who I am. I know you are a very busy man, so I would not bother to take your time if this letter did not concern a matter of national importance.

From watching television behind bars at San Quentin, I've heard politicians talk about the rising crime rate in this country, and that the recidivism rate of ex-convicts is very high. I'm not sure the precise percentage, but I think it's over 50%. Also, the average American citizen constantly complains too that criminals commit the same crimes all over again after they've been set free. Everyone seems to be disturbed, but my question is, is anything really being done about it?

When I was released from San Quentin a couple of weeks ago, I was given two hundred dollars. (I was also offered a new suit, but I didn't need it. My old clothes are fine.) Since I've gotten out, no one will give me a job. This is also what happens to the average ex-convict. And with them, they take their two hundred dollars, get themselves a good dinner and as you probably know, female companionship, and after a few days the money's all gone. Since they can't get a job because they're ex-convicts, they eventually return to a life of crime, which ends up costing this country billions of dollars. I'm not one of them, Mr. President, I'm a born-again Christian, but most ex-convicts aren't.

I understand that the government spends $100 million for each new missile, and that private enterprise spends millions on shopping centers. If our society's complaints about the crime rate aren't just worthless rhetoric, and if we're really *sincerely* serious about reducing crime in this country, the government should do something.

Have you ever thought about this possibility? The government should be required to provide some type of job for all ex-convicts, at least for their first year out of prison or even for just six months. It wouldn't be a gift because we would be contributing to society and earning our money. For instance, aren't we capable of repairing roads or even working on government construction jobs? During this six month or one year period we would be able to 1.) build a little bank account, 2.) develop some self-respect, and 3.) prove ourselves capable of employment by private enterprise. Not to mention, 4.) we'd acquire non-criminal friendships and associations.

Again, Mr. President, my suggestion only has value if this country is really serious about reducing the crime rate.

Yours truly,

Raymond F. Lomak

Ray received a form letter response from the office of the Attorney General of the United States, thanking him for his interest, along with a summary of the previous year's FBI crime statistics in America.

By the beginning of November, Ray was staying in his room all day playing the clarinet and reading his Bible. At night he lay out on the small quadrant of grass behind the apartment building looking up at the stars. He had exactly three hundred, seventy-one dollars and four cents left.

✳ ✳ ✳

Deflecting his anxieties, Ray went down to the musicians' union hall on Vine Street in Hollywood hoping to learn of some place in the city he might play with other musicians. There he was peppered with a fast introduction and rap by a twenty-five year old agent who had been reading the bulletin board notices in the union hall's unkempt lobby.

"Carry the licorice stick wherever you go?" the stranger hauled out the clichéd term three times his age, nodding at Ray's clarinet case.

"No, I keep it in my room," Ray said, earnest about keeping facts straight. "Are you a musician? I wanted to play some music with, uh . . . with people."

"Don't play myself, but I've been in the business quite some time. Gregory Hork," he said, extending his hand.

Ray shook it and replied, "Very pleased to meet you."

Hork put a hand in the flapless side pocket of his tailored sport coat. Though expensive looking, it appeared to have been to every appointment Hork had ever had.

"Sorry," he said. "Your name?"

It had been a long time since Ray had told a substantial lie, and he was surprised by how easily he answered, "Fred," abbreviating his true middle name.

Hork dipped his head slightly, as people do when politely prying. "Fred . . ."

"Freddy Ray," Ray said, rather pleased with his answer.

Hork nodded. "Dynamite name for a jazzman. You play jazz, right?"

Ray nodded.

"I thought so. I represent jazz groups."

Hork shook a pack of cigarettes so one would pop up for Ray's picking. When none did, he shook it several times more before a few finally emerged, staggered. Only then did Ray tell him, "I don't smoke."

"Right. Listen, I'd like to hear you play sometime. Maybe I could work you into one of the groups I'm developing."

"No," Ray answered flatly. "I mean, I'm still just playing for myself. I'm not ready to play professionally."

"I respect that," said Hork unctuously. "Set your own schedule. Listen, one of the fellas I'm planning on representing has some guys over to his place in Venice two or three nights a week. You know, real casual—for the revved-up type that wanna keep going when their gig's done. Let me hear you play, and maybe I can set something up."

Ray agreed, and as none of the rooms in the hall were available, they went out to Hork's battered little Fiat with its Florida plates. Ray sat in the passenger seat, and only had to play for half a minute before Hork took out one of his business cards and wrote the Venice address on the back side.

"Almost any night. Tell them I sent you," Hork said. "I'll be in touch."

Ray tried but failed to screw up the courage to go to the address that same night. Someone there would surely recognize him, he told himself. The next day he went to a drugstore and bought a pair of sunglasses. When he tried them on in front of his chipped bathroom mirror, he thought he looked ridiculous. Three more evenings passed before he finally reached for his coat and hat, put on the dark glasses and boarded a late-night bus for Venice.

The address was to a wood frame bungalow in the black section of the bohemian, oceanside community. A husky black man with greying sideburns and a tuft of beard answered the door. His stubby fingers held dearly to the alto sax that hung strapped from his neck.

Ray announced himself as Freddy Ray, an acquaintance of Gregory Hork's.

"Oh, my, my," said the man named Hugs Buchanan, with a lift in his low-cracked voice. "That little piss-ass still trying to rub-a-dub-dub the cockles of our hearts. Well, come in out of the chill, Freddy Ray—a white man is always welcome at our table."

Hugs walked Ray into the living room with his arm around his shoulder and introduced him to a half dozen other musicians who relaxed on sofas and bean bags. Two vulnerable jugs of wine sat half empty on the wooden floor. Only one of the jazz players was white, a young guitarist with shoulder length blond hair whom they called Snowflake.

"I want it to go on the record, gentlemen," Hugs said with tart enjoyment in his eyes, "that someday, young Mr. Hork is actually going to *book* a group. Now, what do you think of that? Especially if he can replace enough of you darkies. Let go of my ankle, Samuel," he said to a bass player who had put a flourish to his laugh by falling over sideways. Ray laughed with the others at Hugs Buchanan's rubber tipped barbs.

Never removing his sunglasses, Ray not only kept up with the group's playing that night, he could feel all of their eyes respectfully fixed on him whenever his sixteen bars of solo came around. He belonged.

At the break, the jugs of wine were passed around. Ray asked only for a glass of water.

"The cat *look* cooler than he be!" Samuel, the bass player, gibed.

"My landlord owns a liquor store, you know," Ray told them, thinking of the legitimacy even the Bible gave to wine. "I can get big discounts. I'll bring some tomorrow night."

The next day Hal Lewin flung his answer at him over his shoulder, as he strode down the store's aisles marking figures on a clipboard.

"Are you kidding me? You must be trying to kid me. I already got the lowest prices in town right on the stickers. Don't go trying to take advantage of me, okay, Ray?"

Ray bought five half-gallons of wine at the regular price, and when the musicians paid him back at the discount he claimed to have gotten, he was six dollars short. Zealous for their respect and friendship, Ray continued to supply the wine on all the nights the men got together to jam.

To the other residents in Ray's six-unit apartment, Ray became more of a mystery than ever. He still kept no name on his mailbox, and no one had ever met up with him out on the sidewalk, though all had at some time heard the haunting blues of his clarinet filtering up from his basement room. And now, the ones who were up late enough and who chanced to look out their windows, saw the new tenant leaving the building close to midnight every few nights in his trench coat and unusual black hat. A few of the more restless sleepers heard the desolate footsteps coming back up the walkway and down the basement stairs as late as four or five in the morning.

During a break in one of their jam sessions, a wiry trumpeter named Coley sat down next to Ray and soon got to talking about women.

"You ain't had a woman since you been to L.A.?" he squealed in his high voice. "Oh, man! Hey, we gotta help this man out."

Soon they were all tossing out, with leers and snickers, the names of the pros they knew. Horse-faced Stacy, not worth her asking price; a wildcat who clawed, named Annette; Treak the Deb; a pork barrel named Molly—she liked trumpeters.

"Who's Treak?" Ray asked, twisting the tip of his clarinet into the shag throw rug next to where he sat.

"The debutante?" Samuel cried. "Snowflake, you tell the boy, seein' you know her the best. Heh-heh," he laughed hellishly.

"What's that low-down laugh?" Hugs upbraided his friend before Snowflake could answer. "Why, Treak Johnson is a fine, educated woman. Audited a night course on jazz I taught back in New York. It was too primitive a course, I guess, for that fancy Sarah Lawrence College she was going to. I gotta say I was surprised to hear what line of work she's into these days."

"Yeah, and if you forget your five fins at home, she might even extend you some credit, isn't that what you told me, Snowflake?" Samuel persisted.

Coley shook some spittle from his trumpet. "We figure her daddy back in Long Island must have big money."

"Folks," Snowflake finally spoke up. "I like her."

Ray did not leave that night before having Treak's phone number and address pressed tightly in his hand.

The very next night, Ray sought out Treak Johnson. She lived in a run-down clapboard house in Santa Monica. A pair of partially dried panty hose were draped over the water meter, and a rusted-out Continental with tattered upholstery was parked in the narrow driveway.

Treak Johnson, no more than twenty-five, had a fragile, wan face, but to Ray as pretty a face as that of any woman he could remember standing that close to. She wore a silk robe, and offered Ray a chair in the living room, saying, "Don't you believe in calling a girl first, and giving her time to look a little more presentable?"

"I'm sorry, I forgot."

The place was an appalling disarray of blouses and stray shoes on the floor, dying plants, a half-filled watering can sitting on the couch, smudged records out of their album jackets. Treak excused herself and went into the bathroom, leaving Ray to wonder where Hugs had discerned any class in this common slattern. But when he looked around again he noticed that all the indolently strewn clothes were of rich material, and that behind the unemptied glasses on the many little tables were ivory vases, hand carved statues which Ray guessed only people who had traveled extensively would own, and indifferently tossed gold necklaces. In the open hallway closet he even saw a luxurious fur coat.

"Well, as it so happens, you caught me on a free night," Treak said when she came back into the room. "I'm sure Snowflake told you, I don't have many of them," she proclaimed, though something in her voice rang false, insecure. She lit a cigarette and talked to Ray dilettantishly about jazz.

Continuing the charade as Freddy Ray—town-to-town, knock-around jazzman—Ray wove a history for her that began to give him some pleasure, the more tangled and intricate his yarn became. He painted himself as something of an undiscovered genius. Partway through a story about his early years in New Orleans, he thought he saw a different look suddenly fill Treak's big grey, curious eyes. Though he couldn't be sure, he sensed she knew who he was.

Ray paused, then quickly concluded his story.

"You're a rather intriguing man," she came to say. "Do you want to go into the other room now?"

"I don't have very much money," Ray said, coolly regarding the fur coat in the hall closet.

She took his hand and led him into the bedroom. "We can talk about it later."

She was a nymphomaniac, Ray decided, as Treak moaned professionally with the first touch of his hand on her leg.

The next night that the men agreed to jam, Ray swelled with more excitement than ever for the hours of music ahead. He really was one of their group now, he thought, as he ironed a pair of slacks and took a fresh shirt off a hanger. He savored the idea of even letting it slip how Treak had found him so fascinating she hadn't even charged him. Not even a matter of credit—she truly liked being with him. Ray hurriedly tied his shoes and half-walked, half-ran to the bus stop, his clarinet case tucked under his arm.

When he got to Hugs' house, it was dark inside and the front door was locked. He peered in the front window, but nothing inside stirred. He turned back toward the sidewalk, dismayed and hurt—if they had changed their minds about playing that night, they might at least have cared enough about him to leave a note on the door. Turning back again, he walked briskly to the door and knocked one last time. When no one answered, he shuffled forlornly back to the bus stop.

He called Hugs' home the next day and left a message with his nephew for Hugs to call him at a designated time at the pay phone Ray used near his apartment. Ray waited expectantly at the phone booth, but received no call. All that week Ray continued to leave messages with the nephew, but Hugs never called back.

Ray sat alone on his bed, mystified. It was very clear that, for some reason, Hugs and the others did not want him to be a part of their group any more. He had thought that they were his friends, but he was wrong. His already empty life had been stripped of the one thing he looked forward to during the many long days in his apartment.

Could it be that they had discovered who he was? No. He was convinced he had successfully kept his identity from them. As he sat and pondered, the thought of Treak Johnson crossed his mind. Just as quickly, he dismissed it. Though there had been a moment during his evening with her when he feared she knew who he was, he obviously had been mistaken. If she had known, would she have made love to him, and with such apparently deep emotion? Even if, perchance, she had been aware he was Raymond Lomak, he just knew she would never have betrayed him to his jazz friends. She seemed to be a really nice person. And she seemed to care for him.

If they didn't know who he was, what else could it possibly have been, he asked himself. There must be something about him, he thought as he stood for more than a minute in front of his mirror, that put people off.

He walked back to his bed and lay down, tired. In a few minutes, he had escaped into sleep.

The following Sunday, Ray visited Treak again. Her long brunette hair was combed and beautiful. With just a whisper of make-up highlighting her delicate, white oval face, she looked even prettier than before. In the middle of their love-making, she put her arms around his neck and hummed, "Mmm, *Raymond.*"

Immediately, Ray lifted his head to look at her, and Treak held her lower lip between her teeth a little fearfully.

"You do know who I am," Ray said, tonelessly.

Treak only nodded.

"And you told Snowflake and he told the others who I am."

Treak's whole body tightened.

"It just came up," she said, her breath falling short. "It doesn't matter. What do you care what they think of you? You don't need them, you've got me," she beseeched, trying to pull him back down to her.

Ray sat up and stared at the wall, then reached for a pocket in his pants next to the bed. Treak's pale mouth fell open and her sharp, alive grey eyes widened in fear. Stonily, Ray took all the money he had in his wallet—twenty-one dollars—and laid it out on the nightstand. Then he came back on top of her slender frame, and finished—as coldly as a soldier in an enemy village for the night.

As he lay half asleep, Treak tried caressing his cheek and began talking to him. Ray, dreamy, moved his hand over to her leg. Then something he heard, or thought he heard, shook his senses.

"What was what like?" he asked.

"You know," she said, rocking her head and embarrassed now. "What was it . . . like? You know, killing someone."

Ray turned on his side and looked at her—his blue eyes iced. After a moment he began to smile faintly, derisively.

"Why do people want to know things like that? It's an unbelievably frightening thing to end a human life. No one could ever describe it. . . . Or did you just want to know about things like the blood and the screams?"

"Okay, okay, you don't have to get sore. I just wanted to know what it . . . you know, felt like—you know, like how does it feel killing someone in a war."

A minute later Ray entered her again, viciously. But no matter how hard he slammed his pelvis into hers, it only seemed to please her. When Ray realized he was hating her more than anyone he had hated in a long, long time, he suddenly stopped. He held her face in his hands and engulfed her with kisses all over her forehead and cheeks. "I'm sorry, I'm sorry," he panted. "I'm sorry."

"For what?" she smiled.

"I'm sorry," he repeated.

✶ ✶ ✶

When Ray got home late that night, he sat gloomily in his darkened basement room. After a time, he was aroused by the sound of footsteps out on the walkway above him. Moving over to his window and looking up, he saw him—the man with the dark jacket and green badge. A force of hot breath gathered instantly in Ray's chest. Without moving a foot, he pulled his head back, his eyes riveted to the stranger who was also looking up, apparently at the doors of all the first and second floor apartments. In the dim light of the building's outdoor lamps, there was a look of furrowed and dull-witted frustration on his face. He puckered his lips like a fish, wheeled, and walked back toward the front sidewalk. But from the halt of footsteps that Ray heard, he knew that the man had gone back only as far as the bank of mailboxes.

Ray back-pedaled slowly across the room to the bed, where he eased himself down onto the quietly exhaling mattress. He sat there, motionless, as the footsteps returned and the two legs, which were now all Ray could see, planted themselves again in front of his window. The feet turned one way, then the other, remained rooted a long minute, and at last moved away, carrying the night prowler back out to the street. Only after sitting utterly still for another full ten minutes did Ray venture to stand up. The back of his shirt was matted with perspiration.

The next morning Ray cautiously left his apartment and went to the Hollywood Division of the Los Angeles Police Department. There he spoke with a Detective Sergeant Prettel. As Ray carefully detailed the incidents which had convinced him the stranger meant him harm, Prettel, a stringbean fifty year old veteran with a pinched face and a whip-thin belt, sat noncommittally back in his chair.

"Aren't you going to take any of this down?" Ray asked, after a time.

"Yeah . . . sure," Prettel said, still leaning back, but picking up a pencil and scribbling a few words at arm's length.

"My full name is—"

"I know your full name," said Prettel coldly.

Ray glared long and bitterly at the detective.

"I see. I get it."

Doodling beneath the few words he had written, Prettel droned, "I'll see if someone can look into this."

"No, I know you won't, I'm not stupid," Ray spat back. He stood up and marched out of the police station.

In Hal Lewin's back office later that day, Ray approached his landlord deferentially. "I thought maybe a man with all your connections would know where I could get the protection I need."

"Yeah, sure . . . sure I got those connections," Lewin said, avoiding Ray's eyes as he rummaged through some store invoices on his desk. "It's just . . . these things need the right kind of handling. Okay?"

"I don't want any violence, please," Ray said, "I'm just . . . very worried."

"Of course you're worried, that's why you came to me," Lewin swaggered. "You're a good tenant, I take care of my own." He wagged a finger weightily at Ray. "You're family."

"When do you think—"

"Don't worry about it, okay? Store's going to hell, everyone needs a piece of me for *something*. I'll make a few calls—call in a few chits. Now give me a little room."

Just after dinner that night, a fifteen year old lummox of a boy with a few scruffy whiskers and a baseball bat in his hand showed up at Ray's door.

"I think maybe Mr. Lewin didn't quite understand the situation," Ray told the boy politely. "I'm afraid you might get hurt, but thank you for coming, anyway."

Ray stayed in his apartment as much as possible, and when he did have to go out onto the foreboding streets, he did so with a constant eye over his shoulder. At almost every car horn, he jumped, and whenever he turned a sidewalk corner his hand unconsciously rose part way up, protectively, in front of him. At night, he slept fitfully.

But for the time being, the man had disappeared.

AFTER THEIR SECOND SESSION, WHAT STRUCK Richard Pomerantz most about Ray Lomak was that Ray, the man who had said he was in lasting need of a psychiatrist, was not particularly interested in any of Richard's opinions. If they happened to coincide with his own, he nodded approvingly at Richard; if they did not, Ray merely looked at Richard blankly, or in some instances said with total dismissal but no antagonism, "No. No, doctor, that's not it at all."

Toward the start of their fourth session Richard began easily, "Ray, from reading all the reports, I know what you've told others about *why* you did what you did when you were nineteen, but have you ever thought about how you were able to actually bring yourself to do it?"

For the first time in their several hours together, Ray seemed to be caught off balance. He sat back and gazed thoughtfully at Richard. "I don't know, doctor . . . it might sound strange to you, but I never have thought about that."

There was an uncomfortable silence.

"Can I ask you what *you* think?" Ray said with a certain hesitancy.

"Of course. . . . To be really candid with you, Ray, which I think you want me to be," Richard said, scratching his ear, "some people simply have much more of a homicidal tendency than others. Now, maybe my profession should know why this is so, but the fact is, we don't know yet. Which isn't to say there aren't a number of interesting theories, from hormonal imbalances on down. In any event, from what limited knowledge I have of you, perhaps we should give consideration to other factors that may have been at play. Like the fact that you seem to be a person of uncommon intensity."

"Really?"

Richard smiled. "Yes, you are. And unfortunately, I think sometimes the type of intensity you seem to possess causes a constriction of vision—a kind of tunnel vision.

"When you were nineteen, you knew precisely what you wanted to do, but unlike most of us, you didn't temper your instincts with other considerations."

Richard looked for some reaction in Ray, but Ray sat impassively, as if listening to a case study observation about someone else.

"Ray, you know more than I do what was on your mind when you committed the murders, but for instance, I would hazard a guess—and correct me if I'm wrong—that apart from thinking about your main objective and what was going to happen to the victims, you gave virtually no thought to the consequences your act would have on many other people, including yourself if you were apprehended."

Ray looked at the floor, and very slowly nodded.

At their next session Richard said, "It must be hard not feeling a little resentful about being made to still pay for what you've been told you've already served your time for."

"I intend to prove myself," Ray declared.

"Do you think people have enough forgiveness in them to eventually give you the kind of breaks you feel you need?"

Ray looked at Richard before answering. "Yes. I think God at some point reveals to men what they must do . . . and he'll show me what I must do to prove myself to them."

"How do you feel about that man at the apartment house who pointed the rifle at you?" Richard asked.

"He was frightened," Ray said. "I felt sorry for him."

Richard tilted his head and, with a friendly narrowing of his eyes, smiled lightly. It was a look and smile meant to convey that if Ray were not being totally honest, he should feel free to be so.

Ray did not return the smile.

"Why have you chosen to spend so much time with ex-convicts, doctor?"

Richard tossed a hand out nonchalantly. "They're entitled to help the same as anyone."

Ray looked at him in an oddly docile but accusatory way that craftily implied knowledge of Richard's interior.

"People are fascinated by violence, aren't they," Ray said.

Richard knew he should have immediately replied what he thought—that yes, people were intrigued by it for a number of reasons: the distant ominous bell it struck deep in man's aboriginal past; the glimpse it gave of one's own fate (why else would people turn a magazine picture sideways to better see the corpse's face?); the quick curious look at grotesqueness in any form; the unstated euphoria of knowing that after that day's or that movie's body count, they were still alive. But Richard did not respond to Ray for a moment, and the pause, he could see, gave Ray considerable pleasure. He felt a strange, arrogant power in the man across the desk from him and, as if suddenly tongue-tied, answered only, "Yes, many people are fascinated by violence."

Ray began to speak rapidly. "Maybe you even identify with people who commit murder, Dr. Pomerantz."

"I don't think I *identify* with murderers, no," Richard said. "But I think you're right to say I'm interested in them."

"Most of them aren't very interesting," Ray said scornfully. "They're simple-minded. They're people who can't control them-selves."

"Do simple-minded people anger you?"

Ray did not even seem to hear this interruption to his train of thought. "So if *they're* not interesting, it must be what they *did* that interests you. Do you enjoy it if they describe their murders to you?"

Richard chuckled a little, though beginning to feel uncomfort-ably warm beneath his corduroy jacket. In truth, to even contem-plate what some of his patients had done, to conjure up any kind of mental picture of their victims' suffering, was to loathe these ex-cons. And as their psychiatrist, he could not afford to do that.

"If reliving a murder can play a part in helping a patient," Richard responded, " I don't discourage it. But otherwise, no, I don't seek to hear these stories. And to answer your next question, yes, like most people, I haven't gone a lifetime without a violent thought entering my mind. But it's important to dichotomize—to know the difference between our thoughts and what we really desire to act upon."

Richard released the firm grip he had on a Scotch-tape dis-penser, and put it back on the desk.

"I don't ever have violent fantasies any more," Ray said, look-ing from Richard to the tape, and back to Richard. "Are you religious, Dr. Pomerantz?"

"No, not very."

Richard called an end to the session exactly at the hour.

✳ ✳ ✳

The day before Thanksgiving, Richard left his office early and spent part of the afternoon doing wind sprints on the beach with his Irish setter, Paddy. With the chilled water and sand clear of swimmers and sunbathers, they had the place to themselves. Richard's compact legs pumping on torn sneakers, he bulleted from one large rock to the next. Every time he started up again, Paddy bolted out ahead of him, only to slow up after a few loping strides, never quite remembering the limits of his master's speed. It was not Paddy's Irish-setter denseness as such that endeared Paddy to Richard, but rather his slathering, unconditional love, and the absence of a moodiness which would have resulted from even half a brain.

Climbing the uneven wooden steps that led up from the beach, Richard heard his phone ring and bounded up toward the door off his sun deck.

"Hello, Dr. Pomerantz," came a slightly tensed voice. "This is Ray Lomak calling."

"Yeah, Ray, how are'ya?"

"Very well, thank you. The reason I'm calling," he said, "is . . . uh, I wanted to invite you to Thanksgiving dinner. I wanted to know if you'd like to share Thanksgiving dinner with me."

"Oh, that's very kind of you, Ray, I'm very flattered. But I'm afraid I already have plans to go with a friend to her cousin's."

After a short silence Ray said, "Yes, I suppose it's probably late for me to call like this the day before . . . yes, well, um . . . I just thought . . . are you going to be there the whole day?"

Not harshly, but to the point, Richard said, "Ray, you know, it's never a very good idea for psychiatrists and their patients to socialize outside the office. There's just a certain objectivity required in the relationship, if you understand."

"I just thought," Ray spoke again, a little too quickly to have been listening, "that . . . well, you see, you're really my only friend in the city, Dr. Pomerantz, and I just thought if you weren't busy—"

"But Ray—"

"Maybe you could see your cousin later."

"My *friend's* cousin."

"Yes, well . . . I bought a turkey this afternoon, and I just thought if you weren't busy . . . but I guess you are, so . . . um . . . and you think you'll be there the whole day?"

Richard sank down into his easy chair and asked with a concealed resignation, "Would it be convenient if we came in the early afternoon, Ray?"

"Two o'clock, maybe?" Ray said, his voice more relaxed.

"Fine. See you then."

Richard smiled to himself, and after they had hung up he sat for five minutes before picking up the phone again, thinking through exactly how he would extend the invitation to his date, Debra Gordon, an eye surgeon's daughter who knew the menu at Ma Maison by heart, and had season tickets to the symphony.

✶ ✶ ✶

Because Debra had not quite finished brushing out her hair when Richard came to pick her up, they were just a few minutes late in arriving at Ray's.

Ray stepped back with the door as he opened it for them, as might a butler. He wore freshly pressed grey slacks, a white shirt and the same crimson bow tie he always wore to Richard's office. It was obvious he had just run a wet comb through his trim hair.

"Please come in. May I get your coats?" he said buoyantly, before even a hello.

"Hello, Ray," Richard said, stepping into the tidy room. "Happy Thanksgiving. I'd like you to meet Debra."

When Debra extended her hand, it was only after a split moment's surprise that Ray grabbed for it. Men and women had not shaken hands much twenty-one years earlier.

"We're not too late, Ray, are we? "Richard asked." We said around two?"

"We said at two, yes." His little alarm clock on the window sill read thirteen after.

Richard and Debra sat down at the only place there was for sitting, on the bed, while Ray hung up their coats next to his own clothes, on a chin-up bar which served as the room's closet. Looking around the room, Debra commented, "You certainly keep the place clean, Ray."

"Thank you," Ray said politely.

Debra would do her very best, Richard knew.

In front of the bed was a row of three orange crates stood on end, each with its Melmac dinnerware setting atop a paper-towel place mat. Across the room, in a skillet over a hot plate, was a large crinkled globe of aluminum foil, a turkey leg punched through its side. Ray ignored his guests for the moment while he turned on a pocket size radio and played with its directional aerial.

Debra leaned over toward Richard and whispered, "I don't think you can *cook* a turkey on a hot plate." Like a Boston dowager, she always pressed her fingertips to the hollow of her throat when she spoke confidentially; her tea parlor ways were among the many small reasons Richard had for dating her sparingly.

The station Ray had the radio tuned to played jazz and old blues, and when he was finally able to bring in clearly the soulful voice of a female singer whom Richard could not quite place, Ray stood back and looked at the floor as he listened.

"Billie Holiday," he said quietly. . . . "A black genius," he added with great reverence.

When the song was finished, it did not occur to Ray to sit down and engage in any pre-dinner conversation. He set about immediately to serve food on all their plates.

"There. Will that be enough?" he asked solicitously. "There's a lot more."

Debra pointed out, gently, that the meat that was still pink was not yet done, and suggested they carve from the other side. With his three inch knife Ray sawed away at the parts that were white, although dry as firewood. He spooned out the gravy directly from its tin can, as he did the cranberry sauce. Seeing no second can of cranberries anywhere, Richard held up his hand after just one spoonful, and said, "That's plenty, that's just fine."

When Ray sat down, Richard picked up his knife and fork, but quickly put them back down when he saw Ray fold his hands and bow his head.

"Thank you, Lord, this day for our food and sustenance. And . . . uh . . . for the support and friendship of others to share it with. Amen."

With Richard in the middle, they sat wordlessly next to each other on the bed while they ate, as if watching a television set.

"Everything's delicious," Richard broke the silence.

"Thank you," Ray replied. "Seeing it's Thanksgiving, I was thinking maybe I'd make sandwiches out of the leftovers and take them down to skid row. They'd probably appreciate something like that."

"Excellent idea," Richard said. "It doesn't even occur to most people to do things like that."

"People feel impotent about the world's problems," Ray asserted.

Within minutes, Ray had ravished his meal. Without a word, he abruptly stood up and left his guests to themselves while he took his plate and silverware behind the partition, where he proceeded to wash them in the small sink. Richard had only to catch Debra's eye to see she was hoping they wouldn't have to stay long.

Ray sat back down next to them.

"About people feeling impotent, Dr. Pomerantz, I wouldn't think *you* ever would. You're a psychiatrist. You've been to fine colleges, and . . . and things."

Richard shrugged good-naturedly.

"Yale," Debra slipped in.

Chafed by Debra's readiness to impress people without a moment's reflection for its appropriateness (another of Richard's many reasons), Richard added, "A good college. New Haven's a toilet," and crammed a forkful of turkey into his mouth.

"Was your father a benefactor there?" Ray asked.

When Richard shook his head, Ray seemed surprised, almost not even believing that one could get in to those gold-ivied schools any other way. He asked Richard more about his past, nodding politely but silently at what he heard about the quiet wealth of Greenwich, Connecticut.

Richard later had all three of them laughing over the story of two psychiatrists passing on the street, one of them saying, "Good morning," the other muttering to himself, "I wonder what he meant by that." Ray's face took on a rare glow as he saw his little room filled with laughter. He smiled ingenuously, and said, "I told you we'd have a good time."

When some static came over the radio, Ray walked over to it and twisted the aerial around. Getting no results, he began to shake the radio roughly.

"Those pocket ones don't have a lot of power," Richard calmly advised him. "The reception's probably going to fade a little down here."

"No, no," Ray said sternly, glaring at the radio in his hand. "People just don't make things right any more."

He raised his hand slightly, as if contemplating slamming the radio down onto the counter top, but laid it down gently. He let out a long, charged breath and said, "Boy, I don't know. It just . . . it just seems people should care more."

After the radio corrected itself, he sat back down, but eyed it whenever its reception faltered, as a parent might eye a misbehaving child at a party.

When Richard and Debra stood at the door to leave, Ray said effusively, "It was nice of you to come, very nice of you. I don't know how to thank you."

"Well, thank *you*, Ray," Richard said. "It was very kind of you to have us."

As they walked through the carport Debra sighed, "He's odd

all right, but not really a *bad* fellow. It's so strange to think of
. . . what he did."

"Uh-huh," Richard mumbled absently, an ear cocked back toward Ray's room, half listening for the shattering of a plastic radio.

CHAPTER 7

BEING AS CIRCUMSPECT AS HE WAS ABOUT THE
stranger who had been following him, Ray probably should have
noticed the flat faced, crew-cut man. Although the man wasn't
wearing his dark jacket and badge, Ray had even glanced his way.
But because the stranger, who was seated in a car down the block
from Ray's apartment, was talking easily with a couple of gas
company surveyors working out on the street, nothing had registered in Ray.

By the time the man finally saw him, Ray was already standing
on the corner, boarding an eastbound bus. The man followed the

bus as it proceeded to Fairfax Boulevard and then turned south, taking Ray to Los Angeles' famed Farmer's Market, where Ray often browsed through the fruits and vegetables imported from all over the world. Ray was just going through the front entrance of the open air market when the flushed stranger jumped from his car. His green and red checkered short sleeve shirt came untucked as he chased after Ray, a .25 caliber automatic waving freely in his hand.

A woman standing in front of a bin of persimmons screamed, and her small daughter reflexively joined in, but the shrieks in the clamorous market were too far behind Ray for him to hear. It was only as the gun-brandishing man, rapidly closing in, knocked his way through a group of Japanese shoppers and drew the curses of a vendor as he sent a display of cantaloupes tumbling, that Ray turned around to see his assailant running directly at him less than twenty yards away.

"Oh God, no!" Ray yelled, and stumbled behind the closest available person.

The first shot put a hole in the white painted metal of a refrigerated meat counter.

Ray clawed his way past a fat man involuntarily shielding him, and ran down an open aisle, his arms protectively cradling the back of his head. Two more shots kicked up sawdust far off the mark. His pursuer bulldozing relentlessly behind him with the gun held wildly out at arm's length, Ray zigzagged frantically from one little open space to the next. More shots rang out, miraculously missing all living things. Cries for someone to call the police went up everywhere.

Ray did not look back, but darted like a pathetic, doomed desert rat caught far from his hole. His eyes were wide with the hysterical instinct for life.

At the first glimpse of an exit out to the parking lot, he raced madly for it, but tripped over an empty baby stroller and went sprawling. He pulled himself to his feet and staggered toward the street outside.

A pain in his ankle from the fall began to throb, biting into his bone with every additional step. Unable to continue much farther, he hobbled in panic behind a large garbage bin, where he curled up. Within another minute, his heart still pounding feverishly, he heard sirens coming from several directions. Officers dashed from their cars, and out in front of the other side of the market, far from where Ray was hiding, they apprehended the checker-shirted man at his car. The empty gun hanging limply in his hand, he offered no resistance.

"If judges won't do what they have to do," he volunteered evenly to the arresting officers, "then good American citizens gotta do it. I won't go for no attempted murder charge, either, I can tell you that right now. It wouldn't a'been murder. Not for a slime like that. I'll plead guilty to assault."

Fifty-one year old Herbert Drake, a night watchman at a supermarket in Irvine, did not say anything more, but rode without a stir in the back seat of a squad car to LAPD's Parker Center.

An hour after Drake's arrest, as the police continued to roam the Farmer's Market grounds looking for evidence and interviewing witnesses, they found Ray still curled up, hiding behind the garbage bin.

∗ ∗ ∗

The Los Angeles District Attorney's Office wanted to prosecute Herbert Drake for attempted murder, but quickly lost most of its verve for the case when Ray stated that Drake was simply a misguided individual whom Ray, as a Christian, had forgiven. And more to the point, Ray said he was very much opposed to testifying against Drake. Within the week, the DA's office agreed with Drake's lawyer to accept a guilty plea to the lesser charge of assault with a deadly weapon. The remorseless Drake was sentenced to two years in the state prison at Chino.

A week later, as Ray, still unnerved over the shooting, returned to his apartment with a bag of groceries in one arm and a newspaper's classified-jobs section under the other, he found a woman taping a note to his door. She was a beefy woman of middle age, with a bulldog face and short feathery hair.

"May I help you?" Ray asked warily.

"Oh, Mr. Lomak," she said, immediately recognizing him and smiling warmly. "I hope I'm not intruding. My name is Kate Robertson. Reverend Dornan gave me your address. I wanted to call, but I couldn't find a phone number for you."

"I don't have a phone," Ray told her, a trifle embarrassed.

Inviting her in, he dug his hand into his pocket for his key and let them both into his apartment. He still limped just slightly from the severe sprain he had suffered at the Farmer's Market.

Taking a seat on the bed, where she planted her hands on her spread knees and leaned forward like a ballplayer on a bench, Kate Robertson said, "I'm from the First Church of Our Savior in Anaheim, Mr. Lomak. Down in Orange County?"

When Ray, putting the groceries away, turned around with a regardful look on his face, she continued quickly, "Yes, the same one Herbert Drake belongs to, or I should say belonged to. It was loathsome that his membership in our church got on TV and into the papers. Mr. Lomak, I can't tell you how ashamed we all are that anyone who had ever been in our congregation would have done such a despicable thing. We're just . . . ashamed. Please believe me, we don't feel at all like that about you. Not at all. We've followed your personal story and conversion with great interest, with great admiration. In fact, the reason I've come here is to ask you if you would consent to come speak to us, at a convocation we're holding a week from Sunday."

She smiled broadly at Ray. "You're a tre*men*dous inspiration, Mr. Lomak," she said, her hands squeezing her knees, her elbows out at a mannish tilt. "We've all been praying for you. You must say yes. Over two thousand people are coming. We've rented the Disneyland Hotel," she said excitedly.

Ray sat down at the opposite end of the bed, his eyes bright in thought. He licked his lips with interest. Then his face darkened.

"Two thousand people," he repeated. He shook his head with regret. "I'm sorry, Miss Robertson. I just couldn't do that. I'm sorry."

"But why not?" she asked, a tad annoyed at having been led astray by his initial reaction, which had been obvious in his face.

"Because I just have to disappear for a long time," he told her. "I won't be able to get a job if they keep taking pictures of me now. I just want to live in peace," he said, swallowing back the emotion that was pushing up inside him.

"But—"

Kate Robertson was hell-bent on prosecuting her point. Standing before her church committee and convincing them to invite Raymond Lomak to their convocation had been her finest hour. All the enthusiasm, ambition and tenacity that had scared men off for years had found a place and acceptance in the church, and if she could not maintain court as the never failing Kate in the respectful eyes of those powdered, skinny ladies and their broad-girthed husbands, then she had nothing. "Why won't you do this for us?" she persisted mulishly. "Do you know how many people there are in this country whose lives you could change? People who hate their lives and want something better. Who need to be shown they could be happy and saved if they just take Jesus into their hearts. Don't people deserve a little happiness in their lives?"

"People would misunderstand," Ray said stoically, not raising his voice as she had. "People would say . . . I don't know what they'd say. I have to keep to myself. I just want to live like everybody else."

"You're just being selfish, and I won't let you!" the woman stormed. "You're *not* just like everyone else, Raymond. You're special. What has happened to you is a miracle. Jesus has called to you, just as He called down to Saul of Tarsus. You're different than other people. You know that. And now you've been sent back out into the world with a message. Don't turn your back on God, Raymond. Not again. You have to be strong. I'll help you to be strong."

She moved over toward him on the bed, and put her thick

ringless hand on his arm. Instinctively his arm flinched a little, but his head swam with her words—"special," "sent with a message." Although these were the almost erotic words that swirled in his ears, he believed his suddenly burgeoning excitement was due to his having made one of those electric connections with a stranger over a shared subject greater than themselves. It was not what she said about him, he was sure, but rather the mutuality of their love for Christ. The power of God brought people off their remote reefs.

Ray looked around his room, and for the first time since he had moved in, he saw it as a sad lifeless place. He did not want to live so alone, in such hiding. The thought of two thousand people staring up at him made his insides shudder, but he felt himself at the border of opportunity. He looked at Kate Robertson out of the edge of his eye, and said tentatively—egging her on, actually— "You think it's a moral obligation? Do you feel this is something I *must* do?"

"You're the very story of redemption itself," Kate rhapsodized, reviving the phrase that had gone over so well in front of the church committee.

Ray sat considering, second thoughts beginning to wash away the excitement, and blur the vivid picture that had brought him such a radiant moment.

"Things are so hard for me already. I even thought of moving away to South America, but that would be a violation of my parole. If the parole people ever found me . . . I won't ever go back to prison. Never. That's an iron pledge I made to myself.

"What if someone tries to shoot me, with all those people at your convocation?" he asked.

Kate's eyes flashed with anger at just the thought, as though she were ready to annihilate the man who tried it. As the idea started to become credible, however, she withdrew her hand from his arm, as if to put a step between them before they even got to the stage. But in a firm voice to reassure them both, she said, "Shoot you? No, that was poor Mr. Drake. No one else in our group would ever dream of such a thing. These are going to be your friends, Raymond. Our arms are open in *love* to all who are saved." She shook her head resolutely. "Our faith is one of forgiveness. 'For if ye forgive men their trespasses, your heavenly Father will also forgive you.' "

" 'But if ye forgive not men their trespasses,' " Ray added, with a subtleness to his voice, " 'neither will your Father forgive *your* trespasses.' "

"We need each other," said Kate.

"I can't run and hide, can I," Ray said. "It's important that I don't hide."

Kate Robertson nodded, expectantly.

✶ ✶ ✶

It was chilly and overcast, spoiling for a good rain the entire day. But the solid cloud cover was still just a smack too white for that, the kind that made the world seem like a well lit, but indoor place. The ground and trees had that strange, rich glow, as in a greenhouse. It was the kind of Sunday when older people preferred to stay home and maybe play cards. Ray was comforted by the threatening weather, hoping it would mean far fewer people than expected would show up at the convocation that evening.

In fact, he wished there would be a great storm, and the whole meeting would be canceled. All week he had endeavored to write a moving speech, and had come up empty handed, with a wastebasket full of balled-up pieces of paper. Nothing had seemed right, nothing appropriate. First he tried writing down why he thought as he did when he was nineteen years old, but when he read it back it sounded as though he were somehow attempting to justify his crimes. He added a few words like "madness" and "irrational," but these seemed like cosmetic efforts to absolve himself of responsibility. And, in truth, he never really did believe that his murders had been an act of insanity.

He tried to write about love, but it was difficult. He had never really loved anyone, including his parents. (The last time he had even heard from them was during his first year in prison when they had written him a terse, unsympathetic letter. Six months later Reverend Dornan, seeking a rapprochement with them on Ray's behalf, learned they had left the state without a forwarding address.) Wherever they were today—and Ray often wondered— he could not honestly etch onto paper that he loved them. They had never beaten him, or willfully trampled his spirit. They were simply insular people who had never wanted a child, and one could almost feel sorry for them on that count. Once, very typically, Ray remembered when he was eleven and his mother had been sulking around the house on a Saturday morning. When it came out that she and Ray's father had not been able to find a sitter for him so they could travel to the mountains to exhibit some of her canvas oil paintings at an art festival (as he grew older, Ray was often embarrassed by his soft-spoken mother's pretensions about her ringingly amateurish smearings in the garage), Ray told her he did not need a babysitter. But she just shook her head, and secretly Ray was glad for her worry over him.

After playing in the park by himself all that morning, he came home to find a note left by his parents, telling him they had gone away for the weekend after all. If they had completely forgotten about him, he might have hated them. But his mother had gone out and bought his favorite frozen spaghetti dinners—one for Saturday night and one for Sunday. And his father had left two quarters for afternoon movies. They had signed the note simply, "Your M. and F."

Ray had no brothers and sisters, and even before prison, he had never had a girlfriend. Love was difficult to write about.

Then Ray hit upon the obvious, the very reason all the people were going to be at the convocation, and that was the love of God. He began to write down what it had been like five years ago when Ray's eyes had been opened to the simplest, most beautiful realization of his life—that God in heaven loved him. That our parents were only our temporal guardians, and that God was the true father of all of us, that He loved every child He had ever breathed life into—that He loved Raymond Frederick Lomak. Ray would give testimony at the convocation of how he had lain awake all that night in his cell, too exhilarated to sleep, feeling for the first time in his life that he was not alone. He had stared at the ceiling, and the floor, and his own hand, and even at the steel bars that incarcerated him, and he had felt God's presence in all of them. The Lord had been there with Ray during that great test of his life, as He must have always been there, close-by. Everything happened for a reason—everything.

And yes, Ray loved God in return, loved Him so, that he had jumped out of bed in the middle of the night and let out a holler. "Whoo!" A nearby inmate drowsily grumbled, and Ray crept back under his covers. Finally settling himself, he just smiled serenely. Oh yes, he loved God—almost romantically, with a quick pulse and nervous excitement, with an anticipation of waking to Him again in the morning.

Ray wrote all of this down, anxious to relate the experience to the many people at the convocation. But reading it back to himself the next day, he realized his enthusiasm had betrayed him. It was all wrong. He was not going to be speaking to a small group of fellow inmates—rapists, murderers, villainous men who had never carried Jesus in their bosom any more than he had. Most of the people he would be addressing, Ray was sure, had known Jesus all their lives. Just from the way Reverend Dornan had talked about "the world of good Christians," and from the religious shows Ray had seen on television in the dayroom at San Quentin, he had become convinced there really was a second and separate "world" out there, of which he was still not really a constituent part. Not yet.

And so, who was he to tell these already enlightened people of the sublimely ecstatic moment he had experienced in prison, and of his loving God back because God loved him? It was nothing but a story of selfishness. True, he had done some humanitarian things in prison. He had been sincere when he gave some of the money he had earned to charity, and participated in the inmate program counseling juvenile delinquents—but that was in prison, and prison was different. He had no use for the money himself, and had plenty of free time for counseling. What was more, could his motivations be trusted? How could he honestly deny that the earthly reward of an early parole had never crossed his mind?

No, he still had to *prove* himself, just as he had told Dr. Pomerantz. He had nothing to say to these good people, nothing.

Around five o'clock it finally did start to rain. Ray sat on the floor beneath his one window, absorbed in his origami, folding one piece of paper into a horned owl, another into a dolphin. As the rain grew harder and harder, he listened with pleasure to the water splattering on the cement sidewalk outside. Holding a newspaper over his head, he ran to the phone booth on Sunset and called the Disneyland Hotel. "No, of course the convocation hasn't been canceled," the hotel's manager told him.

At six o'clock Ray sat disconsolately on his bed with his trench coat on, waiting to leave for the bus station. (Kate Robertson had neglected to ask whether he had a car, and Ray had been too reticent to request a ride.) He took the freeway express line down to Anaheim.

By the time he arrived at the Disneyland Hotel, the rain was an oppressive downpour. Men and women alike let out little half-jesting yelps as they ran through the uninterrupted sheet of water that swept down the sloped sidewalk outside the hotel's main entrance. Ray scurried inside with the rest of them and immediately shook out his trench coat, unaware of the spray he was sending up around him.

The lobby was a welter of people, mostly families from out of state, the rain chasing them back to the hotel early from their tour of Disneyland a few blocks away. Ray picked his way to the double doors of the hotel's Grand Ballroom, where the convocation was to be held, and he was dumbstruck by what he saw—it was still forty-five minutes before the convocation was even to begin, and already well over a thousand people were patiently sitting in the rows of chairs spread throughout the spacious ballroom.

An urge rose up in Ray to turn and run. He did step away from the doors, his face drained, only to see a five-foot-high poster on a giant easel he had somehow missed. It read: "Convocation of Joined Hands," and below that, "Dr. Donald Gibbs—'Don't Be the Bride of Anti-Christ' "; "Pastor Steven Hale—'The Shroud of Turin' "; and the last, and one would have supposed from the larger letters, the highlighted speaker, "Raymond Lomak—'From the Devil to God.' "

Unable to reach Ray by phone, Kate Robertson had made an educated guess at his topic.

Ray stood at the doors, feeling sapped, when Kate Robertson materialized and took him by the elbow.

"We haven't much time, Ray," she declared. "We have to get you made up, and then you'll have just a few minutes in the green room."

Ray recoiled slightly.

"What's wrong?" she asked.

"Nothing," Ray said, unaware that all offstage waiting rooms were called the "green room," as he thought only of the one green room he had ever heard of—the apple-green gas chamber at San Quentin.

With a tight grip on his arm, Kate propelled him down a side aisle toward a door near the stage. Her pants and matching jacket top were scarlet red as a ringmaster's.

"I have to get made up? . . . How long am I supposed to talk?" Ray huffed as they sped down the aisle.

"Try to keep it under an hour. Excuse us, please, we have to get through here."

In a glaringly lit room behind the stage with a mirror running the length of the wall, Ray was sat down in a chair, where a heavily perfumed woman with teased hair stuffed a paper towel bib into his shirt neck and started brushing his face with a damp sponge.

"Just a little pancake for the lights," Kate assured him, with a pat on his shoulder on her way out.

"You gonna solo with the choir, doll?" the make-up woman asked blandly. Ray shook his head. Sweeping and whooshing around the room were two dozen blue-robed members of the Portland Glory to the Saints Choir.

"Just try not to touch your hands to your face too much after I'm done, okay?"

Ray nodded. After a few minutes in the chair with his head tilted back, he saw the face and collared neck of a minister suddenly appear over him. The face had a tenderness of age to it, and even the trim beard, which had probably been designed to add a few years maturity to his appearance, only italicized the youthfulness. Ray's hand was grasped and shaken by twenty-seven year old Pastor Steven Hale.

"I just wanted to introduce myself and say hello, Mr. Lomak," bubbled Pastor Hale. Ray felt the hands of the make-up woman pause on his face upon hearing his name, then after a brief moment continue their work, slack and with little pressure behind them.

"It's just an honor for me to be part of this night," Steven Hale said. "People are coming to the Word. It's happening all over. Praise the Lord."

There was a joyful vacantness in Hale's eyes and fixed smile, like that of a former flower child who had sat at too many deafening rock concerts and had experimented with too many substances before rediscovering his confirmation Bible in a bottom dresser drawer. But all Ray saw in Steven Hale's face was the depressing reminder of his own age of forty years. It was what he saw every day since he had been released from prison—clergymen who looked like college kids, construction workers with strings of hair hanging out from under their hard hats, baby-faced motorcycle cops. His only memory was of all these people being older than he.

"Well, I just wanted to thank you for coming," Hale said. "And God bless you."

"Thank you for your kindness," Ray said as Hale left.

When Ray took his seat toward the rear of the stage, he saw

that the large crowd had already doubled, and more were still coming in. Unlike the speakers next to him, Dr. Donald Gibbs and Pastor Hale, who had logged enough hours on stages to sit self-assured and poised, Ray sat back against his seat like a first time traveler in a plane about to take off. He used a hand as a visor against the bright lights to better see the faces in the audience. Some had a dewy peacefulness to them, some a perky effervescence. All had a conservative and ironed cleanliness.

Ray looked into dozens of the unthreatening faces, but felt no more at ease.

The theme and spirit of the "Convocation of Joined Hands" were established the moment the First Church of Our Savior's minister, a man in his late fifties named Preston Gilmore, came onto the stage. Raising his arms, he asked all to stand and hold hands in spiritual communion with the people next to them. Gilmore was a short man with thinning hair on top, and though he was beaming a smile, his mouth looked as though it could be stern when necessary. Directly beneath an arresting thirty-foot cross, the organist and choir struck up "Nearer My God to Thee," and the audience spontaneously joined in.

After the hymn, Gilmore stepped magisterially behind the podium which served as the pulpit and led them all in a reading of the thirtieth Psalm. The people followed from mimeographed prayer sheets that had been handed out at the door. Ray could not help thinking Preston Gilmore had especially chosen the thirtieth because of Ray's presence. Grateful, Ray recited the psalm along with everyone in a bold voice. He knew it by heart: "O Lord my God, I cried unto Thee, and Thou didst heal me; O Lord, Thou broughtest up my soul from the nether-world; Thou didst keep me alive, that I should not go down to the pit. Sing praise unto the Lord, O ye His godly ones, and give thanks to His holy name."

Gilmore addressed the audience at some length on the tide of rediscovery and religion that was sweeping across the land in a magnitude almost unprecedented in the country's history, and about the "specialness and uniqueness" of this evening's service.

On those words, hundreds of eyes shifted to Ray. Ray looked down at his feet, thinking, 'God, what do I say to them? I just have to concentrate. I'm going to concentrate now, Lord, and You guide me.' He tried to concentrate, but could not. Almost as if willfully sabotaging himself, his mind flew off to trivial and ridiculous details in his life, like the radio he was going to take back to the store. When he tried to think of who he was, all he saw was the prosaic house on Fourteenth Street he and his parents had lived in. When he attempted to recall the many introspective sessions he had had with Reverend Dornan which he could tell these people about, his thoughts scattered to the slovenliness of the prison laundry rooms where he had worked for a year, and to the yard where he had watched brutish men lifting weights in the hot sun. Ray tried closing his eyes to swab his mind, but it was of little help.

Dr. Donald Gibbs replaced Reverend Gilmore at the podium. He spoke primarily to the women in the audience, exhorting them to not be "brides of anti-Christ." Although Dr. Gibbs started out with a religious address, the recently divorced psychologist, without blushing, ended up in an undissembling blitz on women's liberation. At the end he led them in a prayer, and Ray seized the opportunity to look out from the stage again. All heads were bowed, even those of a family that had wandered in out of curiosity and now stood at the back, near the doors. Having just come back from Disneyland, their clothes were drenched from the rain, and in the middle of the prayer the father leaned over and curtly plucked the mouse ears from his small son's head.

Pastor Steven Hale, the last before Ray to speak, was plainly enthusiastic about his topic, "The Shroud of Turin." Periodically moving up to the balls of his feet, he cited evidence which he said pointed enticingly to the theory that the piece of linen which bore the faint, back and front images of a man was the cloth used to cover Christ's body when it was taken down from the cross. Ray heard only snatches of the speech, which any other night would have awed him. He sat hunched forward, his eyes on the floor, digging the heels of his hands into his thighs. He was approaching a state of virtual panic.

When Hale finished, there was generous applause, as there had been before and after each of the other persons who had taken the podium.

But when the church's minister, Preston Gilmore, introduced Raymond Lomak—with such phrases as, "to give testimony to the power of God over the shabby cowardice of Satan" and, "this evening which will be remembered as a moment when the forces of good were revealed to be triumphant,"—a total hush came over the audience. Ray stood up.

It was eerie. For a few brief moments, not a cough, not a whisper, not a single shuffled foot. As Ray's heels clicked haltingly toward the center of the stage, two thousand people sat staring.

Only in Ray's mind was there a roaring cacophony of jumbled thoughts. He walked weakheartedly toward the podium, as if in a trance. When he got there, he took hold of the edges of the lectern and kept his eyes fixed on the glass of water provided him, not daring to look up at the two thousand people or at the glinting microphone that curved up at him. He stood there a moment, head down.

And then something strange happened—something strange and unaccountable and, to Ray's way of thinking, almost mystical. In a single instant, all the dread in him vanished—all the throbbing, all the fear—and a wave of well-being swept over him. His racing pulse suddenly dropped, and his forehead felt cool. These people did not hate him. On the contrary, they were there because of him, to embrace what he had to say, to seek him out for the knowledge only someone who had traveled such a tortuous road could have attained. It was just as Kate Robertson had proclaimed—he was *not* like everyone else. There was a reason they were all down there, waiting on his words, and he was on the stage. When Ray looked up, there was a slight, tranquil smile on his face. And yes, most of the faces were smiling back.

"There's . . . there's so much to say," he began. He cleared his throat and looked out to the far reaches of the immense ballroom, where in the back rows people were craning their necks to see him. In that moment of inexplicable peacefulness, Ray had thought, just for a second, that he might have actually been drawn up into the hands of heavenly inspiration, and that the words were going to flow through him, as through a divinely chosen instrument. But it was not to be. The words came agonizingly to him.

"Twenty-one years ago I knew what it was to hate the way the devil hates. I . . . um . . . what I did . . . you see, I can't say I'm sorry because sometimes those words don't mean anything. How can I say I'm . . . uh . . . what I want to tell you people about is about finding God, because God is everything. I know that now. I . . . didn't know that then."

Ray paused and gulped some water.

"When I was nineteen years old I was living for myself. What I mean is . . . is I thought I knew how everything in the world was supposed to be. But it was all just in my mind. I made it all up, I didn't know . . . or, I mean I didn't think about God, and that God had already told us, He told us in the Bible how . . . how the world was supposed to be."

Ray looked back down from all the attentive faces, aware that he had been stammering. He grabbed hold of the glass of water again, and drank thirstily. For a long moment he stared at his hands as they lay on the lectern. They were beginning to tremble, and his breathing quickened.

"There's . . . there's nothing I can say or do to bring six innocent people back to life . . . um . . . oh God, I've dreamed of that, I . . . if there was anything I could do, anything in my power, I . . ." His eyes still cast down, he shook his head. "You see, I didn't want to come here tonight and . . . Words don't change things," he sputtered, his voice beginning to break, though he fought it. "Some . . . sometimes prayers don't change things. They're supposed to, but they can't bring people back to life and . . . I . . ."

He stole a quick glance up at the audience and immediately looked back down again. To steady himself, he leaned on the lectern. Still, he could not catch his breath.

"It . . . it was so long ago, it . . . it was like another person, but it wasn't. It was me, and, and . . . and I have to live with that . . . and . . ."

Ray tried desperately not to cry, but the tears were already at the rims of his eyes. He put his hand up to his forehead, shielding his face from the unrelenting lights, and in a gaspy little whisper only to himself, said, "Please help me, God."

He took his hand away and, taking some deep breaths, was able to blink back the tears. For a few moments he did not speak again, but only stood there inhaling more and more deeply until he finally began to feel steady. He stood up a little straighter, and looked back out on the landscape of faces. Some of their eyes, too, were shining, and it gave Ray a sense of place and connection—that he was different, but not a freak. He spoke a little more easily.

"All this week I asked myself, why am I coming here to speak to you? Why after . . . after everything, have I even been allowed to continue to live? And then that made me ask the question, why was I put on this earth in the first place? Or . . . or why were any of us put here?

"I know now that it's to find God, and do His will. His son Jesus will come into anyone's heart if you just let Him. There are so many important things that have to be done while we're here on earth, and there's so little time. I think when God creates each of us He's giving us a chance to do all the good we can, and He's watching us. And if we sin, we have to right our wrongs . . . before it's too late."

Ray's curling fingers began to scratch excitedly at the top of the lectern.

"Why did God send Jesus to me if it was already too late? He finds people everywhere, He even finds them in prisons. Even great men have gone to prison. Sometimes because what they did, they didn't know it was wrong. They thought what they did was right. And maybe that's why God gives them another chance.

"People don't forgive like God forgives. The Lord is merciful, I want all of you to know that tonight. He's given me a second chance to prove myself and . . . and to earn His forgiveness. We have to earn it, you see, because no one goes to heaven just because of who he was born, or who his family was.

"I know a lot of things I didn't know before. I know no matter what you've done, there's redemption if you *believe* . . . if . . . if you have faith and you pledge yourself to try to make up for what you've done. If you at least try," he said.

Ray lowered his eyes a last time and, suddenly realizing he had nothing more to say, the power in his voice left him.

"I can't ask you for your forgiveness, but . . . but maybe if you would pray with me for His, pray to help me earn it . . ."

People in the audience were leaning from their chairs and turning their ears toward the stage, trying to hear Ray's voice, which had become nearly inaudible. Ray took a full breath, as if to speak again, but without as much as a nod, only turned and walked away from the podium.

Reverend Preston Gilmore jumped to his feet and flung his arm out toward the choir, which promptly resounded with the stirring first bars of "A Mighty Fortress Is Our God." Two thousand people rose as if sprung from their chairs, and joined in the jubilant song. They clapped their thighs, and in their eyes there was joy and brotherhood, and self-congratulatory forgiveness. As Ray walked toward the back of the stage, Pastor Hale clasped him about the shoulders, and one young girl in the front row of the choir reached out just to touch his arm.

Ray did not smile; all he wore on his face was addled amazement. He walked right past his chair, while everyone from Kate Robertson to stage hands to Dr. Gibbs' grandmother, whose wheelchair was provided a special place off to the side of the stage, took a squeeze of some part of his arm or hand or back.

"God bless you," people said. "God be with you, Ray."

Awkwardly, Ray brought his hands up from his sides once or twice to briefly touch someone in return for a hug, but all the while kept working his way to the rear exit door. No one followed him, as every well-wisher assumed he was headed for something or

someone very important, when in fact, not knowing or even thinking about where he was going, all Ray was headed for was a back
parking lot, where he stood by himself under a slow drizzle and
dark sky.

His hands and feet prickled, and he strode down one of the
rows of cars, head down, shaking his hands out a couple of times
like a swimmer before a race. Silently he repeated many of his
speech's phrases to himself. When he reached the end of the
parking lot row he turned and walked up another. "How everything in the world is supposed to be," he muttered, unaware he
had said it aloud. As he came near the rear exit door again, he
stopped and listened to the flourish of two thousand untrained
voices singing, muted by the concrete walls. Ray, who had always
found being in a crowd a suffocating experience, felt a vibrant
sensation around the nape of his neck at hearing this one from a
distance. He turned to walk down the rows some more, when he
saw a massive figure of a man dressed all in black coming toward
him. As the man drew nearer, Ray saw his dress was that of a
liveried chauffeur. The fact that he walked pigeon-toed made him
only slightly less imposing.

"Mr. Lomak?" the man said, giving off a faint odor of alcohol.
"Mr. Harnett would like to see you, if you gotta moment."

Ray looked over the chauffeur's shoulder and saw a burgundy
red limousine parked around the side of the building, its motor
purring, its headlights and windshield wipers on. In the back seat
was the silhouette of a barrel-chested man. Ray did not know
anyone by the name of Harnett, and edging a step closer back to
the stage door, asked, "Is he the man on the radio who talks about
how people shouldn't drink and things?"

"Tex Harnett doesn't think people should drink?" the big chauffeur snorted. "Gimme a break."

"Tex Harnett," Ray repeated the name. "The cowboy movie
star?"

"Come on," the chauffeur said, with a friendly laugh and a little
wag of his big hand. "He wants to say hello."

Ray hesitated momentarily, then followed the heavy-footed driver to the car. As the chauffeur reached for the handle to the rear door, the door opened from the inside, and the interior lights blinked on around Tex Harnett. The once lean hero of twenty-seven hoof pounding, Abilene-to-Laredo movies, now considerably padded by over two decades of lobster, steak and retirement, grunted from having reached across the seat to open the door. He sat back up, and there was no mistaking the twinkling hazel eyes or the solicitous smile of "the gentleman cowboy," as he had been so dubbed by the same studio heads of the forties who had replaced the big Oklahoman's name of Clarence with Tex.

"Well, h'very kind of you t'come say hello," he greeted Ray, stretching a tan and pudgy, liver spotted hand out to him. There was no loss of vitality in the sixty-nine year old man's grasp. "Come in out of that soup. Very kind and generous of you indeed."

"I'm extremely honored to meet you, Mr. Harnett," Ray said, sliding in beside him on the sweet smelling leather seat. Tex Harnett frowned.

"Oh my, we're not such fancy-dans around here. I'm just Tex, and I'd be pleased to just call you Ray, if that's all right. And I know you've already met Ron."

"How are ya?" Ron said, glancing in the rear view mirror.

"Very well, thank you," answered Ray.

"Ron was quite a tackle few years back," Tex said with a great warmth. "Very fine tackle. Hard worker. Always very proud of him."

Ray nodded, though he had no idea what Tex Harnett was talking about. Having never had a palate for sports, he had certainly never heard of Ron Bruckner, whose oxen strength and training camp diligence had never quite made up for his pigeon-toed clumsiness during his two seasons as a pro. Nor did Ray even know that Tex Harnett was the owner of Los Angeles' professional football team. He only knew there was an intangible something about the older man that he immediately respected and felt akin to.

Tex was a jowly man, his head seeming to rest on his broad shoulders without benefit of a neck. From out of the fleshy folds beneath his chin emerged a string tie which was almost as incongruous with his dark, expensive all-wool suit as were his cowboy boots, though the boots were of the finest calfskin leather and studded with blue lapis lazuli down the sides and buttons of green jade around the buckles. Tex scratched at the thin wisps of hair left him, and said:

"I was so very impressed with your speech tonight, Ray, why I just wanted to shake your hand. I know all the good people were very appreciative. They're a good sort of folks down here. That's why I come, you know, do what I can to help Reverend Gilmore's little church. And say, isn't it growing, it's not such a little church at all any more, is it."

"No, it's not," Ray agreed. "But I didn't expect to meet a famous man like you down here," he added obsequiously.

"Well, people say, 'Tex, why don't you join up with one of those churches near where you live out on the peninsula,' and I just smile and say, 'But those aren't my kinda folks.' All that high society, high Episcopalian cow manure. I don't like 'em any more than they like me. Oh, I know I look like some kinda big shot in my limousine, and owning the team in town and all, but the truth of the matter, Ray, is I'm just Oklahoma."

"I'm sure the people down here appreciate having someone like you a member of their church," Ray said.

"My kinda people down here," Tex went on, "and if they don't believe it they'd best look at their church bank records and see where some of those checks have been comin' from, and see if I'm just talking through my hat."

Ron Bruckner nodded a few times into the rear view mirror, and when he could, turned the page of a *Playboy* magazine he had on the front seat.

"You work hard all your life," Tex said, "you don't always have time for church and things. I'm not saying that's right. No, sir. Every man should have time for God. All I'm saying is that maybe

I'm not proud of everything I've had to do in my life, but I'm prouder than some of those others who maybe were trying to keep me from just putting a little bread on the table. Like you said tonight, it doesn't matter if you come to God the day you're on your deathbed, just so long as you do come to Him."

"I don't think I said that," Ray corrected him.

Tex's jowls sagged, as he looked a shade hurt. "Oh. Maybe Gilmore said it last week."

Tex put his hand on Ray's wrist and gave it a fatherly pat. "You were very young when the . . . the tragedy occurred. I believe it takes a great deal of courage what you're doing now. I just wanted to wish you all the best. Getting back on your feet now? With a good job, I mean—very important for a man to have his feet firmly planted in a good job."

"I have some good leads now, yes," Ray said, ashamed to tell him he still had not found work, and thinking of the three help-wanted ads he had circled that afternoon as keeping his answer from being a lie.

"Good. Very good," Tex commended him. "And a decent place to live? A man can't think his life out straight 'less he has a nice clean pillow to rest his head on every night. 'Til I was twenty-five I didn't know anything but a bunkhouse all of us horse breakers kept to. Can't think much about ambition in a place like that. Gotta get yourself clear out of that kinda place."

"I have an apartment in West Hollywood," Ray said with dignity.

"Hmm, Sunset Strip area," Tex harrumphed. "What kind of work you looking for, exactly, if you don't mind my asking?"

"I'm a welder by profession," Ray said, nodding confidently. "I've been going around to quite a few companies."

"They turning you down 'cause you're not good enough, or 'cause of who you are? Only two reasons a man gets turned down for a job."

Ray looked down; he did not want to sound bitter.

"So little forgiveness in the human heart, isn't there," Tex said with a touch of cynicism. "Just how long you figure your money to hold out?"

The already calculated figure rolled promptly off Ray's tongue. "Three weeks."

Tex looked out his window, very thoughtfully. For several seconds he did not say anything. Then he turned to Ray, and his smile was just a bit devilish and self-satisfied.

"There isn't a man or woman alive who hasn't needed a little time to get back on their feet at some point. We've got an awful lot of room at my place now that the kids are grown and moved out. I wouldn't consider myself any kind of Christian if I didn't insist you come stay with us 'til you get things a little straightened out."

"That's very generous of you, but I don't really think I could, I . . . uh . . ."

The gentleman cowboy could make his voice as soothful as the rustling willows when he wanted. "Well now, of course you can, Ray. Why can't you? A few weeks free rent never hurt anybody."

Ray lowered his eyes humbly to his own lap.

"Ron," Tex drawled, getting more southern in his mood, "you just point this thing toward West Hollywood. I imagine there're a few belongings we have to pick up on our way out to the ranch."

Unable to say simple words of emotion, even thank you, Ray continued to look down, and pressed his lips in a vague display of gratitude. As the limousine pulled away, his energetic mind broad-jumped far beyond the offer of a several week stay as a house guest, to the heady notion that a famous and influential man had spotted the burning, patient light in him.

CHAPTER 8

TEX HARNETT'S SPRAWLING HOUSE WAS THE LAR-
gest home Ray Lomak had ever been inside. His first morning he
awoke with a start, a moment of disorientation for being in a
strange place.

He sat up in bed and looked carefully around his room, which
until recently had belonged to the cook. The cook had quit for
want of better pay out of Tex.

"You'll take . . . uh, the cook's room," Tex had said, unable to
remember the man's name, even with Ron Bruckner's reminding
him of it twice on the long drive out to affluent Palos Verdes

Estates in the southwest corner of greater Los Angeles. Still, on arriving at the house, Tex had said, in bidding them both a pleasant good night, "Ron, why don't you show Ray to . . . uh, the cook's old room."

The room, which was at the rear of the house, was as compact and spare as a motel's, with a hard chartreuse carpet that had barely any pile to it, and matching, stiff chartreuse curtains. Aside from the bed and dresser, the only piece of furniture was a child's scratched up desk, which had once belonged to Tex's son. The adjoining bathroom, for lack of even a throw rug or a shower curtain, echoed when Ray walked in. Just the same, Ray could only marvel at what fine lodgings had befallen him.

After showering and dressing, he left his room to survey the rest of the house. Unlike the old Spanish homes of the area, whose arched windows and terra cotta tiled roofs could be seen nestled in the grassy coastal hills, the twenty-five acre Harnett ranch centered around an electronically over-convenienced (and in the neighbors' opinions, hideously modern looking) flagstone dwelling that would have been the reverie of every rising professional in the 1950s.

Ray walked through the broad rooms and long hallways, confused at first by the several ways to get to any part of the sixteen room house, half condemning anyone's need for such large scale living, and half in awe. Circular, white marble fireplaces monopolized the centers of three separate rooms. Everywhere were expansive picture windows, some looking out on the Pacific Ocean, some on the imposing, half Olympic sized pool, others to the white, split rail fence that enclosed a stable and corral.

In the kitchen Ray ran into a young Mexican housekeeper named Esperanza.

"My name is Ray," he said, staring a moment at the woman's bare, light brown forearms, and at her full bosom.

Esperanza smiled, a gap between her front teeth.

"I'm a guest. I've been invited," Ray said.

"Sí, sí," Esperanza smiled, nodding vigorously, though Ray

doubted she understood English very well.

"You don't have to clean my room," Ray said loudly, trying to overcome the language barrier through volume. "I've already made my bed. You don't have to go into my room."

Esperanza continued to smile and nod.

"Have you worked a long time here?" Ray asked. "Worked here? For Mr. Harnett? A long time?"

Esperanza's eyes darted defensively from Ray's. "Sí. I work here. Sí." She turned back abruptly to cleaning the stove top, and Ray, to whom it did not occur that she was in the country illegally and without a work permit, left the kitchen feeling personally rebuffed, and with a passing thought of ungentle sex with Esperanza.

He entered a den whose walls were bedecked with photographs of Tex as a young cowboy movie star, some of them taken candidly on the sets, others in studios with Tex leaning into the picture with his winsome smile. Not that Ray would have thought to look for any, there were no trophies or awards for acting. One wall was taken up almost completely with a glass encased collection of guns, many of them antique six-shooters. Ray promptly left the room and went outside.

A man with a severe limp, and a belly hanging over his belt like molasses just starting over the rim of a jar, was dragging hoses across the enormous, sloping front lawn.

"Finally got here to fix the pool pump, huh?" he called to Ray. "Well, I don't want to hear about it's me jamming up the filter with grass and leaves. I use that Power-Boy over there with an automatic catch. Cost me three hundred fifty dollars. You just go look and tell me if you find a single blade of grass in that pool."

Ray walked closer before answering. "I'm not here to fix the pool."

The gardener studied Ray's face, thinking he recognized him, but not sure. "Oh. Never see anyone use it, anyway. It's colder'n a monkey's ass." He looked another long moment at Ray, then went limping away with his hoses.

Ray walked over to the pool, which was slimed with algae. He kneeled down where a small recess was cut into one of the tile sides. Though he was unfamiliar with swimming pools, he assumed the opening was part of the filter system. Putting his hand a few inches into the green murk, he felt no suction. Pumps were pumps, Ray thought, as he glimpsed an opportunity to impress Tex with the smattering of mechanical training he had received, along with his welding, in prison.

"Where's the motor for this?" Ray called over to the gardener.

Hoisting his hoses over his shoulder, the gardener pointed down at the ground, and Ray realized he was kneeling next to a cement slab that lifted up like a kind of manhole cover. He slid the slab away and climbed down a narrow ladder into what was actually a small room, with a pump, heater, fuse box, and even a plate glass observation window looking into the pool. Ray would later learn from Tex's son, Dean, who at times savored his father's more foolish moments, that Tex had ordered the pool built by a company which specialized in swimming pools for athletic clubs and schools, the window designed for training purposes. When they had asked Tex if he wanted this deluxe model, he had answered, "Well, of course, we want to go deluxe," never thinking of how an observation window would be of any use to him. Tex made the extravagance up to himself by never heating the pool.

After being directed by the gardener to the tool shed near the stables, Ray again went down beneath the pool with wrench, pliers, and Phillips screw drivers, and patiently dismantled the pump motor.

That was where Ray was when Tex finally emerged from the master bedroom late in the morning. Tex never came out of his room until he was shaved and smelling of lotion, his hair neatly parted, his string tie centered. He went into the kitchen, where he gave Esperanza a handful of coupons he had snipped from the morning's newspaper.

"And how are you this morning, Esperanza?" he crooned, smil-

ing warmly. "My, aren't you pretty in that blouse. Sleep well? Uh
. . . dormiste bien?"

"Sí, sí. Gracias."

"Now look at this, Esperanza," Tex said, touching his forefinger
to one of the coupons. "That's quite a buy, wouldn't you say? New
kind of ketchup, I think we ought to try it. Uh . . . el ketchup,
pienso . . . tratamos esto. You take care of that today, dear."

"Sí. I do dees today," Esperanza smiled gratefully. Despite the
grumblings she often heard from Horace, the gardener, and Luis,
the stable hand with whom Tex sometimes had sharp words, Esperanza could feel only affection for the paternal elderly man who
had given her a job and always spoke kindly to her. She lost her
temper whenever Luis proffered his opinion that Mr. Harnett had
hired her only because illegal aliens worked for lower wages. That
the cupboards of such a costly house were filled with off-brands—
runny ketchups, harsh and pungent shampoos, stiff waxy toilet
paper—was no concern of hers. Nor that cooks walked out in a
huff, and pool men were slow to show up because Tex was slow to
pay. Nor, as a speculating Luis had once tried to put a flea in her
ear, that Tex's wife, before her death, had left him because of his
penurious ways with her.

Esperanza saw only a man who still watched his money, and
probably would have felt the same about him even had she known
that Tex owned no less than thirty-two million dollars worth of real
estate in California and five southwestern states.

Until noon Tex made his morning calls—to Carl Miller, head
of daily operations at Harnett Enterprises; Chet Hargrave, general
manager of Tex's football team, a flashy league leading club whom
Tex never referred to by any other name than "the boys"; a brief
and edged call to his twenty-eight year old son, Dean, who was
second in charge of the team's publicity department and who had
failed to purchase the proper amount of advertising space in the
Los Angeles Times for the coming Sunday's game; and last (always
last, to unknot his nerves), to his daughter Jenny who, he forgot,
was down in San Diego auditioning for the Shakespeare festival.

Tex left a message on her machine: "Oh say, sweetheart, I plum forgot you were gone today. That's right, you told me. Well, I just wanted to say hello and . . . now are you taking care of that cold, or are you just running around without a lick of sense? By the way, I hope you don't mind—I gave your number to that Bill Hogarth fella. Remember that fine young fella, he's building all those condominiums over in Hawaii? I told him you're particular about who you go out with—my little girl isn't one for pig'n-a-poke blind dates. I don't say go out with him. I just think nice young people like you two might be friends. How long does this darn tape thing run, anyway? Well, if it's still going, I love you, sweetheart."

Tex's contented little smile stayed with him all the way out to the pool.

"Now what in the good Lord's world . . . Ray?"

Ray climbed part way up the ladder. "The filter got all clogged up, and the pump overheated and burned out."

Tex sat down on one of the deck chairs. "Well, how in . . . ? Christ Almighty! Oh, excuse me, Ray. Bad habit of mine. Very bad habit. How in . . ."

"People are sloppy," Ray said, holding back a contemptuous smile. "They don't care about anyone but themselves. If your pool man had to swim in this pool, you wouldn't have this problem."

"I think you've hit it right on the head," Tex said, wiping a few drops of sweat from his neck with a handkerchief. "Yes you have. My very own son, Dean—we used to call him Deanie when he was little, and he's not so little any more—all he cares about is just getting by. Just get by. How's humankind gonna survive, just getting by? That's what I want to know."

"There'll always be more men like you," Ray said, looking away, as if to make the comment more offhanded than it was.

The two were silent a moment. Then Ray said, lowering himself back down the ladder, "This shouldn't take more than another half hour or so."

Tex stood up. "Well, that's just fine, Ray." He called in to Esperanza to fix a sandwich and bring it out to Ray, then wished

Ray a good afternoon with an offer to have Ron drive him anywhere he needed. Tex had his own lunch on the sun porch inside,
and after a stroll around the ranch, returned to his bedroom for
his afternoon nap.

Ray worked for another hour on the pump, until it hummed
cleanly and efficiently. Absorbed by his project, he forgot about
the sandwich that grew warm and stale in the mid-afternoon sun.
Ray was pleased with himself—with the impression he felt he had
already made on Tex, and with the possibilities for work he
thought might come through this new and fortuitous connection.
He thought of how his entire life would have been different had
he, instead of this Dean fellow, been brought into the world by Tex
Harnett.

* * *

Ray rarely strayed far from the house, and when he did wander
out toward the ranch's pastures, he kept a good ten feet between
himself and the horses inside the split rail fences. Some of Ray's
fears were almost mild phobias—of horses, and flying, and unin-
habited reaches of land—fears of a lower class city boy who had
always lived around the close smell of familiar cement streets.

Because Ray was always around the home, and Tex himself
spent most of his time at the ranch (normally leaving only for a few
regular events like attending the church gatherings or flying out
of the city on a Saturday and returning Sunday night whenever
"the boys" were playing a road game), the two men were often in
each other's company. In dungarees and a red lumberjack shirt
given him by Tex, and with a rollaway tape measure hooked over
his belt, Ray moved from project to project, wherever he saw the
need for some handiwork around the house. And Tex sometimes
followed him about like a boy home sick from school, bored and
lonesome, making friends with the family help.

Ray noticed a few other childlike qualities in the aging cowboy
star—his plain delight over Ray's building a new mailbox; and at

times a child's lack of urgency or purpose, as when Tex sat contentedly watching Ray fix the kitchen disposal.

Fearing that Tex might suddenly announce that his stay at the
ranch was at an end, Ray was not above offering smarmy flattery
to the older man whenever he could. Ray reasoned that his blan-
dishments were not really lies, in that he truly did admire this
self-made man, and even if at times it was a calculated play to a
retired actor's sweet tooth for praise, no one was harmed by it.

It wasn't long before Ray, who was well aware of the money
he was saving Tex with all the free work he was doing around the
ranch, was no longer even looking in the newspaper's classifieds.

"Did you have a lot of women after you, I guess, when you were
a movie star?" Ray asked one afternoon, hungrily, having secretly
watched Esperanza that morning stooping and bending as she did
the laundry, filling out her blouse in a way that made Ray feel
randy.

"Oh, well now," Tex smiled smugly, "that's a whole other matter." Tex looked up at the sky and caressed his throat. "The movie
business is a very social business, you know. Yes, there were quite
a few dandy gals around then. But I'll tell you one thing, I never
let it interfere with the family. No, sir. Some of those fellas, as soon
as they'd get their wife off on a trip somewhere, they'd have
women scamping around right in their own house. Not me. Helen,
she was gone more'n I was. She was a make-up artist, and had to
go all around with those movie companies. I made twenty-seven
films, and every one of 'em we shot right out there in the San
Fernando Valley. Never lost a penny on one of them, either. We
didn't waste money. But not once in my life did I ever bring a
woman back here. Not in the house where my own kids were
raised. And if friends stayed over after parties, why, if they weren't
married, they knew it was just gonna have to be separate bed-
rooms. And my friends know it's still that way. Not in *this* house,
no sir."

A few minutes before six each night, wherever the two men
were and regardless of the discussion, Tex would agree with what-

ever was being said and retire to the den where he sat in front of his four foot by six foot television superscreen to watch the evening's local news. Tex usually watched the channel which, no matter how weighty the more important events of the day might be, began its telecast with graphic film footage of a bank robbery shoot-out, or a mental patient on a ledge threatening to jump, or maybe a domestic quarrel that ended with three family members being killed. Tex sat straight and alert in his favorite chair, as if personally involved in the news stories. If Esperanza or Ron or Ray were in the room with him, he would soberly predict the incident's outcome.

"Hostages all free, they're not about to let that fella stay in there past dark. They'll be in there for him 'fore the hour's up."

Sometimes, just after the news and before dinner, Tex would go into his bedroom and call his top man, Carl Miller, at home. As though drained by the news, Tex would talk to him in a subdued voice about their taking a more conciliatory approach with some of their business adversaries. Several suits against Tex, Ray soon learned, had been caroming about the courts for seven or eight years, but now Tex was beginning to talk about giving up the fights and settling.

"A time comes in a man's life for healing, Carl," Ray heard Tex say one evening as Ray lingered outside the bedroom door repairing a hallway light switch. "Hell if I don't think we're in the right, but I guess I can see where these persnickety banks might misinterpret some of our actions."

Late at night Ray often went out to the dark hillside lawn by himself, wearing a baggy sweater he had found in Dean's old bedroom, and lay down on the grass. As he stared up at the stars in the cold, dead, black space, his mind became filled, as it often did, with the stories of Greek mythology he had learned in school. The hot palpable forms of life and passion—of Pegasus, the winged steed, and Artemis, the huntswoman, and Aphrodite, the goddess of love "born of the foam" off the island of Cythera. He visualized many times their stories of combat and love, promises and secrets, deceptions and loyalties, all within the closely woven kingdom of Mount Olympus. The dramas had always seemed to Ray what he imagined family life in a small village must be like, where everyone had a hand in everyone else's affairs, and all were inextricably bound to each other—both enemies and friends—in a way Ray had never been close to experiencing with anything or anyone his entire life.

Late one night Tex wandered outside, a tall conical glass of dark ale in his hand, his fourth of the evening, and sat down next to where Ray lay on his back. For a few minutes Tex said nothing as he took sparing sips from his glass. When at last he spoke, his voice was very subdued and tentative.

"Ray, that . . . that night when you, when you went out with the gun . . . weren't you afraid of getting killed yourself?"

Ray continued to stare up at the sky, as though not intending to answer. Then, evenly and detached, he said, "Getting killed never occurred to me. That wasn't what I was thinking about."

Tex nodded and then, as if he needed it, took a large swig of ale. He held the glass down at his side and asked, "Are you afraid of dying, Ray?"

"I never think about it," Ray answered him.

Tex stammered, "I . . . I've been, oh my, I've been gettin' to think about it all the time. It's . . . it's a terrible thing to be on the mind so. Terrible thing."

"It doesn't have to be, Tex," Ray said, aware of making the inflection in his voice more gentle than was natural for him. "Think about doing the Lord's will, and the eternal life you'll receive for it."

Tex nodded, but uncertainly.

"You believe in heaven and hell?" he asked. "I mean, as actual places?"

"I do, yes."

"And you truly are repentant . . . you weren't overdoing it just a little down in Anaheim?" Tex asked.

Stung, Ray closed his fingers on handfuls of grass. "I meant every word I said."

Oblivious to his offense, Tex took in a satisfied breath and let it out slowly, as a kind of sigh. "I believe we can make up for the wrongs we've done in our lives. I truly believe that."

Tex looked down at Ray, expecting warm confirmation from him, but when Ray slowly turned his head from the heavens to look directly at Tex, there was a cold and distant shine in Ray's eyes, and an eerie reflection in them from the lights inside the house. Tex felt Ray's eyes boring clear through him, as if Ray knew without the least doubt that Tex was talking about himself, not Ray —as if Ray knew of every questionable, rascally business transaction, every hardnosed bargain he had forged in the amassing of his fortune.

"I believe that, too," Ray said, and with his eyes never leaving Tex's, added, "Everyone would do something different if they had the chance."

When the two bid each other good night, Ray went back to his room feeling that although for the first time he and Tex had cut rawly toward each other's source, it had probably drawn Tex closer to him.

And Tex, as he groggily pulled the covers part way over his ear, went to sleep with the wholly comforting sensation that if Ray Lomak could make it to heaven, *he* sure as hell would.

$$\star \quad \star \quad \star$$

Ray lied the day he told Tex he had obtained a new driver's license. His license had been suspended ever since he was nineteen when, navigating in another realm for the months leading up to his rampage, he had committed a number of moving violations and ignored the traffic warrants against him. Ron Bruckner had been driving Ray in the limousine to necessary appointments (psychiatrist, parole agent), but the day Ray wanted to borrow Tex's country station wagon on his own, he was not uncomfortable in lying about the license, reasoning to himself that a license was just a piece of paper and all that was important was that he drive safely.

Ray also told Tex his errand was to pick up a saber saw, when in truth it was to buy flowers for Esperanza.

When Esperanza found the flowers and attached note in her maid's quarters that night she went to Ray's room to thank him, just as Ray had hoped she would. Ray had a decanter of bourbon from Tex's liquor cabinet and two glasses waiting in the bottom dresser drawer. Whenever Ray went into the bathroom to refill their glasses, he poured his own from a pitcher of tea.

Esperanza was a good-spirited but lonely girl of eighteen. Sitting next to Ray on his bed, she laughed coyly whenever it was apparent they were understanding only a fraction of what the other was saying. Ray's hands quivered with eagerness as he eventually removed the barrette from her hair, letting the sheeny, black swaths, youthfully thick, fall down past her shoulders and onto his forearms. Having made love so very few times in his life, Ray possessed no smoothness or ability to heighten the effect with restraint. He quickly plunged his lips and face to as many parts of her flesh as possible, like a thirsting man on his hands and knees at the side of a river, half crazed, not fully enjoying what he was getting because of the distraction of what he was missing. Peculiarly, Esperanza faintly hummed a Mexican melody to herself, as though that was all Ray had left her to do, or as if she had to re-create a scene from her childhood to feel secure in this unknown man's arms.

Ray moved his open, hungry mouth up her legs and thighs, to a brown belly that jiggled a little like gelatin.

"We can't do this in the house often," he gulped feverishly, thinking of Tex's attitude about extramarital sex in his home. "Only now and then."

Esperanza, not comprehending, wrapped her arms around him tightly and murmured, "Sí. Te amo, te amo."

When Ray finished he lay on his back, away from Esperanza. At forty years old, he still was not attuned to a woman's climax.

When Esperanza tried tickling him into more love-making, he perfunctorily stroked her forehead a couple of times, as though removing dust from it, and said, "You better go now. You . . . should . . . go . . . now," he tried to make her understand.

Somberly, Esperanza gathered up her clothes, stumbling slightly from the bourbon as she put them on, and went wordlessly back to her room. She fell asleep that night softly crying, clutching the cross around her neck.

Over the next several days Esperanza often tried to catch Ray's eye, but Ray, who was almost always in Tex's company, only looked away. A week later, when the urge for sexual release was again spreading inside him like wild roots, he left another bouquet of flowers in Esperanza's room, along with a delicately folded piece of origami, a sea shrimp made of pink paper. He attached it to the rubber band that bound the flowers, and that made it a *noshi,* the Japanese ornament for good fortune which traditionally accompanies gifts.

To Ray, relations between men and women were no more subtle or complicated than a simple tribal barter system. He had seen the blowzy, housecoated wives in the fringe neighborhoods he had grown up in step outside their little humdrum houses to get the morning paper, and he had seen the trim women, as pretty and young looking as their daughters, end up in the gardens of Pasadena mansions. Nothing was going to persuade him that men and women operated by any value system more exalted than that of the marketplace.

He was genuinely surprised when Esperanza did not come to his room that night. Prideful, he had nothing more to do with her. Nor did she with him. Neither would enter a room until the other had left. As soon as he had steady use of a car, he decided, he would start seeing Treak again.

The more important matter that occupied Ray was the phone call that Tex received from Morrow Walters, the closest neighbor down the road from the Harnett ranch. Walters, a banker whose family had owned portions of the Palos Verdes peninsula for nearly sixty years, had expressed in a full-throated, baritone voice his "profound dismay" over Tex's having taken in a house guest the likes of Raymond Lomak. Walters' wife, Bette, who came onto one of the extension phones, was nearly hysterical. She threatened to take up a petition, and by the end of the conversation her husband Morrow was talking of "legal action."

"Go to hell!" Tex thundered, and scraped a knuckle slamming the phone down.

It was a matter of principle with Tex, or as Ray had said at the convocation in Anaheim, a matter of putting actions behind words. And what was more, for Tex it was a sumptuous opportunity to not cooperate with the neighbors who had never in twenty-three years invited him and his wife, Helen, to a party, or even over for a drink. The Brooklyn-born Helen Karaganas had claimed it was because she was Greek. Tex, whose feelings were just as deeply wounded, insisted it was because they considered him an Okie who happened to hit it rich, but who still should have been consigned to the flats of North Hollywood.

When Tex started to tell Ray about the phone call, Ray cut him off by suddenly standing up and announcing he would be packed and gone by morning, though he paused an appreciable moment where he stood.

"You're not goin' anywhere," Tex commanded him, flapping his lower lip. "Don't go tellin' me you think I'd even give people like that the time of day—bunch of medium rare hypocrites." Tex took his steaks well done and had somehow come to use medium rare as synonymous with pretension. Clasping his hands high on his chest, he steered his head one way and then the other, as if centering it, and said, "Sit down, Ray, you live here."

Ray sat back down and managed to maintain a look of solemn indecision, though what danced through his mind was the tingly realization that the Walters had virtually assured his stay would be a long one.

Over the next week, as word of Tex's houseguest ricocheted throughout the community, not a day passed without a group of teenagers driving slowly up the road, four or five sets of wide eyes staring out the window as the car made its cautious turn in front of Tex's house. One day a group of them parked and nervously handed a pair of binoculars from one set of perspiring hands to the next. When Ray saw them from the living room, he fetched his pocket Bible and marched out toward the car, stirred by the chance to do both himself and a few youths some good.

"Oh, God, that's him!" a boy in the back seat shouted.

"He's got a gun in his hand!" one of the girls screamed.

The car tore away in a fishtail, and only after they were a mile and a half down the road did the boy in the back seat say, low and cocky, "Looked to me like a snub-nosed .38. Wouldn't have had a chance against us at that distance."

The Harnett ranch was never pestered by curiosity seekers again. Horace, the gardener, who learned from other people he worked for in the neighborhood why the face had originally been so familiar to him, did not come any more, either. Ray assumed the duties of attending both the grounds and the pool work. And Tex, who was just as happy to have axed those monthly expenses, had by the end of the week forgotten the gardener's name.

CHAPTER 9

ON THE LAST SUNDAY IN DECEMBER, TEX'S BOYS
clinched the National Football Conference's western division
championship. In celebration, Tex hosted a barbecue at his ranch
that started late in the afternoon. It did not end until the team's
front office, coaching staff, invited guests, and most particularly,
the awesome-appetited forty man squad had consumed 110
pounds of Kansas City strip steaks, 90 pounds of baby back ribs
marinated in Tex's personal beer-and-honey sauce, a tub of three-
bean salad, 30 loaves of kouloura bread (there to convey to his
daughter Jenny that Tex had not blotted out her Greek mother

from his memory), 20 gallons of chocolate ice cream, and 13 cases of beer.

Giant men with bruised faces and hands chafed red, many of them dressed fashionably in tailored European-fit shirts or dark blazers, and a couple of them in red and gold African dashikis, meandered about the spacious house and grounds. Joking and talking loudly, most were still too aloft on their own adrenaline or the team doctor's shots to feel the pain yet of the violence visited upon their bodies that afternoon.

Tex moved from group to group like a fat old general back at camp, but in a splashy plaid sport jacket, the thick crease of his double chin even seeming to smile. With what was for him a herculean effort, he had committed to memory the names of every one of his players' kids. If there were no kids to ask about, he asked about the house that was being built out in Malibu or Hidden Hills, or if not that, the chicken farm back in Arkansas.

As at all other celebrations, Tex spent more time with the unsung footsloggers of the line than with the higher paid, higher publicized quarterbacks and runners. Tex had always been a greater admirer of brute strength than finesse. If he had wanted finesse, he often told friends, he would have bought a badminton team.

When he excused himself to go to one of the less frequented bathrooms near the back of the house, Tex found Ray down on his knees, sleeves rolled up, fixing the toilet.

"Oh my, now what in the Lord's world are you doing back here, Ray?"

"Needs a new seal," Ray said earnestly. "That's why you have to jiggle the handle."

"But now? There's an awful fun shindig going on, if you hadn't noticed. I want you to have a good time, Ray. You don't have to do this now, do you?"

"It won't take much longer," Ray said, his voice deadened by the water tank he peered down into.

"No, no, no," Tex said, "I'll use it as is. I want you to go get yourself a plate of food and enjoy yourself. Look at you—no heftier than the day you got here. Come on now, git." He prodded Ray up off his knees and out the door. Being in a merry, ale-sloshed mood, it did not occur to Tex until later that Ray had been hiding out of shame. So used to Ray's new existence, he sometimes forgot just how infamous the man's past was, how recognizable he was to strangers, and how real were the shivers of loathing and apprehension that he caused. Rosy-faced, and made richer by the day's game, Tex at the moment was aware only of how peaceful and private the feeling was of being alone in the bathroom while the sound of a party went on outside. Looking into the mirror, he lifted his chin and stroked his throat, thinking he looked gol darn handsome for a man who would turn seventy in another few months.

Outside, Ray put a small amount of food on a plate. In his work clothes and with his rollaway tape measure forgetfully still hooked over his belt, he sat by himself near the pool. He saw in many of the faces what he had expected—constrained shock that Tex had not sent him away for the day, and in some cases stiffened anxiety.

"Gives me the goddamn willies," one black halfback by the name of Tommy Chesser whispered to his wife. " 'Bout time we get home anyway, huh?"

With a postured casualness, some people sidled away from the pool, as if just by good fortune to be at the other end of the house if and when old man Harnett's pet folly went berserk for a second time in his life. Some drifted closer to the pool, to show everyone, and Tex in particular, they believed a man's past was his past. One balding executive from the team's front office nudged nearer to where Ray sat to somehow prove something to his attractive wife, who had been coquetting for over an hour with a rookie tight end.

Ray watched the party's shifting population quietly and without bitterness. Eventually a couple of people came up and introduced themselves. Tex's daughter, Jenny, whom Ray knew immediately from the photographs around the house, smiled sympathetically and asked whether he wanted anything more from the barbecue. Jenny was a jaunty girl, with coffee brown eyes and delicate fawn colored hair that brushed her shoulders whenever she turned her head to greet another of her father's friends. In her mid-twenties, she seemed a bit shy, more a party listener than a talker, though her avid laugh and slightly mischievous smile led people to feel she had said more than she really had. She was too slender for Ray's taste, but the flush of natural color in her face and the simple, puff-sleeved peasant dress she wore, obviously not new, made her to Ray's way of thinking the most refreshing looking woman at the party. When Ray declined more food and thanked her just the same, she smiled again politely, and quickly left.

The only other person to come up to Ray was a young player from Georgia, a born-again Baptist whose physical trimness was more suggestive of a natural clean liver than a consciously trained professional athlete. Gingerly, he sidestepped anything to do with Ray's personal past. After a five minute discussion about the virtues of Tex Harnett and Southern California weather, he shook Ray's hand heartily and returned to a group of friends.

Ray wandered off by himself toward the corral, away from the party. Seeing Tex's herd of horses grazing at the top of the far grassy hill, he ventured into the stables, which were dim grey in the hastening dusk. Kicking through the hay on the floor, he saw a light on in a back room. Not hearing Luis anywhere around, he went to turn it off. At the doorway he came upon a group of men who were in the room and who had kept still as soon as they heard footsteps. One of them, with broadly flared pants and a gold chain hanging down onto his tan, open-shirted chest, and holding a gold cigarette case filled with white powder, broke the silence.

"Hey, how you d-doin'?" he stuttered with a big lopsided smile, flipping the cigarette case shut. "It's okay," he said to the other three men, one of whom was Luis, who sat on a sack of feed and leaned against a stall post, his glazed eyes shamefully averted from Ray's. The other two men were football players.

The young man with the gold chain, only in his late twenties but already paunchy, stepped forward and said, "I'm D-dean Harnett."

"Yes, I know," Ray said icily. "I'm sorry for interrupting."

He turned and started to go.

"Hey, you don't have to go," Dean Harnett said. "You're welcome to j-join us, y'know?"

"Thank you, no."

"S'okay. . . . How's living out here at the old ranch? Outstanding place, huh? You ought to g-go on up to the old well over on the other side of the grazing hill. They dug it in 1881. Water's got a great taste to it. Or hey, how about those grapefruit trees around the side of the house—give some of those a try some morning. Outstanding, no kidding. I'm a lot like Dad. I just kind of get a feel for people, and something tells me you're the t-type of man that'd appreciate some of the natural things around here like I do. Dad says you really know how to work with your hands. God, that's great."

The eager congeniality was a strained forgery of his father, Ray thought. Ray walked back toward him with an outstretched hand.

"Here, you don't need that kind of stuff," he said, reaching for the cigarette case full of cocaine.

"Hey, h-hold on," Dean exclaimed, moving the little gold box behind his hip, but still smiling.

The two football players moved uneasily, as if wanting to leave.

"I'm not going to tell Tex about this," Ray said quickly. "It would hurt him too much. I'm doing this for you. You don't need it."

Dean stopped smiling, and his face grew bright red within a second, just as it always had since he was a chubby weak-limbed boy who had learned to strike back with a ready tongue. "You g-guys are really something, aren't you? Get that religion all of a sudden and . . . h-hey, save it for my old man, I don't bother anybody, y'know? I don't have to spend *my* life apologizing for anything."

The two players, knowing very well who Ray was, held their

breaths for just a moment. Ray did not so much as move a muscle, but they saw a controlled scorn very slowly fill his eyes. Just as gradually, it passed. Ray looked at the ground and nodded, then turned and left.

'They stagger because of strong drink,' he silently recited Isaiah to himself with an inner hiss of satisfaction as he walked back toward the house and his own room. 'They reel in vision, they totter in judgment. For all tables are full of filthy vomit, and no place is clean.'

That night after all the guests had departed, Ray sat in the living room in front of the roaring fire he had built in the slick, white marble fireplace. Tex teetered in with a glass of dark ale in hand and sank heavily into the billowy white couch with the finality of a rock into wet snow.

"Is your team the champion now?" Ray asked peevishly.

"Not quite, not quite," Tex grunted. He quaffed some ale along with most of the light brownish head and, turning around, whacked the pillow behind his back. "They have to win a couple more yet. If they do, they'll probably all want a fifty percent raise next year."

"Why do you own a team," Ray asked, "if it doesn't make you happy?"

"Did I say that? Maybe I did. Football's a great game, that's why. Or at least it used to be. I don't know, nothing seems the same to me any more. You want to know what's changed? It's the spirit that's changed. Everyone wants more money for less work. You should see some of the things those boys and their Century City agents want in those contracts. Fewer practice hours, the right to take a separate flight to a road game if our charter flight interferes with some God-blessed TV commercial they're doin', the right to not appear in the Pro Bowl. Can you imagine that? The right to *not* appear in the Pro Bowl! Well, I guess maybe I'm a little behind the times. I somehow had the notion it was an honor to be picked to play in the game."

Tex struggled to his feet and shuffled over to the wet bar where

he got another bottle of ale from the refrigerator below. When he
sat back down with it he saw he still had three quarters of the old
one left in his glass.

"Say, here's a bottle of cold ale I got for you, Ray," he said
obligingly. "Thought maybe you'd like to join me. Go get yourself
a glass over there."

"No, thank you," Ray answered. "You know, Tex, you don't
have to stay in businesses that aggravate you. You don't have to
do that any more. There are so many good things you could do
with your money. So many important things to be done in this
world."

"Oh, well now, I don't believe I can be faulted when it comes
to charity, if that's what you mean. I believe I'm thought of rather
well in those circles." Tex held his glass on the shelf of his stomach,
where it rose and fell with each heavy breath.

"I know you are, Tex. You're a very admired man, and you
should be. All I mean is sometimes don't you . . . don't you—" Ray
paused to think it out clearly. He sensed he was on to something
he did not quite have a grasp of yet. He got up to pace.

"Don't you sometimes think things would be better if *you'd*
decide where your money goes and how it's used, not all those
people in the charities. Sometimes they do good things, and sometimes they don't."

"Seems to me," Tex said, "you just can't make all the decisions
there are to be made. You gotta rely on other people somewhere
down the road, now don't you?"

"But didn't you tell me one time," Ray was quick to interject,
walking about the living room, touching vases and tables he
passed, "that things always went wrong when you let the managers and lawyers make all the business decisions for you?"

"Well, now there's my point," Tex said affably, "I've got to
spend my time looking after those business interests. My goodness,
I can't get personally involved with all those charities. Oh, I'm not
saying I have to spend every second just making more money until I
d- . . . for the rest of the days the Lord will see fit to give me. I've

got a few pennies saved up here and there. I just don't want to start ignoring things so much, that I lose it all 'fore I'm gone. A man likes to leave a little something, you know."

"How much money do you have, Tex?" Ray asked matter-of-factly, as though inquiring about how many steaks there were in the freezer.

"Oh, well now, let's see . . . uh." Tex cleared his throat. "That's a little hard to say. There's, uh, that land up north—real pretty redwood stuff. And then I've got a few acres over in Arizona and Nevada and a couple of those other states, you know. And there are the stocks and bonds, of course. So that'd be about—oh wait, I'm forgettin' the team. Fella offered me about twenty and a half for the boys awhile back. Oh, I guess all in all about sixty-two, sixty-three."

"Million?" Ray asked.

"Why yes, million, of course million," Tex said, opening the new bottle of ale and pouring it sloppily into his glass. "Inflation's so bad, you can't hardly be talking about thousands."

Ray sat down, but almost immediately felt compelled to stand up and walk about some more.

"You've made your mark in business, there's nothing more there for you to accomplish," he said with conviction.

Tex shrugged, but made no effort to contradict him.

"Men like you have to move on," Ray continued, "to even greater things. To the work of the Lord," Ray said, turning and looking down like a preacher from a pulpit to where Tex sat staring into his glass of ale. "Could you imagine the things that could be done with the money you have? The churches that could be built? There are *souls,* thousands of souls you could save from an eternity of damnation. There are poor kids all around this country who want to believe, but how can they believe in anything when no one helps them get a job or go to college, or anything? What we need is someone of vision, someone like yourself," Ray said, head down as he paced.

"It's not like you'd even have to give up your house or anything like that. Just maybe some of that land up north that you were talking about. Let someone else cut down redwoods and build shopping centers or whatever they do with redwoods. Our Lord Jesus doesn't care about shopping centers or football teams or . . . Tex, you're too important to be doing what you're doing," Ray now exhorted, running his hand through his shock of hair, which was blonder for having been out in the sun the past month.

"All the Lord wants to know is what good we accomplished on earth," Ray said gravely.

"I imagine maybe there is more I could do," Tex conceded.

"What's going to happen when you . . . when you pass on? The government's going to take most of your money anyway, aren't they?"

Tex's eyes grew beady at just the reminder.

"That's why I have to make sure there's enough left over for my children. Jenny," he said fondly, "and . . . and Dean, too. I can't give everything to charity."

"There'll be more than enough for your family," Ray countered.

"Well, I suppose there's some truth to that."

Ray sat down and remained silent for a short time. Then, his voice tempered, he said, "All great men have left their mark in this world. But no one remembers who once owned a football team or some land in Nevada. Why shouldn't this country remember you just like . . . Rockefeller or . . . or that man they named that theater in New York after?"

"Carnegie," Tex said sourly, though the distaste was only on general principles—he had never met any of those pedigreed eastern families. "Well now, I admit it wouldn't be like giving *all* the money away—there is the tax thing here to consider," he said, growing just a little interested. "See, Ray, you probably don't understand all that fancy-dan financing, and God bless you for it, but this can be done with a few advantages along the way."

Ray leaned forward, licking his lips, his eyes glimmering. "The tax thing," he repeated after Tex, studiously.

"Well, that's what some of those bigger money fellas do, anyway," Tex said, backing off a hair. "Christ Almighty, those ribs make you thirsty! See if there's another bottle of ale down there, would ya, Ray? And help yourself to one. You look all keyed up."

Ray poured Tex another glass of ale, but took nothing for himself.

"Your son doesn't care much for religion, does he."

"Oh, I s'pose I'm partly to blame for that," Tex lamented. "We didn't bring our kids up with any kind of churchgoing, I guess."

"The Harnett name should always mean something in this country," Ray went on.

"That would be nice," Tex agreed. "That would be nice." He closed his eyes and even seemed to doze off for just a moment. "Ray," he said drowsily, his eyes still closed, "would you mind goin' to the phonograph over there and puttin' on that Bill Boyd and his Cowboy Ramblers album. That would sound awful pretty right now."

Ray went over to the shelf of record albums and flipped through them impatiently. When he found Tex's choice he took the album out of its cover, completely slit down three sides, its cardboard edges rubbed to a fuzz, and put the record on at a low, soothing volume. The lonely cowboys harmonized dolefully about five months of sleeping out on the range. Seeing that Tex wanted to relax, Ray circled about the thick white carpet at the far end of the living room.

After a few minutes Tex roused himself from his light sleep and began singing along wistfully with the melancholy tunes.

"Yes, that would be nice," he came to say, and Ray had to think back to what part of the conversation they had ended on. "And the name should mean something to my grandchildren, too. Dean, I don't think, is even the marrying kind," Tex continued. "It hurts me terribly. Jenny, now she's going to have a fine bunch of children. I only pray I'm here for it. Like to make 'em proud of who they are."

Ray came and sat down on the couch with Tex, closer to the

old man than he was accustomed to sitting with people. Tex
opened his eyes and looked into the tapering fire.

"I could do a lot more than I am. That's so, isn't it, Ray?"

"It could be a whole new life for you," Ray said. "Just like
starting over."

"That's what keeps men goin', you know. That's what keeps
men goin'," Tex sighed, repeating himself as older people who
have grown sure of their observations are wont to do.

"The *Harnett Foundation,*" Ray said, sacredly.

Tex smiled. He put his glass of ale down, sobered by the magnitude of what they were discussing. His few minutes' nap had him
feeling quite fresh.

"It could be glorious. Doin' the Lord's work . . . couldn't it?"
he asked, as if seeking a guarantee.

"In the end it's all that counts," Ray said, almost a thread of
warning in his voice. "The Bible tells us so in black and white."

Tex nodded. "You think that was so gol darn big a thing for me
to ask Dean to take me downtown for my doctor's appointment,
my physical? Just a couple weeks ago, when Ron was takin' his
vacation. Was that so big a thing? Said he had a lunch date and why
couldn't I take a cab. Twenty miles, I'm supposed to take a cab."

"You could have asked me," Ray said, then felt obliged to add,
"It's more convenient for me than Dean."

Tex waved away the excuse for his son, and Ray did nothing to
defend Dean further.

"Jenny's not selfish like that. No, sir."

"I could tell just from meeting her."

Tex patted Ray's lap in appreciation of his perceptiveness. "I
don't know what makes one child selfish, and not the other. Maybe
I'm to blame. Dean was our first, you know. Maybe I just didn't
spend enough time with him."

Tex lifted his chin and scratched at some stubble. As he looked
back into the fire, there was a measure of exhilaration in his eyes.

"We could do a lot of good things for all sorts of people, couldn't
we?"

"We could, yes," Ray agreed eagerly.

"The Harnett Foundation we'd call it, huh?"

"The Harnett Foundation," Ray auditioned the sound of it once more, his heart beginning to pound. Tex's use of the word *we* had not been lost on him.

Tex clapped his hands together. "It'd be a whole big national thing. We'd call a press conference to announce it."

"If that's how these things are done," said Ray.

"Well sure, that's how these things are done!" Tex bellowed, beginning to take charge. "Doesn't even have to be that much. Four, five million dollars set aside as the Foundation's principal, invested at ten percent, would mean four, five hundred thousand every year doin' the Lord's work."

Tex got to his feet energetically, and with a blackened poker stabbed and hacked away at the logs that were charred into a pattern of little squares, like a quilt.

"Gotta go slow on this kind of thing," he said. "First thing we do, see, is call Carl Miller tomorrow. Gotta sit down and think through the tax situation we're talking about here, understand? No need to not to be level-headed, even when you're answerin' the Call."

Tex went and started the record over again.

"Oh, I feel very fine tonight, Ray. Doctor says I'm goin' to be around a good long while. Highest priced doctor in Los Angeles. The Harnett Foundation, huh?"

He sat down and laced his hands over his thick chest. His smile was almost kid-like, a smile he hadn't had for years, not since the day he had bought his football team.

Despite the air of excitement, or perhaps even because of it, Ray suddenly felt tired, from head to foot. But blinking back his longing for sleep, he was determined to stay up and keep Tex company just as long as the old cowboy wanted him to.

PART TWO

CHAPTER 1

THE HARNETT FOUNDATION'S MULBERRY CAR-
peted offices occupied a quarter of the floor directly below those
of Harnett Enterprises, the latter taking up the entire thirty-first
floor of one of the sleek Arco Towers in downtown Los Angeles.

The larger front offices of the Foundation were reserved for
one full-time lawyer, several bookkeepers and secretaries, and a
woman in charge of public relations. At the very end of the hallway was the small undecorated room which served as Ray's office.
As both he and Tex were sensitive to the need for him to keep a
relatively low profile within the Foundation, at least for the first

couple of years or so, Ray was more than happy to sequester himself in the unassuming back room. By phone conversations with applicants for Foundation funds, and by his closeness to Tex, he was a fulcrum of influence within the Harnett Foundation.

Only behind Ray's back did the Foundation lawyer quip to another employee, "Now Tex is even letting him sign some of the checks. Why not? He's just a murderer, not a thief."

Dean Harnett made it clear to his father from the start that he thought the Foundation was a far-flung, indulgent idea. Even three months after it had gone into operation he continued to openly hammer away at the subject with Tex, as if refusing to accept it as a fait accompli. He questioned its effectiveness, its grandness of scale, and most of all, the genesis of its inspiration.

"Just how much money are you g-going to spend to help Lomak salve his guilt?" he asked with reddening, adolescent frustration in his face.

On one of the rare nights when he came out to the ranch for dinner, he asked to speak to his father alone in the den, where he launched into the newest financial reasons he had come up with for convincing his father to disband the Foundation. But Tex wasn't even listening—his eyes were fixed on his wall collection of guns where the centerpiece attraction, the pearl-handled Colt that he had twirled in all his movies, was missing.

"Maybe your friend Ray L-lomak took it," Dean sniped.

"Well, now why would . . . oh Dean, you're not tryin' to say—"

"People don't change," Dean said.

"I heard that, Dean," Ray loured darkly, walking into the room.

Dean swallowed. "Do you always eavesdrop on p-people? Jesus." He rubbed nervously at his mouth with the back of his hand.

"I wasn't eavesdropping. I was repairing the hinge on the hallway door, and I heard what you said, Dean."

"Yeah, I'll b-bet you were repairing the hinge on the door. There isn't anything wrong with any g-goddamn hinge on any g-goddamn door, and you know—"

"Aw-right, both of ya now," Tex interceded. "Just get ahold 'a yerselves. Now, all I wanna know is what happened to my Colt. Maybe Ron took it down to clean it."

"Why? You haven't fired it in years," Dean said curtly.

"Well, I guess that's so," Tex acknowledged, seeming more puzzled than disturbed.

"I didn't take your gun, Tex," Ray said, but looking steamily at Dean.

Dean looked at the floor with a smirk, but when he lifted his head and saw Ray staring at him, no longer hotly but with such composed, dead eyes, even Dean's brazenness vanished into a shiver.

"Whole house gives me the c-creeps," he said, picking up his coat and storming from the room. He slammed the front door behind him.

Late that night Luis weaved his way tipsily through the house to the den, Tex's pearl-handled Colt slapping against his thigh in a low-slung, torn leather holster. The loose spurs he wore clinked along the floor and brought both Tex and Ray immediately out of their rooms.

"So you're the one!" Tex roared. "Might'a figured it'd be you. Do you know the fight you just managed to cause around here? Just what do you think you're doin', taking one of my guns without asking like a normal thinkin' person?"

Luis looked as though he had just gulped down his thick tongue. "I din' take nothin'," he insisted, his red eyes cast sullenly on the floor. "I just . . . take it to a party. They all wanna see Tex Harnett's six-shooter."

". . . Well . . . and take those sharp spurs off in this house," Tex bawled. "Gol darn you, Luis."

Luis sank down into a pile on the floor and struggled to remove his spurs. "I din' think you lemme . . . lemme have it," Luis mumbled the ending, thinking he was only getting himself in deeper.

"He didn't mean any harm, Tex," Ray said. "He just wanted to borrow it to show his friends. Don't be angry with him."

Tex looked Ray's way a moment and then, turning back to Luis on the floor, said, "I s'pose that's so. . . . I'm . . . I'm sorry if I was gettin' rough, Luis, but gol darn it, ask next time you want to borrow something that doesn't belong to you."

He started back toward his bedroom, but at the den's doorway turned and said, "And I guess Dean owes you a man-sized apology, Ray. If he doesn't say it, I'll say it for him—I'm sorry for the words that got said to you."

Ray looked at Tex with great tranquility and answered, "I'd never have my father do something I should do. But thank you." He added, not quite as sincerely, "I'm sure Dean didn't mean it, anyway."

Tex looked at him, nodded, and went back to bed.

★ ★ ★

Richard Pomerantz for the first time began to be a little troubled about his patient.

Four months earlier, when Ray had begun work with the newly formed Harnett Foundation, Richard had been encouraged by the potential that work offered Ray in his social adjustment. Permanent employment had been a palliative for Ray's anxiety, and the expanded intercourse with fellow employees had manifested itself favorably in him on a steady weekly basis. Having overcome his fear of flying, Ray did some traveling to interview prospective recipients of the Foundation's money, and he seemed more confident now of his ability to interact with other people, with strangers. No longer was he always pressing so much to make a good impression.

That, however, had been during the first three months of Ray's involvement with the Foundation. What weighed on Richard's mind presently were the subtle changes in Ray's orientation over the last four or five weeks. Whereas he had earlier been eager to talk about the various personalities he was coming into contact with—the likes of Alex Scholt, who wanted a loan to enlarge his religious articles store in St. Louis, or Danny Langton, the asthmatic choirboy who needed money to go to school in hot dry Arizona—his conversation in therapy of late had turned more to the importance of the Foundation itself, as if it was a breathing, mammoth creature all its own, separate from the tangible faces and voices of the people it had been set up to help. What Ray mostly talked about now was getting Tex Harnett to commit more money to the Foundation; already he had convinced the old man to increase the trust fund from four and a half million dollars to eight million. Whenever Ray even uttered the words "the Foundation," one could almost hear the capital F in it.

And oddly, if Richard had initially also been encouraged by an apparent lessening of Ray's absorption with himself, that change had carried itself to a curious, sometimes disturbing extension. Not only was Ray no longer as willing to discuss the details of his life history, but now he virtually ignored his past, including the night of December 24, 1959, almost as if it had never existed.

As Richard returned to his office building on an afternoon late in April, he saw Ray sitting in the front seat of a sporty compact parked at the curb. In the driver's seat was a young woman who was listening and nodding, but appearing uneasy as she held on to the wheel with both of her slender hands. When Ray spotted him, Richard merely flicked his finger in greeting, not wanting to interrupt them.

Ray rolled down his window and said, "Good afternoon, Dr. Pomerantz. Please come say hello to Jennifer Harnett. She was just out visiting her father at the ranch and was kind enough to give me a lift into town."

Richard went over to the driver's side of the car and shook Jenny's hand.

"How are you?" he said, brightening his smile a bit, as she looked a little grim.

"Fine, thank you," she answered him distractedly. Her blondish-brown hair hung limp and uncombed, and she held her chin protectively tucked in toward her chest.

"You live here in L.A.?" Richard asked.

She nodded.

After a moment's silence, Richard tapped the roof of the car and said, "Swell. Nice meeting you. See you upstairs, Ray." He swung his sportcoat over his shoulder as he headed for the building's front doors.

As soon as Ray strode into the office, Richard could see he was agitated.

"Something is obviously bothering you," Richard said.

"You weren't very nice to Jennifer Harnett," Ray answered him coolly.

Richard drew his head back. "I wasn't very nice to her? I don't think she seemed all that anxious to talk to me, Ray."

Surveying one of Richard's lithographs, Ray nodded, but in the way one nods and looks at something else only to convey that much more pique.

"Is it important to you that I like Jennifer Harnett?" Richard asked.

"She's Tex's daughter," Ray said, beginning to roam about the office. "I'd appreciate it if you'd do everything possible to be friends with her. You don't really approve of my relationship with the family, do you. I think it's the work the Foundation does that you don't approve of."

"Number one," Richard said, "I think your association with the family has been a good thing for you, and number two, of course I don't disapprove of the Foundation's work."

"You don't disapprove that all the money goes just to Christian causes? I thought you once told me you weren't very religious."

"I'm not, but as a matter of fact, I contribute to several religious charities."

"I'm glad to hear that," Ray said.

"Do you see Jennifer socially?" Richard asked.

"Of course not," Ray scoffed, then looked at Richard for the first time. "I have a girlfriend."

"Terrific," Richard said. "I don't believe you've ever mentioned her."

Ray went back to looking at the pictures. "Her name is Treak."

"What's she like?"

"She's very pretty." Ray tried to think of more to say, but only shrugged.

"What does she do?"

Pretending not to hear the question, Ray bent down to retie a shoelace that did not really need retying, and said, "She's very nice. She lives in Santa Monica. I don't think a deep emotional involvement would be right for me . . . uh, not now, I mean. Carl Miller, the man who's in charge of the Foundation's finances, asked me recently if I wanted a raise. I don't think he believed me when I told him I didn't even really want as much salary as I'm getting now. Maybe everyone should spend a little time in prison. They'd see you don't need a lot of clothes and cars and all those things. I take the money they give me now and just put it in a bank."

Ray finally sat down.

"I've moved to a bigger room in the house, though. I moved into Dean's old room."

Richard raised his eyebrows. "How do you feel about that, moving into Tex's son's old room?"

Ray did not answer right away, then said, sharply, "He's not a good person—Dean." When he saw Richard studying him intently, he added, "What I mean is, he's not a very good son."

At 5:30, after Richard had finished with his last patient of the day, he found Jenny Harnett sitting in the waiting room. She had changed into jeans and hiking boots, and had a moss-green knapsack on her lap.

"Hello again," Richard said quizzically.

"Hi. Can I talk to you for a sec?"

The somber visage was gone, replaced by a fetching smile. Around her neck was a lovely silk scarf, and her hair, now washed and blown dry, tossed soft and free. She was really very pretty,

Richard thought as he sat down with her on the cherrywood settee.

"I'm glad to see you looking a little more cheerful," he said.

Jenny blushed instantly, all the way to her ears, as she reached up and fingered her scarf.

"Yeah, I, uh . . . was a real charmer this afternoon. I'm sorry if I was rude. I was kind of in a funk. I promise I'm much better now. One thing that always seems to do the trick is to drive to the Angeles National Forest and walk around awhile."

"Was it nice up there today?" Richard asked.

"Oh, it was wonderful," she said enthusiastically, but in a demure and shy way, glancing down. "It was so cloudy and quiet." She paused and, unable to think of any easy conversation, added only a contented, "Mmm."

"Well," Richard said, helping her out, "is there anything I can do for you?"

Jenny nervously touched her scarf again. "Oh, I don't even know," she said apologetically. "I wasn't sure if I should come here. I feel it's a little improper, really. The thing is . . . well, all right, the thing is this—this Ray Lomak. I mean, he seems like a well-meaning enough man, he tries to be nice, but . . . when I think about who this man *is*—"

"Or at least was," Richard interjected.

"I don't know. . . . Have you ever noticed that sometimes when you're talking to him, he just keeps looking at you and never looks away? It's the most uncomfortable feeling I've ever had. You almost sense that he's learning things about you for some purpose," Jenny said, cringing her shoulders.

"Yes, I've noticed," Richard said noncommittally.

"My father's kind of getting on in years. He's only sixty-nine, I know, but sometimes Dad doesn't even remember things an hour later, and . . . what I mean is, this taking Ray Lomak in as a house guest, it's so . . . strange. Sometimes I think about it, and it makes my skin crawl. Am I just being cold and unforgiving? I worry about Dad. I worry every day just thinking about him being under the same roof as that man."

Richard sat back on the settee with a sigh. "So you want to know, is it okay, is your father safe?"

Jenny nodded and, suddenly much bolder, said, "Yes. Very definitely I want to know. I realize psychiatric matters are confidential and all that, but yes, I do want to know—is it safe?"

Richard sat forward again, elbows on his knees, and rubbed the palms of his hands.

"Look, psychiatrists aren't soothsayers. We're not too bad at describing human behavior, and in some cases treating it, but as far as divining the future it's largely one guess against another."

Jenny smiled. Richard was used to the reaction. People smiled at his candor with a sort of fond amusement.

"Now, as far as Ray Lomak goes," Richard went on, "I'm not quite sure what to say to you. You know the man's history, and it would be ludicrous for me to tell you there's absolutely no cause for concern. Of course there is, there always is in a situation like this."

Playing with the loose end of the knapsack strap, Jenny began whipping it lightly against the knapsack. "Well, thanks for putting my mind at ease," she laughed.

He laughed with her. It seemed to dissolve a barrier they were both aware of.

"That was the bad part," Richard said. "The good part is that, yes, I share your concern about Ray, but I also assure you he hasn't been sent back out into the world without any precautions being taken. He reports to his parole agent once every two weeks, and once a week I see him for an hour. Believe me, if I saw him begin to display anything that even *might* bode ill for the future, he would be back on a plane that day for a new parole hearing. Okay? Feel a *little* bit better?"

Jenny cleared her throat and exhibited a faint sassy smile. She moved as if to get up.

"So what kind of work do you do?" Richard asked.

"Oh, I uh . . . um . . ." She squirmed a midge in her seat, then owned up with a quick garbled, "I'm sort of trying to act a little."

"I see. Is 'sort of trying to act a little' the same as trying to be an actress?"

"Yeah, I suppose it is," Jenny acknowledged. "It's just that . . . well, I don't know, it makes me sound like every third person who gets off the bus in L.A. There's something about saying 'wanting to be an *actress*' that makes people immediately react a certain way. 'Trying to act a little,' I kind of come in under the radar."

A sense of humor—five beads shot over on Richard's private abacus.

"Your father should be able to help you at least meet some of the right people, shouldn't he?"

Jenny smiled to herself. "He's so funny. He's got this idea that show business is beneath me. Anyway, his only contacts at this point are old cowboy movie producers who haven't worked in twenty years. I hope this doesn't sound pretentious, but I'm trying to be a serious actress."

"Then shouldn't you be getting your training by doing stage work in New York?"

Jenny frowned and said, "Oh, you're one of those eastern snobs, huh?"

"Well, come on," Richard retorted laughingly, "you can't help noticing when you drive into this state that they confiscate all vegetables and books at the border."

And so the facile banter over each other's geographical backgrounds continued for a while—two strangers interested in each other, overhead-smashing their senses of humor, and too ill at ease to break out of the routine they had set for themselves.

"You have a fair amount of contact with Ray Lomak?" Richard got around to asking seriously.

"No, virtually none, and I don't intend to."

"Good, because if you did, it probably wouldn't be advisable for me to ask you out to dinner . . . which I think I just did."

"Yes," Jenny said, "I think you did."

They drove to an east Indian restaurant in Hollywood.

"I imagine the seasons must be beautiful in a place like Connecticut," Jenny opined, a bit taut and not eating much. "And those grey and white Cape Cod colonials really are gorgeous."

"Yeah, it is nice," Richard agreed. "Of course, you can get some of that old-world charm in Los Angeles, too—the Spanish homes, and places like Hancock Park are great."

"Mmm," Jenny agreed, rolling her brown eyes.

Richard tossed his napkin onto his emptied plate. "We're really cute, what we're doing here. Talking about climate and architecture and everything else, thinking we're being so casual, when all we're doing is giving each other the big compatibility quiz. Okay, so far we've established that you wouldn't be too unhappy living in Connecticut and that conceivably I could see continuing to live in Southern California."

Richard loved Jenny's laugh. It was a natural burst that brought her leaning forward from the waist.

"You *are* cynical," she said, launching into her meal as if seeing it in front of her for the first time. At that moment, watching her with her mouth happily full of food, Richard wanted only to reach across and plant a big kiss on her cheek.

When he dropped her off at her apartment, the upstairs of an old, port red Mediterranean duplex—endearingly small, Richard thought, for a girl with an eight hundred thousand dollar trust fund—they kissed tentatively beneath the hallway light. But for all the sexual pull Richard had felt toward her the entire night, what Richard now experienced was not lust, but rather an emotional warmth. He was only slightly embarrassed when a group of passers-by saw him skipping down the stairs to his car.

✷ ✷ ✷

Richard's and Jenny's love was beautiful and plagued all in its own ways.

Jenny was an adventurer, like her mother who had traveled out west to work in the movie business, eventually marrying one of that industry's more engaging and backwatered stars, Tex Harnett. Because of Jenny's energy, there wasn't a weekend that Richard and she did not travel somewhere out of the city, to clean air and a more physical living. Often they drove to Palm Springs, where Jenny's father had a second home. On some of the afternoons there, they went horseback riding through the dusty flat desert with its creosote and burro bush. Jenny educated him on the wild flowers that were in their late springtime bloom.

At night they read or sat with gin and tonics in the giant indoor Jacuzzi that occupied a good portion of the game room in Tex's desert home. At the flick of a switch the panels of roof directly over the Jacuzzi slid back, revealing the clear, starry sky.

"Pretty decadent, huh," Jenny said. Richard agreed, and neither of them gave it a second thought.

It was on their first weekend in Palm Springs that Richard and Jenny made love for the first time. They caressed each other gently and, before going further, looked for a long, perhaps even forced moment into each other's eyes. They both glanced away.

"Maybe we shouldn't rush things," Richard said softly.

Jenny nodded and smiled sweetly at him, then kissed him on the forehead and said, "I'll tell you a scary bedtime story instead."

Jenny propped herself up on an elbow and, with obvious relish, narrowed her eyes and began with a biting, "It was a cold and rainy night in March, on an island off the coast of Newfoundland. And it was *dark* outside, my friend."

The story, culled from Jenny's childhood at summer camps, was a deliciously twisted gothic tale involving a one-armed old farmer with yellow teeth who was invariably seen gazing at the eleven year old, blue-eyed, pony-tailed heroine from atop a bluff, or perhaps behind a silo. It being a story for eleven year old camp girls, there was of course the wonderful ambiguity as to whether the farmer wanted to murder the girl or deflower her. Shutters swung wildly in the wind, floorboards creaked, doorknobs were turned by unseen hands from outside. When Jenny finally built to the scene of the girl lying in her bed at night and suddenly feeling something moving beneath her mattress springs, Richard sat up and exclaimed, "Son of a bitch, this *is* scary!"

"I know!" Jenny cried and threw her arms around him. They kissed and fell back onto the bed, undressing each other. As they rolled over, Jenny's sun-streaked hair fell down across her shoulders. Her abdomen was as flat and creaseless as a teenager's. Richard was stunned by the exquisite curves Jenny so modestly kept under her everyday clothes. He could have almost ravished her, had his emotions not dictated that he love her more tenderly.

An hour later, as they lay snuggling, he knew it had been the love-making of two people who wanted very much to please each other, who already cared deeply—and that it was between two people who had both been around the block a few times.

"I love you," Jenny whispered.

Richard stroked her hair, somehow mildly troubled to hear her use such a word after so little time.

✷ ✷ ✷

Richard enjoyed listening to Jenny's colorful, if too magnanimous, descriptions of people. A producer who had been one of her father's best friends, and who in fact was truly a dirty old man, was in Jenny's words, "a lonely sort of dirty old man who was just too bright to have ever be⌒n happy with the nubile young things he kept getting attracted to."

Yet somehow, for all of her articulate observations, Jenny's fertile, day by day living and openness to all of it kept her from reaching any enduring judgments or conclusions. Thus did she soak up Richard's self-assured and logical perceptions of life, remarking ingenuously, "You're very wise, you really are."

Spending more and more time with Jenny, eventually uninterrupted days and nights (having fallen undeniably in love with her), Richard soon discovered the untraceable sadness that sometimes collected in her. It was nothing so superficial as a fleeting malaise, but rather a gloom that enveloped her from the moment she awoke and did not dissipate until the next day. Richard, being even-keeled by both inclination and training, saw the shift with the first morning's glance. Her brown eyes rueful, Jenny moped through the rooms in her black and orange, ugliest housecoat, managing weak smiles when she otherwise would have laughed.

"Is it me?" Richard asked solicitously the first time he witnessed the descending depression. "Is it us?"

"I suppose," Jenny said, holding his hand.

Richard in time realized it was not really he as much as it was Jenny's nature of hoping for too much from every new and promising unfoldment in her life, with the inevitable letdown when reality seeped through. Richard's rocklike dependability, which she had at first sung paeans to as the stabilizing force she was searching for, she began to rebel against as Richard's "premature, middle-aged staidness." And his confidently held views, which she had once seen as "wisdom," she came to regard during her darker moods as simple "closed-mindedness." And there was some truth to it, Richard thought. She just exaggerated it beyond reason.

Their baptizing argument came one weekend night in the bedroom of Jenny's apartment. It started over a friend of Jenny's named Maxine.

"She's been seeing a psychiatrist for a couple of years," Jenny said.

"I'm sorry to hear that," was Richard's response.

Jenny said nothing as she sulkily packed some clothes for a several day stay out at Richard's place in Malibu. Finally she turned to him and said, "You act like she's diseased or something. You—of all people. So, she's seeing a psychiatrist."

Richard put his fingertips to his forehead, a confused smile on his face. "Yes, and all I said was, I'm sorry she needs to see a psychiatrist. If you had said she's been going to an orthopedist for her back, I would have said the same thing. If people need to see a doctor, they should go. But obviously, it's better if they don't have to."

"Everything's always so 'obvious' as far as you're concerned,"

Jenny rejoined. "Maybe some people like Maxine are just a little more complicated than you, a little more emotional," Jenny said with tears already beginning to well up. "I've never met such a critical person. You must be the most putrid psychiatrist in Los Angeles."

Richard could not help his burst of laughter, which didn't amuse Jenny in the least.

"Are you so completely critical in your office, too?"

"Who in the hell is being critical? And for your information, I happen to be extremely supportive in my office. I'm also one of the best goddamn shrinks in this state, so you can go fuck yourself with that little crack of yours before."

"Good! At least I'm able to say something that gets some fire out of you."

"You're ridiculous sometimes," Richard muttered.

He slouched in his chair, and said quietly, "I will admit I do have a tendency, now and then, to form opinions a little too quickly in my private life. I work on that, believe me. I'm a lot better now than when I was twenty and immediately assumed anyone who drove a sports car had a sexual problem."

Jenny was forced into a tepid smile.

"Well, keep working on it," she said. "You're so cold and objective about who you are and who everyone else is. Don't you feel anything deeply enough—way down in your insides—to just be plain irrational about it?"

"Oh, Jesus," Richard sighed. "What do you want me to do, throw you around the room a little?"

"Maybe just be a little passionate once in a while when you make love."

On that, Richard got to his feet. "Are you serious? I don't think this is cute any more. Who's the one who always wants to make love?"

"Just because you're a man and you have to get relieved once a day!" Jenny shouted, slamming the top of her suitcase shut. "Not because you love me. I never feel any real *love* from you!"

"I can't even answer something like that," Richard fumed. "You're just going crazy now."

"And of course you don't want anyone who's not perfectly normal and dull. If you really loved me, you'd love me with all my emotions."

"Well, I'm very sorry, but no, I don't love *all* your emotions."

"Then don't put up with any of them!" Jenny yelled.

"Not tonight I don't care to," Richard said. "There are about half a dozen old flames I'd rather wake up with tomorrow."

With one swift motion Jenny brought the flat of her hand smacking across Richard's cheek. Never in his life had Richard been slapped by a woman, or as a kid even socked on a playground. Before he could think, he grabbed Jenny by the wrists and threw her over the backrest of the couch. Her shoulders hit the seat, and only by the quickest reflex did she snap forward, preventing her head from cracking against the coffee table.

"Oh, God," Richard panted, vaulting over the couch and taking her in his arms. "Are you okay?"

Jenny collapsed in tears against him, and as she sobbed, tears came to Richard's eyes, too.

"I love you, Richard," she murmured.

Richard squeezed her tightly, until he felt her ribs and every heave of her stomach against him. "I love you, too, sweetheart. You're so precious to me. I swear to God I've never loved anyone so much in my life."

After a few minutes of silence, Jenny rubbed the shoulder she had landed on, and sniffled, "Fucking animal."

Richard roared with laughter, and Jenny, trying to laugh between her sniffles, only got a bad case of hiccups, which she couldn't shake until they had driven almost all the way out to Malibu.

✳ ✳ ✳

"You've gotten to like Jennifer Harnett, I understand," Ray said.

Richard nodded, watching Ray carefully across the desk from him.

"She's going to inherit a lot of money, I guess," Ray observed flatly.

"I suppose so," Richard said. "She never talks about it. I don't think she's the kind of woman who even thinks about it much."

"Her brother does. It's all he thinks about, the money that's going to the Foundation instead of him. He's trying to discredit me in Tex's eyes. He tells lies about me."

"Perhaps we should talk about your feelings toward Dean," Richard said.

Ray looked away and shrugged. "I'll take it up with him myself."

Ray had become more and more closed to Richard, and it was but one of the reasons their sessions were beginning to show strain.

The following week Richard found Ray sitting in the waiting room at eleven in the morning. His appointment was always for one o'clock.

"Aren't you awfully early today, Ray?" Richard asked with a perplexed smile.

"I have a plane reservation at one," Ray said, snapping shut a new attaché case of his he had been looking through. "I know this wasn't one hundred percent proper, and I apologize, but I told that Mrs. . . . Lasky, is it? I told Mrs. Lasky, who was waiting out here, that you had been called away and that you'd see her at one. I didn't think you'd mind."

Astonished, Richard looked hard at him. "I do mind. Why should Mrs. Lasky be inconvenienced?"

Ray returned his look with a knowing little smile, like that of one executive to another, in the washroom away from the stockholders.

"She didn't look like a woman who had very much to do. She can go shopping in Beverly Hills for a couple of hours, can't she?"

"That's not the point," Richard asserted.

"I don't understand why it's such a big problem. It worked out fine for everyone," Ray said innocently.

"The problem," Richard said, bracing one hand against the doorjamb, "is your incredibly bold lie."

Ray shook his head incredulously. "Well, I suppose you could call it a lie, but I guess I just don't quite see it the way you do."

He looked at the floor. "I've been doing some thinking lately that maybe I don't need a psychiatrist any more."

Richard decided not to remind Ray of his own statement a half year earlier that he would need a psychiatrist all his life.

"Whether you do or not, Ray, as you know, this is a condition of your parole."

". . . Yes . . . I know. . . . It was a foolish thing for me to say."

CHAPTER 2

IT WAS IN THE MIDDLE OF AUGUST THAT RAY,
feeling secure in his mooring at the Foundation, embarked upon
a private project he had not discussed with Tex. On a Friday
morning, he boarded a plane for Milwaukee, Wisconsin. From the
Milwaukee airport, where he rented a car (having gotten his
driver's license several months earlier), he drove the thirty miles
north to the one-yellow-page town of Slinger. Ray had learned
through a tracing service he had hired that a young man by the
name of Kevin Fahey was living there, and working with the U.S.
Highway Department.

During the entire drive up through the rolling farmland on this sweltering August day, Ray felt the clothes he was wearing. Funnels of gnats spun about over the ditches between the highway and the fields of corn, as if perpetually going down a drain. It was already late afternoon by the time Ray reached the Highway Department's branch office and was directed to where Kevin was working that day. A fast rain had begun to fall, and Ray drove slowly over the narrow back roads, trying to follow the scribbled instructions he had been given. The route took him around several birch-lined lakes whose motorboats were covered with green tarps and tied to the piers, and over a gravel road that led through a thickly wooded area. Finally he came to the temporary road sign which read: 'Men Working.'

Ahead were several trucks carrying tar and cinder, a large steamroller, and a half dozen men with shovels laying down a blacktop over the rutted road. One of the workers, who was strapped snugly into a lemon-colored slicker with a matching sou'wester that dripped and hung down over his ears, smiled cheerfully at Ray and held up a red sign that said: 'Slow.'

"I'm looking for Kevin Fahey," Ray said to him, rolling down his window.

The young fellow grinned and nodded. Ray waited, but getting no answer, repeated himself.

"Uh-huh, that's me," Kevin Fahey said with a little guffaw.

Ray looked at the bright-eyed young face that had a sort of rubbery nose and ears and a smooth beardless chin, and though Ray thought he had prepared himself for this moment, he discovered he had not. A tense knot in his throat, he stared at the young man who had, in the maid Mary Fahey's womb, survived the black Christmas Eve of 1959. Rubbing his hands on his thighs, he said, "Can I talk to you when you're through working? I traveled a very long way to see you."

"Uh-huh. Sure," Kevin said with his big smile. "I have to work until five, though. Mr. McCarty, he's the foreman, he lets us go right at five because he says you don't owe anyone a minute more just because you work for the government. He's the one over there in the blue jacket."

"Well, that's only about a half hour from now," Ray observed. "I'll just wait here in my car for you, all right?"

"That's all right, uh-huh," Kevin said.

Ray pulled off to the side of the road and watched the men finish their day's work. They were all a fair number of years older than Kevin, and they all seemed to like him—even to regard him as a kind of mascot, once in a while tweaking the floppy brim of his hat when they passed, or playfully swatting his rump with a shovel.

At five o'clock Kevin jumped into the front seat of Ray's car, and they drove to a small diner Ray had passed back near Slinger. Ray's name drew no recognition from Kevin.

What struck Ray about Kevin was how young he seemed, even for a twenty-one-year-old. At the diner, listening to Ray's explanation of the Foundation, Kevin grew inattentive, wiping his runny nose against his shirt-sleeve or looking about the restaurant.

"Do you think maybe you'd like to go to college?" Ray asked. "We could arrange that."

Hunched over his cheeseburger, Kevin bobbed his head and said, "Golly, I don't think I could do that, Mr. Lomak, I'm not smart enough for that."

"What about your job?" Ray asked. "Are you satisfied with your job? They can't pay you much—you're probably going to be wanting to start a family soon."

Kevin laughed his short guffaw again. "Aw, I really don't like girls all that much. They're always talking kind of silly. I like my job okay. They don't let me run any of the machines because on account of they hired me because of this special program. I just hold up the sign. They all think I'm the best one at it, anyway."

Ray began to study Kevin, puzzled by him.

"Maybe you could just accept a gift from the Foundation," Ray said. "Would you let me send you some money every now and then, Kevin?"

"Oh golly, that would be great!" Kevin exclaimed. Distractedly, he felt for something in his pocket and pulled a baseball card part way out, which he glanced down at briefly and slipped back into his pocket. "There are an awful lot of things I want to get. I want to get a bicycle on account of they don't let me drive."

Ray put his fork down, and looked bewilderedly at Kevin. "What did you mean before, the special program?"

Kevin stopped smiling, and looked away at the floor. One leg started to jiggle, and distorting his face into a frown, he said, "I'm not real smart, Mr. Lomak. My mother was real sick or something when I was born. She even died later. That's why I'm never going to be too smart, I guess. That's what they told me a long time ago."

Blood rose into Ray's face and turned the tips of his ears hot. He stared aghast at the boyish-man across from him, finally realizing the obvious. Kevin Fahey was somehow retarded, brain damaged, and there was no one in the world except Ray Lomak who was responsible for it. Ray's face broke out in perspiration.

Kevin went back to eating his cheeseburger.

Ray's eyes darted about the restaurant. It seemed to him as if everyone knew, that everyone was looking at them, though nobody was. A tattooed man behind the counter was turning sizzling bacon, and at a table in the corner a flabby-armed woman in a pink work uniform poured beer from a pitcher for herself and three other women.

Mumbling a few syllables, Ray excused himself and walked back to the restroom behind the kitchen. Shaking, he bowed his head against the powdery metal top of the soap dispenser. The cool metal felt good against his forehead. Suddenly, he turned and walked out of the restroom. Head down, he veered for the diner's rear exit, knocking the receiver off a public wall-phone as he went. The muggy air outside was even more suffocating than that inside.

Ray started the car with a great roar and shot out of the pebble parking lot, swerving onto the highway with one hand on the wheel, the other rolling down the window. At seventy miles an hour he leaned his head out the window and felt his eyelashes flurry in the rush of air.

His head eventually began to clear. It simply could not be, he started thinking, that the boy would have been brain damaged because of him. Why hadn't the papers, which had all been eager to paint him as one of the most evil men to walk the earth, ever reported such a thing? At the time of the murders, Ray had read every newspaper and magazine article written about the case. They all said the baby was born healthy. A nun had called it a testament to the poor Catholic maid's faith. True, Ray thought, it may have been discovered only several years later that the boy was retarded, but why hadn't he learned about it at that time? The possibility that there had been a small article on the matter which hadn't come to his attention, he dismissed from his mind. No, there was something missing here, and as Ray streaked down the darkening highway he was determined to come up with the answer.

A contemptuous satisfaction soon came to Ray's face. He believed he knew—the surgeons at the Pasadena hospital had been at fault. Having once been a hospital orderly, Ray was certain he was right. The baby could have been delivered normal and healthy, but some inexperienced intern had probably failed to supply the infant with enough oxygen. So concerned had they been with saving the mother's life, they had not followed simple, proper procedure with regard to the baby. When it was subsequently determined that the boy was brain damaged, the newspapers had conveniently looked the other way. Ray nodded to himself. It was the same old story—one little club.

Poor kid, Ray thought. A victim of the self-righteous men who claimed to care so much about human life, when in truth an operation meant no more to them than another pair of diamond earrings for their wives. If he were expected to own up to his deeds, why wasn't everyone else as well?

Ray drove the car hard over the country highway, but finally began slowing as he saw the approaching lights of Milwaukee's northern suburbs. He was not going to let himself get stopped for speeding this night. He could just imagine how a bunch of local gendarmes would love to get him into their jail for a night or two.

What a feather in their small caps—Raymond Lomak, *the* Raymond Lomak. They would question him about every crime committed in the last twenty-four hours in the entire state. Well, he wasn't going to give them a chance. He had a new life now. His life was the Foundation.

The poor kid should someday know the truth about those doctors, he thought, as he carefully steered the car onto the off-ramp for the Milwaukee airport.

★ ★ ★

Ray worked seven days a week, fourteen hours a day for the Foundation, from eight in the morning until ten at night (except Wednesdays when he had a regular eight-thirty appointment with Treak Johnson). Aside from his weekly visits to Treak, there was nothing else personal going on in his life to distract him.

He read over all the diverse requests for money that came into the Foundation's office, and discussed them with Tex, who in turn discussed them with Carl Miller. He flew to Bozeman, Montana, to meet with a pastor who wanted to build a one room addition to the church school; he went to Atlanta where he watched in awe as a paisley shirted, flare-cuffed evangelist, who had failed as a nightclub singer, touched the brows of dozens of his weekly audience of five thousand, miraculously healing them all of cancer and multiple sclerosis and diabetes. In San Diego he met with a woman whose disco played Jesus-rock and served only soft drinks, and in Newark, New Jersey, he vigorously shook hands and promised money to a black community organizer who was teaching pre-school kids to read, using the Bible instead of Dick and Jane.

Ray visited with the sincere, and visited with the hucksters, and rarely could he smell the difference. They all spoke with deep fervor in their voices about spreading the Word, and that was really all Ray cared about. Back in Los Angeles, about half of Ray's recommendations were turned down by Tex after Tex had consulted with Miller and the Foundation lawyer.

As the months passed, Ray began to see that although he personally had little use for material possessions, without them he was not always being accorded the respect he felt he should have been. Many applicants, seeing him in his old formless trousers and worn sweaters or driving up in the used Datsun he had bought for trips near Los Angeles, invariably got around to asking the name of the person in the Foundation they were "eventually" supposed to deal with. By winter, one year after the Foundation had been started, Ray told Carl Miller he was ready to accept the substantial salary increase he had been offered.

Despite a few maudlin protests from Tex, Ray used part of the extra money to move to his own one-bedroom apartment in West Los Angeles. In time, he also bought a week's rotation of reasonably handsome clothes at a downtown Los Angeles store, and leased a Chrysler for himself.

At the end of January, after another football season had passed and Tex's mind was no longer on his team (which had once again made it to the division play-offs and no further), Ray approached him about an idea that had been gestating in him for some time.

"I don't think we're doing any good with all our college scholarships," Ray said, irritated, and pacing Tex's living room. "We're not doing any good at all, I can tell you that right now."

"Oh no, now why's that, Ray?" Tex asked, concerned.

"It's a disgrace what goes on around American campuses. It would be better if the kids never went there in the first place. Don't you even know, Tex, about all the drugs and the drinking? And in some places these boys and girls even live in the same dormitories. Haven't you even read about it?"

"Well sure, sure I've read about it," Tex said. "Bad situation, this drug thing. . . . Living in the same dormitories too, huh?"

Ray told Tex of his idea.

Harnett College, an adjunct of the Harnett Foundation. A place where kids would once again be taught the rudiments in education, and would be given a moral beacon to follow, as well.

Bible classes, dress codes, rules governing social conduct, athletic programs predicated upon Christian sportsmanship. Ray pointed to colleges just like it that had been built recently, and were flourishing.

"Could start a sports program right from scratch," Tex added himself, his eyes gleaming. "Teach the kids what it is to play for pride, not just this gol darn money thing."

"It should be someplace where the air is clean and healthy," Ray chimed.

"I like it," Tex said. "I like it. Harnett College. I like it."

Over the next few months all the officials of the Harnett Foundation were drawn into discussions about the ambitious concept for the college, and by spring, firm plans had been formulated for a school to open within the next year and a half. It would be humble at first—fifteen hundred to two thousand students. A parcel of income-barren land Tex owned just outside Palm Springs was chosen as the site, and single-story prefab structures were erected as temporary student living quarters and classrooms. Not far away, the bulldozers and steam shovels dug the foundation for the permanent Spanish style administration building, Harnett Hall. Three church-going associate deans were bibled away from the state university system, and it was their job to set up the initial faculty. Ray sat in unobtrusively on a few of the interviews. At one of them he spoke up.

"Do you think a school should take some responsibility for the students' moral education?" he asked a young mustachioed professor whose tweed coat, Ray noticed, was rather shabby, and whose shirt cuff even had a small ink stain.

The professor rolled his tongue around inside his cheek and answered, "As long as you don't take away academic freedom. No, I have no attitudinal objection to some of the other teachers conducting . . . Bible classes, if you will."

"Our beliefs wouldn't be a problem in regards to your own . . . uh"—Ray looked down at the professor's resumé on the table —"biopsychics course?"

"Biophysics."

"Yes, biophysics, the 'h' is a little smudged here," Ray blushed.

The professor smoothed one side of his mustache with a finger and replied, "Just so there's sufficient intellectual play. I don't mean to lecture you here, but I'm sure you're aware it's rather difficult to obtain a respectable faculty without this."

"Well, you would know more about that than me. I never even went to college," Ray said with a brief smile. "But actually, I was told there were quite a few good teachers around these days looking for any kind of employment at all."

The young professor looked down at his belt buckle. The next day Ray used his influence to insure that the professor, whose religious underpinnings seemed anemic, was not hired.

That evening Ray arrived, as always, precisely at eight-thirty for his weekly appointment with Treak Johnson.

"You're the most famous, unusual man I've ever been with," Treak said, massaging Ray's feet.

"It's even more important than before," Ray said, "that you don't go telling people about us. Now that I'm going to be so involved in the operation of a college."

Tex and Ray had long since agreed that Ray was not qualified to have any kind of active hand in the running of the school, but as far as Ray was concerned, he was the institution's moving spirit.

CHAPTER 3

"WE'S ALL VARAH PROUD TO HAVE YOU HERE, YES suh," the effusive sexton of the Tabernacle of Faith Baptist Church in Baton Rouge, Louisiana, warbled with a close, tobacco breath in Ray's ear as he ushered him up the bright yellow steps of the church. They left behind the laughter and clack of billiard balls coming out of the open-doored tavern, catty corner, as they entered the air of sweet smelling perfumes inside the crowded little sanctuary. Except for some scattered men sitting close to their wives, the congregation was mostly women—black lardy women with comely daughters-in-law and a brood of children on one side of them, and perhaps their own grey-haired mothers with their prim bifocals, on the other.

From the pulpit a seventy-two year old reverend by the name of Franklin Hewitt, thin-wristed at the ends of his billowy black robe sleeves, and with a scratchy dire voice, hurled down the Word.

"Go on, reverend!" the ladies called out. "Thaz jez what the Lawd said, reverend!" And if Hewitt stumbled over a word, or had to swallow and catch his breath, a red-dressed woman in front could be counted on for a, "That's a'right, reverend!"

The sexton showed Ray to a pew toward the back, and it wasn't long before many of the younger little girls in the congregation, their shiny processed hair put up in braids, were stealing glances or even turning around in their seats to gaze back at the only white face in the church. Their older brothers cast cooler, less interested looks over their shoulders.

Ray smiled acknowledgingly at all of them.

After the first half an hour of sermon, a young man with a trim Afro and three-piece suit who had been sitting poised at the organ, put a hand up to the bass end of the keyboard and waited. When the reverend raised his finger to the sky and got to the part where Moses reached the mountain top, the organist batted out a low bluesy riff, just loud enough to be heard beneath Franklin Hewitt's straining vocal cords. At that, Reverend Hewitt snatched the microphone from its stand, stamped a few steps back and forth behind the pulpit and half-sang, half-talked the remaining hour of his preachments. The women started rocking in their seats. "Amen, reverend, amen," they continually joined in.

The organ came up full and soulful behind.

"And what did the Loorrrd say to Moses?" Hewitt whipped them up like the leader of a field holler a century earlier. "What did the Lord teeellll His child?"

Women clapped above their heads and shouted their answers back at the old man.

"Only told him the truth, reverend!"

"We listenin' *now*, reverend!"

Ray, too, began nodding his head and unconsciously tapping his foot to the spills of jazzed-up organ music.

"A stranger shalt thou not wrong or oppress, for ye were strangers in the land of Egypt!" Hewitt sang out, clutching the microphone in one hand, a gathering of robe at his hip in the other. "And the ones who curse their mothers and fathers gonna surely be put to death!"

"Mercy, mercy, *mercy!*" a short round woman whose legs barely touched the floor cried aloud, putting her hand to her forehead.

The little children in the church stared agape at the reverend, while their mothers rolled their heads back and hummed along with their eyes closed and their grandmothers nodded sagaciously at the floor.

Ray was filled with happiness for all the people.

By the end, two of the larger women had fainted. Another had lapsed into a kind of trance, yelping like a dog, with tears running down her cheeks. All three were given smelling salts and helped from the church by the half-dozen women who were dressed in white, nurse-like uniforms.

The sermon concluded, the congregation, led by the thumping organ and a full-bodied choir, sang lusty hymns that set the church joyously vibrating with rhythm.

After the service, Ray shook Reverend Hewitt's bony hand back in the cluttered private quarters of the rectory, and marveled, "It was very powerful. It was . . . wonderful."

Hewitt nodded ceremoniously, while Willard La Peer, the sexton, spoke up as if on Hewitt's behalf.

"Thank'ee. We's all varah proud to have you here," he repeated himself.

The two men gave Ray a tour of the damage done to the church (pronounced amusingly to Ray's ears by southern Louisianans as a Brooklynese "choych") by Hurricane Julie the previous September, the reason for which Ray had come to offer the Foundation's assistance. Reverend Hewitt kept his eyes averted from Ray's as he pointed to the broken plumbing, the boarded up windows in the basement classrooms, the water buckled floors. He showed Ray the workmen's estimates. When Ray promised the $8,000 that had been discussed over the phone, Hewitt nodded and said distantly, "You will thank everyone at the Foundation for me." Then he turned and went back to his quarters, where he thought searchingly about the morality of accepting money from a man such as Ray Lomak. Ray took Hewitt's reserve as ministerial sobriety. It was Willard La Peer who remained and gushed ebulliently, "Isn't this a joyful day! Isn't this a day to praise God!"

Ray smiled with gratification, and La Peer stepped closer, lowering his voice intimately. "Not many white folks would be helpin' a choych like ours, y'know. You're a righteous man, Mr. Lomak. We knows all 'bout yer troubles. The reverend'd be the foyst to say any community be proud to have you one o' their own. Yes, he would."

Later, as Ray was leaving the church, La Peer caught up to him on the front steps and gaggled excitedly, "The reverend wants you to be comin' to his sister's fo' dinner! Sent me out special t'invite you!"

That night Ray enjoyed a merry dinner at the home of Franklin Hewitt's sister, Adelle. Nephews, aunts and cousins passed around deep dishes of crawfish, crisply fried mushrooms, ham hocks in a gumbo, and pounds of buttery mashed potatoes.

"Give our fine gentleman guest some more mushrooms, Louise," sister Adelle said, smiling maternally at Ray.

Willard La Peer, whose truckling, Uncle Tom ways were good-naturedly tolerated by all that night, lofted grand compliments about Ray to the Hewitt family members across from him, just loud enough for Ray to hear. And a thirty year old niece sitting next to Ray beamingly showed Ray pictures of her two small children.

When the subject of music came up, and Ray admitted to having a clarinet in his suitcase out in the car, there rose a chorus of requests for him to go out and get it. Obligingly, Ray fetched his clarinet after dinner and seated himself between two older aunts on the living room couch. His back straight, he closed his eyes and brought forth into the hushed room a vulnerably beautiful rendition of "Amazing Grace." He trilled the high notes of the spiritual as if they could reach up to heaven itself. By the end, sister Adelle and a couple of the women had tears in their eyes.

Needing little encouragement, Ray soon launched into some jazz and Dixieland, and before long the room was filled with clapping and stomping. No one there noticed how the elder Reverend Hewitt, sitting in the corner, eyed Ray dispiritedly and stared for long moments out the window. In time, he rose and, extending his hand to Ray very formally, excused himself for the evening.

Ray stayed past midnight, playing a few more songs, but mostly talking to everyone about their families and their jobs. By the time it came for him to leave, he felt like a family member. All the relatives pumped his hand and hugged him at the door, telling him how moved they were by what he had made of his life, and wishing him Godspeed back to Los Angeles.

As he drove toward the hotel where he was to stay before catching an early morning flight back to California, it occurred to Ray that what he had been waiting almost a year and a half for had finally come to pass. He had, over that time, proven himself. In the eyes of good decent Americans, he was not a monstrous aberration or a suspect appendage to the Harnett Foundation, but truly someone to be befriended and accepted, to be asked into one's home like anyone else.

For over a year he had scudded around behind the Foundation's name like a gnome, carrying on his work diligently, but afraid to trespass into the light of the larger world. The time had now come, he told himself, to walk as other men walked—to venture beyond the tight-ringed perimeters of the Foundation, born-agains and old time religionists. It was time to hold his head high to all the public, to introduce himself to his apartment neighbors back in Los Angeles, have parties, maybe join a political club. Perhaps it was even time to take a wife and have a family.

The thoughts and plans that burst into his mind like fireworks kindled his imagination. As he drove swiftly along one of Baton Rouge's main arteries, an intriguing idea fell upon him with all the weight of the billboard that had suggested it: he was only eighty miles from New Orleans, cradle of Dixieland jazz. So preoccupied had he been with his purpose for coming to Louisiana, the proximity of the two cities had never occurred to him. Now he smiled at the thought, at the opportunity of seeing some of the great jazz-men, and maybe—just possibly—even jamming with one of them. Unlike his usual self, he heaved aside his previous plans without a second's consideration, and after stopping briefly to cancel his hotel and flight reservations, headed for the interstate highway.

★ ★ ★

Because he hadn't gotten into his room at a small hotel in New Orleans' French Quarter until almost 2:00 A.M, Ray slept uncharacteristically and luxuriously until ten the next morning. When he awoke, strains of jazz were already bending their way up to his second story balcony from Bourbon Street just around the corner. Ray threw back the curtains and looked down onto the slate sidewalks crowded with tourists. Two little black boys were tap-dancing in the narrow street, while an old man kept up a beat for them on a homemade drum set of tin plates and soup spoons.

Showering and dressing quickly, Ray hurried down the hotel stairs into the straightening February morning air. He strode down Bourbon Street, past nine foot high, dark green shuttered doors, and beneath the wrought iron railinged balconies two and three stories above him. Out-of-towners like himself, whose sweaters would soon come off in the midday sun, were pausing at the open doorways of the saloons to listen to the few Dixieland bands that had already started up. Most of the music this time of the morning was still coming from jukebox records.

Ray stopped in front of Pete Fountain's club, and looked long at the picture of the famous clarinetist. The roundish man with the goatee that was his trademark smiled puckishly in the picture, his clarinet held at his side, his wrists adorned with gold bracelets. Ray noted the show times for the night, and walked on.

Wanting to do the things he thought tourists did, he found his way to Decatur Street and ordered a breakfast of beignets and hot chicory coffee, then wandered through the open-air French Market to Jackson Square. There, he stood still and watched a makeshift symphony of pudgy pigeons, drifters, and nomadic artists with chalk on their fingertips perform their functions, then compete for bench space.

When he returned to his hotel at the end of the day, Ray sat next to the window folding one sheet of paper after another into his little origami animals, while dusk fell on the way-down-yonder city. He did not turn on any light, and when his room at last filled with darkness he lay down on the bed and closed his eyes, atingle with the possibility that Pete Fountain might actually let him play with him for a number or two.

Ray got up and showered again, then stood in front of the mirror combing his damp hair until there wasn't an errant strand. He got dressed carefully, straightening and examining each piece of apparel as it went on. After buttoning up the pink shirt a store clerk had once talked him into buying, he flushed hotly with embarrassment, thinking it was too flashy. He stripped it off and put on a white one instead.

Once tucked into his charcoal grey suit, he fastened his crimson bow tie and looked at himself a last time in the mirror. He allowed himself a partial smile, and picked up his clarinet case. Outside the hotel, he walked indivertibly past all the nudie show barkers, tour leafleteers and sidewalk souvenir hustlers—all incongruous neighbors, he couldn't help noticing, to courtyarded French restaurants—to Pete Fountain's Bourbon Street club.

Having asked to see Fountain's manager, he told the hurried young man, "I'd like very much to play a tune with Mr. Fountain at the end of his set. Would that be possible?"

The manager smiled politely and answered, "I'm sorry, but Pete's got a couple of shows to do tonight. We have to keep the program kind of tight, you know?"

"I'm very good," Ray continued. "Would you like to hear me play? It would be very entertaining for your audience to hear Mr. Fountain . . . Pete and me play a clarinet duo together. I just thought I could help you entertain your audience."

The manager laughed good-naturedly. "Well, we appreciate that, but I'm afraid it just wouldn't be possible. . . . Billy!" he called over to the club's head usher, "you show this gentleman to a good seat, hear? He's a big fan of Pete's."

Ray ignored the usher and followed the manager the few steps to a back stage door.

"It would be very unusual. It might even get into the papers. See—"

"Hey look," the manager said, turning around abruptly, "I'm very busy now, okay? Just be a good fellow and buy your ticket, and enjoy the show, okay? Okay."

He disappeared through the door, and Ray, heavy-heartedly laying out his money for a ticket, let the usher show him to a seat at a front table. As it was still an hour before the first show, Ray sat in the nearly deserted club by himself, his clarinet case across his lap, his eyes fixed forlornly and patiently on the bandstand's lowered curtain.

In time the place began to fill up. Ray sat sipping his 7-Up as his one-drink minimum, while the people around him tossed down shots of bourbon and Scotch and became louder with each swing through of the waitresses. From the conversations he overheard, most of the people there seemed to be either tourists or conventioneers. When a waitress accidentally tripped and sent her trayful of drinks spraying over the table of patrons who had been waiting eagerly for that round, Ray's face stretched red and his shoulders began to jiggle with silent laughter. Lowering his watery eyes to his own table, he quaked without anyone's ever noticing him.

By eight o'clock the club was packed, and as the lights began to dim and the curtain lifted, Ray sat back with a flutter of anticipation, his disappointment over not being allowed to play, behind him. His eyes were riveted to the stage as Fountain, planting himself jovially in front of his emerald shirted band, dipped down at the knees and tickled some of the most fun loving jazz out of his clarinet that Ray had ever heard. The crowd whistled and cheered at lively numbers like "Running Wild" and "High Society," and let their sodden hearts be tugged when Fountain eventually slowed things up a little with "Basin Street Blues" and "Do You Know What It Means to Miss New Orleans?" Ray sat mesmerized, looking up at the accomplished jazzman only a few feet away from him. Seeing that attentive face below him, Fountain even looked down once at Ray and winked.

After the show was over and the place had cleared, Ray stayed in his chair and asked one of the waitresses wiping off the tables if he could remain for the second set.

"For another twelve dollars, darling," she smiled sweetly.

Ray nodded forebearingly, paid her the money, and ordered another 7-Up.

During the second show, Pete Fountain looked down at Ray several times with something of an amused smile. At the set's conclusion, Fountain stepped to the rim of the stage and asked into the mike, "Now, you got me wondering just what that might be laying across your lap—that ain't no set of baby kettledrums in there, now is it?"

The audience laughed, and Ray edged forward in his chair.

"Well, it's getting kinda late," Fountain said, a bead of sweat trickling down into his shirt collar, "but I think I know what's on your mind, and maybe these good people wouldn't mind hearing you join us for one last toot."

Ray was up out of his chair at once, heading for the side steps to the stage as he screwed together the two pieces of his clarinet. Fountain turned around to his band with his eyes rolled wide, and gasped privately, "Hope this dude can cut it."

Ray mounted the stage and nervously shook hands with a few of the band members he passed on his way to joining Fountain at the microphone.

"What's your name?" Fountain asked, tilting the mike Ray's way.

"Ray."

"All right, Ray, you call the shot."

As Ray stood pondering a moment which number to play, a green suited bottling-plant foreman from Syracuse, New York, sitting with his wife near the back of the club and loaded down with six stiff bourbons, slurred to no one in particular, "Ho'y shit . . . 'at's, 'at's what's-hiz name, 'at's . . . goddamn, 'at's Ray what's-hiz name."

" 'Muskrat Ramble'?" Ray asked Fountain buoyantly. "In B-flat?"

"Hey!" the man called to a nearby waitress. "Wha' hell kinda place iz'iss? 'At's Ray Lomak up 'ere. Don' you know Ray Lomak?"

The few people who heard him moved uneasily in their seats, unsure whether to tell a probably mistaken drunk to shut up, but unnerved by what he was saying.

Oblivious to the slight commotion, Pete Fountain nodded to his piano player for a four-bar introduction, and told Ray, "Take it to the bridge."

But before the piano player had even rippled his way through the second bar, the man at the rear was shouting, "C'mon, Ray, gonna knock uz dead wi' your clar'net? What's madder, forgedd your guns at home?"

Ray froze where he stood, his hands stuck to his clarinet as if to an icicle.

"Don't ever mind the hecklers," Fountain said to him cheerfully, but seeing Ray standing there motionless, the clarinet far from his lips, he cautioned his piano player from the side of his mouth, "Better take another four."

The club bouncer lumbered toward the back table, but the potted patron got to his own shaky feet, temporarily warding him off, and pointed wavily at the stage.

"Wha' hell kinda place iz'iss? Led Ray Lomak, a goddamn fuggin' mur'erer, go up there an' play his clar'net. Should be shamed 'a yourselz. . . . Go to a gaz cham'er where you belong, Lomak, you goddamn—"

The man pulled his wife up roughly by her hand to leave with him, and suddenly the club was filled with murmurs of Ray's name. Even Pete Fountain shuffled a small step back from Ray, helpless and not knowing what to do.

For another moment Ray could not move. It was a nightmare. He turned to Fountain, who was now standing away from him. Ray's eyes were imploring.

In another second he walked quickly from the stage to the nearest exit door. As he ran down a darkened side street, his fierce eyes burned against the chilled night air. Halfway down the block he stopped and, taking the clarinet in both hands, swung it with all his might against the corner of a brick building, smashing the instrument into two pieces.

He hated them, all of them. It wasn't fair.

At the crowded corner of Toulouse and Dauphine, Ray stopped and bent over, sucking air down into his lungs. He continued on, pushing his way past clogs of night revelers. He was too humiliated to even go back to his hotel for his suitcase or his rented car, and when he spotted a cab he fell into the back seat, sputtering, "Airport. Just take me to the airport."

By the time they arrived there, he had calmed himself. Sitting erect in the back seat, he stared coldly out the window. The world out there was sick with hatred. He had learned his lesson. Never again would he forget. Never.

The Foundation was his home.

✳ ✳ ✳

Dean Harnett wanted to speak to Ray to try to stitch up their differences, but Ray did not want to speak to him. He preferred to despise Dean from afar.

"He told Tex I was just trying to get myself into his will," Ray confided to Jim Brill, the born-again football player who had started up a conversation with him at Tex's barbecue a year and a half earlier. "It's pathetic," Ray said. "The will is the only thing he ever thinks about, so he believes that's all everyone else thinks of, too."

Ray explained to Brill what a danger Dean Harnett could be to the work the Foundation was accomplishing, and asked for his help in bringing a few things to Tex's attention.

"Dean's an immoral person," Ray said. "Tex has a right to know that. It could embarrass him someday in public. That cocaine and everything . . . There's probably a lot more that could hurt Tex," Ray said. "I don't suppose there's really any way we could find out, though? What do you think?"

Brill put Ray on to a secretary in the team's front office who was known to sing in her church's choir. When Ray called her, she was short with him and to the point.

"I consider myself a good Christian, Mr. Lomak, and I don't go around spying on my fellow man. Now, if you'll excuse me, there's another call I have to answer."

Brill asked around a little on his own, but all he could fish up was that Dean stayed out of the office for the better part of the afternoon several days a week, and because he was the owner's son, no one questioned him about his long lunches or wherever it was that he spent his time. Ray decided to find out for himself.

One afternoon he waited in his car across the street from the team's Westwood offices. When Dean emerged and got into his black, racing-striped Trans Am, Ray pulled out and followed him down Wilshire Boulevard. Dean drove east through Beverly Hills and on toward the city's older mid-Wilshire district. There he zipped into a space in front of a real estate office, went inside, and a few minutes later swaggered out with two voguishly dressed young men about his age. Laughing and loosening their ties, the two got into Dean's car with him, and for the rest of the trip down

Wilshire, even staying four cars behind them, Ray could hear loud pop music blaring out their open windows.

Eventually, the three got onto the Pasadena Freeway. The moderate midday traffic breezed along, and Ray had no trouble keeping the Trans Am in sight. He followed them onto an off-ramp and down a series of out-of-the-way, tree lined streets. Wherever they were going, they seemed to know a shortcut. When Ray realized they were in Arcadia, he relaxed his grip on the steering wheel and smiled to himself. So sure was he of their destination, he knew he almost did not have to trail them any farther.

A few minutes later they arrived at Santa Anita racetrack. Ray pulled out of the long line that was forming to get into the parking lot, turned his car around amid the honking and cursing of people who did not want to miss the Daily Double, and with the pleased smile still on his face, headed back toward Los Angeles.

"Did you ask him why he wants to borrow on his trust fund?" Ray posed the question to Tex that same night.

"Oh, he said some friend of his is a little short. That's the funny thing about Deanie—always soft-hearted when it comes to his friends. Always has been. Probably a little *too* generous," Tex mused philosophically.

"One of his real estate agent friends, no doubt," Ray trumpeted.

Tex looked at him with surprise. "Why yes, I believe he is a broker. How did you know that?"

"Everyone down at the team office knows that Dean and his friends go to the track," Ray said. "At least three times a week. He shouldn't take advantage of you like that—just because you're not as active down at the office anymore."

Ray let Tex sit and stew for a few minutes, then asked the crowning question: "Is that what's going to eventually happen to all the money you worked a lifetime for?"

An hour later, as Ray sat by in the den, listening, Tex bleated at Dean over the phone.

"Is that where all the money's going to go when I'm gone?

Have you ever once in your life thought about what it is to go to work at five in the morning for years, just to provide a few comforts for a family? . . . Ray Lomak? No, hell no, Ray has nothing to do with it! Everyone down at the office knows! Who d'you think you been hoodwinkin'?"

A minute later Tex hung up on his son, and Ray, sharing his vexation, remarked, "There's no excuse for deceiving someone in your own family."

* * *

Over the next several months Tex would liquidate a good number of his stocks, bonds and real estate holdings, putting the proceeds into a greatly expanded Harnett College. New construction sprang up in every corner of the sprawling, landscaped campus— from an enviably equipped microbiology department, to a one hundred unit on-campus motor lodge for visitors, to a four-tier indoor swimming and basketball complex.

CHAPTER 4

SEVERAL TIMES RICHARD BROUGHT HIMSELF TO
the verge of sending the parole board a letter requesting them to
have their own panel of prison psychiatrists reexamine Ray. He
had even composed and typed the letter, but still, it lay in the
middle drawer of his desk.

Although Ray had chosen to communicate less and less with
Richard, it had still become clearer every month to Richard what
had been transpiring. A few comments here and there, an inflection in Ray's voice, at times a certain look in his eye, had been
tattling on Ray's progressive emotional seclusion, feelings of resentment and instances of elastic morality. By an unmindful slip

Ray had even let Richard know about following Dean around town.

"I saw him at Santa Anita with my own eyes!" Ray had exclaimed in trying to convince Richard that he was right about Dean. Seeing the disquiet in Richard's face, Ray quickly changed the subject.

"*Reaction formation,*" Richard wrote in his letter, "seems to me to be in evidence here. Ray has professed a religious love for his fellow man, and at a certain level, he sincerely acts upon this feeling. I must question, however, if it is not in truth an overcompensating reaction that he uses to repress his much stronger instincts, which run in just the opposite direction."

Richard read his letter over and over again. Although he was only seeking a reexamination of Ray, and some other outside opinions, he knew that in fact he would possibly be initiating the first step in the revocation of Ray Lomak's parole. Because of the magnitude of what could result, Richard had to ask himself a very simple question: what had Ray actually *done?* Since his release from prison, other than some untoward conduct and attitudes, what actual harm had he caused, or even given any indication he might cause? With the heavy distress of having to make such a decision weighing cruelly on him, Richard slid the letter back into the drawer of his desk.

Compounding his frustration, because of the doctor-patient privilege, Richard could not breathe even a word of his concern to Jenny, even though her family was so intimately involved.

★ ★ ★

"Our children would be smart and pretty good-looking, wouldn't they," Jenny said one day with a shameless grin.

"Yeah, when do you want to get married?" Richard asked, not even looking up from his book. "Sometime this year?"

"Yeah, maybe December," Jenny answered, echoing his infectious casualness as she watered his plants, which she accused Richard of swinishly neglecting. In a small, meaningless spat weeks later, she would claim that his lack of romanticism drove her crazy and that, yes, she wouldn't have minded a slightly bigger production over a subject like marriage. The next day Richard bought a tastefully modest diamond ring, a bottle of Perrier-Jouët champagne, and a red velvet pillow on which to kneel as he asked for her hand.

"And this isn't all just for a laugh," Richard said, putting the back of his hand gently against her cheek. "I do love you, Jenny —very, very deeply. So I'm asking you humbly—will you marry me?"

The tears came instantly to Jenny's eyes, and all she could do was nod her head.

✶　✶　✶

On a brisk night in May when the wind strafed the beach and pushed in on the French doors of Richard's bedroom, Jenny slipped into a robe and started for the bathroom. Two steps from the bed she let out a startled, frightened sound.

"Richard!" she gasped. "There's someone down on the beach there. There's some man down there looking up at us."

Richard stood up on the bed to look out, instinctively reaching out to pull Jenny away from the French doors. Sixty yards down the beach, partly in the shadows of the shoreline's largest mossy boulder, a man in a long coat stood still as a dock post. The lights from the coast highway reflected off the foamy surf and caught the whiteness of his face, revealing that he was indeed looking up at their apartment.

"It's a public beach, honey," Richard was quick to say. "He's probably just looking around. There, see? He's leaving. He probably just stopped to look at the ocean for a while. Maybe he thought the grunion were running. He's going, no big deal."

Jenny pulled the collar of her robe tightly to her neck with a shiver and went into the bathroom. Richard continued to watch the man as he climbed back up the rocky incline to the coast highway. He watched him move down the shoulder of the highway until he disappeared behind the bend. Richard sat back down on the bed, feet together, grasping his cold toes. It had not, of course, been some man aimlessly looking for grunion. A long coat was not all he had been wearing. Atop his head had been a dark hat with a round brim.

As soon as Ray sat down at his next session, Richard looked him straight on and asked, "Why were you out at my place the other night, Ray?"

Ray met Richard's eyes with an almost convincingly bewildered look, and declared, "I wasn't out at your place the other night."

"Is it because of Jenny and me?" Richard asked. Angry, he added, "Do you think maybe we're meeting with Dean and plotting something against your Foundation? I don't like my patients spying on me at my home at night. Am I making myself clear?"

His own voice becoming sharp and indignant, Ray said, "I was *not* out at your place, Dr. Pomerantz."

Unsatisfied, Richard goaded Ray that session to talk about something other than the Foundation, to discuss his past—and his feelings about ends justifying means.

"You're morbidly fascinated by the murders I committed, aren't you, doctor," Ray said. He leaned just slightly forward in his chair and, coolly and emotionlessly, said, "Let me tell you something, Dr. Pomerantz. Anyone's capable of murder . . . even you."

Richard thought a moment, and said, "Most people are capable of *killing*, such as in self-defense."

"They're also capable of *murder*," Ray repeated, decisively.

Richard typed up a new letter, which included a reference to the incident on the beach, and mailed it that afternoon.

✶　✶　✶

Three psychiatrists separately examined Ray over the course of a five day period in San Quentin's minimum security West Block. The psychiatrists—Dr. Louise Dickerson, the woman who had treated Ray the last seven years of his imprisonment; Dr. Emanuel Barrera, a San Francisco forensic psychiatrist; and Dr. Norman Linder, a professor of psychiatry at the University of California at Davis—filed their reports with Howard Reiner and the other two parole board members in charge of Ray's case. Linder discussed at some length what he saw as Ray's penchant for "concretistic thinking," a forcing of facts to fit his own view of things, while Barrera dwelt more on Ray's "self-idealization," sometimes referred to as neurotic pride. Dickerson, who found no heightened psychopathology in her former patient, whom she had recommended for parole a year and a half earlier, passed along to the board Ray's own observation about Richard: that as the fiancé of Jenny Harnett—the potential inheritor of the money that was being channeled into the Foundation's programs—he had an unavoidable conflict of interest in the case.

The incident on the beach, the three examiners noted, had been vehemently denied to the point of trembling indignation by Ray Lomak. Dr. Barrera wrote, "I cannot in good conscience recommend a revocation of parole on such speculative evidence as a nighttime observation of an unidentified man sixty yards away wearing a hat similar to the kind worn by Mr. Lomak."

All three examiners agreed that although Ray Lomak was a highly unusual person, he appeared to pose no demonstrable threat to society.

Ray was released from West Block on June 12, and given a plane ticket back to Los Angeles. At his own request, he was assigned a new therapist.

"Your cronies," Howard Reiner told Richard disgruntledly over the phone, "said some of your observations—like this reaction formation thing—they said it was just too difficult to establish."

"They're right," Richard sighed. "What else is new about psychiatry? Well, it's probably better he have a different therapist, anyway. His point about the money is a lot of bilge, but emotionally I *am* too close to this whole Harnett situation. Okay, thanks for calling, Howard."

Two weeks later, in early evening, as Richard locked his car in the dim garage below his apartment, he had the strange sense of something being different. He glanced about, but everything seemed to be as it had always been. The rusted saws, loose-lying hammers and bolts, and slopped-over buckets of paint all lay along the homemade shelves of pine planks on cinder blocks. In the corner was his grandmother's vacuum cleaner with its iron-based front, as bulky and treacherous to furniture as a diesel train. Garden hoses, rakes and brooms were everywhere. The place was anarchy, but it was his anarchy, one he passed through every morning getting into his car and came home to every evening, and like an old nag in its same squalid stall for ten years, he had an almost unconscious sense of it.

But now there was something there that had not been, or perhaps it was something missing; it was a new smell, or maybe one now gone. Someone or something had been in his garage.

Richard pulled the door down and walked around the side of the building. The fenced-in yard where Paddy romped during the day was empty, the swing-gate open. His heart beginning to thrum, Richard looked back out toward the highway, where cars and trucks thundered around the bend in the coastline at frightful speeds. There was no sign of Paddy in either direction, or across the road. Richard leaned his briefcase against the fence and started down the wooden steps to the beach.

"Paddy! Hey, Paddy!"

What Richard saw when he was halfway down the steps took the breath out of him like a knee in the stomach.

"Oh God," he gasped, grabbing hold of the handrail.

Fifty feet out from the shore, just downwind from a man-sized boulder that stood dry and exposed at low tide, but at this time in the evening revealed only a tip of its anemone-encrusted surface, Paddy's limp body rose and fell lifelessly with the ocean swells. His long beautiful red hair fanned out and swirled with the current. Around his neck was a rope whose other end was tied to the tip of the boulder through one of its eroded crevices. It was the rope that had hung coiled in the center of the garage's front wall.

✷ ✷ ✷

Richard sat behind the one-way mirror-window looking into the interrogation room at the L.A. Sheriff Department's Malibu station, where Ray Lomak was being questioned by Hugh Vortner, a plain-clothes detective. Sitting with Richard in the hidden alcove was a sergeant in his mid-forties by the name of Thompson. Thompson's ruddy face showed a combination of boredom and resentment for a case involving nothing more than a dog.

"So you think it's a matter of this Dr. Pomerantz having it in for you?" Vortner's voice came muted through the alcove speaker.

"I do, yes. This is correct," Ray answered flatly. "He tried to have me sent back to prison, but three psychiatrists there verified that he's a bitter, prejudiced person. I can give you their names if you like."

"They know this Pomerantz?" Vortner asked.

"Well, no, but . . . but when they found there's nothing wrong with me, I think it's a pretty obvious conclusion. I'm being blamed for my past, you see, for the illness I suffered when I was young. It's Dr. Pomerantz who likes violence. He spends half his time with violent people, you can check this."

Vortner glanced at his watch and said, "Well, I think we've pretty much covered it, Mr. Lomak. Thank you for coming down. I'll show you out."

Sgt. Thompson flicked on the overhead light in the alcove. "Is it possible that one of your other patients doesn't much care for you?" he asked. "Some of these group therapy people?"

"I doubt it," Richard said. "At least not to this extent." After a moment, he asked, "No fingerprints anywhere in the garage?"

"Nothing readable," Thompson said, suppressing a yawn and scratching at his cheek. "Dr. Pomerantz, I've been on this force a few years, twenty-one come September, so let me pass on a rather simple observation, if I may. The fact that this person, or persons, who did this thing used a rope from your own garage, indicates to me that this person didn't even know what he was going to do until he got to your place. He didn't come with any kind of a weapon or instrument of his own. You know what that says to me, Dr. Pomerantz? Especially when it's summer? It says vandals, teenagers. Vicious teenagers."

Richard thought, then nodded. "Yes. Vicious."

On the front decking of his apartment, Jenny and Richard sat together in a lounge chair, Jenny between his legs, leaning back against his chest. They faced the sinking sun which, because of their location on the shoreline, did not set over the ocean, but over the sun parched hills beyond Malibu. Though neither of them had said it, they were not much in the mood, anyway, for more than an occasional glance at the water out front—at the horrible, harmless-looking rock that emitted such peaceful lapping sounds.

"Maybe it wasn't Ray," Richard said. "Would revenge be so important to him that he would risk going back to prison?"

"Maybe his aim wasn't revenge. It could have been to warn you," Jenny said somberly. "To tell you to stay off his back. He doesn't want you to pursue this thing with the people in Sacramento any more."

"And now I've just had him brought down to police headquarters," Richard added ominously.

"When I told Dad about this, all he said was, people should stop harassing Ray and stop punishing him for his past."

Jenny kissed Richard's forearm, and laid her cheek against it. Her voice quavered. "I'm really frightened, Richard."

Richard pressed his face against the soft nape of her neck, and held her tightly. After a minute's silence, he said anxiously, "So am I."

Ten days later it arrived in the mail—a typed-out, one line missive: "Psychiatrists are dispensable."

"Let him be!" Jenny cried. "Take the warning and just let him be, Richard! If he doesn't think someone's trying to put him back in prison, he won't do anything. He'll go his crazy sanctimonious way. He'll work for the Foundation until he's eighty."

Richard carefully lifted the note by its edges, as if it were a phonograph record, and placed it on a sheet of kitchen cellophane. He unrolled another piece of cellophane to lay on top. Jenny stood with her arms akimbo. Her eyes were puffy from lack of sleep. She sat down with her head in her hands while Richard dialed Sgt. Thompson in Malibu.

The Latent Prints Unit of the Sheriff's Scientific Services Bureau found no fingerprints, except Richard's own right-thumb print from opening the letter. The typewriter used was determined to be a portable manual, in all likelihood a Smith-Corona. Richard had Jenny call one of the Foundation's secretaries and, on the pretext of wanting to borrow one of their typewriters, ask about the kind used in the office. All were IBM electrics.

"I'm no good with electrics. Thanks anyway," Jenny said, and hung up. "This is stupid, Richard. If he really intended to do anything to you, he wouldn't warn you in advance. He just wants you to leave him alone."

Richard nodded absently.

"So let's leave him alone!" Jenny screamed.

Richard was already dialing again. He spoke with Howard Reiner, while Jenny sat on the couch as if expecting a crash, knees drawn up, her forehead against her thighs.

"This fucker belongs in prison, Howard!" Richard fumed. "Now, what are we going to do about it?"

From the other end came the dampened popping sound of a pipe being lit; Reiner had been trying to give up cigarettes. "If you can get something substantial, we can take him in front of the board again. It doesn't even have to be conclusive. We don't operate by the same rules of procedure or evidence as the courts. But it has to be substantial, Rich—much more than you have."

"By that time it might be too late," Richard groused. "Do I have to wait until the bullet's on the way?"

"I don't know what to tell you," said Reiner.

"You tell your two buddies on the board who sopped up every-thing those three incompetent shrinks said," Richard continued, "that if anything . . . *any*thing at all happens, I'm bringing a negligence suit against them and the whole goddamn state."

"So noted," said Reiner.

"My observations were too difficult to establish, huh?" Richard vented a little more bile. "Well, I don't much care for shrink talk, so let me be as direct as I can. Ray Lomak is a madman—bonkers, nuts, off the wall. Got that for the record?"

"Got it. And listen, Richard, if Lomak has become who you think he has, don't go start playing on his home court. Know what I mean? You take care of yourself. I'm very serious about this."

Richard calmed down a shade. "Yeah, I will, Howard. Thanks. Talk to you later."

Jenny still sat with her knees drawn up, her eyes closed.

"You don't want me to do anything more? All right, I won't do anything more," Richard said to her.

"Good. Except one last thing."

"What?"

"Buy a gun."

When Richard realized she was serious, he snorted a poking laugh. "I'm not going to buy a gun. You really are Tex's daughter, aren't you."

"Laugh your condescending little laugh," Jenny said, her voice drained. "I don't want you to do anything but buy it and keep it in a drawer—if you expect me to spend one more second in this place. In fact, I want you to move away from here as soon as possible."

✷ ✷ ✷

Jenny accompanied Richard in looking for a new apartment for him, and it was she who asked all the pertinent questions about utilities, parking spaces, and the like. For the most part, Richard would test a few cupboard latches, and wait in the hallway. He resented being forced out of his home by fear.

As the days went by without further intimidation or communication from Ray of any kind, Richard began to agree with Jenny's theory about Ray's acts. They had not been for the purpose of reprisal, but were warnings, and as Richard took no additional actions in response, there seemed to be an end to them. After a month of half-hearted apartment hunting, the subject of moving began to fade from Richard's and Jenny's conversation. Richard did, however, agree to purchase a gun.

The clerk at the gun store put a coal-black Iver Johnson .22 caliber revolver in Richard's hand.

"They're heavy," Richard remarked.

"That's the first thing they all say," the clerk said with a languid smile. "No one's gonna take your stereo when you got this thing in your hand."

"They can have my stereo, pal," Richard said, and filled out the application form.

After the fifteen day waiting period in which the state Bureau of Criminal Identification and Investigation made its routine check of Richard's name against its lists of convicted felons, known drug addicts, and adjudicated mental defectives, Richard picked up his gun from the store and placed it queasily in the nightstand drawer next to his bed. No great believer in the manufacturers or their safety devices, he pointed it away from the bed, toward the wall. He tried to forget about it, but its presence in the room remained felt, like a black lethal creature living two feet from his bed.

On the off chance there was some merit to Sgt. Thompson's question about other patients' having acrimonious feelings toward him, Richard began to closely scrutinize the faces of the ex-cons at his group therapy sessions. He looked for a hint of some kind suggesting that, just perhaps, one of them was his dedicated terrorist. An evil serenity in the eye for having eluded detection, a gloating lip, a nervous kneading of the thighs under Richard's lingering gaze. But if any of them was his anonymous enemy, he remained under veil.

A night Richard came home late from his office, he caught sight of the shadowed outline of a man crouched low to the ground, motionless, around the side of his garage. The back of Richard's neck went clammy.

"Evenin', doc," came a familiar voice.

Richard did not move.

The man let out a raucous laugh and stood up to his full six-foot-four-inch height. It was Bernard Townsend, black as a tree in the night.

"We heard what's been goin' down the past month," he said with a friendly snarl. "Jive dude come around again, we brothas explain t'him how things are, see. Wring the mothafucka's neck."

Richard's laughter was an eruption, releasing in himself weeks of caged tension. Bernard Townsend put his heavy arm across his shoulder and said, "You sleep easy, doc, we be takin' turns out here each night."

Richard did not object—for his own sake, and for the sake of the rough-edged men who obviously wanted some way to repay him for being there when they were the ones in need. After another uneventful week and a half, however, he dismissed his motley sentries with gratitude.

Over the next few weeks Jenny tried to reunite Tex and Dean, but ever since the horse track rhubarb, neither of them would be the first to pick up the phone and call the other. It was thus only through the newspapers that Dean, like Jenny herself (with whom Tex never discussed business), learned of Tex's grand and sudden decision. It was there in the headline of the Monday morning sports page: Tex was selling the team to a New York lawyer, and was going to be putting the money from the sale into Harnett College.

"Few years from now," was one of Tex's quoted comments, "you see if our kids aren't beating Notre Dame and the whole lot of 'em."

The next morning Dean Harnett, who had over the course of

the last year and a half seen his inheritance whittled down to one twentieth of what he had once expected—and who now found himself without even a job—called his own lawyer in Century City. Stammering hopelessly, he asked about forcing his father to a competency hearing, and dissolving the whole Harnett Foundation.

CHAPTER 5

WHEN DEAN CALLED RICHARD THE FOLLOWING
night at his apartment in Malibu looking for Jenny, Richard told
him that she had decided to go out and relax at their father's ranch
while he caught up on some of his patients' files. The scalding hot
summer day had worn Jenny down, and she wanted an hour's
swim in the pool.

"I c-can't call her there," Dean sputtered. "I don't want to talk
to Dad, and he d-doesn't want to talk to me."

"Your dad's not there," Richard said. "He's in New York with
that fellow who's buying the team."

"This L-lomak, this murderer," Dean continued, working himself into a lather, "he's pulled the hood over Dad's eyes, he's taking advantage of him."

"I appreciate what you're saying, Dean, but this probably really isn't any of my business. Call Jenny out at the ranch, okay? She'll be there in about half an hour."

Jenny arrived a little after nine at the ranch, and felt regenerated almost the instant she stepped out of the car and pulled her sticky halter top away from her skin. Jenny had been told that Ron Bruckner was in New York with Tex, and that Esperanza was visiting her cousin for two days, leaving only Luis at the ranch. She could see Luis' bunkhouse light down at the stables a quarter mile away. Jenny let herself into the house and went into her old bedroom to change into a bikini.

When the phone rang, it was Dean. Jenny sat on the bed with the phone, trying to soothe his bruised, angry feelings.

"You and Dad are going to make up like always, you know that, Deanie," she said. "You're a capable person. If you want, you'll get a job with another team, probably a better job. You'll show everyone you can do it on your own."

"Dad's not r-rational," Dean said, almost in tears. "He doesn't care about his own f-f-fam—"

"That's not true, Dean. Apparently this is something he feels he has to do. And it's his money, you know."

"I t-talked with my lawyer," Dean said, trying to make his voice sound firm, his decision clear and unemotional. "If Dad's not c-competent, we can stop this in court."

"Oh, are you serious, Dean? Well, you'll have to do it without me. I'm not about to stand up in front of Dad and tell some judge that my father's senile, and that his whole Foundation should be disbanded. You have any idea what that would do to Dad?"

"D-don't do it if you don't want to, but I am. It's for Dad's own s-sake. This Lomak is behind all of this. Lomak just wants to t-take all of Dad's money."

Jenny sat back against the headboard and wearily blew a strand of limp hair off her forehead. She sighed, "I know Lomak is behind it, but Dean, come on, you just can't do this to Dad. It would kill him, it would literally kill him to see his kids go into court and say something like that. Listen, why don't you come out here tonight, and we'll talk about it, okay?"

"I've already m-made up my mind, Jenny."

"Well, come out anyway, and we'll just talk. I was going to take a swim—I'll wait for you, all right? We haven't gone swimming together since we were kids. Just come out, and we can talk about it. Please? I'll wait for you."

"Okay," Dean said, and hung up.

When Jenny put the phone down, she thought she heard someone's footsteps padding quietly down the carpeted hallway, away from her room.

"Luis?" she called out, hesitantly. There was no answer.

A little frightened, she walked timidly to the door and poked her head into the hallway. It was dark and deserted. At the far end of the house, the living room lamp she had turned on burned brightly, reflecting off her father's chrome-and-glass furniture and the large picture windows looking out into the night's blackness. Uneasy now about being alone in the big house, Jenny locked her bedroom door. She sat on her bed reading a book, her knees drawn up close to her, waiting for Dean to arrive.

Half an hour later she heard a key in the front door. She recognized the sound of Dean's footsteps, a familiar trudge that hadn't changed since he was twelve years old. Jenny opened her bedroom door. "Boy, am I glad to see you. I thought I was hearing things."

"Hi," he said morosely.

Mimicking his sullenness, Jenny grunted a truck driver's hi back at him. "Come on, nothing's all that bad," she found herself borrowing Richard's basic philosophy, though Richard always added parenthetically, "because nothing's all that good."

Dean got into his swim trunks, wearing them high on his paunch like a man twice his age. Jenny took his arm with sisterly affection as they walked out to the pool. At the cabana she flicked on the switch to the underwater light. The turquoise pool gleamed like liquid treasure in the ebony night. Despite Tex's not heating the water, after two months of summer, its temperature had reached the midseventies. Jenny dived in with a clean zip, while Dean shivered slowly down the steps. He watched Jenny's effortless stroke, and had a moment's pride at how beautiful he thought his sister looked, slender and glistening in her bikini. Dean paddled about in what he considered to be a breaststroke, or treaded water near the middle of the pool with Jenny while they talked seriously about the problem.

Jenny loved swimming at night. Somehow the water always felt heavier, more enveloping, like velvet. She rolled backward from Dean and, gliding down to the soundless privacy of the bottom, kicked her way along the sides.

When she saw it, her whole body recoiled in fright. In the observation window was a face.

She never saw the crowbar come breaking through the underwater light, whose metal back was in the observation room. As the current instantaneously shot out through the water, it snapped her head back, and Jenny's entire body jerked into a rigid spasm. Within a second her heart muscles went into a wild fibrillation. Her fingers, locked and bent as claws, tore away at nothingness—at the invisible killer the water was sending through every fiber in her body.

Near the center of the pool, his head still above the surface where he had been treading water, Dean let out an inhuman, deathly wail. Within seconds, he was unconscious. His vacant glassy eyes looked upward, but they saw nothing—not the peaceful beauty of the stars sprayed across the black sky, nor the bows of the lacy pepper trees gently lifting and falling with the summer night's first breeze.

In a minute, it was all over.

In her tiny maid's room at the back of the house, Esperanza, who had not gone to her cousin's that day, but had been in bed since mid-afternoon with the flu, awakened slowly, lethargically, unsure whether she had actually heard a scream or had only dreamt it. She pulled her blankets more tightly around her shoulders, feeling cold and feverish. As she stared blankly at the wall, she heard the sound of the garage door going up and a car starting.

Stumbling out of bed and into a robe, she minced down the long hallway to the living room and peered out the front window. Ray Lomak was backing his car quickly down the driveway, having to go slightly onto the grass to maneuver around Jenny's and Dean's cars, which were parked in front of the garage. Hugging the robe closer to herself, Esperanza went quickly through the den and kitchen and looked out toward the side yard—to where she believed she had heard the scream come from. Though her eyes were watery and still unfocused, she thought she saw a shadowy mound of something floating in the middle of the pool. She pressed her face to the window pane, then tremulously let herself out the service porch door to the yard. Haltingly, she drew closer, until there could be no mistaking the figure in the pool.

"Oh, hees son! Hees son! Nooo . . ."

Running back inside to the kitchen phone, she dialed the operator with shaking hands. "Oh please—doctare—please," she moaned. It took a full minute for the operator to get the ranch's address correctly from Esperanza.

Esperanza sat trembling in the kitchen, and waited the ten minutes until she heard the siren of an ambulance streaking up the ocean-bluff road to the Harnett ranch. It was 10:19 when it arrived. She met the two white-clad paramedics out in the side yard.

In walking swiftly alongside the pool, the taller, gaunt-faced paramedic received a jolt as he brushed against the handrail of the pool's ladder.

"Jesus!" he shouted, jumping back.

"Don't go near the water," he barked at his partner and Esperanza. He recalled a brief mention in his paramedic's training about finding a body in a darkened pool. At least a couple of times a year in Los Angeles County, someone died accidentally because of an underwater light's short-circuiting.

"Where's the light?" he asked Esperanza. "The light . . . to the pool."

"Oh, thee light," Esperanza panted, and hurried to the cabana. She moved the switch up and down, but nothing happened.

"Get the gaff out and just hold onto it," the paramedic told his partner.

"I see him," Esperanza said. "I hear yell, and thane I see him out the weendow go away."

"You saw someone?" the tall paramedic repeated. "Okay, you'll tell everything to the police. When the police come. Do you know where the fuse box is, miss?" he asked, drawing a rectangle in the air. "The fuse box or the circuit breakers," he said, exasperated by Esperanza's dazed look. She only shook her head.

Though he thought there was little chance of still saving the man's life, the paramedic sprinted to the ambulance and pulled a flashlight from its pincer bracket on the door. Quickly, he shined the darting beam all around the cabana and nearby bushes looking for the electrical equipment for the pool.

"Polees come?" Esperanza asked the other man.

"Be here in a few minutes," he answered her dryly.

Esperanza wandered off a few steps, attempting to think clearly in her ill, disoriented state. She had seen things tonight, and the police would ask questions. And they would ask her all about herself. If only Mr. Harnett were home, he would protect her. He wouldn't let them know she was an illegal alien. Tears came to Esperanza's eyes. They would deport her. Maybe they would even throw her in jail. She had heard stories. Her hand cupped to her mouth, she continued aimlessly away from the pool, trying to think.

"Here it is," the taller medic with the flashlight called out to his partner. He lifted the slab of cement away and started down the ladder. Halfway down, he shined the beam at all the room's equipment, realizing he knew almost nothing about electrical circuits. Water was spilling onto the floor. Suddenly he felt qualmish about even being in contact with the ladder rung he was standing on. When he heard the siren of the approaching police car, he scrambled back up out of the hole.

"Wha'ss goan on?" a voice called out to him from the darkness. It was Luis, tramping up the hill from his bunkhouse. Before the paramedic could answer, he saw two officers from the Palos Verdes Police Department running toward him.

"You guys know anything about electrical things?" he blurted out to them. "There's a goddamn current going through the water. Must be a fuse box down there someplace," he spewed on. "Maybe it's in the house, I don't know."

One of the police officers, not saying a word, shined his flashlight down into the room. Curling his lip, he did not venture down into the room himself. He swiveled the light onto the body in the middle of the pool. Unlike the paramedics, he thought to also inspect the rest of the pool along the bottom with his flashlight. As he did, he spotted the second body—the young woman who, in contrast to the limp form at the surface, lay at the bottom frozen grotesquely, knees in, mouth open, her bent arms and clutching hands splayed out from her sides.

"Oh, dear God," the officer said almost in a whisper.

The officers radioed their watch commander to call the Los Angeles Sheriff's Department for one of their electricians. While they waited, one of them went into the house through the open service-porch door and looked for the maid. She was nowhere inside nor, curiously, could they find her anywhere on the grounds.

When Sgt. Parsons, the LASD electrician, arrived, he turned off all electricity to the ranch through the main switch inside the house, and at last the paramedics dragged the inert bodies up onto the ground with their gaff. Parsons let himself down into the equipment room next to the pool and, after just a few minutes, climbed back up.

"Looks like we've got a homicide here," he told the patrol

officers. "Crowbars don't drive themselves on their own through the backs of underwater lights. And no one accidentally prevents a current from shutting off by replacing the fuse with an unmeltable strip of copper wire. Christ, what kind of a mind would it even occur to, to kill someone this way?"

PART THREE

CHAPTER 1

JENNY IS DEAD. THE PERSON YOU LOVED IS NO
longer. Your future . . . well, there will be a future for you, Richard.
Though you don't believe it right now, you will wake up again on
Sunday mornings with a light-headed anticipation of brunch with
friends out on your decking, and you will attend psychiatric conventions, and even go on picnics with other girls. They'll be very
pretty and vibrant, and some will have cute senses of humor. But
their liveliness and laughter will only make it worse. For months,
maybe years, you'll come home after work, fall on your bed, and
cry for the only one you had ever truly wanted.

My poor beautiful Jenny. I was going to hold you in bed every night, and protect you all your life. You left me too early, Jenny, years and years too early.

Alone in his apartment, Richard held many complete, not always coherent, conversations with himself.

Having canceled all appointments for a week, he stayed in bed until noon every day, his head foggy from the alcohol he had poured down the night before just to get to sleep. Each morning when he awoke, there was that one split second of life as normal, before the white-hot realization of what had happened came flooding again into the core of him.

What always came back in that first instant was the retching memory of the brief grim phone call from the police. They believed it was accidental, they had said. (Not until the day before the funeral would Richard learn that the police had withheld the truth so as not to tip their hand to any possible suspects.) Though the following week would become a blur of emotion in Richard's memory, the phone call itself would be with him, indelibly. A cataclysmic event telescoping itself into the moment of learning about it. Having finished his office paperwork, Richard had been sitting at his kitchen table reading an article in the *Atlantic* about the Mayan ruins and sipping a glass of pineapple juice when the phone had rung. The smell of pineapple juice would forever haul him back to the night of Jenny's death.

At the cemetery Richard and Tex had wordlessly embraced each other, the older man's bearish arms pressing Richard to his bulky chest. When Richard started to pull away, Tex held onto him. (The few occasions Richard had spent any time with him—two dinners along with Jenny at the ranch, and one afternoon in Tex's stadium box at a home football game—Richard had had a slight feeling that Tex did not approve of his daughter's plans to marry a psychiatrist instead of some enterprising young businessman.)

When Tex finally released Richard from the embrace, he looked toward the grave sites and, his voice choking, said, "Never got the . . . the chance to set things right with Dean. Just . . . and Jenny . . . dear God, Jenny."

Beginning to cry, Tex's face bunched up as he wept loudly, pawing at his tears with his pudgy hand. After a minute, he patted Richard's shoulder and slowly wandered off.

Scattered over the shady knoll where Jenny and Dean were to be buried stood retired cowboy movie producers wearing dark ascots, aging stuntmen, staff workers from the Foundation and college, many of the football players who had played for Tex, and even Bernard Townsend and a couple of the others from the group therapy sessions who had met Jenny the few times she had occasion to pick Richard up at the halfway house. The one person glaringly absent was Ray Lomak. The day before the funeral the police, who had uncovered certain facts which they were still not divulging to the public, had taken Ray into custody.

After twenty-two years, Ray Lomak had again managed to become a page-one story throughout the country. Though Ray was not at the funeral services, there was, in the mortuary office on the cemetery grounds, the stark irony of his picture in the morning's *Los Angeles Times.*

Still staggered and grieving, and unable to think of anything beside Jenny, Richard did not yet have the room in his emotions to truly and deeply hate Ray Lomak.

After everyone had left the cemetery, Richard sat immobile in his car, gazing at the grave site where T-shirted workers were preparing to lower the coffins by a winch and straps into the ground. He could not take his eyes from the bronze casket that Jenny was inside. The reality was unspeakable. When one of the workers threw back the lock on the winch, and the casket began to sink smoothly, Richard finally had to look away. He started his car and drove slowly through the cemetery's wrought-iron gates.

Richard wished the religiosity of the ceremony had given him solace, but it had not. Offering up words to an unknown Being, he had always told friends, seemed to be nothing more than "institutionalized insanity," but now that clever, sometimes glib lack of belief left him only empty and envying those who had walked away from the pastor's words somehow sustained.

Richard wanted to be alone, but could not quite yet bring himself to return to his place on the beach, where half a batch of Jenny's peanut butter cookies they had stuffed themselves on a few days earlier remained atop the breakfast-nook table, and many of her lovely dresses still hung in the closet. He drove instead to his office in Beverly Hills.

Because it was a Sunday, the entire building was deserted. Richard ranged aimlessly about his office, pausing now and then to look down on vacant Rodeo Drive where the chic boutiques were all closed, or miles east, where he could see the grey summer peaks of Mt. Baldy. He picked a copy of Menninger's *Man Against Himself* off his desk, and as he reached up to put it back on the bookshelf he saw that his hand was shaking. Closing his eyes, he lowered the book to his side.

Turning, he stared at the chair where patients sat—where Ray Lomak sat. In another second he pulled back his arm and heaved the book at it. The book skipped off the armrest and went sailing into the corner. Tears boiled up into Richard's eyes, blistering his vision. He sat down and breathed deeply, trying to quell the nausea.

✱ ✱ ✱

Joe Grife, the fifty-six year old Los Angeles County deputy district attorney assigned to the Harnett murder case, was a sometimes cranky, always overweight man who felt little excitement for being given the high publicity case that was his gold watch for three decades of service. Twenty years earlier, the case might have meant something to Grife's career.

The first time Joe Grife asked Richard down to his office to talk about the case, he mumbled vague condolences.

"Mr. Grife, do you mind my asking how much evidence you've got against Lomak?" Richard inquired.

Grife turned open the folder of police reports with the obligatory air of a store owner facing a customer who has a valid warranty.

Like many prosecutors, he had a courthouse ripened disdain for psychiatrists—most of whom, he believed, pampered and shielded the guiltiest of defendants. But Joe Grife's crankiness, Richard soon decided, was a more pervasive and lifelong fixture, like the mole on his neck Grife had never bothered to have removed.

"Plenty," Grife said, squinting at the police reports on his desk. "No jury's gonna acquit a guy like this, don't worry. Already stands convicted of six murders—unbelievable."

"Well, what do you have in *this* case?" Richard pressed the issue.

"A woman in the neighborhood saw a car like Lomak's, which is a 1981, dark blue, four door Chrysler New Yorker, driving away from the Harnett ranch right after the time of the murders. After being advised of his rights, Lomak admitted he was at the ranch that evening. We already knew that. Old man Harnett told us he called Lomak from New York the day of the murders and left a message on Lomak's answering machine. He asked Lomak to find some papers for him in the den at the ranch dealing with the football team, and to read some paragraphs to him over the phone the next day. The morning we arrested Lomak, we listened to that taped message—Lomak hadn't erased it. Tex tells him in it that no one's going to be at the house, and that the key would be in the usual place.

"Lomak claims he left the ranch before Dean and Jennifer ever got there. When the detectives asked him where he went, he told them he'd rather not say. That'll come back to haunt him." Grife flipped a few pages. "A secretary down at the Harnett Foundation told Lieutenant Bollinger—he's the officer from the Palos Verdes P.D. heading up the investigation in this case—"

"Yeah, I know," Richard said. "I've already talked to him. It's probably in your report there."

"Oh. Well, the secretary told Bollinger that Lomak once asked her to kind of spy on Dean Harnett, find out if he was doing anything immoral his father should know about. This goes to motive, ill feeling between them. Turns out, Dean talked to his lawyer the day before his death about initiating competency hearings against his father, and forcing a dissolution of the whole Harnett Foundation. The kid made some pretty bitter accusations against Lomak, apparently."

Joe Grife sat back in his chair.

"I hope there's more," Richard prompted him.

Grife flipped more pages. "Tex Harnett, who's not a very cooperative witness, by the way—he seems to believe Lomak is innocent—did admit that Lomak was familiar with the workings of the pump room beneath the pool. The light was broken from the rear by the pointed end of a crowbar, apparently knocked through by a sledge hammer. Both were taken out of the toolshed. A Luis Peralta, the stable hand, says he saw Lomak in the toolshed dozens of times when Lomak lived there."

Grife ran a finger between his white shirt collar and his neck for a little air. In time, Richard would discover that Joe Grife wore with almost amusing regularity what he was wearing that day—white shirt, brown suit, brown shoes, and a forest green tie, its two lengths hanging separately down his shirt front. Grife was from Cedar Rapids, Iowa, ate one of two different lunches—grilled cheese with bacon and tomato, or fish sticks—nearly every single day at Ed & Tina's Diner, two blocks from the Criminal Courts Building, and every Sunday religiously took a drive with his wife down Sunset Boulevard to the beach and back. His wife drove while Joe tried to relax.

"Police found an eleven inch tire track on the edge of the lawn next to the driveway," Grife continued. "Harnett's sprinklers go on automatically every evening around seven, that's only about three hours before the murders. The ground would have still been wet. When Bollinger questioned Lomak two days later, Lomak's got four brand new tires on his car. Bought 'em the day before.

Quite a coincidence. Says he sold the old ones to some stranger—doesn't know his name."

Grife snorted contemptuously. "You think any jury's going to believe that?" He cuffed the police reports with the back of his hand. "It's all here, doctor. All right here."

He tossed the reports back onto his desk and poked his tongue into his cheek, distending it. "One small problem—we'll clear it up soon enough—we don't know where our chief witness is. Tex Harnett's housekeeper, Esperanza Gomar, was the one who called the ambulance. She disappeared before the police arrived—apparently she's an illegal alien. The guys with the ambulance say she said something about quote, 'seeing him out the window go away,' unquote. We find her, we have our frosting on the cake of who the 'him' is."

"Seeing '*him*,' " Richard said, thinking, "sounds like she knew him. She knew Lomak, of course."

"We're well aware of that, Dr. Pomerantz. But only Esperanza can testify to what she saw."

A secretary bobbed her head in the doorway of Grife's office. "Lieutenant Bollinger is here," she said.

"Thank you, dear," Grife answered her warmly, with his morning's first gentility. "Send him in, will you?"

Phil Bollinger was an athletically framed man of forty whose sport coat tugged across his shoulders and chest. With a sincere smile and mutinously extended, reddish-brown sideburns, he considered himself an ideal bridge between the younger and older cops on the nineteen man Palos Verdes police force, and had told his wife many times when he stayed up late reading books on criminology that the position of police chief would be his if he could just improve his rather mediocre exam scores. He shook Richard's hand as he had the time before, with confident energy.

"Phil tried questioning Esperanza Gomar's cousin. Lives over in East L.A. What's his name again?" Grife asked.

Bollinger took out a pocket notebook.

"Felipe Gomar. 2248 Ramboz. All I could squeeze out of him was that Esperanza didn't come to stay with him the night of the murder because she had the flu. He claims he doesn't know where she is. I tried to convince him how important it was for Esperanza to come forward, but he won't help us. Heck, I understand his concern, and I told him so. Tough situation, this immigration thing."

Reappearing at the doorway, the secretary asked if there were any takers on coffee, and brought them each a steaming cup. Grife poured enough milk and sugar into his to make it more like melted toffee ice cream.

"Whole thing doesn't make sense, anyway," Grife said. "Why would Ray Lomak leave a witness? Why didn't he kill this Esperanza too? That's one of the things we hoped you could help us with, Dr. Pomerantz. Know anything about their relationship?"

"Obviously, I'm the last guy in the world who would want to thwart this investigation, but the doctor-patient privilege is still involved here, isn't it?" Richard cautioned.

"Well, yeah," Grife nodded. "Section 1014 of the Evidence Code gives Lomak the privilege of preventing you from testifying in court to any confidential communication he made to you. But number one, we're not in court right now. And number two, there's an exception to the Code, cases too, which say that if someone is a threat to the person or property of another, not only *can* you go to the authorities with information you've gained as his psychiatrist, you're legally obligated to."

"Yeah, I know all about the *Tarasoff* case, but Lomak's already in custody. Who's the threat to here?"

Grife held his hands out. "For starters, what about Esperanza? Lomak had the right to see all the police reports, so now he knows she was there that night and can probably identify him. You think Lomak's above trying to hire someone to knock her off? And I understand you got a nicely put death threat yourself not too long ago. If that's not enough, let me ask you this. Is there any doubt in your mind that if he walks out of court on this rap, he'll probably murder again someday?"

Richard shook his head. "Not a lot of doubt, no. . . . Put it this way, as far as my own profession's ethics go, I don't believe that under these unique circumstances there would be any problem in my getting involved in this case outside of court. I looked up the AMA's Principles of Medical Ethics last night. Section nine clearly states that in a situation like we have here, I'm allowed to take an adverse position against my own patient. But as far as the courtroom is concerned, you're the lawyer. I'll leave it up to you and the judge what I'm legally permitted to say. Actually, as far as the murders are concerned, there's probably nothing of any relevance from my sessions with Lomak I could testify to, anyway."

"Okay, doctor. When we get to the trial, if there's anything you can testify to, we'll play it by ear. For now, let's go back to my last question about Lomak's relationship with Esperanza. What do you know about it?"

"Well, Ray only mentioned her once or twice. But I got the impression they didn't much like each other."

"So in your opinion, it's not likely she'd cover for him?" Bollinger asked.

"No."

"That's what I thought," Grife grumbled . . . "I'll tell you, we've got enough evidence, but there are unanswered questions, too. How the hell did Lomak find out about Dean's plans to force his father to a competency hearing—if that, in fact, was the reason he killed Dean and Jennifer?"

Richard's body chilled at the open mention of Jenny's murder.

"I also think we could know a lot more about exactly what happened that night," Grife went on, "if we knew who arrived at the ranch first—Lomak, or Dean and Jennifer?"

"If that was Lomak's car that made the tracks on the edge of the lawn," Bollinger pointed out, "then he probably arrived at the house before Dean and Jennifer and parked in the garage. Dean's and Jennifer's cars took up the width of the driveway, so Lomak, in backing out when he left, had to go onto the lawn a little to get around them."

"Great," Grife grunted. "Now tell me why he would have put his car in the garage when he was just going to pick up some papers, and the whole driveway was free when he got there?"

"I don't know, but he not only must have put his car in the garage," Richard interjected, "but he must have pulled the door down, as well. Jenny knew Ray's car, and I can assure you she wouldn't have gone into that house if she had known Ray was there."

"Maybe he pulled the garage door down because he knew somehow they were coming later," Bollinger speculated eagerly, scratching at a sideburn.

Richard explained how that was impossible, in that Jenny's decision to go out to the ranch had been made on the spur of the moment, and that even Dean did not know she was out there until he called Richard at Malibu, trying to find her. "Has to be some other reason the garage door was down," Richard pondered.

"Beats me," Grife said. "And what about this? If Lomak had arrived at the house before Jennifer . . . Jenny, then the lights would have been on when she arrived, and she would have known someone was there. Instead of going swimming, why wouldn't Jenny have hightailed it out of there the second she walked through the door and saw it was Lomak? If she had this fear of him, as you say."

"Look," Richard said, "seems to me it all comes down to getting Esperanza Gomar to come out of hiding. Why can't you clear it with the, whatever it's called, the Immigration and Naturalization Service? See to it she'll be assured she won't be deported if she comes forward to testify."

Bollinger pointed a finger at Richard, and nodded. "There you go."

"I was going to do that," Grife said, ". . . later."

He picked up the phone and called the immigration department, but after talking to five different people over the course of half an hour, the most he could extract from them was a promise to allow Esperanza to stay in the country long enough to testify. They insisted they would still have to deport her after the trial was over.

"Why don't you give me Esperanza's cousin's number," Richard said to Lieutenant Bollinger. "Maybe he won't arrange for Esperanza to meet with the police, but he might let someone like me get a taped statement from her."

"Doc," Grife smiled tolerantly, "even though there's no legal problem with your investigating things on your own, I'd appreciate it if you'd leave the investigation to us."

"Just a couple of things where maybe I can help. . . . What do you think?" Richard persisted, reaching for the phone.

While Bollinger sat by intently, Grife agnostically, Richard called Felipe Gomar's home and was given the number of an automotive center where Felipe worked. When he finally got Felipe on the line, the lightly Spanish-accented young man was suspicious, but the personal tone in Richard's voice reassured him. He told Felipe that Esperanza was the only living witness to a terrible tragedy, and that without her, a murderer might be set free. When he promised Felipe that he only wanted to get Esperanza's statement on tape and would not bring the authorities with him, Felipe agreed to arrange a meeting between Richard and Esperanza for the following night at his house.

At seven o'clock the next evening, Richard arrived with a portable tape recorder over his shoulder at Felipe Gomar's runt of a house in the heart of Los Angeles' barrio. Though it was a worn stucco dwelling with a small weed-choked yard and a crack down the front outside wall, it was still made a touch special by a stained-glass window and iron-bell wind chimes hanging outside the door.

Felipe Gomar, a deeply brown-skinned man with smooth muscles beneath his T-shirt, stood behind the screen door, not opening it for Richard.

"Esperanza is not here," he spat angrily. "You are not welcome." He gestured toward the end of the block where two men sat in a cream-colored Plymouth parked around the corner.

"Two hours they are. You think whee do not know police in our neighborhood, vato? Somos pobres, no somos estúpidos. Whee are poor, whee are not stupid!"

"I didn't know anything about this," Richard apologized earnestly. "You might not believe that, but it's true."

Felipe studied him a moment.

"Maybe . . . maybe not. It does not matter, anyway. She is gone."

He slammed the front door in Richard's face. His hands in his pockets, Richard strolled with a menacing casualness over to the Plymouth. As he drew close, he could see Phil Bollinger sitting innocently behind the wheel. Another plain-clothes officer, Sergeant Hubbard, one of the several detectives on loan from the L.A. Sheriff's Department for the case, was in the front seat next to him. Richard ducked his head down to window level and asked evenly, "What the hell are you guys doing here?"

Bollinger muttered something incomprehensible, knowing very well what had happened. He collected himself and said, "It so happens, you know, that our coming here was perfectly proper. Esperanza is a material witness. If we have the chance, we intend to take her into custody until she testifies at the trial."

"Are we communicating in a different language or something —I thought I was going to get a tape-recorded statement from her *for* you guys."

"Doctor, I know you're not in the law, sir, but someone's tape-recorded statement wouldn't mean beans in court. Even I know it's just hearsay. You have to have the live witness," Bollinger replied.

"And so you and Grife knew you were going to pull this while you were sitting there yesterday listening to me tell Gomar I'd come alone."

Bollinger shrugged. "C'mon, Dr. Pomerantz. When you're going after a dangerous criminal, you don't always follow Queensberry rules."

"Well, tonight may have been our only shot for at least establishing contact with her," Richard said. "So just go back to your criminology books and look up what it says to do once you've lost your star witness for good."

Richard threw his hands up and walked away.

$$\star \quad \star \quad \star$$

It was on a Saturday morning in his Lexington, Kentucky, law office that William "Trotter" Smith received a phone call from Ray Lomak. Smith, a 1949 graduate of Princeton, Korean War hero, former prosecutor, and two-term United States congressman, held the phone with a thumb and a finger of his large handsome hand and listened with interest.

"I'm innocent," Ray told him, talking rapidly as he always did when speaking long-distance. "Will you take the case?"

Trotter Smith was too much of a gentleman to mention legal fees in a first conversation. By the time he was ten he had as firm an appreciation of matters like appropriateness and refinement as most boys had only of stolen bases and pup tents. He doubted Ray could afford his normal six-figure fee for major murder trials, anyway.

"I'd most certainly be interested in at least coming out to Los Angeles to talk to you about it, Ray," he said, leafing through the pages of his desk calendar. Smith had acquired only a felicitous trace of a southern accent while growing up in a family that owned the third largest horse farm in Kentucky, and at Princeton had eradicated even that last tincture of identifiable speech. In court he wore tweed jackets and three-piece, Savile Row tailored suits, and when he came to the office on Saturdays he scuffed around in the same attire he had sported during all those house party weekends at Princeton—white duck pants with a pink pin-striped shirt, burgundy sweater tied over the shoulders, hard-soled moccasins without socks, and tortoise-shell glasses slipped rakishly part way down his nose. He was one of a small silver-templed breed who could look youthful and distinguished at the same time.

The most worldly member yet of his seventh-American-generation family, Smith appeared to be from anyplace where fine wines were drunk, though at Lexington public affairs he judiciously wouldn't have considered asking for anything other than Kentucky bourbon.

The next afternoon Trotter Smith caught a plane for Los Angeles. If Ray Lomak knew of his reputation as one of the finest defense lawyers in the nation, he assured himself, then he also probably knew of the former prosecutor's refusal to defend anyone he believed guilty of a violent crime, unless there were substantially mitigating circumstances.

Smith never criticized other lawyers for defending people they believed were guilty of such crimes, and he had always averred publicly that if no attorney were to step forward on behalf of such a defendant, he would do so himself—the right to counsel was a sacred right. But short of that extreme situation, he elected personally not to be a party to releasing dangerous individuals back into society. To the argument thrown up to him by other lawyers at clubhouse smokers that no one is guilty of a crime unless a judge or jury finds him to be, Smith would counter with a convivial smile that under that line of reasoning Adolf Hitler and Jack the Ripper weren't guilty of their crimes.

This long-standing practice of his was only underlined by his realistic appraisal of his ability to beat virtually any prosecutor in court. The principle had limited his practice, to be sure, but then again, when money wasn't a necessity, there was just as much challenge to be had from a month's sailing expedition across the Atlantic as from any thirty days in court.

Challenges were Smith's life-drug, what kept his six-foot-two-inch frame trim and his smooth shaven cheeks full of color. As a kid he had insisted to his parents that he be allowed to help train the trotting horses, though when it came to the actual races, from the Hambletonian on down, he knew that as a minor he had to sadly let that final glory fall to all those little adult Cubans his father hired. By the age of eighteen, Smith had decided that the nickname "Trotter" had enough class to it to become his legal name.

Trotter Smith and Ray Lomak first laid eyes on each other in the visiting room of the Los Angeles County Jail, where Ray was being held without bail.

"So our friends in blue have got the wrong man. Well, it's not the first time something like that has happened, is it," Trotter said with an inbred tolerance for all parties concerned.

"I'm being punished for my past," Ray said crisply.

Ray's outrage at having been arrested permeated everything he said in response to Trotter's questions. He was an angry bitter man, and after only an hour interview, Trotter was better than half-convinced he really was telling the truth—that a previously convicted multiple murderer, who seemed to be the only one with any motive for these heinous killings, and who admitted being at the Harnett ranch shortly before the murders took place was, against almost all the arithmetic, in fact innocent.

"I'm not rich," Ray said with an edge, having already learned of Smith's own wealth. "I've saved over half of what the Foundation paid me, though. I can give you four thousand dollars. And *Esquire* magazine has offered me twenty-five thousand dollars for an exclusive interview. You can have that, too."

Trotter shrugged and nodded affably. Twenty-nine thousand dollars for him in a case of this magnitude and prominence was a joke. But there was an uncommon challenge offered by this case —convincing a jury that a notorious, convicted mass murderer was as guiltless as they were of the terrible charges brought against him.

"Once you're acquitted, maybe we'll work something additional out on a long-range basis," he said. "One last thing, Ray, before I give you a definite yes," he added, as if offhandedly, as he stood to leave. "Just for my own final satisfaction. Will you take a polygraph for me?"

"Yes, of course," Ray answered without hesitation. "If that's necessary."

"I'd like you to," Trotter said balmily. He touched Ray's arm and showed himself out past the guard.

Four days later Trotter flew Charles Hecker in from Cleveland. Hecker was one of the nation's foremost polygraph examiners.

"I'm going to hook up a few of these gadgets here, Mr. Lomak," he said, sitting Ray down in a chair next to the instrument and its graphs, "but I'm not going to turn anything on until later. Now, there's nothing in this machine that will cause you any pain, or anything of the like."

Hecker, a rugged ex-marine and former policeman, nonetheless had a light-handedness in wrapping the blood pressure cuff around Ray's arm, and the rubber accordion-like pneumograph tube about his chest for measuring breathing irregularities. Lastly, he applied the silver metal tabs to two of Ray's fingers to register any change in the skin's electrical resistance.

Hecker then proceeded to tell Ray the exact questions that would be asked. It was a standard procedure that tended to put the truthful subject at ease as it eliminated anxiety over surprise questions, and to increase the tension in the would-be liar as he anticipated his deceptions. Most important in the pre-test interview was trying to find a "control" question to ask, the one Hecker was satisfied the subject would either lie about, or would at least have great doubt about his answer's truthfulness. The control question would establish, first, whether the subject was a "responder," as opposed to one of those rare individuals who evince no physiological response to the telling of a lie; and second, the degree of that response as a point of reference with which to compare his responses to questions concerning the crime under investigation.

"Have you ever in your life stolen anything?" Hecker began, in working toward the proper control question.

"Yes, as a child I stole another kid's bicycle," Ray answered promptly.

"Aside from that, have you ever stolen anything?" Hecker asked.

Ray thought a moment. "Well, maybe small things as a child. I don't remember."

"Aside from the bicycle and aside from small things as a child, did you ever steal anything as an adult?"

"No."

"Did you ever *try* to steal anything as an adult?"

"No."

"Have you ever *thought* of stealing anything at all as an adult?"

"No."

Hecker nodded, and ceased his questioning. He thought he may have had his control question.

Hecker inflated the pressure cuff around Ray's arm, turned on all dials on the polygraph machine, and started in on the actual test.

The first two questions merely concerned Ray's proper name and age, just to get a graph reading of his normal blood pressure and breathing patterns. Hecker's third question was the crucial one. Like any experienced examiner, he never used words like "murder," or "rape," or even "embezzle," as they were too open to moral and legal interpretation. He stayed strictly to phraseology that would preclude the subject's rationalizing away his acts.

"On the night of August 20, did you cause the deaths of Dean and Jennifer Harnett while they were swimming in Tex Harnett's pool?"

"No," Ray answered calmly.

The response on the graph was negligible, easily within the allowable range of innocence.

"Have you ever thought of stealing anything at all as an adult?" Hecker followed up immediately with what he was using as the control question.

"No."

The pen tracing Ray's blood pressure swung upward, the baseline moving a full inch higher on the graph. At the same instant, the pen tracing his respiration suddenly held steady at the end of an exhalation, showing a momentary, but clear suspension of breath by Ray. Both signs were clear indications of deception; Ray appeared to be a responsive subject to his own lies.

Hecker concluded this first test with a few more irrelevant questions, and Ray's graph recordings returned to normal.

Hecker turned off the machine.

On a second test ten minutes later, Ray gave the same answers to all the questions and, again, his physical responses recorded on the graph were essentially the same. All indications were that he was lying in answer to the control question, and telling the truth when he denied involvement in the Harnett murders.

That evening Hecker phoned Trotter Smith with his findings.

Seeking assurance of a fact he was already well aware of, Smith asked, "Your polygraph tests have a better than ninety-percent accuracy rate, am I correct?"

"This is correct," Hecker said, chewing a turkey sandwich in the lonely silence of his hotel room. "It is my considered opinion that Ray Lomak is innocent of the crime he has been charged with."

The next morning Smith visited Ray again at the county jail and informed him of the polygraph results.

"I'm going to take the case, Ray," he said with a patrician smile.

"I told you I was innocent," Ray said, then added passingly, as though there were nothing peculiar about his not having mentioned it in their first conversation, "I have a witness who can testify I was nowhere near the Harnett ranch at the time of the murders."

CHAPTER 2

THE MORE CONTACT RICHARD HAD WITH JOE

Grife, the more he worried about the prospect of Ray Lomak's walking out of court a free man. Though Grife seemed to be a competent lawyer, he was, in some discouraging senses of the term, a company lifer. When Richard suggested he read through the 1960 court transcript of Ray's first murder trial to glean what further knowledge he could about Ray, Grife said he would, but when Richard called back a week later, Grife had not done so. Nor had he done so two weeks after that. Richard finally went down to the attorney general's office and plowed through the five thousand pages of transcript himself.

The first of many unsolicited memos that Richard dropped off at the deputy D.A.'s office read: "With respect to our last conversation about the unlikelihood of a criminal's being aware of leaving tire tracks and therefore disposing of the tires, as Ray did, see page 3,782 of *People* v. *Lomak*, Superior Court Case #17204, 1960. A crucial piece of evidence against Lomak was the shoe print he left at the home of Parmer Cale. *This* criminal would be aware!"

Though Lt. Phil Bollinger was an energetic and dedicated police officer, Richard had problems with him as well. He tended, just from what Richard could observe in discussions with him, to often slap along the factual surface of situations, never wading deeper during his interrogations for the psychological profiles that could possibly explain many occurrences.

Richard took it upon himself to visit Tex in an attempt to elicit more information from him, even though Bollinger had already interviewed him.

Tex was sitting motionlessly on one of the wicker chairs in the back yard, absently staring out over the ocean that was a mottle of green and cobalt blue off the Palos Verdes peninsula. Tex almost never left his ranch any more.

"Sit down here with me awhile, Richard," Tex said hoarsely, gently tapping the armrest of the chair next to him. He sipped from a tall glass meant for ale, but containing only water.

"You have to get this out of your head about Ray. I . . . I don't know who took my children from me, but I know in my heart it wasn't Ray."

"I'm just trying to get at the truth," Richard said regardfully. "Will you tell me a few things, Tex? So we can both learn the truth, whatever it is, about what happened?"

After a pause, Tex tipped his head slightly.

"I want to know," Richard said, "about when Ray lived here, what some of his habits were. Ray's a very precise man, he does a lot of things the same way. In my business, you might even call him compulsive."

Tex looked askance at Richard, but Richard, cupping his hands together, pressed on.

"I'm not saying some of his habits don't make sense, but I want to know about a certain guess I have. Was Ray extremely conscientious about not wasting things—say, like water or electricity? Think back, Tex. If you ever saw him brush his teeth, for example, did he make sure to turn the water off until he rinsed? Or for instance, if he were to walk through the house on the way to the den," Richard continued, thinking of the possibility that Jenny never knew Ray was in the house that night, "would he be likely to turn off the lights behind him? Try to remember, if you can."

"I don't have to try to remember anything," Tex said, a little gruffly. "Sure he'd turn a light off after himself. He's like me, knows the value of things. Not like so many other people these days—see their houses, you'd think they were hostin' an inaugural ball every night."

"Did he *ever* leave lights on, in a hallway, or in a room he wasn't using?"

"Hell no. Why should he?" Tex asked, drawing his head back. "Why should anyone? You call it a compulsion, if you like, I call it just plain good sense. Even complimented him on it once."

"Very interesting," Richard said. "One other thing. When he came to visit, after he had moved to his own place, did he always put his car in the garage if there was room?"

Tex sat and thought, more and more perturbed by the whole interview. "I don't know. I suppose maybe sometimes he did, I really can't tell you now."

"The reason I ask," Richard explained, "is because Ray once mentioned that your neighbors didn't like it when he lived here. They even threatened to take up a petition."

"Walters! Morrow Walters!" Tex hooted. "Medium rare phony down to his socks. I straightened him out right off."

"But when Ray came to visit later," Richard asked, "did he put his car in the garage and pull down the door so not to rile the neighbors who might pass by?"

Tex looked glumly at him, then back out at the ocean. He stared off toward Catalina Island, and his face sagged. "I don't know. I'm tired, Richard. I want to nap now. I just want to rest a little."

The visit was abruptly ended as Tex stood and, putting his hand momentarily on Richard's shoulder, walked on into the house.

The next night, Richard drove out to the ranch again and, getting Tex's unenthusiastic permission, turned off all the lights in the house except the one in the den, where Ray would have been on the night of the murders, going through Tex's papers for him. Just as Richard had expected, the light in the back den was not visible from the driveway, nor from the hall or living room, or Jenny's bedroom.

On the night of the murders, because of Ray's habits and the physical setup of the house, Richard surmised that Jenny never knew Ray was there.

As he went back out to his car, Tex called after him wryly, "Sure *you* wouldn't best see a psychiatrist, Richard?"

The next memo Richard left on Grife's desk answered Grife's question as to why Jenny hadn't "hightailed" it out of the ranch if Lomak was there when she arrived, as believed. Richard suggested Bollinger be sent out to the ranch to confirm Richard's findings, as Richard's testifying to them could appear suspect to a jury. "I might add," Richard postscripted his memo, "that since Esperanza had the flu that day, she could very well have been in her bed with the lights off in her room, and thus, in Tex's sixteen room, labyrinthine house, neither Jenny, Dean, nor Ray knew she was there."

✶ ✶ ✶

Richard had, by increments, become obsessed with the trial of Raymond Lomak. What had started out as a few isolated efforts to help the prosecution's case, soon metamorphosed into a driven state of mind, resulting in an indefinite leave of absence from his own practice in order to pursue the man charged with his fiancée's murder. Through his own interviews—not entirely unaided by his training in psychiatry—Richard delivered small shards of evidence, but mostly just theories to Grife's office on an almost weekly basis. Some of his suggestions were helpful, many of them were not.

Whenever he showed up at the doorway to Grife's office, the deputy D.A.'s bushy eyebrows contracted with resentment, though he never declined to hear what Richard had to say. Only once did he comment on Richard's ardor for the investigation, striking a chord of truth, if indelicately. "I wonder how many of your colleagues would be so sympathetic to some of these guys," he mumbled without looking at Richard, "if they had suffered a personal loss like you."

When Grife announced to Richard, and not without a grain of belligerent pride, that Bollinger and he had unearthed their best witness yet, Richard drove out to talk to that witness himself. He was Morrow Walters of Palos Verdes. Like many others, Walters respectfully consented to speak to the grieving survivor.

"In this time of tragedy," banker Walters intoned soberly, swirling a small glass of port, "I'm not about to tell Mr. Harnett, 'I told you so.' But I must say this man should have known better —even given his . . . well, background . . . his, shall I say, limited education."

Richard pushed his foot up against the hassock in front of his chair. "You told Lieutenant Bollinger you had a clear look at Lomak's face as he drove away from the ranch that night."

"Car and face, that's correct."

"Even though it was dark by then?" Richard asked.

"I was close enough," Walters declared. "I was just starting out on my after-dinner walk."

"Can I ask you, Mr. Walters, why you didn't immediately come forward with this information? I don't doubt you had your reasons, but it seems like three weeks was a long time to wait."

Walters nodded seriously. "I suppose it was fear, Dr. Pomerantz. Who knows if this Lomak fellow is really going to be put away for good this time. But then when I heard that Mrs. Kirkham down the road was willing to testify she saw a car 'like' Lomak's driving away that night . . . well, Mrs. Walters and I discussed it, and I decided it was time for me to stand up and be counted, too. We all have children in this neighborhood, you know, Dr. Pomerantz. I still have a teenager at home myself. A couple of murders have just been committed virtually next door, and I understand Harnett is *still* on good terms with this fellow." He shook his head to himself.

"Yes," he said, looking into his glass, "I suppose it was just fear."

The "suppose" chafed Richard's instincts. Normally, one did not "suppose" a sense of fear; it was usually a discernible and recollectible emotion.

"Do you feel biased in any way against Ray Lomak?" Richard asked. "Do you think maybe you had any bad feelings toward him before all this happened?"

"No, no, good heavens no. I didn't even know the man."

Richard looked Morrow Walters straight in the eye. "The reason I ask is that I was told you and your wife tried to pressure Tex Harnett to get Lomak out of the neighborhood a year ago."

Unruffled, Walters took a sip of his port. "That was another matter, Dr. Pomerantz. I had imagined you were on the same side of this case as I. I must say, your tone of voice at the moment indicates otherwise."

Richard attempted to sound less hostile. "I just don't want any inaccurate testimony to hurt the prosecution's case."

Walters' defensiveness grew geometrically. "You're accusing me of fabrication, I think that's quite plain." Then, with a civilized smile, "I think you'd perhaps best show yourself out, doctor."

Richard smiled back. "Do me a favor, Walters," Richard said, "and stay off the stand." On their soapy smiles, Richard set out to find the front door of the Walters mansion.

Richard told Grife he thought Morrow Walters was lying and

should not be called as a witness. "If Trotter Smith is one third the lawyer he's supposed to be," he noted, "he'll make parade confetti out of Walters."

For the first time, Grife became openly inimical to Richard's meddling.

"In thirty-one years I've never suggested or in any way encouraged a witness to perjure himself. Morrow Walters is our best witness, so why don't you just once acknowledge you might not know everything, and let the jury decide if he's telling the truth."

"Fine, swell," Richard ended the conversation glibly. But the nearness of what Grife said, to Jenny's accusation of his always being so sure of himself, stung Richard with a sharp haunting pain.

Richard did not, however, cease to meddle. Through the new team doctor who had been hired after Tex sold the franchise, Richard tracked down the two players, Roger Ferris and Billy Mews, who had been present when Ray and Dean had first met each other back at the stables the day of Tex's barbecue.

Both corroborated stable hand Luis Peralta's statement to Lieutenant Bollinger that there had been an immediate antagonism between Ray and Dean over Dean's use of cocaine at the party, although both Ferris and Mews, with an eye on their careers, denied they had taken any of the drug themselves.

To stay out of Joe Grife's way for a while, at least physically, Richard left his latest memorandum (containing a summary of the players' statements) on Grife's desk at half past noon—when Joe was dependably at Ed & Tina's having his grilled cheese with bacon and tomato.

✱ ✱ ✱

September 28, the Los Angeles County grand jury convened behind closed doors. Although Joe Grife called his witnesses in a somewhat confusing order, the next afternoon the twenty-one grand jurors, to no one's surprise, handed down their indictment of two counts of first degree murder against Raymond Frederick

Lomak. The jury found there was "probable cause to believe" Lomak committed the murders. The case would go to trial. (As a matter of course, the original murder complaint upon which Ray had been arraigned the day after his arrest was dismissed and replaced by the grand jury indictment.)

The morning Ray Lomak was arraigned on the indictment, he stood stone-like before the presiding judge, Nicholas Hartamian. When asked what his plea to the charges was, Ray answered stoically, "Not guilty, Your Honor."

Back in Ray's cell, Trotter Smith said, "Ray, I want you to pretend now you're on the stand, and answer a question I'm going to be asking you at the trial."

"You want me to testify at the trial?" Ray interrupted, a little alarmed. "I don't think most good defense lawyers put their clients on the stand, Mr. Smith. This is something we used to discuss up at San Quentin."

"That's quite a reliable sample of opinion," Trotter chuckled. "Men who had lawyers that managed to get them into San Quentin. I'm not most good defense lawyers, Ray. You have any idea how it appears to a jury when a man who claims to be innocent won't even get up there and tell his own story and answer a prosecutor's questions? In answer to your question, Ray, you *will* testify.

"Now, I want you to pretend the jury is over here, and the judge is sitting here, just a few feet away, all right? I want you to truly visualize it, Ray. I'm going to ask you a question I'll be posing to you in court."

While Trotter took a few roaming steps toward the back wall of the cell, Ray closed his eyes a moment, concentrating, and then opened them. Trotter came back to where Ray was sitting, and put his foot up on the frame of the cot.

"Mr. Lomak," he said pointedly, "did you kill Dean and Jennifer Harnett?"

"No," Ray answered him, dispassionately.

Trotter took his foot down and stood back up, a shadow of

dismay in his face. He stroked near the corner of his eye with a forefinger and said, "End of rehearsal, Ray, and not at all to my satisfaction. When I ask you that question, the jury is going to be watching you as they will watch no other witness giving any other piece of testimony. An innocent man who has been charged with murder and very possibly faces a sentence of death could be expected to lend a little emotion to his denial of guilt."

"I don't see—"

"Good God, Ray, *tell* that jury you didn't do it! Tell it because you want the entire people of the state of California who've accused you of this dastardly crime to know that you didn't do it! When we first met, you were very vehement about your innocence. You don't have to become devoid of emotion just because you're in a courtroom and there's Latin etched above the doorway, and a judge wearing a black robe.

"I'll see you tomorrow morning at seven. Don't plan to see any visitors until I tell you, because you won't have any time for them —we're going to be working over the weekends, as well."

To better insulate himself from hounding reporters and provide as much undistracted time as possible for the case, Smith instructed the switchboard operators at the Biltmore Hotel where he was staying in downtown Los Angeles only to take messages and not to ring his room.

Taking his first and last several hour break from the Lomak case, Trotter Smith flew to Palm Springs, where he had been invited to address the California Trial Lawyers' annual convention. When asked during the question and answer period after his speech what his tactics were going to be in the Lomak case, Trotter smiled benignly at the five hundred members present and said, "Almost entirely scrupulous."

✳   ✳   ✳

The jockeying for appointment to the high visibility trial among the few more ambitious Los Angeles County Superior Court judges began immediately. Judge Nicholas Hartamian, who would make the appointment, even received a phone call from a state legislator in Sacramento who recommended Judge Arnold Stokes as a "dedicated, fair-minded man." The legislator did not mention in the call that Stokes had proven his fair-mindedness to him two years earlier when he gave probation to the lawmaker's son, who had led police on a 95 m.p.h. chase through Redondo Beach, away from the fading racket of a supermarket alarm bell.

But Hartamian, an independent sort, chose a judge who was experienced, quietly respected and, as far as anyone knew, not planning to seek higher office; the judge was a forty-eight year old woman named Dorothy Penstrake.

Smith made very few pre-trial motions. One was a motion under Section 995 of the Penal Code to have the indictment dismissed for lack of sufficient evidence, which was denied; another, for a change of venue because of inordinate publicity in the Los Angeles area, was denied all the way up through the California Supreme Court, all seven judges concurring that the entire state had been so saturated with publicity about the case that Lomak was no less likely to receive a fair trial in Los Angeles than anywhere else in the state.

As Ray did not want to waive his constitutional right to a speedy trial, Judge Penstrake set the trial date for November 25, less than two months after the indictment.

Two weeks before the trial was to begin, Smith met for a prolonged session with Tex Harnett. Though Tex shook Trotter Smith's hand vigorously and welcomed him to California, as he thought a good Oklahoman should do for any boy out of Kentucky, it soon became apparent to both of them just how many borders existed between the bluegrass pastures of Lexington, Kentucky, and Tex's Enid, Oklahoma. The rapport they both expected and fought for in the first five minutes was stillborn.

"I used'ta ride in all the gymkhanas when I first came out here, y'know," Tex crowed. "Palominos and paints, mostly. You got a special horse down on your farm you like to saddle up, I imagine?"

"Sure do," Trotter smiled. "A Tennessee walker, stands over sixteen hands tall."

"Oh . . . yeah," Tex said, looking down, embarrassed that in all his years he had never gotten around to riding so blue-blooded a horse as that. "Fine animals, I understand . . . those Tennessee walkers."

Trotter tried his best to make Tex comfortable, but could see that the older man was simply ill at ease in his presence. Trotter went quickly on to business.

"You're a very important friend to Ray," he told him. "Right now I think he needs you more than he's probably ever needed anyone in his whole life."

Tex nodded, with great concern. Trotter did not spell out the coldly pragmatic fact of the matter that the victims' own father taking the stand in Ray's defense would carry enormous weight with the jury. He did not have to spell it out; by the end of their talk he knew Tex already believed wholly and sincerely in Ray's innocence, and could be counted on to the denouement.

When Richard first ran into Trotter Smith on the steps outside the Criminal Courts Building, he felt the lawyer to be a basically decent man.

"I want to tell you how profoundly sorry I am for your loss," Trotter had said to him, shaking his head ruefully, a saddened stillness in his grey eyes. "I truly hope you'll understand my role here as defense lawyer."

"Yes, of course," Richard assured him. "Thank you for your sympathy." He walked Smith part way down the sidewalk.

Not above trying to use Trotter's decency to his own advantage, Richard continued, "I hear Ray passed the polygraph you gave him."

"Yes, he did. According to Charles Hecker, who doesn't satisfy easily."

Richard nodded.

"I realize, of course," Trotter said, "there's always a certain small inaccuracy rate with those tests."

Richard walked with his hands in his back pockets. "Yeah, right." He looked across the street and added casually, "And then, of course, Ray's precisely the type of person who might be able to beat the lie detector."

Trotter turned his head toward him, with a slow interest.

Richard tossed a hand out, humbly. "Well, Ray's an exceptionally intense individual. Some psychiatric case studies have shown that people like Ray might very well know they're lying when they deny committing a crime—he's not psychotic, after all, he has a sense of reality—but they feel they were so justified in their actions, so much the wronged party in the first place, that their subsequent crime becomes practically irrelevant. The crime, so to speak, carries so little significance in their mind, they don't even respond on the polygraph when they lie about it."

It was only a pinch of a frown that Trotter showed. "Yes, well, from *all* the evidence, I have enough reason to believe in the probability of his innocence to offer him the best defense I can."

"I understand," Richard said uncontentiously. "Well, I'm parked over here. It was nice meeting you." Richard turned to go, believing he had dropped enough scabrous seeds for one day in Trotter Smith's enthusiasm for his job. Then he turned back with a last observation: "You and I have more in common than you think."

Trotter waited on him with an attentive smile.

"I tried to help Ray Lomak, too." Richard raised an eyebrow a moment and then walked to his car.

CHAPTER 3

ONCE MORE, RAYMOND LOMAK WAS AT THE
center of a nationally publicized trial. As no cameras or sound
crews were allowed inside the courtroom, the technical apparatus
of the media were set up in the corridor outside the fifteenth floor
courtroom. Network sketch artists, L.A. bureau correspondents
for *Time* and *Newsweek*, wire service reporters, and stringers for
several of the larger papers in the country were given daily passes
to assure them seats inside.

From the day jury selection began in Department 133 at the
Criminal Courts Building, an extra detail of the L.A. County She-

riff's Department was assigned for added courtroom security. Five anonymous phone threats against Ray's life had been received, and on the day the *voir dire* (questioning) of prospective jurors began, a leathery faced old man in Biblical robes barged through the hallways swinging a club-headed staff and screaming he had to see his son, Raymond Lomak, before the crucifixion. He was grabbed and carried off kicking by three armed deputy sheriffs.

The days of high ceilings, globes of muted light, wood paneling and carved spires had long since vanished from most cities' places of justice. Department 133 was a modern courtroom, brightly lit by recessed fluorescent tubing. On the floor was a tight and springy, yellowish carpeting; on the back wall, a newfangled numberless clock; protruding from the front of the judge's bench was an electronic emergency call-box in case of any trouble in the courtroom.

Ray sat at the defense table assiduously writing notes out to his lawyer, completely oblivious to all the simmer his trial was causing. He did not even take much notice of the packed courtroom. Many of the curious were young lawyers and law students who had come to see Trotter Smith at work.

Rising early in the morning, Richard was seated among the first several rows of spectators every day. During jury selection, Grife had even asked him to be there for his help.

"Maybe you can give me an opinion on some of these people," he had suggested begrudgingly. "Lawyers have been known to use psychiatrists for this stuff, right? Jurors have always really thrown me, I'll tell you. My wife, she can figure people out right away, just talking to them in the market. Not me."

"You want some quick pigeonholing, huh?" Richard said skeptically. "I'll do what I can."

"You offended by it?" Joe Grife asked. "As a psychiatrist and all?"

"Offended by it?" Richard smiled. "Not at all. I'm just not sure an observant cabbie wouldn't be just as qualified for this type of on-the-spot assessment as I am."

Trotter Smith was hard to match when it came to canvassing the arbiters of Ray's fate. "How are you this morning, Mr. Peters?" he asked a prospective juror, just as he began warmly with all of them. "I know it's awfully hard to concentrate right away, after coming through that miserable traffic this morning, so if anything I ask is even a little bit confusing, you just stop me and ask me to clarify. Will you do that?"

After a half hour of questioning the jurors, Smith came back to the defense table and said *sotto voce,* "Ray, I can't be quite sure, but as I'm questioning each juror, you seem to be looking at them absolutely without letup. I think some of them are becoming very uncomfortable."

"I'm sorry," Ray said, surprised. "I was just interested in what they were saying."

Over the course of *voir dire,* Smith would ask the jury panel any number of questions, from whether they would have any negative feelings against a defendant who regularly went to a prostitute, to what their attitude was toward anyone who had ever needed psychiatric care. But before any of those questions, he addressed a major issue head-on, realizing full well it would not evaporate simply because he ignored it. Penstrake had ruled that based on a California Supreme Court decision, the facts of this case disallowed Grife from asking the defendant, were he to testify, whether he had ever been convicted of a felony (in this instance, six murders). Smith, however, knowing the jurors were aware of Ray's past anyway, decided to broach the issue himself. For the defense, it was by far the most critical question during the entire process of jury selection:

"I'm sure all of you know at least something about the crime for which my client was convicted many years ago," Smith said. "With this in mind, I'm going to ask each of you, one by one—and you are, of course, under oath—whether you will let your knowledge of Raymond Lomak's past in *any* way influence you in reaching a verdict in the case presently before you. Frankly, I believe it would take an unusual person not to be influenced, but we are going to hunt until we find twelve such unusual people."

Already Smith had helped endear himself to whichever twelve people would eventually be chosen, as he had, ahead of time, complimented them for being "unusual."

"Because of its singular importance," he continued, "during my final summation, I intend to remind you of the commitment I get from you today to judge Mr. Lomak purely and exclusively on the evidence that comes from the witness stand in this courtroom."

Nearly half the jury panel candidly admitted that their knowledge of Lomak's past might influence them, and they were excused "for cause." One of them, a TV repairman, went so far as to say, "You want to know the truth, Mr. Smith? I think he should have been hung twenty years ago."

As the repairman reached for his cap amidst a mixture of surprise, amusement and opprobrium in the courtroom, Judge Penstrake, confirming the man's appraisal of his longevity as a juror, stated: "On the Court's own motion, Mr. Simpson, you may be excused."

A percentage of the jurors who did profess an ability to be completely objective in the case, Smith worried, may have just been kidding themselves.

On the second day of jury selection, Grife asked a fluttery-eyed, sixty year old housewife from Covina, "Mrs. Childress, as I've pointed out in my previous questioning, if the jury in this case returns a verdict of first degree murder against Mr. Lomak, the prosecution, in the penalty trial that will immediately follow, will be asking for the death penalty. Knowing this, do you have any objection to the death penalty that would prevent you, under any circumstances, from returning a verdict of death?"

Mrs. Childress blinked nervously. "Oh my. Well, I voted for the death penalty in the last election." She paused a moment, and added, "I did vote against the right to smoke in public places, though."

Several jurors looked in puzzlement at each other, trying to figure out the connection.

At the next recess Grife asked Richard, "If Smith doesn't use a peremptory on her, think we should keep her? Seems sympathetic to the prosecution."

"She's also a moron, of course," Richard murmured. "If truth is on our side, don't you think we'd be best off trying to impanel people whose minds work somewhat logically? Let Smith look for the unpredictable ones, not us."

Grife nodded, slowly, and dismissed Mrs. Childress from the panel.

The jury that did finally emerge after three days of *voir dire* was, at least to the naked eye, neither obviously unpredictable nor unintelligent. They were seven women and five men, ranging from a twenty-six year old substitute school teacher to a sixty-eight year old retired mailman. One thing not known about any of the jurors was his or her feelings concerning the matter of religion, as Judge Penstrake had not allowed the lawyers to inquire into that area. Neither Grife nor Smith was particularly distressed by the court's ruling. An irreligious person, Smith reasoned, would probably not hold Ray's religious fervor against him, while a devoutly religious juror's state of mind, both attorneys decided, could cut either way. Just as he might sympathize with Ray, so too could he find the defendant to be an embarrassment to churches everywhere. Neither Kate Robertson nor any of the other First Church of Our Savior pious could be found within miles of the courthouse during Ray Lomak's trial.

✶ ✶ ✶

At 10:40 A.M. on November 28, the prosecution opened its case.

Judge Penstrake, a serious minded woman who considered touching up some grey in her black wavy hair an example of a private wild streak in herself, leaned forward and asked: "Will there be an opening statement, Mr. Grife?"

"Yes, Your Honor."

Although argumentation is not allowed in opening statement, there was little question among the courtroom regulars that Joe Grife was doing just that. He pounded the lectern and raised his voice as he outlined what he said were no fewer than a dozen separate pieces of evidence that pointed irresistibly to Ray Lomak's guilt. The network sketch artists sitting in the front row tried to snapshot with their colored pencils the first drama of the trial—Ray Lomak glaring intently at his accuser, Joe Grife, as the prosecutor capped his brief, fifteen minute statement by promising the jury that the evidence "would prove Ray Lomak's guilt in these two horrifying murders not just beyond a reasonable doubt, but beyond all doubt."

Trotter Smith elected to waive opening statement, prompting a mild stir among the capacity spectators. They had prized their seats even more than usual this morning, as they had expected to hear the famed Kentucky lawyer's first oratory of the trial. Though Smith enjoyed playing to courtroom galleries, his primary audience was the jury—and for impact, he wanted the powerful testimony of Lomak and the other defense witnesses to be virgin to the jurors when it came from the witness stand, undiluted by any preview from him first.

The opening witness for the prosecution was Stuart Michaels, senior member of the paramedic team that responded to the emergency call on the night of the murders. If Richard had worried about Grife's being an unimaginative, albeit aggressive, plodder, he soon realized it was the deputy district attorney's same straightforward, artless ways that effectively conveyed to the jury a simple man's deep outrage at the crimes committed against innocent human beings.

Q. "Mr. Michaels," he asked, "did you feel there was any chance in the world to save those two young people, Dean and Jennifer Harnett?"

A. "Well, not with that juice going through there like it was."

Q. "The juice?" Grife asked. "You're referring to the electricity that went through the bodies of those poor people?"

A young woman juror's shoulders rose in a cringe. Although Smith considered objecting to Grife's attempt to inflame the passions of the jury, he elected not to.

A. "Yes sir, the electricity," Michaels answered, more respectful of the loss of life they were discussing.

Q. "People don't necessarily die instantly when they're electrocuted?"

A. "Not necessarily, no, sir. These underwater light things happen a couple of times accidentally every summer. Sometimes the victims are even still conscious when the paramedics get to them."

Grife was not thespian enough to look over at Ray with revulsion. But he shook his head with abhorrence and asked:

Q. "Dean and Jenny Harnett could have been conscious and aware for some time as that electricity passed through their bodies?"

A. "Yes, sir," Michaels answered, his own voice now with some pity.

Richard could only put a hand to his brow, and look down at the floor.

On cross-examination, Trotter Smith went to work on the witness who Grife hadn't thought could possibly be conscripted for defense purposes.

Q. "This Mexican-American woman who led you to the pool, Mr. Michaels, you say she spoke very little English?"

A. "That's right."

Q. "Did she ever tell you who she was?"

"Your Honor," Grife interrupted, pushing off the armrests in getting his extra pounds up out of the chair, "I'm going to object to this line of questioning. Mr. Smith knows very well who that woman was."

Judge Penstrake curled a finger for both of them to come to the bench. Once there, standing next to the taller, pin-stripe suited Smith, Grife, who held his arms stiffly and stared at a spot near the bottom of the bench, looked like an Iowa farmer in his brown

Sunday suit on the day he was raked over by big land interests, and vowed to never come into the city again for justice.

"Mr. Smith has seen all the police reports," Grife fumed. "He knows very well that the housekeeper, Esperanza Gomar, was there that night, and that the description of the woman who called for an ambulance fits Miss Gomar to a T."

"Joe . . . Joe," Trotter lullabied, putting his hand on Grife's arm, "Miss Gomar is only *alleged* to have been at the house, and the description of the woman *allegedly* fits that of Miss Gomar. Now please, Joe, you'll only be hurting yourself in the eyes of the jury if you start objecting to everything."

"I'll try my cases my way, Mr. Smith. I've won a couple of them over thirty years."

Judge Penstrake glanced over at the court reporter, who was taking all of it down. "I think we've wasted just about enough paper and ink on this point, gentlemen. Objection overruled."

Smith set about immediately to test Penstrake's boundaries.

Q. "On direct examination you testified that this woman was wearing a housecoat. Could you see what she was wearing beneath the housecoat?"

A. "I don't recall."

Q. "Could it have been pajamas? A party dress?"

A. "I don't know. But it sure didn't look like any party was going on. The whole house was dark."

Q. "By the time you were called, yes, but then again, there had been at least two people in the swimming pool that evening, isn't that correct?"

A. "Yeah, sure, the decedents."

Q. "Could have been more before you got there?"

A. "I wouldn't know."

Q. "Did this woman say anything about friends of hers or friends of the Harnetts' having been over earlier that evening?"

"Objection. Calls for hearsay."

"Sustained."

Q. "In any case, Mr. Michaels, you don't know that other people hadn't been there and cleared out before you arrived—all you do know is that this woman of unknown identity for some unknown reason vanished before the police arrived, is that correct?"

A. "Yeah, I guess that's correct."

Q. "Thank you. No further questions."

Smith sat down, while law students in a back row scribbled in their notebooks.

★ ★ ★

As Los Angeles County Deputy Coroner, Robert Hakato, described the condition of the bodies and the cause of death due to electrocution, Richard had to leave the courtroom for several minutes.

On cross, Smith asked:

Q. "Establishing time of death was rather difficult in this case, wasn't it, Dr. Hakato?"

A. "Yes, this is true, although we certainly know the deaths had been recent—that is to say, not *too* long before the bodies were discovered."

Q. "When you say, 'not too long,' you mean it wasn't a matter of days?"

A. "No, certainly not days."

Q. "There was no decomposition or skin discoloration, correct?"

A. "Correct."

Q. "But when you say 'recent,' Dr. Hakato, isn't the fact of the matter, you really can't pinpoint the time of deaths to within, say, even six hours, one way or the other?"

A. "Well . . . this would be difficult, yes."

Q. "Would you please explain to the jury *why* this was difficult, perhaps you might even say impossible?"

In answering, the conversationally awkward deputy coroner studied his hands, which curiously caused several of the jurors to also gaze at them, as if believing that the habitué of the morgue had perhaps forgotten to wash them before coming to court.

A. "A common way to determine time of death is by the degree of rigor mortis, which usually reaches its peak about twelve hours after death, when it begins to subside again. In this case, however, both bodies had been subjected to what we call a tetanic current—this is an electrical current that is strong enough to cause a muscle contraction that remains for a period even after death and after the current has been removed. This was more present in the woman than the man, as she had apparently been near the bottom of the pool closer to the drain, which was the closest electrical ground. The current, you see, would have traveled from the broken light socket to the drain pipe at the bottom of the pool."

Q. "And in determining time of death, there's also the test of tissue temperature, isn't there, Dr. Hakato?" Trotter Smith asked, walking in front of the jury as he demonstrated his knowledgeability, conveying the impression he already knew every important fact in the case and was not groping his way toward the truth, as was the jury. "Would you explain the problem there?"

Hakato adjusted his thick black-rimmed glasses and brought his hands to a steepled position.

A. "Bodies after death cool at a certain rate, determined partly by the temperature of their surroundings. But in this case, the temperature of the pool water was never taken on the night of the murders, nor do we know how long the victims had been in the water, either before or after their deaths."

Smith walked up to the witness stand and put a hand confidently on the arm of the box.

Q. "Dr. Hakato, medically speaking, isn't it possible these deaths occurred as early as, say, 4:30 that afternoon?" he asked, knowing Ray could prove he had not left for the Harnett ranch until 6:30.

A. "Medically speaking, yes, this is possible," Hakato admitted.

After Hakato, Grife called LASD's electrical expert, Sgt. Mel Parsons, who testified to his finding a 1/16 inch strip of copper wire in place of the pool's fuse, which would have blown and stopped the flow of electricity the instant the underwater light was broken. Parsons insisted the rigging could have been accomplished by anyone with an elementary knowledge of electrical wiring. But explaining it to the note taking jury, and answering Smith's imaginatively extraneous questions, took up over an hour.

(Showing more thoroughness than Richard had expected from him, Grife would call a San Quentin vocational instructor the following morning for his testimony that Ray, in addition to learning welding in prison, had a course on practical, household handiwork. The course spent a week on basic electrical repairs. Grife would later inlay a telling piece to the mosaic when he elicited Tex Harnett's admission that Ray had made several repairs on the pool during his stay at the ranch, and was thus familiar with the room where the lighting equipment was housed.)

Sgt. Parsons also testified to his having found the sledge hammer in the underground equipment room, along with the crowbar that was still lodged in the metal-plate backing of the underwater light. The rear end of the bar was resting on a footstool, indicating the murderer had used the stool to support the electrically conductive crowbar so he would not have to touch it himself as he knocked it through the light fixture.

Shortly afterward, sequin-shirted Luis Peralta, who had made himself eminently available to the TV reporters in the hallway—lingering even as they folded up their tripods, should a last vagrant question be asked—took the stand. He testified that the stool, sledge hammer and crowbar had all been regularly kept in the ranch's toolshed, and that he had seen Ray in the shed on any number of occasions looking for tools with which to do his handiwork around Tex's ranch.

As a way of establishing credibility with the jury, Trotter Smith did not believe in brawling with facts that were irrefutable, and thus did not even cross-examine on the damaging links between Ray and the physical means of the crime that were going into the court record. Ray sat next to his lawyer growing more and more agitated until finally, after the jury had filed out at the end of the day, but within earshot of everyone else in the courtroom, he turned to Smith and lashed out, "You don't care what happens to me. All you care about is the money. It's all people like you ever care about."

If Smith was startled by Ray's outburst, he didn't show it. "Was Luis Peralta lying?" he asked in a discreetly lower voice.

Ray only looked away, angry.

"And as far as the money, Ray," Smith went on, "I could be making more back in Lexington having a nice three hour lunch with a couple of real estate developers. If you're dissatisfied with my services and want another lawyer, you only have to say so. I'll be in my hotel room tonight studying today's transcript if you care to reach me."

★ ★ ★

Feeling a sense of momentum, Grife charged on with his case, anxious as he always became once a trial started for a jury to know his side was in the right, and for justice to be dispensed. Joe Grife wanted quick clean resolutions to life's moral traumas. Lethargic in pre-trial preparation, and impatient with the long, post-trial appeals process, Grife was at his best in the heat of mid-trial, calling his witnesses for the hard plain facts, dogging the opposition like a crouching graceless fighter who looks down at the canvas too much, but keeps the tough little punches coming.

Grife recalled to the stand paramedic Stuart Michaels, who identified a photograph of Esperanza as the woman he talked to on the night of the murders, thus neutralizing the implications raised by Smith in his earlier cross-examination of Michaels.

Late that day after court, Richard joined Grife and five other deputy D.A.'s in the more comfortable office of Lou Selby, head of the Trials Division. The place was a regular hangout for prosecutors to exchange war stories at the end of the day. Most sat around eating peanuts and swigging bottles of beer from the re- frigerator in the small room across the hall known as "Selby's Deli."

"Police making any progress in locating Esperanza?" Selby asked Grife.

Grife cupped a handful of peanuts into his mouth and chewed disconsolately. "I've had two men from our bureau assigned to tracking her down. She's just plain disappeared—probably not even in the state any more."

"I've even knocked on a few doors in her cousin's neighborhood myself," Richard added.

Grife glanced Richard's way, but muzzled his exasperation over Richard's continued extracurricular activities with another handful of peanuts.

In the third week of trial, Lt. Bollinger, coming to court in a new camel-hair sport jacket, told the jury: of finding the tire tracks, and Ray's claim he had sold his old tires to a stranger; of Ray's admission to having been out at the ranch the night of the murders to pick up papers for Tex; and of Ray's "I'd rather not say" comment to the question of where he had gone after leaving the ranch.

Grife anticipated Smith might argue that if Ray had been at the ranch when Jenny arrived she'd have seen the lights, and discovering it was Ray in the house, would not (because of her ill feelings toward Ray) have stayed to swim. Grife therefore had Bollinger testify to one's inability to see the den light from out front or from most areas in the house.

Concerning the taped message Tex had left on Ray's answering machine, Bollinger testified, "Within the parameters of our investigation at that stage, I spoke to Mr. Harnett, who told me, actually very reluctantly, that—"

"Motion to strike the words 'very reluctantly,' Your Honor," Smith said pleasantly, not even looking up from the papers he was reading through the tortoise-shell glasses perched on the end of his nose. "And we also seem to be getting into a best-evidence rule problem here. May we approach the bench?" he asked, finally looking up.

At the bench, Smith remarked, "I assume Mr. Grife is going to have Bollinger testify about Mr. Harnett's taped message to my client that no one would be at the main house of the ranch that night."

"That's right, Your Honor," Grife agreed.

"It's probably not hearsay," Smith acknowledged, "because Joe obviously isn't offering this to prove no one was in fact there—he's just presented evidence the maid was—he only wants to prove that because of the message, Mr. Lomak *believed* no one was there, nor was anyone about to come. I guess that's supposed to convince the jury that my client was lulled into thinking he could commit a witnessless crime that night. In any event, under the best-evidence rule, the jury should hear the tape itself, not Bollinger's recitation of its contents."

"Well, I think you're clearly right, Mr. Smith," Judge Penstrake said. "You'll have to play the tape for the jury, Mr. Grife."

Grife looked away sourly. "Lt. Bollinger seems to have temporarily misplaced the tape."

Trotter Smith's smile twinkled waggishly. "Bollinger lost the tape?"

Grife gazed up at the ceiling, not answering.

"Well," Judge Penstrake sighed, "has Lt. Bollinger listened to the tape?"

"Yes, Your Honor," replied Grife, reanimated.

"Then, in the tape's absence," Judge Penstrake said, "the best-evidence rule would permit Bollinger to testify to the contents of the message. But instruct your witness, Mr. Grife, to not make any more comments insinuating that Mr. Harnett has been at cross grains with the police in this case. In the meantime, I'll instruct the jury to disregard the conclusionary words, 'however reluctantly,'. . . for whatever good that kind of instruction ever does."

Before turning away from the bench, Smith said genially, "And Joe, I know that ever since the word got misused during the Watergate hearings, everyone has been following suit, but you might tell Bollinger that the word parameter is strictly a mathematical term—I believe the word he means is perimeter."

✳ ✳ ✳

After Bollinger testified to the tape's contents, Joe Grife introduced what he knew very well to be one of the most damning pieces of circumstantial evidence he had against Ray Lomak—Lomak's purchase of four new tires for his car just one day after the murders. It was with a righteous pleasure that Grife dwelled on the point in his examination of Ted Stiegel, owner of Stiegel Tire Center.

Q. "What was the condition of the old tires on Mr. Lomak's automobile?"

A. "Like new. Just like new. Hardly any mileage on them. I remember the whole transaction very well. I remember Mr. Lomak. Had a way of really looking at you when you talk to him. But those tires were good as new."

Richard could see from many of the jurors' faces that they considered Ted Stiegel, in his black wash-and-wear slacks and open-collared white shirt, to be the kind of unaffected, dependable sort who strode down his store's aisles quoting facts and figures from thick catalogues, and who would tell the unvarnished truth from the stand.

Q. "Like brand new, you say," Grife repeated. "Did you offer to give him something for them as part of the deal?"

A. "Oh, yeah. Oh, sure. Trade-ins are standard in our business. But he wouldn't hear of that. Insisted on taking them with him. We had a heck of a time getting them in the trunk. He didn't want to get the carpet in the back seat dirty."

After a few more questions of Stiegel concerning the fact that Ray had paid for the four new tires with cash, Grife turned the witness over to Smith.

Even Richard had to smile a little to himself at the charismatic class and breeding that Trotter Smith exuded in something as ordinary as standing up and preparing to ask a first question. Straightening his body flowingly to its full height, pausing to remove his reading glasses and slip them into his suit's breast pocket, he took measured steps over to the witness stand. There was no cheaply theatrical or self-conscious attempt to make people wait for him, but simply a southern peacefulness and a robust Ivy League ego that made him feel wanted wherever he was, and therefore in no need to rush. Believing the man on the stand was just a jot too anxious to aid the cause of justice, Trotter Smith met Ted Stiegel's eyes for a couple of seconds, and smiled faintly.

Q. "Mr. Stiegel, I believe you're an honest businessman," he began in his resonant, congressional voice. "Have I made an accurate appraisal of you?"

Joe Grife moved forward in his chair, his eyes shifting suspiciously.

A. "Yes, sir, you have," Stiegel answered.

Q. "You're not the kind of man who would take advantage of a customer, exploit a situation. You offer fair value at fair-minded prices, am I correct?"

A. "Yes sir, you are."

Q. "And I know you wouldn't want to do anything to make people in this city begin to think different of you."

A. "I try to provide the best service I can," Stiegel agreed, with a glance toward the spectators.

Q. "You were in your office when you and Mr. Lomak began talking prices, isn't that right?"

A. "That's right."

Q. "And a former employee of yours by the name of Gerrard Mantee was also present in the office at that time, is that correct?"

Stiegel paused a moment.

A. "Yeah . . . yeah, I guess that's so. Uh-huh."

Q. "Right. Now, I know your next answer will be as accurate as memory will allow, so I'm sure I won't have to call Mr. Mantee to the stand. Mr. Stiegel, please try to remember, and tell the jury: how much did you offer Ray Lomak for his used tires?"

The only discernible change in Stiegel was that his baby finger lifted up and immediately came back down on the armrest.

A. "Well . . . as I say, Mr. Lomak didn't want to sell them, but . . . let me think here, if I recall, it was about fifty or sixty dollars."

Q. "Fifty dollars apiece?" Smith asked, a near perfect imitation of being in the dark.

A. "No . . . no, for the four of them. . . . And now I remember, it was sixty dollars."

Q. "I see. Fifteen dollars apiece. Mr. Stiegel, I called—let's see here—ten, elev . . . twelve retail tire stores in Los Angeles, one dozen stores, and all dozen of them told me—which I'll authenticate if Mr. Grife objects to the hearsay—that they'd give me about fifty percent of the original list price on a trade-in if the tires were, as you described Mr. Lomak's, 'just like new, hardly used.' On a seventy dollar radial tire, which was the original list price on the tires that came with Mr. Lomak's car when he got it, that would be thirty-five dollars. Yet you only offered Mr. Lomak fifteen dollars for each of them, over fifty percent below your competitors. Now, I *know* you're an honest, fair-minded man—"

A. "That's right," Stiegel jumped in. "Now, you gotta understand, when I say 'like new,' I mean they were in pretty good shape, but they were still used tires, they—"

Q. "Had some wear on them?"

A. "Well, sure they had some wear on them. And I guess Mr. Lomak probably isn't the best parker in the world—white walls had some scuff on them. I wasn't going to be able to sell those tires as if they were actually new, you know."

Q. "Of course not," Smith sympathized. "So maybe you were being just a little bit loose in your choice of words when you said 'just like new.' What you meant was, they were in *pretty decent* shape. Is that right?"

A. "That's right, they were in decent shape."

Q. "Oh. In *decent* shape. Moving on, Mr. Stiegel, do you get a certain number of people coming in for new tires even though their old ones are in decent shape, but they don't think decent is good enough, especially when it comes to automobile tires, where safety is involved?"

A. "Oh yeah, we get a certain number of those people."

Q. "Thank you, Mr. Stiegel. No further questions."

At the recess, after Smith finished talking with Robert Gurney, an author from Charleston, South Carolina, who had been sitting in on the trial for a book about the case, Richard strolled over to

Smith and said, "I guess you don't have to study psychology to cross-examine. All you have to know are the facts."

"Yep," Smith said, putting papers back into his Moroccan leather briefcase. "If you have the facts, they can help a little."

CHAPTER 4

AS THE PROSECUTION CONTINUED ITS CASE AF-
ter the ten day Christmas recess, Mrs. Elaine Kirkham of Palos
Verdes took the stand. She told what she believed to be the unas-
sailable truth when she testified that while sitting on her screened-in
veranda with her dog, Caspar, on the hot summer evening, she
saw a car "like Ray Lomak's" speeding away from the direction of
the Harnett ranch just after 10:00 P.M., the approximate time the
police believed the murders took place. Not even Trotter Smith
could get her to retreat one millimeter or contradict herself in any
way. When he showed a number of pictures of various automobiles

to Mrs. Kirkham, a handsome woman of fifty-seven with demanding hazel eyes, she shook her head in annoyance and said, as he flipped from one picture to the next, "No . . . no . . . my goodness, no. . . . Take your thumb away, Mr. Smith. . . . No . . ."

Her glance up to Judge Penstrake, which bore the triumph of having rejected the most dashing man at the party, was one that only another woman could appreciate.

When Smith asked her if it wasn't in fact very dark in the area, Mrs. Kirkham replied, "There's a quite sufficient lamp hanging over the road at our mailbox, and I didn't say it *was* Mr. Lomak's car—I said it was a car very much *like* his."

On redirect, Grife brought out the fact that the road which led to the Harnett ranch was marked as a 'No Outlet' dead end, and that therefore very few unknown cars ever came through.

Gaining speed, Grife called Morrow Walters to the stand over Richard's last-ditch, unwavering protests. Erect and dignified, Walters told of having just started out on his after dinner walk (which he referred to unflinchingly as his "postprandial" walk) when Ray Lomak sped past in the opposite direction.

A. "It was rather fleeting, but I was only about six feet away, and there is simply no question about it—it was Mr. Lomak's car, and it was Mr. Lomak behind the wheel. In fact, for some reason, I don't know why, the overhead interior light was on in his car, and this is how I discerned Mr. Lomak to be the driver."

On cross, Smith, finding Walters' story egregiously pat, mocked, "There didn't happen to be a floodlight mounted backward on the dashboard, did there, showing what type of fountain pen Mr. Lomak had in his shirt pocket?"

Judge Penstrake clasped her hands and said, "That'll be about enough of that, Mr. Smith."

Joe Grife, who had stood up, about to object that Smith was badgering the witness, sat back down.

Q. "You say you started out on your walk that night, Mr. Walters, around 10:00?" Smith resumed his questioning, unfazed, having seen a good nine or ten guarded smiles in the jury box.

A. "Yes, it was right around 10:00. We had had a late dinner that night."

For half an hour, Smith could not wheedle any kind of admission from Morrow Walters that there was a possibility of error as to what he had seen that night, and at last, seemingly giving up, he asked idly, "Are your walks very long, Mr. Walters?"

A. "Fairly long, yes."

Q. "How long?"

A. "My walks are never shorter than forty-five minutes. It's a little over a mile from my house to the road's dead end, where the Harnett ranch starts. It takes me almost exactly forty-five minutes to walk down and back."

Q. "You're sure about this?"

A. "Absolutely."

Q. "So on the evening of August 20, you claim you were walking on the road which leads to the Harnett ranch between approximately 10:00 and 10:45. Let me ask you this. Did you see the ambulance on its way to the Harnett ranch? It went down that road, arriving at 10:19 P.M."

A. "Yes, I saw the ambulance."

Q. "How about the police car that came a few minutes later?"

A. "Yes, of course. In fact, as soon as I got back to my house, I called the police department to ascertain what had happened. They wouldn't tell me anything."

Q. "If you went out for a walk that night, as you claim you did, I take it then that you also saw the fire truck that was called when they thought the short-circuited wires might lead to an electrical fire, and which arrived at the ranch at 10:33 P.M.?"

With a look of confused apprehension, Joe Grife turned quickly to Lt. Bollinger, seated to his left at the counsel table.

Walters paused briefly. "Yes, I did."

Q. "Are you sure?" Smith persisted.

A. "Yes. Isn't this getting a little tedious?"

Without a smile, and genuinely incensed for the first time in the trial, Smith whipped his head toward Joe Grife and said, "May it be stipulated that on the evening of August 20, no fire truck ever went to the Harnett ranch."

Joe Grife, not wanting the jury to observe his intense dismay and embarrassment, answered calmly, "So stipulated, Your Honor."

Morrow Walters, his face watermelon red, volunteered, "There were a lot of sirens. I must have confused a fire truck with the ambulance."

"Very understandable," Smith rejoined. "A lot of ambulances carry forty-foot ladders and a hose."

*   *   *

Testifying that when he met Ray Lomak he believed him to be a reformed and well-intentioned man, born-again defensive back Jim Brill was bitterly remorseful on the stand that he had ever agreed to help Lomak find out about some of Dean Harnett's private indiscretions—all for "the sake of the Foundation." "Bad son," and a "drain on Tex," were the phrases Brill now recalled Ray's having used when discussing Dean.

Grife had little trouble showing Ray's hostility for Dean. After Brill, he called Nancy Wyatt, the secretary in the team's front office, for her testimony that Ray had also asked her to spy on Dean so he could "bring appropriate matters to Tex's attention." Grife then called football players Roger Ferris and Billy Mews to the stand, as well as recalling stable hand Luis Peralta, for their testimony concerning the bristly confrontation at Tex's barbecue between Ray and Dean over Dean's use of cocaine. Ferris and Mews categorically denied they had partaken of the cocaine themselves, only to have Peralta testify a few minutes later that the two players were snorting like crazy that afternoon.

Ray's face radiated a pleased haughty glow, first as Peralta, a prosecution witness, impeached the credibility of the two other prosecution witnesses, and then as Smith squeezed a few candy flowers onto the cake by asking Peralta:

Q. "You say this is the only time you ever tried cocaine, Mr. Peralta?"

A. "Yes, yes, never again," Peralta said, eager to convince his employer, Tex Harnett, who sat attentively in the courtroom, that this was so.

Q. "Why's that?"

A. "Oh, is bad stuff. Makes you can't theenk right."

Q. "Makes you kind of out of it, Mr. Peralta?"

A. "Yes, yes, out of it. Whew."

Q. "And this was the shape you were in when, even though neither Ray Lomak nor Dean Harnett raised a hand against each other, or even threatened each other in any way, you somehow thought there was some kind of bad feeling between them?"

Peralta looked down into his lap. "I do not theenk they liked each auther," he insisted humbly.

The instant a few spectators laughed out loud at Peralta's words and inflection, bailiff Kip Duncan, who liked to run a tight court, shot them a mean, frontier-marshal look. Occasionally playing a bailiff for a few extra bucks out at Paramount Studios, Duncan was known to stand on the studio set with his arms across his chest and, sometimes forgetting where he was, glower admonishingly at spectator-section extras for starting up conversations between takes.

In the sixth week of trial, Joe Grife sought to introduce testimony that was perhaps more crucial than any other to the prosecution's case. It was almost a *sine qua non*—the testimony of Steven Broder, Dean Harnett's lawyer, that Dean called Broder the day before the murders telling him of his desire to initiate competency hearings against his father, and to dissolve the Foundation.

In the most pitched legal battle of the trial, Smith argued in Judge Penstrake's chambers that the proposed testimony was not only inadmissible hearsay, but that it was totally irrelevant since there was no evidence that Ray Lomak had ever learned of Dean's intentions.

"You're just desperate to give Lomak a motive for these murders," Smith, out of character, pointed a finger at Grife. "And you apparently don't care how you get it in."

After two hours of sophisticated legal theories from both sides began to cloud the judge's chambers like the smell of spent gunpowder drifting across a battlefield, Judge Penstrake overruled Smith's objection to the testimony. An archly flabbergasted Trotter Smith declared, "Judge, I can tell you right now, if you let Broder take the stand, I'm going to be moving for a mistrial."

"And I can tell you, Mr. Smith," Judge Penstrake replied, "that that motion will be denied."

Steven Broder took the stand and testified to Dean Harnett's call—and thus the prosecution got before the jury what they believed to be the motive for the murders of Dean and Jennifer Harnett.

⋆ ⋆ ⋆

Grife called Richard to the stand as the final witness for the prosecution. Smith had objected to Richard's being identified to the jury as anything other than the fiancé of one of the victims, arguing that if the jury were to know he had also been Ray's psychiatrist, they might easily infer that since he was testifying for the prosecution, he must know something about Ray that indicated his guilt. While appreciating the problem, Judge Penstrake still ruled that Grife could ask Richard whether he had been Ray's therapist, in that the question by itself did not violate the doctor-patient privilege. And Smith's fears about prejudicing the jury, she added, were too conjectural.

Smith sat stolidly in the courtroom, planning his counterattack, as Richard told the jury that he had indeed been Ray Lomak's psychiatrist.

Intermittently staring down at the defendant as he spoke, Richard did nothing to hide the accusation in his voice in every answer he gave from the stand. Ray did not flinch beneath the stare, but returned the look with a stony antipathy of his own, for just as long as Richard cared to continue.

Richard's testimony concerning the night of the murders contradicted the hypothesis posed by Smith in his cross-examination of deputy coroner Hakato that Dean and Jenny could have been killed as early as 4:30, which was before Ray had left the Foundation's headquarters for the ranch. Jenny had not left for her father's home, Richard testified, until 8:15 P.M.

The only other incident Richard was allowed to testify to was the windy night in May when Richard and Jenny saw a man on the beach peering up at the apartment.

Q. "And who was that man?" Grife asked.

A. "I can't give a positive identification. But from the dress and especially the unusual hat, I can give you my good-faith belief it was Raymond Lomak."

Q. "Did you ever confront Mr. Lomak about this?" Grife asked.

"Your Honor, I hate to object, particularly in a trial before a jury," Smith said, "but if this occurred during a therapy session, I believe any conversation that may have taken place would be privileged."

Ray leaned over and whispered urgently in Smith's ear. Before Judge Penstrake could rule, Smith called up, "May we have a moment, Your Honor?"

"Yes, of course."

After a quick consultation with Ray, Smith said, "Your Honor, my client waives his patient privilege regarding this matter."

Grife repeated the question and Richard answered, "Yes, I did, Mr. Grife. Ray Lomak denied it was he."

At the end of his cross-examination, Smith asked with a friendly glint in his eye, "You wouldn't think about taking liberties with the truth about this 8:15 P.M., would you, Dr. Pomerantz?"

A. "Mr. Smith, I think it's obvious to everyone in this courtroom that you do your homework, but if you'll look at the police reports that I'm sure you've been provided with," Richard said without a puff of irritation, "you'll see that long before Dr. Hakato's testimony at this trial, I told the police Jenny left my place around 8:15 P.M."

"Thank you, doctor," Smith smiled. "I guess I'll have to stay up even later at night than I do."

After Smith sat down and Richard left the stand, Grife conferred briefly at the prosecution table with Lt. Bollinger, then rose and, to Ray Lomak's noticeable relief, announced: "The People rest, Your Honor."

✶ ✶ ✶

Principally to rebut the accusation implicit in Richard's testimony, Trotter Smith decided to commence the defense's case with testimony which, as far as could be determined, was bereft of legal precedent. Smith proposed to call several inveterate defense psychiatrists to testify that based on their personal examinations of Ray Lomak which Smith had had them conduct individually, they seriously doubted Lomak presently had the requisite tendencies, predisposition or emotional makeup to commit a premeditated murder. Ray Lomak, they believed, was a rehabilitated man.

Grife, aghast at the mere suggestion of such testimony, called for another conference in chambers.

"Judge," Grife pleaded, "as Mr. Smith very well knows, in addition to a lot of legal scholars, many psychiatrists themselves believe psychiatric testimony has no place in a courtroom, even where there's a defense of insanity or diminished mental capacity. And in *those* defenses, the defendant is never claiming he didn't commit the act. The only issue is whether he had the necessary state of mind to be fully responsible. When we're talking about state of mind, at least psychiatrists have some training and expertise in this area. But here, Smith wants to have his shrinks testify they don't think Lomak *committed* the act. There's absolutely no authority for this. This is ridiculous."

"I have to tell you, Mr. Smith," Judge Penstrake said respectfully, putting on the silver-rimmed glasses that hung from a chain around her neck, "that what you propose to do is quite novel."

"Your Honor," Smith retorted, "if psychiatrists are permitted to testify to a person's state of mind, and if we acknowledge that all conduct springs *from* state of mind, why is it so ridiculous for a psychiatrist to testify that because of the *lack* of a particular state of mind, certain conduct would have been very unlikely?"

"Because it is," Grife muttered.

"I don't think it's unreasonable at all," Smith continued confidently. "Certainly, a neurologist would be permitted to testify that a paraplegic defendant wouldn't have had the capacity to perform a certain physical act. But acts aren't dependent only on physical capability, they're dependent on mental capability as well. Would anyone question the right of a psychiatrist to testify he didn't believe a mentally dull defendant had sufficient intelligence to perpetrate a highly complex corporate fraud? And if he can testify to intelligence, why can't he testify to other conditions of the mind that would make other conduct unlikely?"

"An extremely interesting, although exotic, argument, Mr. Smith," Judge Penstrake smiled appreciatively. "I've never heard it made before. I'm going to have to think about this one overnight."

The next morning Judge Penstrake stated that, although she had serious reservations about the validity of such psychiatric testimony, she believed that Smith had made a case for its admissibility, and that she would allow it in—but only with the proviso that defendant Lomak also agree to be interviewed by psychiatrists chosen by the prosecution.

After Smith's three psychiatrists, not one of whom had ever testified on the side of the prosecution, offered their testimony on Lomak's behalf, Grife would, in the rebuttal phase of the trial one week later, call his three psychiatrists who, not coincidentally, had never once in their own careers testified for anyone *but* the prosecution. Sounding as sober and thoughtful as the three before them, they informed the jury of Ray's "violence prone personality." Richard shrank in his spectator's seat, ashamed of what he felt was just a parade of hired guns from both sides of the courtroom and of the burlesque this type of courtroom psychiatry made of his profession.

In the seventh week of trial, Smith called the first of his only three non-psychiatric witnesses. In twenty minutes, Smith and that witness, Treak Johnson, altered the complexion of the entire trial.

At Smith's private insistence, leggy Treak Johnson left her short dresses at home and came to court instead in the navy-blue pleated skirt and white blouse she had left Long Island in three years earlier. (A few days before, Smith had employed a small video-taping company to set up their camera equipment in his temporarily established office suite next to his room at the Biltmore Hotel, and used it to show Treak exactly what she would look like in court. Nervous habits were spotted; an appearance of sincerity and forthrightness encouraged. Ray Lomak would go through the same procedure before he testified, but back in his jail cell.)

In court, with her hands folded in her lap, Treak spoke softly from the stand.

Q. "You have been a companion of Ray Lomak's over the last year, is that right?" Smith asked, going to the far side of the courtroom, forcing her to speak up clearly and more compellingly.

A. "Yes."

Q. "You have been a paid companion of his?"

Treak lowered her eyes.

A. "Yes, sir."

Q. "Where do you live, Miss Johnson?"

A. "Santa Monica. 521 Seafarer Avenue."

Q. "Miss Johnson, this jury has heard testimony from Dr. Pomerantz that Jennifer Harnett did not leave for her father's ranch until 8:15 the night of August 20. By use of a scaled map, there has been a stipulation that the distance from Dr. Pomerantz's residence to the ranch is approximately twenty-eight miles."

A. "Yes sir."

Q. "Therefore, I think it would be fair to assume that Jennifer would probably not have arrived at the ranch before 9:00."

Treak nodded.

Q. "Do you understand that you've sworn under oath to tell the truth?"

A. "Yes, I know that."

Smith paused, and looked sternly at Treak Johnson.

Q. "Where was Ray Lomak on the night of August 20?"

A. "He was with me at my place. It was a Friday night, and that's the night Ray always comes over," she said, adding two days to the truth.

Q. "What time did he arrive?"

A. "The same time as always, 8:30. He's never even five minutes late. He's funny that way."

Q. "And where was he at 9:00, around the time Jennifer Harnett would have arrived at her father's ranch?"

A. "With me."

Q. "And where was Ray Lomak at 10:00, when Mrs. Kirkham said she saw a car speeding away from the Harnett ranch?"

A. "He was with me, Mr. Smith."

Q. "And at 10:19, when the ambulance arrived?"

A. "He was with me until almost midnight."

Q. "Do you swear that's the truth, Miss Johnson?"

A. "Yes, sir. I swear to God it's the truth."

Trotter Smith sat down amidst the silence of nearly one hundred stunned people in the courtroom. Even Joe Grife, his jaws straining, sat still a moment. He had heard a thousand friends of defendants perjure themselves, but rarely with such an openfaced, convincing sincerity. He snapped out of his own dazed suspension quickly enough, though, and trudging belligerently back and forth between the prosecutor's table and the witness stand, barked questions at Treak Johnson for over an hour. But the more clamorsome his voice, the softer hers became. It was a matter of her word against no one's, and at the end of the hour, exhausted by her silken voice and timid imploring eyes, he sat down with his arms folded, staring at Judge Penstrake.

Out in the parking lot, Richard dodged half a dozen cars and caught up with Treak Johnson as she was getting behind the wheel of her own ten year old Continental and nervously lighting a cigarette.

"Okay, look," Richard panted, "we both know you lied in there, so there's little point in even discussing it. I just want to know what I have to do to get you to come back tomorrow and tell the truth. Did he pay you? I'm sure we can arrange it with Grife so you won't be charged with perjury."

"I wasn't lying. Now please get away from my car," she said with a brass edge one wouldn't have thought possible from the woman who had just been on the stand.

"Of course you were lying. Like I said, there's no sense in our debating the point. I'm here to bargain, understand? Did he threaten you?"

From the look on her face, Richard could see he had hit it on his second try.

"Don't you see, the only way he can harm you is if he's set free. Tell the truth, and he can't hurt you. He'll go to prison."

Treak Johnson looked up at Richard with an almost pitying smile and, just before pulling away, said, "He will, huh? How long you figure before they let him out this time?"

✶ ✶ ✶

Richard tried calling Treak Johnson, but she wasn't answering the phone. Twice he went to her house, and the one time her car was parked in the driveway, she wouldn't open the door. That weekend, Richard sat out on the Malibu Pier with an unwatched fishing line flung over the rail, trying to devise ways to break her story. By Sunday morning he thought he had it.

When he showed up at the Grifes' green-shingled home in Pacific Palisades, Joe was directing his wife out of the garage as he did every Sunday morning.

"More to the left. Okay. Okay. More to the left. *Turn it to the left!*" he shouted in a moment of unwarranted panic. When he saw

Richard, he held up his hand to his wife to halt. She always indulged his sense of importance over this weekly procedure.

"Listen, Joe, we can't completely discredit Johnson's story," Richard started right in on the man who didn't require morning pleasantries, "but we might be able to maul it up pretty good."

Grife looked from the car to Richard. "Yeah? How's that?"

"My guess is that the first thing Lomak would have thought of after he got away from the ranch that night was to try and set up an alibi for where he was that evening. He probably went over to Treak Johnson's immediately, but it seems to me he would have called first to make sure she was there."

Expressionless, Grife gazed across the street at a neighbor mowing his lawn, and Richard asked, impatiently, "Well? You with me so far?"

"Yeah. Yeah, go on. I'm listening."

"Okay. Now the thing is this. I've already checked this out. Palos Verdes and Santa Monica are in different toll call zones, and the phone company would have a record for any call made between those two areas—you know, for billing message units. Okay? Palos Verdes is just a tiny part of L.A. County, so if we can find a record of someone calling Treak Johnson's number around 10:00 from a Palos Verdes phone booth, or from anywhere en route, I think you could be pretty persuasive arguing to the jury that it would have taken an incredible coincidence for that someone to be anyone other than Ray Lomak."

Grife rolled his tongue around his mouth awhile and asked, "Why would the phone company keep records on a public phone booth? They get the money right there, they don't have to bill anyone."

"Well, we'll find out with one call to the phone company Monday morning," Richard said. "My hunch is that they do keep records. How else would they know if the right amount of money is being turned in from those boxes to the company?"

When Grife looked at Richard, there was even some hint of a congratulatory smile.

"We'll call first thing tomorrow," he said.

"And if the answer's yes," Richard smiled back, "we'll have to determine every major driving route Ray could possibly have taken, and give those street names to General Telephone so they can check the records of the public phones along the way."

Grife nodded, and Richard slapped him on the shoulder. "Great day for a drive," Richard said. He waved good-bye to Mrs. Grife, and halfway to his car heard Joe call after him, "We take Sunset. Very pretty."

General Telephone in Los Angeles did indeed keep a computerized record of toll calls made from all public phone booths, the time of day the calls were made, and the length of each call.

Richard, Lt. Bollinger, and Sgt. Hubbard spent most of that Monday night searching out the routes Ray was likely to have used between the ranch and Treak Johnson's residence.

Pens and note pads in hand, they wound their way down from Tex's ranch in the hills, first to Palos Verdes' intimate main plaza, with its center fountain replica of Bologna, Italy's La Fontana del Nettuno, and then on to less precious scenery as they moved away from the idyllic peninsula, north toward Santa Monica.

The next morning, Sgt. Hubbard took a list of streets, boulevards, and designated stretches of Pacific Coast Highway to an executive at General Telephone headquarters in Santa Monica. Within an hour a computer chuffed out the information that 375-7983, the number at a phone booth outside an Arco service station not far from Palos Verdes' shopping district, had been the initiating point of a call made to 458-0216, Treak Johnson's number, at 10:08 P.M. on the night of August 20. The call had lasted less than a minute.

When Richard learned of the find, he was very excited. But there was no smile—if anything, he had only a deeper feeling of contempt, and loss, and rage. At home, he walked the beach, through the razor chill of the December night.

The following day, with the permission of Judge Penstrake, Grife recalled Treak Johnson to the stand for a new round of cross-examination. Richard sat poker-straight in his spectator's seat, his eyes fixed as often on the back of Ray's head as on the witness. After marking the General Telephone record as an exhibit, Grife asked:

Q. "Miss Johnson, People's exhibit number 43, this phone company record here, indicates that someone called your residence at 10:08 P.M. on the night of August 20. The call was made from a public phone booth in Palos Verdes, stipulated by counsel to be exactly two and six-tenths miles from Tex Harnett's ranch. Who was that who called you?"

Treak glanced uneasily at Trotter Smith. Smith's own look darkened as he realized his star witness may have possibly been lying.

A. "I don't know," Treak said softly.

Q. "Well, do you know anyone who lives or works in that area? Anyone who might have called you from Palos Verdes?"

A. "Not off the top of my head, no."

Q. "You were in the middle of your weekly exercise with Ray Lomak," Grife continued with raw sarcasm, "and someone interrupted you. You don't remember who?"

A. "That was months ago," she answered, regaining some composure. "It could have been anyone. Let me see. There's a guy named Tom. I think he mentioned living in that area. You know —the Rancho Palos Verdes, Rolling Hills, Portugese Bend area. The last time I saw him was about a month ago. He said he was going to move back east. And there's an older gentleman named Edgar. I believe he's a widower who lives alone in a big mansion in that area. If you want any more information about these people, I honestly don't have it."

Q. "Do you at least have their phone numbers?" Grife asked, a smirk for the jury's ingestion.

A. "No, I don't need theirs. They just need mine."

Q. "This older fellow named Edgar, who lives by himself in a mansion, does he normally sneak down to the Arco gas station to call you?"

Treak smiled saucily. "Sneakiness is part of the fun. I've seen kinkier."

"I'm sure you have. No further questions, Miss Johnson."

Realizing how rigidly he had been sitting, Richard let out a knot of breath and relaxed, nodded at Grife, and for the first time in days allowed himself a small smile. Although Treak Johnson had rebounded somewhat, exhibiting a greater sense of balance than he would have expected, Richard felt that Joe Grife's handling of her on the witness stand had infected her credibility with substantial doubt, and that the phone call evidence had introduced the aroma of a contrived defense.

CHAPTER 5

SKETCH ARTISTS FOR THE THREE NETWORKS SPIR-
ited their pencils across pads like fevered war correspondents the
morning Ray Lomak pushed himself back from the defense table
and walked briskly to the witness stand. The pose they all chose
to show to millions of Americans in their living rooms that night
was the one Ray struck the moment he sat down in the elevated
chair, and maintained for much of the questioning—leaning forward, his eyes unblinking and intense (as though they, and not his
ears, were his devices for listening), one hand taking hold of the
stem of the microphone before each answer as if afraid someone

was going to snatch it away from him.

Trotter Smith's first question was the one he had told Ray he could count on. He asked it from over near the jury box so that Ray, in looking at him, was also showing his face completely and clearly to the twelve jurors.

Q. "Ray . . ."

Smith paused, gripped the rail of the jury box firmly with his left hand, and returned Ray's keen look with his own, staring at his client as if he were not his lawyer, but rather on the opposing side—a hard-bitten detective, through with the balderdash and wanting a straight answer. "Raymond Lomak, did you kill Dean and Jennifer Harnett?"

A. "No! No, I did not," Ray almost shouted, then lowered his voice. "I swear in the name of God I didn't. I'm innocent. This isn't fair, it isn't just. I'm being punished for my past. I—"

"Objection, Your Honor," Grife croaked with disgust. "The question was simply—"

"No! You can't object," Ray said, pulling the microphone closer. "Don't let him object, Your Honor. He's put me through hell. He should be disbarred, this man."

"All right, that's enough," Judge Penstrake interceded, holding up her hand.

"Your Honor, the grounds for my objection—"

"Your Honor, I'm sure my client—"

"If people knew what getting out of prison—"

The court reporter, a petite middle-aged woman named Peggy Phelps, slumped back from her stenograph machine in futility. "Your Honor, I can't take down what twenty people are saying at once."

For the first time in the trial, Judge Penstrake rapped her gavel. "Yes, gentlemen. Let's calm down here. . . . On my own motion, I'm going to instruct the jury to disregard those last remarks by the witness concerning Mr. Grife. Hereafter, Mr. Lomak, please confine yourself to answering your counsel's questions. However, within those limits, I will let you express yourself as fully as possible."

"Thank you, Your Honor," Ray said. "I feel you're conducting this trial with great dignity. Thank you."

Penstrake nodded listlessly at Ray, and instructed Smith to carry on. Smith did so with considerable artistry, taking Ray hour by hour through the day and evening of the murders, making a special point of directing Ray into a discussion of his laudable activities that afternoon at the Foundation.

"At 4:30 I believe I was still on the phone with Reverend Bryant in Montgomery," Ray informed the jury. "Mr. Harnett had given me permission to talk about the possibility of giving some help to a new senior citizens center down there. It would have been the largest one in Alabama."

Where possible, Smith asked questions that allowed for emotional answers. Ray was at his best when swept up by his own ardor.

Q. "Did you hate Dean Harnett?"

Ray shook his head as if stunned by the suggestion.

A. "Oh, no. No, sir—the time I talked to him about the cocaine, I was just trying to help him. I felt he was very lonely and mixed up. It's a very hard thing having a great man for a father."

Q. "Did you hate Jenny Harnett?"

A. "We were friends. Very *close* friends. Jenny drove me to my appointments with Dr. Pomerantz. That was of course before Dr. Pomerantz turned her against me and before the parole board declared Dr. Pomerantz incompetent and—"

Grife's motion to strike Ray Lomak's gratuitous comments about Richard was granted. Again, Judge Penstrake instructed Ray Lomak to restrict himself to only answering Trotter Smith's questions. This time her admonition was more forceful, and Ray did not thank her.

At the next recess Smith advised Ray: "Look, I know you're angry at Dr. Pomerantz and Grife, and some of the others opposing you here, but try not to show quite so much hostility on the stand, all right, Ray?"

"I thought you wanted me to be sincere and forthright."

Smith thought for a moment, with a frown. "Well, when it comes to people you don't like, let's just say sincer*ish.*"

Smith kept Ray on the stand for two full days, and by the end, the transcript of his testimony was embroidered by nine mentions of church and community projects he was involved with around the country, five references to Harnett College, two quotations from Luke, one from Matthew, and fourteen utterances of the Lord's name. When Smith finally concluded his examination, nodding, "You may take the witness," Grife jumped to his feet like an eighteen-year-old signing up to fight the Huns.

Q. "Mr. Lomak, three psychiatrists brought to this courtroom by your attorney testified you were a rehabilitated man, and remorseful for your crime twenty-two years ago. I'm curious to know what that means. Have you ever once taken flowers to the grave sites of Paul Morrison, Laura—"

"Ho!" Smith hooted, actually with a laugh, he was so jolted. "Ob-*jec*tion, Your Honor. Objection, objection. May we approach the bench, *please?!*"

At the bench, Smith closed his eyes and pinched the bridge of his nose like a man who has just seen double.

"Joe, I don't believe you asked that. I really don't."

"Your Honor," Grife fulminated, "the defense opened up the matter of rehabilitation on direct examination, and it was allowed into the record. I'm entitled to cross-examine any point brought up on direct."

Dorothy Penstrake remained silent for a moment, looking genuinely disturbed, and it was partly over her own judgment.

"Mr. Grife, I did allow the psychiatrists to testify to rehabilitation and remorse," she said. "But those references were only admissible as a partial basis for their ultimate conclusion that Mr. Lomak couldn't have committed these murders. I may have made a mistake allowing that testimony in. But in any event, you can't now use those references to rehabilitation and remorse as your anchor for dredging up details of the past obviously intended to inflame the jury."

"Your Honor," Joe Grife began . . .

"I don't even want to hear argument on this point, Mr. Grife. Your question was flagrantly objectionable. Proceed to another line of questioning."

Back behind his table, Grife was only more fired.

Q. "Mr. Lomak, if you didn't feel any hostility toward Dean Harnett, as you claim, why did you ask Jim Brill and Nancy Wyatt to spy on him?"

A. "I didn't ask them to 'spy.' I asked them if there were things his father should know about. It's important for fathers and sons to talk about problems they have."

Q. "Dean Harnett was twenty-eight years old, Mr. Lomak. He was an adult."

Ray kept his eyes acutely on Grife, listening for more, and when none came, said, "You haven't asked a question, Mr. Grife."

Q. "All right, let me be a little more accommodating. Just one day after the murders, you suddenly needed new tires on your car. Was that really a day to go shopping for automobile tires? Weren't you the least bit upset or grieving over the deaths of Tex Harnett's children?"

A. "They were gone, they were in God's hands—"

Q. "And you needed new tires. Right. How did you go about finding a buyer for the old ones—a buyer whose name you testified on direct examination you don't even know, or anything else about him?"

A. "I tacked a few flyers up on trees in the neighborhood."

Q. "And how long did you spend with this mystery man? How long did the sale take?"

A. "I'm not sure, I suppose about half an hour."

Q. "And in half an hour's time, his name just never came up?"

A. "No."

Q. "Or where he lived?"

A. "No."

Q. "Or where he worked?"

Ray paused. "I think he said he worked for a home security company. One of those places that installs alarms and then keeps an eye on your house."

At the first opportunity, when the proceedings were momentarily interrupted for the bailiff to quiet curiosity seekers in the hallway who had not been able to get seats, Richard passed a note via a spectator in front of him, up to Grife's table. Grife read it, and asked as his next question, "What did your father do for a living, Mr. Lomak—in between his two jobs at service stations in Pasadena?"

Ray looked at Grife, his eyes surrendering nothing, and answered calmly, "He worked for a home security company."

In his final summation, Grife would argue that people fabricating stories often freckled them with details from their own past, small particulars that sprang quickly to mind.

Lomak repeated his direct examination testimony that he left the ranch for Treak Johnson's, a little over twenty miles away, about 8:00 P.M. on the night of the murders, explaining his "I'd rather not say" statement to Bollinger as a matter of embarrassment over his visit to a prostitute. Ray's uncomplicated version of his activities on the night of August 20 gave Grife, who nonetheless made a long effort, little room for entrapping cross-examination.

Q. "You were quite familiar with the workings of the pool out at the Harnett ranch, weren't you, Mr. Lomak?" Grife switched directions, snapping back the pages of his yellow pad as he searched for his scribbled questions.

A. "Yes, I was. I don't deny it."

Q. "Because you lived for some time out there, right?"

A. "Yes, Mr. Harnett had been good enough to—"

Q. "Where exactly in the house did you stay?"

A. "In the cook's old room."

Q. "The whole time?"

A. "Later I moved to a room off the back garden."

Q. "Right. That was Dean's old room, wasn't it?"

A. "Yes."

Q. "You kind of took Dean's place in a way, didn't you? Sort of became a son to Tex Harnett?"

Ray did not answer right away. He glanced over at Tex, who sat near the back of the courtroom looking down at his hands in his lap, his liver spotted forehead marred with grief. Tex picked vacantly at a diamond ring as though it were worthless glass.

A. "With all respect to Mr. Harnett, I don't think it's fair to—"

Q. "I'll withdraw the question. You and Dean Harnett were in competition for Tex Harnett's money, isn't that the fact of the matter?"

A. "Money's never meant anything to me."

Q. "Just as soon see it burned?"

A. "The world might be better off that way."

Q. "Where did you get that suit you're wearing today?"

A. "I don't honestly remember. Someplace downtown, I think. Bullworth's or something?"

Q. "Bullock's?"

A. "Yes. I think that's it."

Q. "That's a fairly high-priced department store, isn't it?"

A. "I don't know. I suppose it is."

Q. "What kind of car do you presently drive, Mr. Lomak?"

Ray licked his lips anxiously, a gesture that always made Trotter Smith shudder inside.

A. "I have to visit groups that—"

Q. "Excuse me, but the question was what kind of car you drove."

A. "A New Yorker."

Q. "I'm not too familiar with those fancier cars," Grife said, just a little bitterly. "Is that a Chrysler New Yorker?"

A. "Yes."

Ray went on to explain that his leasing of the Chrysler was to secure the respect of the people he dealt with on Foundation business.

Q. "The Harnett Foundation was your entire life, wasn't it?" Joe Grife continued, a rolled-up sheet of legal pad paper in his hand, like an agitated bettor at a track with his racing form.

A. "Well, you see, the work we do—"

Q. "Just answer the question yes or no, Mr. Lomak," Joe Grife interrupted sharply.

"Your Honor," Trotter Smith began with an assured intonation that portended authority. "I know of no rule or law in this entire land that says a witness has to answer *any* question with a yes or no answer. That's just a legal myth that curiously keeps perpetuating itself."

Judge Penstrake cogitated a few seconds, then with a bemused smile, nodded. "You may answer the question, Mr. Lomak, the way you intended to," she said.

A. "The work we do is very important," Ray started over again. "And so the Foundation is very important to me. But I don't know exactly what you mean by 'my entire life.' "

Q. "What I mean is that you worked there from eight in the morning until ten at night. Often seven days a week, many times when no one else was there, isn't that true?"

A. "I believe in hard work, if that's what you mean."

Q. "It was your home. You had *nothing* else. Isn't that right?" Ray's neck reddened.

A. "I've always had a lot of friends. And I play the clarinet."

Q. "Who are your friends, Mr. Lomak? Tell me the names of three close friends." Grife's eyes had grown brutal.

A. "Mr. Harnett—"

Q. "Your boss, and director of the Harnett Foundation. Who else?"

A. "Miss Johnson—"

Q. "A paid prostitute. Yes, who else?"

A. "Um . . ."

It was a grim silence in the courtroom as Ray tried in vain to think of a third friend.

Q. "Dean Harnett was going to take the Foundation away from

you, wasn't he?"

A. "He never told me so."

Q. "No, but you knew he was going to initiate competency hearings against his father in an attempt to dissolve the Harnett Foundation. You knew that, didn't you?"

A. "No. How would I have known something like that?"

At the recess, Joe Grife walked over to Ray Lomak at the defense table and said with a deep quiet anger, "I don't know how you knew . . . but you did."

★ ★ ★

In a day and a half of cross-examination, Grife captured bloody little high ground for his efforts. As each hour on the witness stand passed, Ray Lomak looked more confident and at times actually grateful for the chance to prove his innocence. Richard could only sympathize with Grife, knowing the prosecutor had a man on the stand who probably believed most of what he was saying.

When Ray finally sat down and Tex Harnett shuffled somberly to the stand as the defense's last witness, Tex put his hand on Ray's shoulder as he passed, obviously more convinced than ever of his innocence.

If Trotter Smith had been unable to establish much rapport with Tex in the privacy of his office, he did not let the opportunity escape him a second time. As Tex answered his questions with simple, rural candor, Smith himself waxed more and more southern. For the first time in the trial, he took his suit coat off.

Q. "Did Ray Lomak seek *you* out, Mr. Harnett, or were you the one to introduce yourself to *him*?"

A. "Why, I asked to see Ray. He's not the kind goes pushin' himself on you, no sir."

Q. "He never asked if he could stay at your house awhile?"

A. "Hell's bells, no. Oh, excuse me, Your Honor," Tex said, looking up at the judge, who smiled back understandingly. "Bad habit of mine. No, sir, I asked him to stay."

Q. "Just a matter of plain old hospitality," Smith added, taking on the very slight tinge of his boyhood southern accent.

A. "That's right."

Q. "Ray minded his p's and q's, did he? He was always respectful of your family, and the fact he was a guest in your house?"

"Objection, Your Honor, the question is leading," Grife said.

"Overruled. You may answer."

A. "He always acted properly."

Q. "Never once lied to you, did he, Mr. Harnett? No two ways about that, now is there?"

"Same objection, Your Honor."

"Overruled," Penstrake said mechanically.

A. "Never lied to me. No, sir."

Smith put his foot up on the base of the witness stand, and pretty soon he and Tex were just two good ol' boys jawin' away up there.

Q. "About how many sees down the road is the Walters place?"

A. "Oh, guess 'bout two."

Q. "Two sees, you say? Well, if a car were—"

"Your Honor," Grife felt compelled to speak up, "I have no idea what these two men are talking about."

Judge Penstrake had herself been captivated by the rather soothing lilt of the conversation, and only now leaned forward to ask, "What are 'two sees' exactly, Mr. Smith?"

"Two sees, Your Honor," Trotter said with seductive charm. "Look up the road as far as you can see, and that's one see. Go to that spot and look again, and that's two sees."

The love of quaintness registered itself on every face in the courtroom. Judge Penstrake, as taken by it all as anyone, inquired deadpan, "Does it make any difference, Mr. Smith, whether you're nearsighted or farsighted?"

In the course of the afternoon, Smith established before the jury just what he wanted—that Tex Harnett, the father of the victims, the man who had spent more time with Ray Lomak than anyone, would have mortgaged his own life on Ray's innocence.

On cross-examination, Grife asked Tex if Ray had been the one who told him about his son Dean's gambling on the horses. Tex scratched foggily at his thin strands of hair and answered, "Well, I don't 'xactly recall how I first found out, but . . . but I know I talked to Dean myself about it. I . . ."

Tex's thick neck began to pulse, and his eyes became a little wet.

". . . We talked between ourselves, you see. We . . . we were closer'n a lot of people thought."

Tex looked away, and Grife let the question lie. When asked about the alleged hostility between Ray and his son, Tex reflected upon the past with the softest light, telling the jury that if the two had had differences, they had simply been between two hard-headed but sincere people. Grife knew better than to push or badger this witness in front of the empathizing jury. He was just as happy to let Tex leave the stand as soon as possible, and to hear Smith announce: "The defense rests, Your Honor."

Outside the courtroom Grife grumbled to Richard, "I don't understand that Tex Harnett. Defending Ray Lomak."

"He has to believe in Lomak's innocence," Richard said. "For him to believe anything else would be admitting to himself that he was partly responsible for his own children's deaths. Who else brought Ray Lomak into their world in the first place?"

CHAPTER 6

ON THE WEEKEND BEFORE FINAL SUMMATIONS
were scheduled to commence, Trotter Smith met with Ray back
in his jail cell and told him, "If the jury were to vote right now,
I believe they'd convict you."

Ray was stunned. "But how could they?"

"Because I think the prosecution has offered enough evidence
to make them believe you did it. But fortunately for us, the question of whether or not you did it isn't the issue."

"It's *not?*" Ray said, totally perplexed. "What are you talking
about?"

"Something really very simple that virtually no defense lawyer in this country seems to have a complete grasp of."

Ray stood up. "Wait, what are you trying to do here? I'm not a guinea pig, you know."

"Calm down," Trotter said, and picking up his coat, tossed out with a smile, "Listen to my final argument."

Across town in the Grifes' modest home, Richard was a guest at a dinner of lamb chops, corn on the cob and baked potatoes.

"If Lomak walks out of court, it will be the greatest parody of justice ever to come out of an American courtroom," Richard offered.

"It would be terrible," Claire Grife shook her head.

"Smith will be clever. Apparently he always is," Joe Grife acknowledged, rolling his corn liberally in the butter dish, "but the one thing he can't change is the facts. Lomak is so guilty, he stinks up the courtroom."

"The main thing that concerns me," Richard said, a nagging crease to his brow, "is that these facts you talk about are all circumstantial."

Joe Grife patted his mouth with his napkin. "Circumstantial evidence cases are tough to win, but over thirty years, even a common workhorse like me learns a trick or two. Give the jury a nice little comparison of what circumstantial evidence really is and you'd be surprised how far it goes."

"For a common workhorse, I hear you've won your share of the big ones," Richard said.

Grife shrugged. "Well, one thing I've always found pretty successful down the years is my sort of describing circumstantial evidence for the jury like the spelling of a word. One letter by itself could be the first letter of thousands of words. But with the addition of each letter, see, you narrow the number of words those letters can belong to. Pretty soon, there's just one word you can be spelling.

"Now likewise, one piece of circumstantial evidence, standing all by its lonesome," Joe Grife said, pausing to shake some more salt on his ear of corn, "may point towards innocence as well as guilt. But with the addition of a lot of other pieces of evidence, eventually they can only spell just one word, and that's *guilty.*"

★ ★ ★

In his opening argument before a jammed courtroom that was flush with moral support for his task, Joe Grife told the seven woman, five man jury that Ray Lomak not only had the means and the opportunity, but only he had the motive to kill Dean and Jennifer Harnett.

Deciding to save his more thumping, emotional appeal for his closing argument, when he would have the last word (after Trotter Smith's summation), Grife summarized the testimony of the key witnesses in the case. Rarely leaving the lectern, which held his sketchy notes, he first got the psychiatric testimony out of the way, dismissing all of it (candidly including the testimony of his own psychiatric witnesses) as "twentieth century witchcraft" and "as useless to this case as buttons on a hat."

The prosecution, he went on, had not only presented by far the greater bulk of the evidence in the trial, but the state's witnesses had given solid testimony that without exception pointed inescapably to the defendant's guilt.

Leaving his lectern one of the few times during his argument, he approached Ray Lomak, who sat motionless at the counsel table. "Now, let's look at the defense," Joe Grife gestured toward Lomak and Trotter Smith. "Other than Mr. Lomak himself—who you could expect to lie to you—their only important witness was Treak Johnson. And the yarn she told you folks from that witness stand, even her mother wouldn't believe," he scoffed.

"How convenient her testimony was about these two mysterious men she claims she used to see from the Palos Verdes area— doesn't know their last names or phone numbers or their addresses. What a joke. One of them is now supposedly back east, and the other is an elderly man who lives alone in a mansion with probably two phones in every room, but who still has to go out in his robe and slippers to an Arco gas station to call her.

"Even if these two phantom customers of hers do exist—and I'm sure none of you believe they do—isn't it an astounding coincidence that one of them would have called her from a location just two and six-tenths miles from the Harnett ranch at 10:08 P.M. on August 20, which is around the exact time that prosecution witnesses put Ray Lomak in the same area?"

Joe Grife concluded his forty-five minute address to the jury by telling them that the prosecution had presented a very strong case of the defendant's guilt and now it was their job to see that justice was done.

★ ★ ★

Commencing his final summation that afternoon, Trotter Smith stood in the very center of the courtroom, looking about him like a Kentucky rancher who knows that all the terra he surveys is his. He smiled briefly, as if to himself, and gazed out the window toward the San Gabriel Mountains east of Los Angeles.

"You know, just about this time in Kentucky," he began in his deep, dulcet voice, "you see strips of white canvas covering the land for miles and miles—covering that broadleaf burley tobacco. Pretty soon, on toward spring, the strips come off, and down along the Kentucky River the redbud and jonquils come out, and you even start to smell those honeysuckle vines and cedar trees."

Grife swiveled his chair away from the jury and looked at the spectators with a barely perceptible shake of his head, as though asking them if the jury could possibly be buying such alligator dung.

"Like I'm sure *you* do," Smith went on, "I have a great love for my home, and it's not often that I leave it." That was quite simply a lie. Smith had not acquired a national reputation by trying grand-theft auto cases in places like Lexington and Louisville, though that fact had not prevented him just five months earlier from beginning a final summation with the exact same homesick words to a jury in Philadelphia.

"I leave it only when I feel there is a great and important reason to do so," he continued melodiously, as if telling a story to twelve bibbed children. "Only when there is danger of a terrible injustice being done.

"I've come to California because, based on the evidence, Raymond Frederick Lomak is innocent.

"According to the prosecution, there's only one side to this case —theirs. But like Eddie, a ranch hand I know back in Kentucky, says, 'No matter how thin I make my pancakes, they always have two sides.' "

Smith looked at the jury a moment, then began a slow, pensive walk about the territory.

"My good friend, Joe Grife," he said, as Grife slouched irritably in his seat, "wants you to convict Ray Lomak because, as Joe says, 'who else could have committed these murders?' As long as no other suspect has appeared on the scene, why then, Ray Lomak must have done it.

"Just must have," Smith said with a small, ironic smile. "Well, that's not quite how our system of justice works. We don't come into court to determine if the defendant is the most likely suspect, and then hang him from a lamppost in the town square, providing no one better has stumbled along. We're here to determine if the defendant has been proven guilty. Proven beyond a reasonable doubt."

He turned to Grife and held up his hands. "Joe, where's the proof? The man who saw Ray driving away from the Harnett ranch just minutes after the murders? He also saw a fire truck that didn't exist. He lied, Joe, and when this trial is over I'm going to ask your office to file a criminal complaint for perjury against him."

The testimony of Elaine Kirkham, Smith dismissed lightly, in that she hadn't seen the defendant driving away from the ranch, only a car that looked "like" the defendant's. "How many of you," he asked the jurors, "can even in broad daylight, much less at night, distinguish from a brief look at a distance the various models of a Buick or a Chevrolet, a Chrysler or a Plymouth? Since there's no indication that Mrs. Kirkham is any kind of a car enthusiast, and given the power of suggestion witnesses are subject to, we simply cannot give meaningful weight to such testimony."

Smith went down the list of witnesses for the prosecution, reminding the jury of each and every fissure that had appeared in their testimony once subjected to cross-examination.

"And what about the one person we *couldn't* cross-examine?" he asked, his eyes dancing tantalizingly. "The woman who called the ambulance. Let's accept, for the time being, the prosecution's theory that that was Esperanza Gomar, the housekeeper. Fine and well, I say. That *all the more* points to Ray Lomak's innocence. Whoever committed these murders, I believe would almost assuredly have seen her. And if that murderer had been a stranger to the Harnett ranch, as I also believe is the case, he would have been much more likely than Ray Lomak to have left a living witness like Esperanza. Would Ray have left her? The one woman who could immediately identify him to the authorities? The answer throws itself upon us. If Ray had been the one to murder Dean and Jenny Harnett, as the prosecution contends, he simply would not have left Esperanza Gomar alive.

"We're talking about a man's life here, ladies and gentlemen. We're talking about possibly sending a man to prison for the rest of his days or even to the gas chamber. And on what evidence? Because Ray Lomak bought new tires for his car shortly after the murders? Well, there's nothing like cross-examination to reduce exaggerated statements to their true dimensions. By the time we had finished with that Mr. Stiegel, who originally claimed Ray's old tires were 'like new,' I think you'll agree we had worn those treads down a good three-sixteenths of an inch.

"And good Lord, think about this a moment. We have absolutely no sure way of knowing who left that small, eleven inch tire track—it could have been the fleeing murderer, and it also could have been someone just out for a drive, someone using Tex Harnett's driveway to turn around in. Yet the prosecution wants you to believe that not only did Ray Lomak leave that tire track, but then—here's what makes my head swim—even though this one solitary tire left the driveway pavement for only a split second, leaving a partial print not even a foot long, Ray Lomak was somehow so aware of the significance of what he had done in that split second that he rushed out to buy four new tires. I don't believe I've ever met or even read about a criminal in my life who would have been so aware of such a minuscule occurrence as that."

Like Grife, Richard could only sit dourly and swallow the frustration of seeing the jury never know why Ray, the man who had two decades earlier been caught because of a shoe print, *would* have been just so aware.

"What about the grandest question of all?" Trotter Smith asked. "The motive. The prosecution claims the murders were committed because just the day before, Dean told his lawyer he wanted the Foundation dissolved, which would have left Ray out in the cold. Yet there isn't *one* scintilla of evidence indicating that Ray ever knew of Dean Harnett's intentions, or his conversation with his lawyer. Don't we still require evidence in this country before we draw conclusions?"

After pouring himself a glass of ice water from the pitcher on the counsel table, Smith continued into his second hour of summation: "And consider this. Ray Lomak was close to the Harnett family. He was familiar with what went on around the house, where things were, what went on in their lives. Isn't that really all that's been proven by the evidence?

"I want you to think about something very, very seriously back in the jury room during your deliberations. And that's this: Couldn't the exact same kind of circumstantial evidence be brought out against you, every one of you, if someone you were closely connected to were murdered? What if a friend whom you've maybe had a argument with were found murdered? Why, I bet you may very well know where that friend hides his front door key, don't you? So it could be shown in court how you could have let yourself into his house. And if that person had been killed with his own gun . . . well, I don't have to finish the scenario, do I? You knew where your friend kept his gun.

"And let's not even talk about something so fussy as a tiny tire track. Your *fingerprints* would be found all over the house. Pay no mind to the fact that you had been to the house many times recently, and that there was every reason for your fingerprints to be found. The prosecutor's not about to point out all the explanations for occurrences that don't fit snugly into his theory.

"And then there would be the phone records. Documentation, mind you, that you placed a call to your friend's spouse at his or her office on the day of the murder. You were just calling to ask how you could patch things up with your friend, but then again it might look like you were calling to discuss dividing up the insurance money and running off together to Mazatlán."

Smith twiddled at one of his silvery temples and said, "It's one thing if a complete stranger is connected to a crime, but when someone is intimately associated with the victim, we must think twice and three times lest we leap to unwarranted conclusions. We are, all of us, linked to the people we know by more than just emotions—we are linked by literally hundreds of tangible, physical shreds that make up our daily lives. And every connection between you and the people you know is potential evidence in a murder trial."

Trotter Smith, within a week after his arrival in Los Angeles, had arranged for two UCLA law students to assist him in the case. One of their jobs was to peruse the transcripts of final arguments to the jury that Joe Grife had made in past trials, to ascertain his methods, style and pet examples.

"Now, Joe Grife is probably going to get up here during his final argument and tell you that circumstantial evidence is like the spelling of a word," Trotter Smith said, winking surreptitiously at Grife. All thunder stolen from his analogy, Grife sat slightly mystified but mostly crestfallen at the prosecution table.

Smith proceeded to give the entire analogy. "But this example would only apply to a case where all or nearly all of the pieces of evidence, when put together, can spell only one word—guilt. It certainly does not apply in a case where there is also solid, credible evidence spelling out the word *innocence.*"

Smith cited such evidence for the defense: Treak Johnson, being just a hired prostitute, would have no motive to commit perjury for a mere customer, Smith argued, and her testimony alone, if believed, was conclusive evidence of Ray Lomak's innocence; Tex Harnett, the victims' own father, who believed in Lomak's innocence; three psychiatrists who gave their experienced, professional opinion that Raymond Lomak was now devoid of the type of antisocial, malevolent instincts necessary for such a cold-blooded murder (while prosecution psychiatrists testified to the contrary, this merely created a stalemate, and the defendant, Smith pointed out, is always entitled to the benefit of the doubt); and lastly, Ray Lomak's fervent denial of guilt from the witness stand and the inability of Joe Grife, on cross-examination, to shatter or even weaken his testimony.

Smith focused sharply on the instruction the judge would give the jury that if one reasonable interpretation of the evidence in the case pointed towards guilt and another towards innocence, they were legally obligated to adopt that interpretation pointing towards innocence.

Smith walked over to the jury box and looked especially at James Cottler, a marketing executive whose articulate answers on *voir dire* and confident carriage seemed to stand out a notch among the twelve jurors, suggesting to Smith that the jury might very well select Cottler as their foreman.

"If any of you is even leaning toward believing Mr. Lomak is guilty, can you honestly say that you are not being influenced, ever so slightly, maybe even only subconsciously, by your knowledge of Mr. Lomak's past conviction? At the beginning of the trial, each of you gave me your solemn oath that you would bring in a verdict based solely on the evidence in *this* case, and I now remind you of that oath. If this case involved a defendant who had been the purest choir boy and was now the most respected citizen in the community, would you convict that person of first-degree murder based on this kind of circumstantial evidence?

"As you leave this courtroom, look over at that defense table and don't just see Mr. Lomak. See yourself in his place. Envision yourself there, and imagine how you would want a jury to weigh *your* life.

"Mr. Jaspin . . . Mr. Clowes . . . Miss Wingert . . ." Moving from one set of eyes to the next, Smith recited each of the jurors' names with the same sureness that he had, in earlier years, shaken hands with all the people at the end of a fund raiser.

Approaching the conclusion of a stirring summation that had provoked the thoughts of everyone in the courtroom (except, apparently, one male juror who watched Smith's presentation much the way a cow looks at a passing train), Smith devoted ten minutes to a discussion of the presumption of innocence and how that hallowed legal presumption protected a defendant unless it was rebutted by proof of guilt beyond a reasonable doubt. Smith went on, "I want each of you to think very . . . *very* carefully about this thing in our system of justice that we call reasonable doubt.

"The prosecution's burden of proving guilt beyond a reasonable doubt, ladies and gentlemen, demands of them a very high standard of proof.

"I'm going to tell you something now that will probably sound shocking, but it happens to be the law. The ultimate issue for you to decide at this trial is *not:* did Raymond Lomak commit these murders, or did he not commit these murders."

Several of the jurors visibly showed their puzzlement at Smith's statement.

"The ultimate issue," Smith went on, "is whether or not the prosecution met its legal burden of proving Raymond Lomak's guilt beyond a reasonable doubt.

"Let's just assume for the sake of argument that one or more of you feel that Raymond Lomak is guilty. Based on the evidence, I believe Ray Lomak is innocent. I do not believe he committed these murders. But let's just assume that, for whatever reason, one or more of you do. Can you possibly believe it *beyond a reasonable doubt?*" Smith asked, bent forward at the waist, his squinting face thrust toward the jurors, as if questioning someone's absolute belief in a Kansas weather forecast.

"Perhaps the doctrine of reasonable doubt can best be put this way," he said, sitting down on a corner of the defense table, posturing himself conversationally. "If the state of mind of a juror in a criminal case is 'I kind of believe that the defendant committed the crime' or 'if I were forced to wager, I'd bet he did,' that is *not* enough. Under the law, if you don't believe in a defendant's guilt beyond a reasonable doubt, you simply have no choice or discretion. You must, you have a legal duty, to return a verdict of not guilty.

"An example I would like to give you illustrating this principle concerns a former congressman from your own backyard here, Charles Wiggins from El Monte, California, who was a member of the House Judiciary Committee during the impeachment proceedings of President Nixon. As you know, many of the White House tapes were played at the hearing, and on several of them Mr. Nixon made statements which could have been construed to be incriminating, but they were not clear-cut. At the time Congressman Wiggins made the statement I am about to read to you, the tape of June the 23rd, 1972—the so-called 'Smoking Gun Tape' where Mr. Nixon made statements which apparently pointed unequivocally towards his participation in the cover-up—had not yet surfaced.

"Wiggins, a lawyer, told his colleagues on the House Judiciary Committee," Smith carried on, flipping open his eyeglasses, and holding up a sheet of paper in front of him, " 'I cannot express adequately the depth of my feeling that this case must be decided according to the law and on no other basis. If we were to decide this case on any other basis than the law and the evidence applicable thereto, we would be doing a greater violence to the Constitution than any misconduct alleged to have been committed by Richard Nixon.'

"Shortly thereafter, the 'Smoking Gun Tape' surfaced.

"Representative Wiggins went on national TV and with his eyes moist, his voice cracking, called for the President's resignation. Several days later, however, he issued this statement:

" 'I have no apology for the position I originally took. I think my position was legally, intellectually and morally correct. The fact that the suspicions against the President were subsequently demonstrated to be true does not make me feel any more kindly toward those who voted on the basis of the facts *then* available.' "

Smith folded up his glasses.

"Let's tie what Congressman Wiggins said into this case. Maybe, just maybe, there is more evidence against Raymond Lomak which has not been presented in this courtroom—hard convincing evidence such as his fingerprints on that crowbar, fingerprints which were somehow missed by the police; or someone who could come into this court and testify, 'I saw Ray Lomak climbing up out of that underground room next to the pool the night of the murders'; or an admission of guilt by Lomak made to some friend. In light of what we have seen about this case, there is absolutely no reason to believe that any such evidence exists. None whatsoever. But maybe, maybe somewhere, it does. The point is that the prosecution *never presented that evidence here in this courtroom.* And since they did not, they have not met their legal burden of proof and therefore, under the law, Mr. Lomak is entitled to a not guilty verdict.

"Ladies and gentlemen of the jury, if there ever was a case based on assumptions, speculation, and suspicion, rather than upon strong, solid, unequivocal evidence, this is a textbook example.

"I now turn my client's destiny over to your fine hands. Because of who Ray Lomak is, I know it will not be an easy task to vote for an acquittal. But I have every confidence that you *will* return a verdict of not guilty, as I know that all twelve of you have the intelligence, the integrity, and the courage to base your verdict solely on the facts in this case and on the law of the land."

After Smith had thanked the jury for their attention and patience, he sat down amidst a heavy silence in the courtroom. Judge Penstrake recessed the case until the following morning at nine, when Joe Grife would deliver his final argument to the jury.

Normally Joe Grife slept as well at night as the peasants from the Caucasus Mountains who lived to one hundred and ten, never curious about the village they heard of eight miles away. But on this night before his final argument, he tossed in his sleep and awakened several times. Just the same, the next day he was fueled with adrenaline, and angry.

In the earthy, curbside view of Joe Grife, Ray Lomak was an evil, irredeemable human being. Defense attorneys had the duty to represent their clients to the best of their ability, but with a client like Raymond Lomak, he asked himself, didn't an emotional line have to be drawn in the sand somewhere? Trotter Smith had not just argued with persuasive logic but—and this is what disturbed Grife—with conviction and flame. Didn't he know that Lomak was guilty?

Because of the adroitness and force of Smith's summation, for the first time Joe Grife envisioned the dreadful specter of Raymond Lomak walking out of court, free to cruelly end more human life.

Grife rose from his chair at the prosecution table and told the jury that when it came to eloquence, he "took a back seat" to Trotter Smith. "But eloquence is not evidence, ladies and gentlemen, and no matter how fine a talker this man here is, he can't change the facts. The facts show that Raymond Lomak is guilty of first-degree murder and justice demands that he be punished for his horrible acts."

Realizing that the most potent fact the defense *did* have was Trotter Smith, Grife sought to undercut Smith's credibility with the jury. "He told you," Grife smoldered, "that he rarely leaves his home in Kentucky. But where was he just five months ago? Trying another criminal case in Philadelphia. And how do I know this? I was home sick four months ago and saw him talking about it on the 'Phil Donahue Show'—which comes out of *Chicago!"*

Quickly turning his attention to Ray Lomak, Grife argued that if Lomak could viciously murder two human beings, what would prevent him from threatening to murder Treak Johnson if she didn't give "that cockamamie story" she spouted on the stand.

"And Mr. Smith says that Ray Lomak 'fervently denied' he murdered Jenny and Dean Harnett. Well, what kind of evidence of innocence is this? If he wasn't going to deny committing these murders, he would have pled guilty in the first place, and we wouldn't have ever had this trial. As far as the 'fervently' goes, it seems that Ray Lomak pretty much does everything fervently."

Rubbing the side of his neck and dropping his voice, Grife went on, "With regard to Tex Harnett's testimony, well, I just felt very sorry for that man, losing his only two children in the worst way a human being could ever imagine. He most likely testified the way he did because Ray Lomak has pulled the wool over his eyes. One way or another, he's bamboozled poor Mr. Harnett out of everything he's wanted from him. That was the very reason Tex's son, Dean, wanted to dissolve the Foundation."

Tex hunched forward in his seat, trying to catch every word, unconcerned that many in the courtroom were casting sidelong glances his way.

"Mr. Smith said he believes the murderer was a stranger to the ranch because a stranger would have been much more likely than Ray Lomak to leave a living witness like Esperanza. Well, who said that the murderer saw Esperanza? Isn't it just as likely that he didn't? This is a sixteen room home. Esperanza could have heard screams and hidden. Or she could have been sleeping or ill in her room," Grife slithered in by way of more or less permissible speculation a fact he couldn't present from the stand.

"We know from the tape that Lomak never thought anyone would be at the ranch that night, so he probably wouldn't have even bothered to look for Esperanza. We'll never know these things for sure. But are we really supposed to believe, ladies and gentlemen," Grife asked, with his arms outstretched, "that some-

one else came to the Harnett ranch in that short little span of time
—just after Ray Lomak claims to have left, but just before Jenny
arrived—had the knowledge Lomak had of the workings of that
swimming pool, knew exactly where he could find the kinds of
tools he needed, and for completely unknown reasons, killed those
two young people?"

Grife recited the many other pieces of evidence (the friction
between Ray and Dean; Mrs. Kirkham's seeing a car like Lomak's
driving away from the ranch; the call from a pay phone in Palos
Verdes to Treak Johnson; Lomak's selling his tires the very next
day; et cetera) which, if Lomak's innocence were to be believed,
Grife said, would have constituted "the greatest string of coinci-
dences in California criminal history. There is no *reasonable* doubt
of this man's guilt."

By the end of his final argument, Grife had worked himself up
into a state of moral outrage no one in the D.A.'s office could
remember his having ever exhibited before.

"Who in the world would have had the motive to cold-blood-
edly murder these two young people, except this defendant sitting
right here?" Grife bellowed, pointing at Lomak. "This man, this
. . . this hypocrite, this liar . . . out of . . . I don't know what . . .
out of selfish desperation, so cold and calculating, just . . . just
murdered them. Just murdered them.

"This man speaks of love, and . . . well, I don't think he really
knows the meaning of that word. He talks about God and religion,
and it makes my blood boil. I *do* believe in God, and everything
I've been taught says it takes more than just words to bring God
into the human heart. You're not looking at a religious man here.
You're looking at a . . . at a fanatic."

Grife shook his head, and ran a hand through his fashionlessly
cut hair. His upper lip was beaded with perspiration. Sheathing
the sharpest part of his voice, he said, "I don't even know if you
could call Raymond Lomak vicious. Not if I understand that word.
Vicious means emotion. It's his mind . . . his, his . . . the way his
mind works—it's the most frightening thing I've ever seen.

"I ask you on behalf of all the people in this state—I implore you—don't let this man get away with what he's done. Bring back your verdict of guilty. It might be the most important thing you'll do in your entire life."

As Joe Grife gathered up his notes from the lectern, his hands were trembling slightly.

At the recess, as Ray was being led back to the holding tank, he stopped in front of Grife's desk and said, "I think you really believe all those things you said—so I forgive you."

After the recess, Judge Penstrake read the jury the dozens of formal, abstruse instructions concerning the legal concepts of premeditation, deliberation, malice aforethought and the many other points of consideration in a murder trial, and at 3:25 she ordered that the jury be sequestered until they reached their verdict. Turned over to the custody of bailiff Kip Duncan, who always lit up at this proprietary transfer, the jury was taken to the downtown Hyatt Regency where they spent the night. The following morning they were bussed back to the Criminal Courts Building to begin their deliberations on the fate of Raymond Lomak.

✶ ✶ ✶

Richard loitered around the courthouse the entire first day of the jury's deliberations, believing that if the verdict were guilty, it could come in just that fast. He walked the halls, browsed through the morning newspapers in the first-floor cafeteria, and played losing chess with a deputy sheriff by the name of Mackey at the information desk. Richard's mind was inhabited only with the moment the jury would file back into the courtroom. Although he worried about the effect Smith's summation may have had on the jury, the only scene Richard allowed to play through his imagination, over and over again, was the one of the jury foreman announcing that Raymond Frederick Lomak had been found guilty —guilty of two counts of first-degree murder.

Guilty, Your Honor. The look of horror on Ray's face. The

clamor of reporters. Twice Richard caught himself slapping the information desk with satisfaction while waiting for Mackey to make his move.

Richard drove to the courthouse on the morning of the jury's second day of deliberation, but by mid-afternoon and still no word, he went back home. A third day passed, then the weekend, and then a fourth and fifth day—still without word of a verdict being reached. Richard's optimism had long since given way to concern, and the concern had begun to turn to steep anxiety. A first vote certainly had to have been taken by now, and obviously the jury was split. How could it be, he asked himself, and asked Grife as well in late night phone calls. Grife was a stalwart and, in truth, by this point a friend. He counseled patience, trying to buoy Richard's spirits with his thirty years of experience in court and stories of juries that had taken twice this long.

"In a death penalty case, a lot of jurors who just can't make up their minds vote not guilty on the first and second ballots, see, because it's easier, sorta safer. They want to get talked into a guilty vote by other jurors, people like themselves, not lawyers," Grife told him. Like every other lawyer trying a case, Grife had never been allowed back in a jury room, and had only heard this once from a juror seventeen years ago.

By the ninth day of deliberation, Richard was beyond assuagement. The case, it appeared, was probably being decided not by the facts alone, but by the persuasiveness of the various opposing jurors. The verdict was floating in the wind and would fall to earth on one side of the culvert or the other because of elements like the housewife being more articulate than the bookkeeper, or the retired engineer not being as resolute and mentally alert as the machinist, who sat himself next to the coffee urn. It seemed as much a trial of twelve lay peoples' personalities as it was of Ray Lomak.

When the call finally came from Grife on the afternoon of the tenth day that the court clerk had buzzed his office three times, signifying that a verdict had been reached, Richard yanked his car from one lane to the other down Pacific Coast Highway, his feet clammy as though they had no socks. It was a forty minute drive to the courthouse, and by the time Richard arrived he found his path checked by the media horde outside the courtroom. Television cables being tugged past his ankles led into a frenzied, floodlighted world where mass murderers were celebrities.

There being no more available seats inside the courtroom, Richard went back down to the ground floor and hailed Deputy Mackey, chess master of the information desk. Mackey obligingly led him to the prisoner elevator which took them up to the fourteenth floor, where they then walked up the flight of stairs leading to the back door of the crammed courtroom. Even the aisles were clogged with standing spectators, Penstrake having allowed this only for the reading of the verdict. The jury and judge were seated, as was Ray, his head bowed as if in prayer. Smith and Grife stood at the bench talking with Judge Penstrake.

After a few minutes, Penstrake rapped her gavel and, turning to the jury, asked, "Ladies and gentlemen of the jury, have you reached your verdict?"

The foreman, George Gerlach (Smith had guessed wrong about Cottler), rose and answered, "Yes, Your Honor, we have."

Gerlach handed a folded sheet of paper to the bailiff, who passed it up to Judge Penstrake. Dorothy Penstrake unfolded the paper and read its contents to herself without a visible flicker of emotion. She passed it back down to her clerk, James Wren, who stood up and read it for all in the hushed and stuffy courtroom.

"Superior Court of the State of California for the County of Los Angeles. The People of the State of California, Plaintiff, versus Raymond Frederick Lomak, Defendant, Case No. A-462321, Department No. 133.

"We the jury in the above-entitled action, find the defendant, Raymond Frederick Lomak, *not guilty,* as charged in Counts I and II of the Indictment. George L. Gerlach, Foreman."

For several seconds, the courtroom was strangely silent, the spectators too dumbfounded to speak to each other.

Trotter Smith leaned back in his chair with a mighty smile, and put a congratulatory hand out to his client. Not seeing the hand, Ray stared straight ahead and said, with more self-righteous wrath than joy, "Praise the Lord."

Throwing his hands up in the air, Grife looked over at the jury and shook his head back and forth.

Within seconds, a mob of reporters swarmed around Ray and Trotter Smith in a courtroom charged with shock and consternation over the fact that Lomak was again a free man. Sinking inside with revulsion, Richard elbowed his way out of the courtroom, oblivious to the voices of two reporters who were trying to shout over the din for his reaction to the stunning verdict.

CHAPTER 7

ONE OF THE MEMBERS OF THE JURY WAS QUOT-
ed in the morning papers as saying that for all twelve jurors, there had been a reasonable doubt. For Richard, there was none.

He called Joe Grife at home that night.

"Joe, there's no point in lamenting what happened in that courtroom. All I want to know is, can anything be done to get this mutant off the streets? Any legal action at all? Federal or something?"

"Not a damn thing," Grife kicked. "He could call a press conference tomorrow and announce to the world that he murdered

Dean and Jenny. There's no exception in the law of double jeopardy. He can't be prosecuted again. Period."

"And there's nothing else?"

"Well," Joe said, and Richard could hear him turn in his den's easy chair, "being a prosecutor, I hardly ever have anything to do with the parole process, and I don't know that much about all the laws in that area. But I do know for sure—I've even seen this happen—that if any new evidence comes up, it can always be taken to the parole board, and if it's enough to satisfy them that Lomak's guilty, they can revoke the parole on his original sentence."

"It's something to think about," Richard said . . . "I guess."

"In fact, you can send him back to prison if you can find out he violated any of the parole conditions he must have on him. His breaking *any* law would do it."

"Thanks, Joe," Richard said pessimistically.

Richard arrived at the Harnett Foundation headquarters at seven the next morning, before Ray would be able to quarantine himself behind a cordon of secretaries. Ray arrived, alone, a half hour later.

"I want to talk to you," Richard said as they faced each other at the thirtieth-floor elevators, just outside the Foundation's glass front doors.

"I don't wish to talk to you," Ray answered him, moving swiftly to the office doors, key in hand. Richard stepped in behind him. Ray turned and they glared at each other a moment. Richard followed Ray as he went through the doors and walked briskly down a series of hallways to his small office.

Sitting down behind his desk, Ray said, "You're trespassing on private property."

Richard sat down in the chair across from him. He just stared at Ray.

Swallowing nervously, Ray asked, "What do you want?"

"I want you to voluntarily commit yourself to a hospital."

Ray sat very still, his eyes never leaving Richard's.

"You're a sick man," Richard went on, "just like you were when you murdered those six people. You talked about it when you first came to my office—you said twenty years ago you were ill.

"You know what I'm talking about, don't you. When you think about the things you've done, maybe while you're lying in bed at night, what do you say to yourself to turn it off, Ray? 'Don't think about it, don't think about it, don't think about it'—that's the kind of thing you say to yourself, isn't it.

"But you do know exactly what you've done. And you know there's no justification."

He watched Ray for a reaction, but Ray sat rigidly, impenetrable.

Suddenly, Ray looked away. "Is that your expert diagnosis, doctor?" he asked acidly. "I should put myself in a hospital? Hospitals are prisons."

Richard did not answer. Ray wasn't denying his crime; they were at least not shadowboxing with reality.

Richard peered deep into the pupils of Ray's eyes, into the small, round, black gateways that held behind them, safe and hidden, the secrets of every human being's world. Richard detected a spot of recognition in Ray's eyes, but it faded as quickly as a breath upon a mirror.

"Anyway, I didn't do anything," Ray said. "There's no reason for me to go to a hospital."

Richard looked at him another long, tangled moment. "I detest having to beg you, but I am."

"You're wrong," Ray said. "You've really gone off the deep end."

Slowly, Richard rose to his feet and leaned on his hands over the desk, the muscles in his forearms which supported him in hard spirals. It was an effort to keep his voice steady.

"I can barely stand to look at you. . . . I'm going to prove you killed Jenny and Dean. It's that simple—I'm going to prove it."

"You're . . . an arrogant, hateful person," Ray sputtered. "I was found innocent. You're not allowed to do anything more to me."

"Not in court any more, I can't. But there's still the parole board, and they never heard of double jeopardy. And if it won't be for the murders, it'll be for something else, because I'm going to get *something* on you. Cross your eyes the wrong way, and I'm going to be there to see it. You're going back to prison."

"Leave my office," Ray commanded, pointing.

Richard stood up and nodded slowly. At the door, he stopped and turned back.

His face gone pale, he said, "How could you bring yourself to do the things you did, you son of a bitch."

Ray did not respond, and Richard left.

✳ ✳ ✳

In part, Richard had been bluffing; any further attempts to prove Ray's guilt, he felt, would have been futile—just some wind kicking up dead leaves. His threat to catch Ray at something new was similarly empty. For the near future, Ray would make sure to act like a saint. Richard's main hope—and one he specifically did not mention to Ray—was to uncover some transgression Ray might already have committed during his first year with the Foundation. Something small perhaps, something typically Ray—expedient and amoral—something that would have been a violation of his parole conditions.

Knowing Ray's propensities, Richard seriously doubted that Ray would have engaged in any kind of monetary hijinks with the Foundation's funds, but being desperate, he was ready to probe any avenue at all. Richard started with the publicly accessible list of previous Harnett Foundation recipients. In calling them, he was open and undissembling in announcing his purpose.

Assuring a university divinity student in Minneapolis, who had received a stipend to help him write a book, that immunity from prosecution would undoubtedly be granted him if testimony be-

fore the parole board were required, he boldly asked whether Ray
had ever suggested or in fact arranged a financial kickback to
himself for securing the grant.

With a cloistered shyness the divinity student answered, "No,
nothing like that was suggested. I didn't feel Mr. Lomak was the
kind of person who would even think about personal gain like
that."

"Yeah, I know what you mean," Richard said cheerlessly.

A reverend whom Richard went to see personally in San Diego
was less polite. "What are you trying to do to that man?" he asked,
jumping up from his desk in the basement rectory. "I read all
about that trial you had up in Los Angeles. The man was proven
innocent."

"The man was found not guilty," Richard corrected him, having painfully learned the distinction from Ray's own lawyer.

Word started to get back to Ray that Richard had been making
his calls about him all around the country, and in the process not
mincing words over his belief in Ray's guilt for the two murders.

Ray called Richard at his office.

"You can't do this. There are laws against what you're doing."

"Go call the police, Ray," Richard said. "You're just about their
favorite person."

Three weeks of continued effort brought Richard to the frus-
trating conclusion that he was pumping for water in a barren well.
He turned his attentions instead to the Foundation's employees
themselves, though he felt uneasy about taking his case to the
people who worked literally alongside of Ray. The only one to
meet with him (at a lunch spot near the Foundation's headquarters) was the lawyer for the Foundation, who, after getting Richard's assurance that it would not get back to Tex, told him, "As far
as Foundation work goes, I think he played it pretty straight. But
hell, of course most people down here are still suspicious of the guy
about these murders. He's got the benediction of the old man,
though, so no one will speak about it above a whisper. But I can
tell you, one secretary has already left, although she naturally gave

some other reason for going.

"And I might add that applications out at the college have dropped off noticeably since this whole thing started."

As Richard started back toward his car by himself after the lunch, Ray stepped out in front of him from a doorway, as if from nowhere. Richard's breath caught in his throat. Though a feverish hatred had settled in Ray's eyes, his voice was controlled.

"Don't keep this up, Dr. Pomerantz. I wouldn't keep this up."

He eyed Richard another smoldering, ticking moment, then turned and stalked off down the sidewalk.

Richard did, however, continue to pursue the matter, and just as vigorously.

It was on a Sunday morning in mid-April, before Richard had even awakened, that a persistent knock on the door from a process server brought notice of a ten million dollar personal slander suit Ray had filed against him. The next morning Richard learned through an article in the L.A. *Times* that the local attorney Ray had hired was also asking the California Board of Medical Quality Assurance to strip Richard of his license to practice because of "unethical conduct and moral turpitude."

When Joyce Halston, the *Times* staff writer covering the story, called Richard, she asked whether he was considering publicly retracting the statements he had been making about Ray.

"Not a chance," Richard told her. "And you can put it in any story you write that I welcome the suit. I understand from a lawyer friend of mine, who may end up representing me, that truth is a defense against libel and slander, so I'm just going to have to prove in a civil court what should have been proven at the criminal trial. Let's just see what a second jury says."

"And if they say the same thing the first jury said?" the young reporter asked, her voice indicating obvious sympathy for Richard's cause.

Richard paused.

"Well," he finally found the spirit to quip, "after a brief appearance in bankruptcy court, I guess I'll be looking into practicing psychiatry in Japan."

A week later Joyce Halston phoned again, wanting to know if it was true that Richard had "assaulted" a Miss Treak Johnson in the courthouse parking lot during Ray's trial. Every evening without exception Ray had been calling Joyce, who was working the paper's night shift that week, providing her with what Ray termed "background information" on Richard.

"Jeeesus Christ," Richard groaned in disbelief, to which the reporter answered, "Yeah, that's what I figured."

For the patients who had thought enough of Richard as a therapist to wait out his personal ordeal and not transfer to other doctors, Richard began to reschedule hours in his office where, not uncoincidentally, he found himself unusually interested in those patients who were beset with an obsession of one kind or another. Suddenly, that element in the human psyche had garnered Richard's very personal concern. What if a second jury did, in fact, decide that his accusations against Ray were false and slanderous, he asked himself. Would it make any difference if one hundred juries concluded that the authorities had prosecuted the wrong man for Jenny's and Dean's murders? Richard wondered whether he himself was not capable of becoming like the classic example of a man with obsessive, ineradicable delusions who insists that he is dead, and when asked by a psychiatrist whether dead men bleed, responds no. When he is pricked in the finger by the psychiatrist, he still exclaims, "How do you like that? Dead men do bleed."

For the first time since Jenny's and Dean's deaths, Richard questioned whether he had not long since fixed on Ray as an object of such personal enmity, that no number of contrary opinions could disabuse him of his belief in Ray's guilt.

Richard's days of introspection and self-doubt came to a sudden end, with a single ring of his office phone. It was Felipe Gomar, Esperanza's cousin.

"I read Esperanza from the paper. She see what you're going troo, man. She thought even without her, trial send Lomak to jail.

She say she now give you what you want, unnerstan'?"

"Yes! Yes, I understand!" Richard said excitedly. "Where? When?"

"You come here, you come tomorrow night. An' I warn you, man—tape recorder okay, but police come weeth you, man, you're troo."

"No police," Richard swore. "But can I bring a witness, Felipe? Someone from the newspaper. Please, it would be better if I have another witness."

Felipe was silent a few seconds. Richard braced himself for the click of a phone being hung up on him.

"Yeah, okay. Seven o'clock. No tricks, vato, you unnerstan'?"

"Of course not. Understood, completely."

His fingers getting ahead of himself, Richard had to dial twice in getting the *Times,* where he asked for Joyce Halston.

The following evening he met the young, dark-haired journalist in the parking lot at the Union train station, not far from where Felipe Gomar lived. When they arrived together at Felipe's house, Esperanza was already seated on the sagging, cloth-covered couch in the living room, her back nervously erect, her hands folded tightly in her lap. Her beautiful ivory cross hung around her neck. Half a dozen relatives milled about the room, and in the kitchen.

When Esperanza learned that Joyce Halston was a reporter from the *Los Angeles Times,* she shook her head and said meekly, "No, no periódico."

Felipe told Joyce she had to leave, and Joyce, flipping her note pad shut, went outside and sat in a rocker couch on the front porch.

"Felipe," Richard said, "I can understand Esperanza's concern. I give you my word that this tape and everything Esperanza tells me is only for the parole board, and I'll try to see that Esperanza gets as little personal publicity as possible."

Richard placed the tape recorder on the floor in front of the couch, and using Felipe as an interpreter, asked his crucial questions slowly and precisely. Understanding bits and pieces of English, Esperanza sometimes began nodding halfway through a question.

"She say she hear a scream," Felipe translated her soft, swallowed words of Spanish. "Nothing else, man, just a scream, a yell."

"And that's when you went to the window?" Richard asked. "The *window*. You looked out the window?" Richard said, the weight of the moment sweeping him up and impelling him to try to communicate directly with the girl.

"Sí, de weendow," Esperanza nodded.

Richard leaned forward and asked with deliberation, "What did you see out the window, Esperanza? Who did you see?"

Esperanza looked at Felipe for the translation, and when she got it, lowered her eyes and turned her head.

"Thee man," she said almost inaudibly, as if information mumbled would not come back to harm her. "Thee man, meester Ray."

"Ray Lomak?" Richard asked intently.

"Sí," she said, and let out a large breath. Putting her fingertips to her forehead, she began to cry softly. "Sí," she repeated once more.

Less than an hour after Richard and Joyce had met at Union Station, they returned to drop Joyce off at her car. They sat on one of the old walnut benches, the massive carved ceiling overhead, cathedral-like in the nearly deserted station.

"Well," Joyce sighed, "I guess my story will be confined to whatever the parole board makes public."

Richard nodded.

"It's almost over," he said quietly. "It's actually almost over."

They talked for several minutes, Joyce sensing that Richard did not want to be alone just yet. In time she rose, and touching his shoulder, said, "Take care."

Richard used one of the station's public phones to call Howard Reiner at his home in Sacramento.

"I've got the smoking gun on the Lomak case, Howard," he blurted out.

Informing Reiner of the tape, he added quickly, "You told me last year that you people didn't follow the same rules of evidence as a court does, so this tape should be okay, right?"

"Right," Reiner said. "As long as you or this cousin of hers can substantiate that it's her on the tape."

"Don't worry," Richard hastened. "We both will."

"Incredible," Reiner said. "Unbelievable. So that bastard did commit the two murders. I'll set the wheels in motion tomorrow morning for a new parole hearing."

"And I assume," Richard continued, "even your two buddies on the board up there will finally agree to put him back behind bars for good."

There was an unexpected silence on the other end of the line.

"Richard," Reiner finally said, "we used to be able to send someone back for the full amount of his original sentence, which in this case would be life imprisonment. But that's not the law any more. The maximum that *anyone* can be sent back for now on a parole revocation is one year."

Richard stared at the phone dial, incredulous, his eyes growing hot.

"This has to be a joke," he said, almost voiceless. "I can't believe such a law exists." He looked out over the dated, expansive train station to a lonely ticket clerk playing solitaire behind his caged window. Calming himself enough to speak civilly, Richard repeated the implausible words, *"One year. . . .* Howard, why didn't you tell me that's all Lomak could go back for when I contacted you about him a year ago?"

"Because then we were talking about the killing of a dog, a misdemeanor. One year back in prison was probably appropriate, and it didn't seem worth mentioning."

Richard could do little more than look down at his feet and shake his head, slowly, with a suffocated rage. "So in other words the parole sanctions are the same for murdering two human beings as they are for killing a dog."

"Well, in this situation here, yes, because he was acquitted. If he had been convicted, he of course would have received a completely new sentence."

After a long pause, Reiner continued, haltingly, "You know, Richard . . . if I hadn't gotten you involved in this, you never would have gone through all this tragedy. . . . I don't know what to say . . . except I'm very, very sorry."

"That's okay, Howard . . . how could you have known all of this would have happened? I'll talk to you tomorrow morning."

"All right. Good night, Richard."

The drive back to Malibu passed by Richard as if he was unconscious, his starts from a couple green lights prompted only by the car horns behind him. When he arrived home, he sat in the corner chair of his dark bedroom.

At the *Los Angeles Times* building near the Civic Center, a David Porter picked up an incoming call at the city desk.

"I'd like to speak with Joyce Halston, please," a male voice said.

"Joyce isn't here," Porter answered.

"Would you know how I could get in touch with her? I've been working with her all week on a story she's doing."

"I think she's out interviewing someone on the Lomak case."

There was a pause.

"Oh, really?"

"Let me see," Porter mumbled, "I think she left the number . . . yeah, here it is, 751-4612. In case you don't reach her, can I say who's calling?"

There was another pause, this one a little longer.

"Thank you—thank you very much," the man said quickly and hung up.

As he listened between waves to the tick of the turret clock in the hallway, Richard's stomach roiled with anger and frustration. Shortly before ten o'clock the phone rang.

"The crazy man, he call here for your lady friend at the newspaper," he heard Felipe Gomar say, sounding panicked. "I tell him I never let her come in. I send her away."

"Wait. Wait, Felipe, slow up. Who? Who called?" Richard said.

"Lomak, man. They give him my number! What is this? I don't

want no part of this!"

"Okay, just calm down, Felipe. What did Lomak want? What did you tell him?"

"I try and fake him, but it's no good, man. He already guess what's going on."

"Why did you even talk to him?" Richard shot out. "Why didn't you just hang up?"

"He murders all those people, man. I don't want him coming after Esperanza, so I tell him cat's already out of bag—I tell him she say what she knows to you on your tape, and now shees gone. No good coming after her no more. She not coming back, ever." He paused to catch his breath. "Shees my fam'ly, vato—I look out for my fam'ly, huh?"

"All right, all right!" Richard said. "You did what you had to do. Now, when did he call? How long ago?"

"Little while 'go."

"What did he say when you told him about the tape, Felipe?"

"Not much. He just listen. Real strange, man."

"I know he is. Just take it easy, everything's going to be all right. Just calm down, all right? You okay?"

"Yeah, yeah—I'm okay."

"Don't worry about it. He'd have no reason to harm you. I'll call you back later."

Richard hung up, but his hand remained on the phone. He stared at the emergency number for the police. The only person in immediate danger was he, Richard, the man with the tape, the man who had vowed not to rest until Ray was back behind bars. Even if, perchance, Ray knew that the most he could go back to prison for was one year, he would also know just as certainly that were the tape to be made public, he would be through at the Foundation. He would be through everywhere—for life.

Richard sat a full minute with his hand poised on the telephone . . .

. . . then, as if compelled by an eerie and darkly unfathomed stranger within himself, he took his hand away. He sat very still, listening to the drone of cars along Pacific Coast Highway. Slowly he rose, turned on the small light above his bookshelves in the living room and, standing to the side of a curtained window, looked out onto the highway below. Hundreds of beady head-lights, snaking up the coast from as far south as Santa Monica, moved with the illusionary lethargy of objects at a distance. Rich-ard turned off the light and sat down again, in the darkness.

A minute passed, and then several more, and still Richard did not stir. He listened to every sound about him like a forest crea-ture, more alert than intelligent. He began to feel the ramming of his heart. He felt like a hunted animal, but unlike one, he did not move.

Gradually, his heartbeat began to slow, and he even stopped listening so acutely for noises down the stairs at his front door. A strange resignation began to come over him, as when one stops grappling with the wheel to avoid an accident, and accepts in that final moment the inevitability of impact. He rose from his chair and walked back into the bedroom. Opening the nightstand drawer he had not touched in nearly a year, he looked at the gun.

All his adult life Richard had quarreled with people's casting their fates to the wind, yet now he felt himself making the simple willful choice to not weigh his actions. When Richard picked up the gun, he was no longer, as he had always understood the word, thinking. He was merely putting an end to choices and watching life's results.

The gun still felt heavy to him, and foreignly cold. He turned it over in his hand and looked at it as if looking at an odious, dark part of himself for the first time in his life. The perspiration on his palms made it stink of metal. He wrapped his hand about the butt and slipped his finger tentatively up against the trigger. Walking back into the living room, he sat down on the floor in the corner with his back against the wall. With so few strokes of the clock, he had set foot in a new world. He was surprised by how uncom-plicated a world it was, and what little resistance the mind, in a black solitary room, offered against it.

For over an hour, he waited.

When he heard the sound out front of a car quietly rolling to a stop, he did not doubt for a moment that it was Ray. When the slow, muffled creaking of a tire iron wedging into the doorjamb came, he did not even flinch. He was watching results.

Shortly, the door gave way, and soft, guarded steps mounted the stairs. Each shallow breath Richard took brought a burning sensation to his chest. He put both hands on the gun, to steady it. A single drop of sweat, as cold as rubbing alcohol, ran down his side.

Richard stared at the room's arched entranceway, his eyes now sprung wide, as if waiting for an alien creature.

As the shadowy figure of Ray Lomak entered the living room, Richard's hands trembled even as his finger tightened on the trigger. When Ray took his third step in, a shaft of light glinted off his measuring eyes and the knife in his hand. In that instant, Richard's jaw stiffened and he pulled the trigger.

The roar he expected didn't come. It was more a sharp cracking sound, but Ray bent over, a hand to the middle of his chest.

"Ahhh," Ray half-groaned and half-gasped, as if merely having the wind knocked out of him. "Oh G—"

He pitched over into a heap, on his knees, with his head resting against the seat of a chair.

Richard watched in disbelief. Traces of acrid smoke stabbed at his nostrils. Numbed, he lowered the gun, and when he closed his slack mouth, his teeth chattered violently. The tendons in his arms had been frozen so rigidly, they ached.

Weakly, he placed the gun on the floor next to him, and on shaky hands and knees lifted himself up. Gazing at the man whose one eye was closed, the other open a slit and fixed blankly into space, Richard felt neither compassion nor righteousness. He could see from the slight pulsing at the throat that Ray was not dead yet. Within the next minute, the pulsing ceased.

Looking down at Ray, Richard found it almost impossible to believe that there was actually an end to Raymond Lomak—that someone who had wrought so much tragedy in such a short life span, no longer existed in the world.

When Richard called the police, he still could not control the chattering of his teeth, or the tremor in his voice.

"I'll meet you out in front," Richard told them. "I don't want to wait inside here."

✷ ✷ ✷

Sergeant Thompson, the deputy sheriff who had surmised that teenagers were responsible for killing Richard's dog, tossed the responding patrol officers' homicide report on his desk and gulped down another slug of his morning's first cup of coffee. Richard sat on the hard green couch against the wall, heavy-limbed but reasonably awake. He had been up the whole night at the Malibu sheriff's station, his ability to sleep having gone past him like a missed highway exit, with the next one a long distance off.

"There was no need for them to have kept you here all night," Thompson said apologetically.

"It was pretty late when I finished talking to Detective Newhouse. It was my idea to stick around 'til you got here," Richard said.

Sergeant Thompson clasped his hands in back of his head and gestured to the patrolmen's report with his elbow. "It'll be a little while before all the necessary investigation is completed. Just because Ray Lomak was killed here, we're not like some of my friends down in Texas who like to ask at the start of their investigation, 'Did he need killing?' But it's pretty clear to all of us what happened here. I can tell you that the way it looks now, we won't be seeking a criminal complaint against you."

Richard nodded.

"When anyone, much less someone you already know to be a killer," Thompson said, "forcibly enters your home in the middle of the night and comes into your room with a knife, you're entitled to use deadly force in self-defense. Law says you don't have to wait until they strike first."

Richard nodded again, and looked down at the floor. Thompson studied him a moment.

"Something on your mind, doctor?" Thompson asked.

Richard looked back up at the sergeant and hesitated, then answered calmly, "No."

"Fine," Thompson said, and rose from his chair. "We'll be in touch."

They shook hands, and Richard went out to his dewy car in the parking lot. After wiping the windows with a rag, he got onto the nearest freeway, not quite sure where he wanted to go. Driving for a few minutes, he found himself headed east toward Palm Springs, and decided to follow the road out that way. In an hour he was past San Bernardino, and the air became clear and warm. The reddish-roan ridges of the low Sierras that hemmed in the desert were sharp in the distance. The road descended into the hotter dry air which, curiously, made Richard only more awake and sentient. The desert was again in bloom.

At the nearest wide shoulder he pulled off the highway. Stepping gingerly over low-lying cacti, he sauntered along the edge of a dry wash, taking in all the deep blue, fragrant royal-lupine and golden gilia, flowers Jenny had taught him to appreciate. As he bent down and reached out to touch a delicate Mohave aster, his eye strayed from the lilac-colored petals to his own hands. Just for a split second he stared at them, the moment unsettling and without enlightenment. Quickly, he got back in the car, and suddenly more tired than he had realized, headed back toward Los Angeles.

His thirteen year old Buick hummed its sensible, trustworthy sounds. If he didn't mind some people thinking him a little eccentric at age forty-nine, it could last another thirteen years, easy.

✶ ✶ ✶

Four days later, at Westlake Cemetery, Raymond Lomak was buried in a grave left unmarked, for fear of vandalism. Only two people stood at the grave site, a couple in their sixties who did not sign the mortuary register. Immediately afterward, they left in their old station wagon, a car with out-of-state plates and a stack of canvas oil paintings in back.

THE AUTHORS

VINCENT T. BUGLIOSI received his law degree in 1964 from UCLA law school, where he was president of his graduating class. In his eight-year career as a prosecutor for the Los Angeles District Attorney's Office, he tried close to 1,000 felony and misdemeanor court and jury trials. Of 106 felony jury trials, he lost but one case. His most famous trial was, of course, the Manson case, which became the basis of his best-selling book *Helter Skelter*. But even before the Manson case, in the television series "The D.A.," actor Robert Conrad patterned his starring role after Bugliosi. His most recent book, also a best seller, was *Till Death Us Do Part*. He lives with his wife, Gail, and children, Wendy and Vince, Jr., in Los Angeles, where he is in private practice.

KEN HURWITZ was born in Milwaukee in 1948 and graduated from Harvard University. He is the author of two books, *Marching Nowhere* and *The Line of David* (a novel), and co-author of *Till Death Us Do Part* with Vincent Bugliosi. He lives in Los Angeles.